Advance praise for

ECHELON

"A terrifying glimpse into the future. Jam-packed with intrigue, terror, and suspense. Conviser is a writer to watch."
—ALLAN FOLSOM, author of *The Day After Tomorrow*

"This fast-paced info-tech thriller takes your breath away, both with the speed at which events unfold, and the sheer imagination of the author. . . . Ryan Laing is the twenty-first-century James Bond."
—FREDERICK P. HITZ, former inspector general of the CIA and author of *The Great Game: The Myth and Reality of Espionage*

"Breathtaking . . . intensely exciting from the very first page."
—LAIRD KOENIG, author of *The Little Girl Who Lives Down the Lane*

"If William Gibson and Tom Clancy teamed up to write a novel, *Echelon* would be it. Conviser is a brilliant, inventive storyteller."
—ADAM FAWER, author of *Improbable*

"Unsettling and provocative. Conviser gives us a powerful depiction of intelligence-gathering run wild." —JACK McDEVITT, author of *Seeker*

"[A] fast-paced hurtle through a near-future dystopia, in the William Gibson mold—and not so far-fetched as you'd think."
—PATRICK RADDEN KEEFE, author of *Chatter: Dispatches from the Secret World of Global Eavesdropping*

"*Echelon* takes the spy thriller to an almost metaphysical level, exploring what happens when government 'intelligence' becomes 'omniscience.' With simple but evocative language, Josh Conviser brings you into the back room of *1984* and shows just how it would be done."
—GARY GOLDMAN, executive producer, *Minority Report*

Other titles you will enjoy from Del Rey

BY RICHARD K. MORGAN
Altered Carbon
Broken Angels
Market Forces
Woken Furies

BY PHILIP K. DICK
Blade Runner

BY CHINA MIEVILLE
Perdido Street Station
The Scar
Iron Council

BY JOHN BIRMINGHAM
Weapons of Choice
Designated Targets

ECHELON

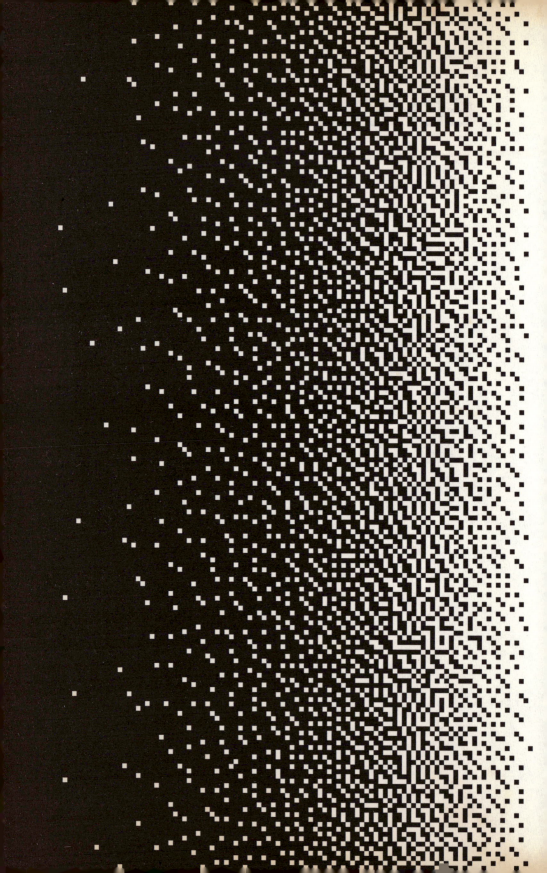

ECHELON

A NOVEL BY

Josh Conviser

BALLANTINE BOOKS
NEW YORK

A Del Rey Trade Paperback Original

Copyright © 2006 by Josh Conviser

Published in the United States by Del Rey Books, an imprint of The Random House Publishing Group, a division of Random House, Inc., New York.

Del Rey is a registered trademark and the Del Rey colophon is a trademark of Random House, Inc.

ISBN 0-345-48502-5

Printed in the United States of America

www.delreybooks.com

9 8 7 6 5 4 3 2 1

Text design by David Goldstein

For my dad, Michael Conviser

ECHELON

I

In the moments after impact, cold fury consumed Ryan Laing. Adrenaline blasted through him. Rage fired hot. Electric pain racked limbs, joints, and bone. His blood flowed, staining the desert earth. Muscles locked in spasm, drawn taut.

Then the shock wave receded. Sensation slipped from his hands and feet. One by one, each point of input faded to static. He felt desiccated, a husk left to California's Santa Ana winds. Only the jagged rocks digging into Ryan's back cracked his isolation.

As death neared, breath came harder—gulps of air drawn through frothed lips. Desert sun lanced him. The granite spire vaulting over his head offered little protection. Seconds earlier he'd clung to that rock, climbing smooth and well. It had taken half an hour to climb the spire. He'd caught the express train down.

Darkness crept in even as memories circled, vague and illusory— the parting explosions of a billion synapses. The flickering images refused to coalesce into a life Ryan could recognize; he felt as if he were watching someone else's childhood vids.

Only the past weeks stood clear. What he'd seen. What he'd done. That memory refused to follow Ryan's pain into oblivion. It bore into him still—as it had during mission debrief. Despite the interrogators' relentless questioning, he'd talked around memories of the old man dying at his feet—and by his hand.

Work defined Ryan Laing, Echelon agent. If Echelon was the puppet master controlling humanity, Ryan was a string linking the manipulator to the puppet. Work outlined the shape and texture of his life. But there were days when it cored him, the brutality of the means he utilized not quite justifying the ends. On those days, self-respect came hard.

During the debriefing, the interrogators had caught onto that weakness and exploited it, blasting him with questions. Ryan had done the right thing; he'd done his job. But guilt ate at him as the debriefing dragged on. The old man's eyes haunted him.

Finally, Ryan cut out. The interrogators had his feed; they could see what he'd seen and didn't need a narrator. He removed his goggles and flow-space blinked out, leaving him alone in the prefab perfection of his Los Angeles apartment. He leaned back in his chair, letting his senses adjust to reality. Hours in the flow affected perception. Ryan tried to shake the old man's death from his mind. It wouldn't budge.

Rarely did Ryan take notice of the cramped space he called home. Most of his domestic life was spent in the flow, or asleep. His flow deck bulged from an alcove next to his bed. As he rose, it recessed into the wall. He slipped past the molded plastic dining nook, which he'd never used, and out onto the terrace. LA's high-rises ghosted up through the smog-strangled air. He took a deep breath, coughed it out, and knew he had to leave.

Rock climbing was part of the cycle. Some people shot chems, some fucked toward a state of grace—Ryan climbed. To set the ledger straight, to rebalance, to avoid a system crash—he climbed. No rope, just hands on rock.

The promise of release pulled him from the balcony, and he was out the door in seconds. Ryan hopped the maglev to Palm Springs, which was difficult to differentiate from Riverside, from Los Angeles itself. For a thousand kilometers in any direction 'scrapers cut up the sky, negating topography. The monoliths blurred as Ryan slid east on the maglev's smooth track. He lost himself in their unbroken consistency.

Ryan imagined the 'scrapers' residents scurrying through a daily grind as constant as the scenery itself. They lived easy, worked their jobs, slurped through bioengineered meals and returned each night to cookie-cutter apartments. Energy contained, harnessed and regulated. As an Echelon agent, Ryan had a lot to do with that consistency. In spite of his own culpability, Ryan shuddered.

In Palm Springs, Ryan caught a scenic shuttle into the desert. Joshua Tree had been maintained as a nature preserve, a pockmark in the urban monotony. Corpulent, tech-junked families filled the shuttle, gaping at the moonscape through rad-filtering plexi. Compressed by sprawl and the relentless drive to build, Joshua Tree remained a living museum of something reckless and carnal long abandoned. The shuttle glided through the park, a canned voice defining each piece of the landscape.

Ryan rose and forced the door, setting off the alarm. Hot air flooded the compartment as the shuttle slid to a halt. Ryan jumped out and scrambled away from the tracks. The shuttle's emergency system warned him to return to his compartment. Scorched earth crunched underfoot as Ryan jogged through crooked Joshua trees. Their rough bark and spindling limbs offered up a dry organic scent that cut through the smog. The shuttle finally gave up on Ryan and moved off, claxon shrieking.

Ryan kept his eyes trained on the valley before him. He could forget the encroaching 'scrapers if he looked in exactly the right direction and kept his eyes down. Massive boulders pocked the landscape, detritus belched from the Earth's core.

From the glinting desert, sheer cliffs vaulted into the sky, slabs of granite forced up by eons of pressure. Laing clambered up the narrow valley, a fissure slicing between two cliff faces.

He reached the base of the climb, letting his breath slow as he gazed up at the familiar route. Ryan saw the cliff as a progression of moves. Left hand high and lunge for the pocket. Balance out, extend, and crimp the flake. The action string coalesced into a single perception. It would be a good climb.

Ryan sat, replacing his blocky street treads with climbing slippers. He laced into them, savoring their bite, the constriction of his toes, then he stood and put his hand to the rock.

It was old granite, knobby and sharp. The decision to begin always surprised him—the shift from passive to active made by some subterranean piece of his 'ware. He reached for the first hold, high and left, and his feet found the vertical.

He coiled his legs into his chest, the tips of his toes plastered to the rock, building energy. Thoughts shoved aside—his concentration filled by the pocket one meter above. Ryan centered on it, dialing life down to a single action. An explosive release, legs pushing, left arm pulling hard. He vaulted into the air. Right hand shot up, driving for that pocket—finding it with the very tips of his fingers. He slapped his left hand up to match his right. The granite's knobbed grit dug into his palms as his full weight bore down. His feet gained purchase, relieving some of the tension. Ryan sucked in huge lungfuls of air, gazing up at the moves ahead.

He climbed with an easy grace—cranking one move into the next.

Space sprawled below, and his world ratcheted down. The climb swelled to become his whole existence. The past weeks dissipated. Shades of gray contrasted out. On the rock, there was only black and white—life and death. The power of this vertical world enveloped him. Freedom.

The scrape of metal on rock pulled Ryan from the zone. Tension pulsed through him. Fingers clenching, Ryan scanned, hunting for the sound's source. He felt eyes on him. Fractured impressions pushed his field training to redline. Then, the granite before him pulsed—searing heat warping the dry air. Ryan's illusion of control evaporated.

Crack. Fear blossomed. Handholds crumbled. Ryan couldn't believe the input—refused to accept it. Adrenaline surged. He raked his fingers over the rock, desperate to regain purchase. Too late. His feet lost their grip. A splash of acceleration and the snap knowledge of doom.

Impact.

Now, the grinding crackle of broken ribs pulled Ryan from memory, initiating him into death's final act. Fear swirled through the pain. The gulping urgency to live stung hard. Seconds passed—an eternity. Then, the pain faded, replaced by a core-deep resignation. Ryan felt his body yield; he was beyond salvage.

The shock-blue sky forced Ryan to squint. A lead-heavy banality settled in. Ryan couldn't believe this was his life, his death. No rhyme or reason, just stupidity and chaos.

Ryan released his final breath. The sun bit into him. Had the past weeks—hell, the past years—been worth it? Worth anything? He closed his eyes against the glare, then made a final choice. He opened wide and stared into the sun.

He died disappointed.

2

"Neil Buist had to die." Sarah Peters let the statement slip and immediately regretted it. She shifted uneasily.

Echelon did not permit its officers to download personal identifiers within its confines. Each virtual desk, each slice of flow-space, maintained a blank, unerring sterility. There was no homeness to the Echelon construct.

Even so, Jason Sachs' workspace felt particularly cold, as if he had skewed the angles of the room to set his visitors off balance. The office glowed white on white, almost blinding. Sarah tweaked the contrast in her goggles, but the room amped with her adjustment. She had to remind herself that none of it was real. She could pull off her goggles at any time and be back in her cozy apartment. The office shifted infinitesimally, triggering a shot of vertigo.

"Is that your opinion, or was it Agent Laing's?" Even in flow-space, where facial features were magnified to counteract signal degradation, Jason Sachs betrayed nothing. Sarah wasn't sure he had emotions to betray.

"It was my finding," she responded. "Laing didn't bother debating the subject."

"Well, something got to him."

Sarah started to realize why Echelon's inspector general was taking an interest in the operation. "You think Laing was so racked with guilt that he killed himself?" Sarah couldn't hold back the sarcasm.

"This being your first experience with my office, I'll cut you some slack. But let me be very clear as to the gravity of this conversation. I am tasked with understanding the events that led to Ryan Laing's death. Any culpability you had in upsetting his stability will have . . . ramifications." Sachs let the last word hang in the air.

At times, Sarah hated Echelon with every atom of her being, but for someone with her skills there was no place else. Growing up, she had craved action and adventure, finding in the flow what her real life as a shy, gangly adolescent couldn't offer. In the flow, she could be strong and bold. And she was good—really good. She felt an affinity for coding and complex mathematics that made the flow her personal playground. Echelon's recruiters had tracked her early romps through this man-made universe. They liked what they saw.

As soon as she had entered college, Echelon approached her and revealed a secret that changed her life. In the flow, meshed into the tangled web of coding that connected humanity, there was a watcher.

Each and every bit of information flitting across the globe ran through Echelon. Encryption and security measures had no effect on its clean retrieve. Even more shocking, Echelon could manipulate the data pool—altering exchanges in real time, with no one being the wiser. Unbeknownst to the countries, corporations and consumers of the world, Echelon controlled the flow of information with a benevolent, if iron, hand. Sarah readily became an analyst for the clandestine kingmaker. How could she not? Within Echelon, she could change the world.

But now, after several years in Echelon's sterile flow-space reading reports, calculating probabilities, and plotting data shifts, she often forgot the on-ground effect Echelon had on the world. Then, she would overhear a conversation at her local coffee shop—customers discussing the Korean unification or Middle East Peace Accords with lackadaisical assurance. In those conversations, she heard a naive faith that conflicts invariably resolved themselves. Madness, terror, greed, and vengeance shaped much of the human condition—but their ramifications only cut so deep. Something always happened to allay crises. Sarah was part of that something. With Echelon at her back, Sarah corralled the horsemen of the Apocalypse.

Often it was as easy as making sure one side understood the other. But Echelon's manipulation could grow intricate, requiring tangled decision trees and RAM-pounding statistical analysis. Sarah's specialty.

Now and then, data manipulation failed. Then reality work became the only option and Echelon's Special Operations unit entered the calculation. When that happened, Sarah got the excitement she had so craved as a kid. It invariably turned her stomach. Hard manipulation meant bloodshed, and it wasn't always the bad guys who had to die. Sometimes, her calculations led to a man like Neil Buist.

Sarah realized Sachs had been speaking. She pulled herself back to the white glare of his workspace. He repeated himself. "The flow funnels through Echelon, Peters. We don't miss a thing. So explain how we didn't pick Buist up months ago. How did he slip our web and necessitate destruction?" Terms like murder weren't condoned in Echelon. "Carrier destruction" sounded so much cleaner.

"The man did it all in his head," Sarah responded.

"I'm sorry?"

"He was deeply paranoid, and beyond brilliant. Neil Buist communicated his discoveries on completion," she said.

"In that case, how did you pull signal intercept?"

"Luck. Pure, dumb luck."

Every now and then, Sarah kicked into the raw data flow funneling through Echelon. Initially, her superiors had discouraged the practice. No one could ingest such a torrent of information. But she had an uncanny instinct for finding those nodal points that shifted the whole. Twice, Sarah had spotted shifts before Echelon's software picked them up. She had uncovered a high-level Japanese plot to pull Antarctica into its natural resource protectorate, a move that would have led to war. And she had unwrapped Neil Buist.

Sarah had been trying to ascertain what his company, Calsoft, had in its pipeline. Buist's ability to work through groundbreaking developments in his head and then present them full-blown made Calsoft a threat to stability. A company of that size, shifting direction with little warning, created huge mop-up problems for Echelon. So, Sarah sniffed around the code emanating from Calsoft.

"I found a voice message," she told Sachs, "sent to the old man from one of his executives, Michael Welton, which struck me as odd. It was a recommendation for a nature vid. Something about a deep-sea animal called a siphonophore."

"What?"

"Basically, it's a massive jellyfish. Like fifty meters long."

"And this caught your attention?" Sachs asked.

"Odd thing to call your boss about, don't you think?"

"I give. What's the connection?"

"The siphonophores themselves. Each individual is, in fact, a colony of smaller beings working in perfect unison."

"Okay . . ."

"I started digging." Sarah said. "Buist's hits in the flow, linked conversations, travel schedule, people he met—they all led to one conclusion. He'd found a means by which millions of independent processors could work in perfect unison, adapting to any given input as a single organism."

"And this is important?"

"It would change the nature of data processing, robotics, and a thousand other disciplines," Sarah replied with a tinge of annoyance.

"Not really cause for destruction."

"Not in itself. But I did a probability run on the most likely buyer of Buist's software. It came up ugly. Pakistan has a substantial force of combat robots. Currently, the Pakistani bots offset India's massive army. With Buist's software, the bots would tip the balance. I found an actionable probability that Pakistan would take offensive action."

"And that gets us to Ryan Laing."

Sarah cringed. Even dead, Laing gave her the creeps. "I tasked Laing with recovering Buist's software," she said.

"And destroying the carrier before dissemination."

Admitting her hand in murder stung, but guilt was part of the job. She bore it grudgingly. Sarah couldn't remember the last time she'd gotten a good night's sleep.

"Yes. The situation mandated such action, and I have the authority to so implement," she said.

Jason stared at her. Sarah shrugged off her guilt and continued. "Unlike most paranoids, Buist wasn't reclusive. He was larger than life, hitting every party and spending lavishly. Laing caught up with him in Miami, Florida, attending a benefit dinner."

"Let's review Laing's sense dump."

A wall in Sachs' flow-space office disintegrated. It was replaced with a recording of the sensory input Laing had ingested during the mission, captured by a disc placed over the agent's temple. The devices were mandatory during such operations.

The wall unfolded. Watching the past as present skeeved Sarah. Entering Laing's feed threw her off-kilter. She breathed deep and let Laing's vision inundate her.

The slick glare of Florida's New South Beach rezzed in. A flotilla of tremendous barges anchored fast, it looked like a chemical hallucination flash-frozen. The sparkling retro-deco behemoths bobbed in the ocean just off the original South Beach, now crumbling into an ocean that continued to rise. Capitalizing on South Beach's historical allure, developers had fashioned the barges to re-create what had been lost to the rising water. The barges sprouted high-gloss 'scrapers, forming a playground of lavish excess.

Sarah clawed up through Laing's input. She spoke over the recall. "Buist liked being the center of attention, publicly and privately."

Jason's voice filtered over the scene. "Clarify."

"He scooped up women, wrung them dry and flung them aside with the rising sun. The man relished consumption."

"Sounds like a real gentleman."

"Never claimed he was a saint," Sarah responded.

Jason flashed forward, sense points tumbling over.

Sarah narrated the fast forward. "The setup didn't take much. Ryan locked Buist's pattern, found the hideout you see here and waited. The gala wound down. At midnight Buist took his latest conquest back to his suite."

Sachs slowed the recording to real time, drawing Sarah back into Laing's past. From a decaying hotel room in old South Beach, Ryan scoped in, his heat-sensitive scope cutting through the one-way plexi of Buist's suite on the barge. In the jittering, tunneled image, Laing watched the two slide close. The woman's head rolled back in laughter, then forward into a kiss. Her lips met Buist's. It was time.

Laing grabbed the stub-short barrel of his rifle, locking the scope onto the gun and loading a mag of swivel-shot. His hands moved fast and steady. He touched the phone in his ear, placing the call. Sighting in, Laing watched the woman pick up the phone and hand it to Buist.

"Hello?" Buist said into the phone.

Laing settled into a firing stance. Three deep breaths, then another held halfway. He pulled the trigger between heartbeats. A soft, metallic ping fractured the room's moist silence.

Designed for silent penetration, the projectile spun on impacting the plexi of Buist's suite, boring through it. Most of the bullet dissipated in the energy transfer. The remaining needle point punctured Buist's neck. He slapped at the irritation.

"Who is this?" Buist asked.

"Hello, Neil. You have just been poisoned."

Through the scope, Laing watched Buist's annoyance shift to fear. He bolted for the bathroom.

Laing sighed and resighted on the woman. He pulled the trigger again, the needle imbedding into the woman's midsection, making her jump. Shock and pain torqued her features. Death came in a series of bone-crushing convulsions. Neil emerged from the bathroom and watched her die, stunned.

The phone hung limp in Buist's hand. He raised it to his ear. "I'm proofed against bioware. Daily updates," he said.

Laing waited until the woman stopped twitching. "Your protection won't hold. You'll be dead in an hour."

"Not possible," the old man sputtered. Hesitantly, he knelt over the woman and put his fingers to her throat. His head dropped and he stumbled back.

Watching, Laing's breath caught. He repositioned the gun on his shoulder, shaking it off. "The great Neil Buist and his whore dead of some designer drug. Tragic." He let that sink in. "I'm in the old Delano Hotel."

Buist wrenched his gaze from the woman and looked out across the water to Laing's general position.

"That's right," Laing said. "Sooner you get here, the longer you'll live."

The scene shook, then blurred out. Sachs sped through Laing's visions—of Buist exiting the suite, approaching Old South Beach in a water taxi, disembarking, and making his way toward the Delano.

Sachs slowed back to real time as Laing negotiated his way down the hotel's collapsing stairwell and entered the lobby. Two bedraggled bums lay sprawled in a corner. Ryan walked through the high-ceilinged lobby, grown over with lush foliage, and onto the sloping marsh that led to the pool.

The pool's edges blurred with the waves washing up and into the lobby itself. Just offshore, the glittering white barges of New South

Beach loomed. Cemented into the pool's shallow end, a wrought-iron table and two chairs were the only pieces of furniture remaining.

Sitting in one of these chairs, Neil Buist looked worse than his surroundings. The toxin ate at him.

Laing sat. "For your sake, I'll get to it. I want your work on processor colonies."

Buist's jaw dropped, revealing bloody gums. "You can't do this."

"Mr. Buist, you're dying. You don't have long." Laing placed a syringe on the table. "The antidote."

A gurgling hack escaped Buist's lips. He coughed blood into the milky water sloshing beneath them, oil black in the moonlight.

"Just talk. I'm rigged to record," Laing said.

"Who are you?"

No response from Laing.

"Jesus, okay. I'll tell you. Processor colonies . . ."

Scene shake and speed blur. Jason punched forward. Sarah spoke over the feed. "Tell me the software's good."

"Madda has it now. He says it's groundbreaking"

Sarah sighed in relief. She watched Neil Buist talk his life away in double time. Intermittently, the man wretched, spewing bile into the water.

Jason locked the scene back into real time.

Sarah watched Buist make a desperate grab for the syringe. Laing was way too fast.

"You're going to let me die," Buist realized.

Ryan said nothing.

"How? How did you know?"

"Siphonophores," Ryan said.

Sarah watched the realization shoot across the old man's features. "Michael's call. Good God."

Pain folded Buist double. Sarah gulped down her nausea as Laing stood, shifting perspective. Through Laing, she watched Buist keel over and splash into the pool. Laing turned to leave, but Buist grabbed his trouser cuff.

"You've got to . . . get Welton . . . ," Buist gargled out. Then he sank below the waterline, a final pulse of bile escaping his lips.

Scene stop—a frozen image of the murdered man. Sarah pulled free, recalibrating her own perception, trying not to let emotion get the better of her. The wall in Sachs' office regained opacity.

"Two days later, Ryan Laing fell off a cliff," Sachs said with cold finality.

"Destroying Buist was a—" Sarah hunted for the right word. "—difficult decision. But his death, and the woman's, saved thousands, maybe millions, of lives. Laing knew that. The op and Laing's accident were unrelated."

"Probably," Sachs responded. "Your destruction order probably cut off an event chain leading to war, but you can't be sure. They might have died for nothing."

Sarah faltered, if only for an instant. She had to remain strong in front of this man. "That is correct, sir."

Sachs bored into her. "You are free to go," he said.

Sarah rose to leave—a formality in flow-space. She could simply cut transmission, but she needed the finality of the physical act. Reaching the door, a nagging tickle in the back of her mind forced her to turn.

"Sir . . ."

He cut her off. "For you, Peters, this case is closed."

Sarah opened her mouth to respond, then thought better of it. She nodded and touched the door.

As her fingers closed on the knob, space shifted. She'd been pulled.

Sarah found herself in a dark room, utterly blank, uncoded. A man emerged from the void. Christopher Turing looked broken. The image made Sarah recoil. Echelon's leader, its heart and soul, looked down at her with bloodshot eyes.

"There's nothing else?" he asked.

"Sir?"

"The report you just gave Sachs. Nothing more you want to add?"

Sarah's skin crawled. Instinct screamed at her to say yes, to reveal the tingle down her spine that Michael Welton's name had brought on. But there was nothing to back up her suspicion.

"No sir."

Turing nodded. "Very well."

The room blinked out, depositing Sarah back into Sachs' office. The pull had taken a fraction of a second in real time. Sachs had no idea she'd been gone. She triggered the knob and exited hurriedly.

Christopher Turing goggled out. He felt old for the first time in his life. No, he felt ancient. He left the cubicle and walked down the hall to a steel door. Cracking it open, he let his eyes adjust to the dim light.

Beyond the corpse draped in a white sheet, the room stood bare. Turing approached and forced himself to lift the sheet. A smile rose up through Turing's sorrow. Even in death, Ryan Laing sported the slightly annoyed grimace that had caught Turing's notice so many years ago.

Turing placed his hand on Ryan's cheek. Dead cold. Turing forced himself to keep it there—better to ponder the decision before him.

Another man entered the room. Turing didn't look up. He didn't need to. He and Dave Madda were the only two people in the complex.

"Will it work?" Turing asked.

"I think so," Madda responded. "Buist's colony software was the final piece of the puzzle. The drones are operational. Untested, dangerous, but operational."

Turing cycled through the ramifications of what he was about to do, possibilities floating into eternity. He let it all go.

Turing walked to the door without looking at Madda. "Do it," he said. Fuck the ramifications. He wanted Ryan back.

3

A searing, convulsive, internal reconstruction drew Ryan from the void. He couldn't see. Couldn't feel. No sound. Shards of memory flaked off and flashed past. Indecipherable. The weight of time settled on him. Each moment stretched into infinity.

Then, the buzzing began. Neither language nor gibberish, it reverberated within him, infused every cell. Laing's sense of self cracked. He felt trapped in something foreign, something other. His mind reeled, desperate for a center. He spun within the blitzkrieg of memories—raging bursts of unconnected images, nothing to ground him.

Ryan couldn't feel the restraints holding him. He couldn't feel the stab of a needle piercing his arm. But in the darkness, he felt a warm infusion of calm. He melted into it. It didn't last. The other—the squirming, pervasive thing inside him—found the fluid and neutralized it. Anxiety and dark fear stormed back. They gripped him, locking Ryan into an impenetrable cycle. He couldn't hold the past, couldn't feel anything beyond the invasion of his flesh. And the buzzing.

—*Ryan? Ryan, I'm with you.*

The thought stream filtered through Ryan's mind, cracking the dissonance. He tried to respond, to latch onto the lifeline, but the current dragged him under. Laing struggled with everything in him—fighting the pull.

—*Ryan, you need to relax. Stop blocking. Let the drones help you.*

The thought stream surged again, punching through Ryan's maelstrom, linking to memory. He grasped the words. Felt but unvoiced, their cadence and tone cascaded through his mind. They held Sarah Peters' imprint. He caught the thread of her thoughts and held fast.

—*Sarah?*

Around him, the tidal surge eased, Laing's internal reality settling.

—*Yes, Ryan, it's Sarah. You're okay.*

—*I'm dead.*

—*Not for long.*

In slow, measured tones, she explained what happened and what he had become.

· · · · ·

The drones repaired him. Flesh revitalized, bones regenerated, cells activated by a new stimulus. Repairing the brain took longer. Drones sifted through his memories; Ryan's violation was total. They found patterns, webs within his mind. They repaired what the impact had torn apart. Death's veil slowly lifted. Memories jigsawed into place, regaining consistency.

Ryan groped back to the being forged from the past he'd lived, the thoughts he'd had, the instincts hardwired within. Sarah talked him through his journey, keeping the terror at bay.

Months passed. Billions of synapses came online. Strength returned. Ryan's corporeal link reengaged and consciousness flooded him. He opened his eyes.

A young man's face greeted him.

"Welcome back, sir," Dave Madda said.

Ryan recoiled. He'd expected Sarah.

"Where is she?" Ryan croaked out.

—*Oh, I'm here. You're stuck with me.* Sarah's thoughts filtered through his mind.

Ryan rose from the bed with Madda's help.

"What the hell is going on?"

"Madda, Dave Madda. You know me."

Ryan looked at the young man, recall locking into place.

"I know you."

Madda's grin widened. "Welcome back to the land of the living."

4

Six months later.

The one-man sub bored through the ocean. Its slick frame slid through black water with the grace of a manta ray. The sub wasn't much larger than the cabin itself—a bullet strapped to a massive turbine. Maintaining control required every scrap of Laing's concentration.

His fingers twitched over the controls. Ability, reaction and luck combined to overwhelm the ocean's chaos, if briefly. Laing's bulky frame ill fitted the hydro's tight confines. Pushing two meters tall and eighty-six kilos, Ryan admitted to himself that the bloom was off the rose.

Resurrection hadn't altered the slight midline paunch that nagged at his ego every morning. At thirty-nine (and with one death already under his belt) he was an old man in his profession. Few could handle the constant stress, the unrelenting risk, the knowledge that any misstep could shove the world into a tailspin. Ryan needed it. Needed Echelon. He was thrilled to be back—released from Madda's subterranean lair and returned to the world.

Indicators monitoring the hydro's speed, pitch and yaw were projected onto the transparent dome, beyond which Ryan saw only black. In the canopy's reflection Ryan made out the curl of his own smile. Not much to look at, but he didn't have much need for looks. Laing preferred a face that blended in, that had all the parts in the right place and was forgotten immediately, melding with the masses. Good cover. Still, he hated seeing the deep fissures creasing his mug. He didn't have any laugh lines, just grooves below the lips. No problem in the hair department, though. He had more than enough. It grew thick, black salted with gray. Had been since high school. Yet another feature that muddled his age. He could still pass for a hard-lived twenty-nine. He could also be sixty.

Black sea contrasted his one distinguishing characteristic. His eyes radiated a stark, high-mountain blue. The eyes of a husky. In his reflection, Laing caught a wisp of gray swirling within one cornea. Resurrection had changed everything. The gray receded, slipping back into a body that was no longer his own. Ryan Laing had houseguests.

The hydro bucked and he shook off his reverie, sinking into the soothing void of concentration. Ryan recalled Madda beaming over the slick beast now wrapped around him. During the months of recuperation, Ryan had had little to do but hang over Madda's shoulder.

Deep in Los Angeles' abandoned subway system, Dave Madda engineered the bits and bobbles that made Echelon agents so formidable. Madda's physical interaction with the agents consigned him to a subterranean existence—a prisoner of his own knowledge. Dave's hermetic life was interrupted only by agents requisitioning gear and his forays into the flow.

By day, Madda toiled for Echelon, meshing pieces of stolen data, technology and insight to leapfrog into the future. By night, he lost himself in another world. From the sense pad in the back of his workshop, under hundreds of meters of earth, Madda fought through the flow. Though his inventions pushed the frontiers of weaponry, Madda's obsession lay in an art whose efficacy died in the nineteenth century: fencing. Had life been different, had he not possessed gifts that confined him to Echelon's version of purgatory, he would have been an Olympian. This fact he repeatedly mentioned to Laing. Someday he would get the chance. Someday they would let him out.

Through his career, Ryan had used Dave like any other piece of equipment. All that changed after the fall. Dave had implanted the drones. Only Dave understood the extent of Ryan's metamorphosis. The thought made Ryan uncomfortable. He guessed it also made Dave a friend.

Laing remembered Madda introducing him to the hydro as if it were a new puppy. He really was a kid. Smart as hell, dangerous enough to be confined, but a kid nonetheless.

Running his hand over the sleek beast Dave said, "Supercavitation reduces hydrodynamic drag. The hydro builds a self-generated bubble of water vapor and air. By traveling inside the drag-cutting gas pocket, this bad boy can move at previously unachievable speeds."

"English, Dave," Ryan said.

"It's warp drive—underwater."

"How fast can it go?"

"Put the throttle down and we'll see. Theoretically, it could crack the sound barrier."

Now running deep off the California coastline, Ryan luxuriated in the hydro's voracious dynamism. He felt weightless, winging through the black. Each twitch of his fingers adjusted the flight. His slightest move drew the sub in sweeping arcs through the darkness. He could feel the speed. He could feel the shift in direction. He just couldn't see where he was going. The sub skimmed the ocean floor, reliant on sense readings. At this depth, any misstep would cause a cataclysmic implosion. Laing imagined the gloom crushing in on him. He had to fight the urge to push the controls over and do a negative-g swan dive into the ocean floor.

Ryan didn't fear heights. He feared an almost irresistible urge to jump. The bigger the cliff the greater the compulsion. That he'd seen the other side, if briefly, didn't slacken the impulse. Maybe this throbbing urge was something hardwired into humanity's genome—a sick need to court annihilation, to knock on Armageddon's door. Ryan was not one to leave the future in the hands of fate. He harnessed his own impulses, controlled them.

Though reinstated to active duty, Laing was being kept on a short leash. Serious assignments passed to others. He got the cripples. In this case, he'd been tasked with reconnaissance on an inconsequential data haven close to home. He'd requisitioned the hydro. The brass had acquiesced as if placating a petulant child. Just one more indignity. Ryan let it go.

The drones swirling through his body offered new horizons, even as they changed him. They tingled within him—an eerie sensation. Claustrophobia haunted him. Nothing to do with the sub. The drones made him claustrophobic within his own skin—as if he were trapped in a foreign body. He should be dead. He knew it. Each and every cell in his body knew it.

Out in the open ocean, the hydro flew within its thin bubble of air. The green glow of the seafloor's image only made the environment more alien. Ryan negotiated the trench, slipped into the channel, and began his ascent. The hydro's propulsion hummed quietly. He watched the depth gauge projected on the dome. Concentrating, he could sense the electrical impulses making up the information sent to his screens. He could read these more quickly than his eyes could process the projected data. That was the drones.

He turned off the projector, and the tingle bloomed into a full connection.

—*Everything okay?*

Sarah's thoughts percolated up. He was surprised the drones could pick up her transmission this far underwater. Unlike standard comlinks, the drones transmitted her input directly into his mind. She injected thoughts—orders—into his head. He thought he'd be alone—at least for a while. He realized he was glad for the company.

—*Fine. I can read the system impulses through my new friends. Just call me the computer whisperer.*

—*The computer whisperer. I like that.*

Besides their drone link, Sarah monitored real-time satellite feeds and the Echelon data pull pertaining to the mission. Sarah's presence within him took some getting used to. He hated having nowhere to run, no place she couldn't reach. But their dialog had pieced him back together. Her words had allowed him to maintain sanity as the drones remade his mind. In moments of weakness, Ryan wished he could match a face to his handler's thoughts, but that would never happen.

—*Who knew you had a sense of humor?*

—*Only you. No one else gets the honor of knocking around in my head.*

He'd learned to control his responses—to keep her from hearing each and every thought in his head. He wouldn't open that abyss for anyone, himself included. Introspection had never been his strong suit.

Ryan imagined Sarah, hunched over her console somewhere in the wide world. Her thoughts floated through the data flow as he did through the water, weightless, leaving no corporeal signature.

His thoughts stopped short as a dark shape materialized from the gloom. Ryan slammed the controls over and rolled left, the g-force crushing him into the side of the cockpit. Despite the snap roll, he slammed into the obstruction. The cocoon of air effervesced, sending the hydro toppling end over end. Pressure pounded down on Ryan, narrowing his field of vision until he could no longer cling to reality. His eyes fluttered back.

—*Laing! Laing?! You okay?*

Sarah's voice reeled him back in. He threw up all over the pristine sub.

—*Fine. Hydro's fine. I'll owe Madda a six-pack for cleaning this up.*

—*What the hell was that?*

—*Whale.*

—*The most advanced technology in the world and you hit a whale? Thing must've had the sonar pinging like crazy.*

—*Sonar's cloudy. Rising through a sharp temperature gradient.*

—*Well, I'm picking up radiation from an active security net, countermeasures charging. We were right; whoever's on that rig doesn't want company.*

He could see the whales now. They loomed over Ryan's hydro: a couple big cows and a calf. Fluid and graceful, the creatures reminded Ryan that he was out of his element.

—*How far to the rig?*

—*Half a klick.*

—*And how long can these guys stay underwater?*

He imagined Sarah typing away at her console, zooming in on the sat feed. He could access the info directly but preferred to hear it from her.

—*They're gray whales. The calf is a couple weeks old. It can stay under for about five minutes.*

Ryan did some quick calculations. Speed. Depth. Currents.

—*Perfect.*

With that, he dove into the whale pod. The mother's agitation grew, and he made sure not to get between her and the calf.

—*Jesus! What are you doing? They'll crush you.*

It took Ryan a couple seconds to respond. He needed every bit of mental capacity not to get belted. He dodged and weaved, keeping himself right in the middle of the pod.

—*Element of surprise. Maybe they'll think I'm a calf.*

—*Oh yeah, you blend.*

—*How much farther to the rig?*

—It's almost on you.

—My mates here aren't going up.

—Break away and return to base. Abort mission.

—No.

—Ryan, it's fine. Let it go and return to base.

Ryan fumed, bristling over his new status as a lab rat. His duties as an agent merely served to field-test the drones.

—I'm going to take a closer look.

—Do not proceed, Laing. Your mission is recon only.

To hell with her. He swung the hydro in a wide arc, barely missing a slashing fin. This wasn't Colorado and he hadn't seen a horse in years, but old habits died hard. He would bend their will to his, drive them up. But these weren't mindless cattle. The whales were smart, agile and keenly aware of their superiority. Ryan dodged and weaved, one minute herding, the next scuttling out of the way. Finally, the pod began to rise.

Ryan made out the rig's outline above him. Constructed in the twentieth to pull oil from the channel, it had been decommissioned when the residents of Santa Barbara deemed the contamination of their beaches unacceptable. Abandoned and too expensive to dismantle, it had become just another decaying formation pocking the channel.

As Laing drove the whales, the ocean floor rose, narrowing his margin for error. He forced the beasts into an arcing ascent, and their fury grew.

A howling sonic squawk pierced his cockpit.

—The rig's sending out sonic blasts. Keeps the sea life away.

—Looks like it works.

—Break off, Laing.

—Just a little farther.

He kept them together for another second. Then, as a unit, the whales pulled into a tight arc and spun away, disappearing into the gloom to continue their migration north. Ryan slingshot off them and flung his hydro at the rig. Just a little farther, then he'd turn around.

—Stop! Sarah's voice exploded through his mind.

He threw the hydro into all stop. It stabilized and hovered with the current.

—It's mined. Big-time.

—What? I don't see a thing.

—Sat feed's picking up slight variations in light refraction all around you. What else could it be?

—Cloaked mines? At some two-bit data haven? Unlikely.

—Want to bet your life on unlikely? This is exactly why we do reconnaissance before engaging.

Ryan tried to shake off the criticism. What did a data rat know about fieldwork? He squinted into the darkness. Nothing. The tingle inside him grew insistent. Suddenly, he felt the mines surrounding him. The subtle electronic voice of each mine acquainted itself with his drones. Expletives tumbled through Ryan's mind. He wasn't used to being wrong.

—So, this is what crow tastes like.

—Ryan, get out of there immediately.

—Not possible. Don't have much wiggle room here.

—I repeat, you are ordered to retreat.

A mine floated straight at the hydro's dome. Ryan's eyes registered nothing. His vision ran beyond sight—a new sense that had no name. Laing flicked the controls slightly, and the mine passed within centimeters of the dome. That close, its cloaking rippled.

—You are ordered to retreat, Sarah repeated with more urgency. *That comes from the top, Ryan. From Turing himself.*

Mines surrounded him. Ryan kicked himself, enraged that he had confirmed everyone's suspicions. He couldn't be trusted. He'd destroy the hydro, and himself, proving it.

—I can't retreat. Totally penned in.

—Then hold position. We'll send a recovery team.

Ryan dodged another mine, but the velocity shift sent him barreling toward several others. Holding position wasn't an option.

—You've got to be kidding me.

Ryan drifted through the electronic aura. He heard, saw, even smelled the chatter of each mine. Amid the clutter, he found it—a single path leading directly to his target, open for the briefest moment. No time to think.

He punched the throttle. An air pocket formed at the hydro's nose, slipped back and wrapped itself around the ship. Then, the turbine engaged and he blasted forward.

He struggled to stay on target. The turbine howled, accelerating within the air cushion. Warning lights blinked furiously. One thousand meters per second—cavitation bucked the craft violently. One thousand two hundred and Ryan nearly bit his tongue off. One thousand four hundred thirty-five meters per second—the hydro punched through the sound barrier. The sub outran the sonic boom's thunderclap. Behind Ryan, the wall of sound blew through the mines, triggering them in an expanding wave of destruction.

Retreat was out of the question now, Laing thought. He clawed his way back to functionality, leveling the velocity out. As the g-force decreased, his consciousness expanded to encompass the world around him. Sarah yelled into his thoughts. He blocked her out. He'd always been able to ignore pieces of his mind. Maybe that made him a master of repression. He didn't think about that either.

Mines exploded behind him, their combined force generating a shock wave of water. A snap glance at his rear monitor was all it took. He lost his bearings for a single instant. Laing sensed its electrical signature a millisecond before the mine slammed into the hydro's dome. It bounced away before exploding, not built to destroy a ship traveling at fifteen hundred meters per second. But the impact cracked the supercavitation bubble, along with the dome itself.

Fighting the water's friction, the hydro's speed drastically decreased. All the blood in Ryan's feet sloshed back up to his head. He felt his heart in his throat, literally. The turbine wailed, churning water instead of air. Jets of seawater shot into the cabin. A crackling web spread over the dome—implosion imminent.

The shock wave gained. A billowing titan, it thundered behind him. Even through the hydro's shell, Ryan felt its power, a raw force—inexorable and seductive. How easy to just let it take him—to jump off the cliff.

Ryan shook the thought away. As the wave neared, an idea snapped into frame. He blew open the emergency speed brakes—small wings that increased hydrodynamic drag. He took aim at the rig, hoping the hydro would hold together. Suspense extended the next moment into a gut-wrenching infinity. Then the shock wave hit.

It caught the wings, and Ryan slammed the turbine into overdrive, desperate to maintain direction. The wave catapulted Ryan's hydro from the ocean in a geyser of foam and force. The dome imploded, shards ripping through Ryan's face and chest. High over the ocean, impact with the water would be fatal. The alternative wouldn't be pleasant either.

The mangled sub slammed into the rig's dry dock, chewing through metal and concrete. The tail sheared, sending the turbine spinning through the mayhem. Grinding cacophony inundated Ryan, destruction spiraling around him. But as quickly as it had begun, the deluge of action abated. The hydro stopped short, impacting a support pillar.

A silence so monstrous Ryan reeled from it. He'd been here before and wasn't thrilled to return. The tingling revived him. It grew stronger. It evolved from itch, to burn, to agony. Ryan's eyes shot open. He tried to scream but couldn't find the breath.

He saw his reflection in a piece of twisted metal, his face ripped to shreds. The bloody pulp shimmered. Drones emerged from abrasions in Ryan's flesh, from his nostrils, his eyes, his ears. The sea of microscopic machines swarmed black—rebuilding what was left of his face.

Fear was a sensation Ryan understood. After twenty years in Echelon, it had become his constant companion and sixth sense. In grudging moments of introspection he admitted that he was an addict, craving its high. This wasn't fear.

This was horror—a brilliant revulsion threatening to eclipse him. Only the pain brought him back. He recognized pain. The monster before him—the swarming, seething froth that shrouded his face—that was the alien. And they pervaded him. Every pore, every cell, infested.

Seconds stretched long. Then slowly, time returned. The drones disappeared as quickly as they had emerged, leaving Ryan with a perfect, if slightly cherubic complexion. He was whole again. Not a single cut. Hesitantly, he touched his cheek. Smooth. Too smooth for a forty-year-old man. He let Sarah's voice back in.

—*Christ! Ryan?!*

—*I'm here.*

—*Status?* Relief flooded her voice.

—*Women everywhere will be envious. I'm literally as smooth as a baby's bottom.*

—*Agent Laing, you disobeyed a direct order. We're on the book now with lots of company. Status?*

Ryan imagined agents all over the world crowding in on Ryan's little piece of the flow—each shocked that Laing, the coldest fish in the pond, would even think the word "bottom." The thought curled his lips into a smile, an expression he rarely indulged in.

—*No major damage. Hydro destroyed.*

He pulled himself free of the hydro's twisted hulk and surveyed the decimated dry dock. Networks of decayed piping funneled through the room. Steam, at least Ryan hoped it was steam, blew from buckled conduits. Ryan's entrance hadn't added much to the dock's entropic clutter. Everything looked long abandoned and unloved. Everything except the Cigarette Boat. At the far end, maybe twenty meters from where he'd made his grand entrance, a boat hung from a cable system. He'd heard about such antiques, even seen pictures. A creation of master craftsman Don Aronow, the Cigarette Boat was capable of great speed, back in its day, and became the ship of choice for the rich and famous. Unfortunately for Aronow, its invention coincided with the first influx of cocaine into America. The Cigarette Boat became the ultimate drug-running vehicle. Aronow didn't survive the transition.

Ryan wondered if the antique still worked, having a feeling he'd need it. It was the only ship in the dry dock he hadn't destroyed. Before he could investigate, the drones jolted a warning into his system.

—*Mercs, coming fast.*

—*You got yourself into this shit storm, Laing. I'd suggest you find a way to slip out—quietly.*

—*Not today.*

—*Ry—*

He cut her out again. He could hear them. Not their steps but the static of their tech. Mechanized warrior men. The new wave in home security for the rich and paranoid. Biofeedback muscle suits made the men strong, fast and impervious to all but the most hard-core ammunition.

In the seconds before they entered, Ryan ripped into the hydro's storage container. He pulled a thin, black device from the sub's innards.

Despite its slender dimensions, the Fat Lady packed a punch. A resonance amplifier, it worked on the same principle that allowed an opera singer to shatter glass—but on a much larger scale. Ryan held it, homing in on its digital signature. When he was sure he could pick it from the swarms of signals inundating him, he slipped the device into a pouch in his jacket.

Then the mercs stormed in, converging on Ryan. He looked each man in the eye—or in the injection-molded, transparent titanium faceplate, as the case may be. The suits did have weaknesses: hinges that could be disrupted, buckles that hid defects. But the men's swagger and nonchalance hid their deepest flaw: the suits made them feel invincible.

"Come quietly," the leader said through the retro-electric voice synthesizer that came standard on all merc suits. The voice evoked a centuries-old paranoia of machines gone wild.

"Not today," Ryan responded.

"Attack mode."

The men's suits pulsed with greased energy. Ryan had sampled the best of athletic-grade steroids as a kid. He'd liked the bulk, the power, but hated the shift in perspective. The suits had a similar effect on these men.

Their jet-black exoskeletons twitched as the mercs amped power. Only colored shoulder markings differentiated one from the next. They moved in, engaging Ryan. The trick to fighting mercs lay in raw speed—and never punching back. No fist could break through the suit. Counterstrikes had to be made with a thumb, a finger, even teeth now and again. The weak points were small, the suits built to withstand high-force frontal assaults, not quick hit-and-run strikes.

The leader attacked first. Basher drawn, he swooped down on Ryan, knocking him off balance. Ryan dodged the strike, careful to throw up a glancing side block—a straight-on block would crack his arm like peanut brittle. The drones couldn't repair such an error in time to save his life. Ryan whirled around the leader, using his own momentum to whip the man to the ground, where he kicked like an upended beetle.

The others descended. Ryan danced between them. He needed this. The merc with blue shoulder markings cocked for a front kick but, at the last moment, hinged at the hip and came in with a side strike. Not bad. Ryan stepped into the blow, melding his body to the merc's. He spun with the force of Blue's kick, jabbing his thumb into the man's neck before spinning clear.

Orange entered the fray. Laing skirted away from a hailstorm of blows and broke for the door, adrenaline suffusing him. He sprinted up the rusting gangway.

Turning a corner, Ryan pulled the Fat Lady from his jacket and slapped it onto a massive support stanchion. The device sprouted spindling pincers that wrapped the column. A slight bulge emerged in the device's center. The generator would analyze the makeup of the stanchion and find the exact frequency that would create harmonic resonance. Once initiated, it would send vibrations through the column—shattering it in seconds. When this fat lady sang, it was definitely over. The mercs neared, and Ryan sprinted on. Intent on their target, the mercs missed the device burrowing into the column.

A barrier field protected the data haven's core from electronic attack, blocking any communication in or out. Its radiation signature sizzled through Ryan's drones. His senses weren't sure how to process this new input. It came as a smell. A particularly agreeable scent—something like a woman fresh out of a hot shower. He hoped Sarah didn't notice his arousal—that would be very hard to explain. Her voice clattered through his mind, teardrops diffusing into an ocean.

Whipping around the corner, he halted abruptly and came to terms with substantial impending pain. More mercs—maybe ten. The ones he'd left in the dock closed ranks behind him. No chance for escape. Might as well get it over with. Laing charged the mercs and they dropped him.

A rainbow of armor-clad fists pummeled him. Ryan tried to cover the sensitive parts—finally giving up on even that. The mercs seemed determined to reduce his groin to mush. So be it. He hadn't had much use for that part of his tackle in years.

As darkness hovered once again (two concussions in a day—a new personal best) he concentrated on the barrier's smell. The suits gave off their own electronic stink of motor oil and synthetics. He'd have to hone the smell thing—figure out what smelled like what. He floated up, sensing a rib crack, the dislocation of his right shoulder. They were thorough. Shadows expanded to black.

· · · · ·

Laing's mind wasn't his alone. Alien dreams flickered within. Images distorted. Faces and memories shifted. The drones' code touched him, their impulses winding through his mind. The hot sting of slaps across his face pulled Ryan from the drones' dark cacophony and back into consciousness.

The beefy man looming over him welcomed Laing back to reality with another fleshy slap. Wrists tied behind him, Ryan had been unceremoniously dumped into a hard-backed chair. The drones had already repaired his rib. The shoulder would take a little more work. He arched up, forcing it back into the socket with a grinding crackle. Pain shot through him, pulling him fully into the moment. No stimulant in the world could beat the searing rush of agony. Ryan took a deep inhale. The smell differed in here. He was deep inside the barrier, his link with Sarah snuffed out. The solitude was intoxicating.

The hulking man before him grinned. Not fat, but defined by an utter lack of tone, he moved with the practiced disdain of someone who'd relinquished the corporeal for the flow. His body was nothing more than a storage device for a mind adrift in data. A code junkie.

"Calvin Shepard," he said. "Mild-mannered techie, proud squatter of Platform Holly, and the man who's gonna end your life."

"Pleasure," Ryan responded.

"Normally, I don't do wet work. All the blood and mess. We're quite disgusting. All of us." He paused, lumbering around Ryan, looming over him. "But my curiosity is itching the hell out of me. How the fuck did you get past my mines?"

"I'm just a fisherman, lost in the storm."

"Nice."

Calvin turned his back on Ryan and hunched over a data terminal. Glossed molding and smooth chrome signaled high-tech 'ware. Too pricey for the biography Sarah had compiled. One more piece that didn't fit.

Calvin gazed off into flow, his fingers flying over the keyboard, linking mind to machine. Data flickered on the wall screen.

"A sub running super-cav. That don't come cheap. Who's supplying your 'ware?"

"I like to tinker," Ryan responded, trying to get a rise from Shepard. He needed to throw the hacker off-kilter.

"Right," Shepard said.

Ryan pulled at the bonds holding his hands. It hurt, a lot.

"Wouldn't do that. That cable is microns thin. It'll saw your mitts right off."

Ryan girded up for the task at hand, letting the drones percolate to the surface of his awareness. Slinging through the flow, goggled in and typing madly was second nature for him. The drones' fleshy, biological interface was another thing entirely. They allowed direct access to the flow. Ryan hated it—the total immersion—only calling the drones to action when absolutely necessary.

He needed to distract Calvin.

"Okay. Truth is I'm just a data pirate, looking for a quick score."

"Don't think so. Not with that kinda 'ware. You're company. You with the Saudis? Canadians? Who?"

Time to rattle Shepard's cage. He wouldn't survive the next few minutes anyway. "Echelon," Ryan said.

Shepard's eyes bugged out. His face washed pale, then curdled into a smirk. "Echelon is a wives' tale. An urban legend hackers tell their kids."

"That so?" Ryan held Shepard's stare.

Shepard's sneer faltered. He looked away, masking his rising anxiety with a coating of cynicism. "The mythical Echelon, unseen hand keeping us little folk from fucking things up. I thought Echelon agents were unstoppable."

"We are," Laing returned, deadpan.

In the flow, Ryan zeroed in on the haven's gate. He inched up to the edge and took the plunge.

"Why any hacker, even a lying, stealing company fuck like you, would say's he's Echelon is beyond me. Am I supposed to be scared? Shit, Echelon is just a pathetic delusion, one more attempt to force logic on chaos. No one's at the wheel; no unseen hand guides us along. There's no God, no Buddha, no Allah, and no Echelon . . ."

Calvin plunged further into his diatribe. Words like "domination" and "freedom," "privacy" and "choice" got past Ryan's block, percolating through his awareness. Same intellectual bullshit he'd heard a thousand times. If these evangelists had any idea how many times Echelon had saved them from doom, they'd shut up and hit their feeder bars for another pellet. That's all they were—lab rats in the great human experiment that was Echelon.

Ryan felt the drones interface with the haven's net. He bounced off several firewalls, skirted some very mean-looking booby traps, saw his hole and plunged in.

The mass of data crushed him. Even by Echelon standards it loomed enormous. What the hell was going on? No one could draw this kind of load without Echelon catching on. Its sheer size meant that Shepard must have been on Echelon's radar for a long time. Why had they waited so long to deal with him?

Torrents of information washed through Laing. He lost himself within it. Calvin's rant faded to background static. Laing groped for something to latch onto—a life raft. Within the data mass, a name flashed past and stuck.

CHRISTOPHER TURING. Why would the head of Echelon have an account in an illegal data haven? Ryan attempted to access the account. The encryption was good. Echelon good. He crashed through the barrier, and information bombarded him. He struck a trip wire, unable to control himself in the sea wash. He had about five seconds.

Back in reality, sirens wailed and an automatic, irreversible destruct sequence initiated. Binary mashers bit into the stored code, reducing everything to zero. As a redundant measure, the data stacks were rigged with packets of phosphorus suspended in water. For those storing illicit info, the only thing worse than losing everything was theft. Laing's incursion cracked the packets. Exposed to air, the phosphorus burst into flame. The data stacks burned.

Ryan dragged himself back to reality in time to see the mainframe begin to smolder. Calvin's eyes went wide. He leaped to his terminal, typing with dazed abandon.

"No, no, no . . ." Calvin frothed. Burning phosphorus' garlic stink filled the room. He looked at Ryan, unable to comprehend. "You?" he said. "But how?"

Ryan smiled. He ripped his hands from the grapples, severing both pinky fingers. He held up the bleeding stumps for Calvin to see. The drones stemmed the twin fountains of blood. Full repair would take some time.

"No! Not possible," Shepard gasped.

With the system crashing, the electronic barrier fell. Sarah's frantic voice flooded Laing. He washed it away, concentrating on the Fat Lady's signature. He found it, and initialized the device. A dull throb echoed as it beat sound into the stanchion. In seconds, the rig began to sway. The stanchion buckled, and explosions slammed the platform.

The ensuing chaos didn't faze Shepard. His world shrank to cover Ryan's fingers alone.

"That's not possible," he repeated. "We don't have tech for that! No one does!"

"Echelon does," Ryan said.

"Holy fuck." The realization slammed through Calvin.

He remained glued to his seat, shock blocking any drive for self preservation. The rig lurched, tipping the stacks and blanketing the control room in a white-hot shower of phosphorus. Chemical fire rained down on Calvin, searing through flesh and bone. Laing sprang for the exit, bursting into the corridor as the control room flared yellow and burned.

He sprinted down the hall, stumbling as the platform ripped free of its moorings. It lurched sideways, tons of steel teetering on the edge of oblivion. Ryan worked his way through the mercs. They were no longer interested in him. Just the same, they couldn't resist a few potshots as he flashed by. He flowed past them, dodging their fire, rolling and tucking.

He entered the dock with seconds to spare. The rig groaned and tilted farther, pulling the dock higher out of the water. Ryan yanked on the cables to disengage the Cigarette Boat. It landed hard on the concrete floor.

Ryan hopped aboard and hit the ignition. Nothing. The mercs stormed him, the boat their only means of escape. They flung their bashers at him, spiraling arcs of electrified metal. Two sailed wide. Laing bent double to dodge the third. The basher continued its flight, spiraling around a stanchion and exploding on impact.

Mercs swarmed, one getting as far as the tail of the boat before the old engine turned over and the props engaged. The howl of prop grinding through merc added to the scene's dissonance.

Another support beam groaned and gave way. The platform swayed wildly. The floor's added slope got the boat moving. It slid free of the rig, and fell, nose canting down. Nothing Ryan could do now; he was just along for the ride.

The platform shuddered one final gasp and buckled. Just below the looming hulk, the boat plunged into the water, its nose boring deep. Ryan felt the props bite and the boat surge forward even as the rig fell above him. He wouldn't make it. Not enough time to get out of the way. The rig loomed. The engines howled; tachometers slammed into the red.

Nitrous! These old guys used nitrous oxide to boost the engine's power. Sure enough, the switch gleamed from the console. Laing jammed it down and felt the hot flood of acceleration. The boat shot forward, rising up out of the ocean, as the rig crashed down, missing Laing by meters. The force bore a hole in the water. A giant wave surged forward.

The wave hit Ryan. He tried to keep the boat on an even keel. It slid up the face, teetered on the flash point, and then tumbled forward, cartwheeling down the wall of water and disintegrating in its trough. The force of impact spit Ryan clear. He dove for the bottom, the wave churning him like a rag doll. Finally, stillness returned. He told his legs to kick. They responded grudgingly, and he rose to the surface. As he broke through, a piece of flotsam nailed him in the back of the head. He struggled through nausea.

Behind him, the entire platform had vanished. Ryan churned water, alone in the channel. His head throbbed. Treading water, he had plenty of time to ponder the information he'd accessed before a nondescript fishing boat retrieved him.

He let Sarah back in once he was aboard.

—*You disobeyed a direct order.*

—*I know.*

—*Not the best way to return to active. Plan on an uncomfortable reception when you get home.*

5

Carved from the bowels of the abandoned subway system running under Los Angeles, Jason Sachs' offices backed up on Dave Madda's. Sachs knew Madda well. As the only other person permitted flesh contact with agents, Dave was a major focus of Jason's surveillance. Madda understood the constant scrutiny he lived under. He couldn't know that the eyes on him were only meters away.

At the moment, those eyes stared through mold-crusted plexi into the interrogation room. Sachs had designed the room personally. Its next-gen 'ware lay hidden under the dirty rot of nineteenth-century asylum decor. White walls and clean, softly whirring tech soothed subjects, convinced them that their torture, though excruciating, was meted out with some modicum of control. Interrogation time plummeted when the room looked like a sewer, and sweaty fear hung in the damp air.

Laing lay strapped to a rusting, pitted gurney, wires clamped onto every inch of his unconscious body. Only a fraction actually carried information. The rest aided in the subtler arts of intimidation and fear—tools that Sachs wielded with a master's touch.

Jason's father had taught him all he needed to know about fear and intimidation. From outside the white picket fence, Jason's suburban childhood would have appeared idyllic. A perfect house—cleaned spotless. A doting mother and successful father. No siblings. All of it an eggshell veil, hiding a rotted core.

Sachs men had an instinct for ferreting out weakness and an irresistible drive to dominate. Jason's father was no exception. The old man's meek exterior concealed a zealous compulsion to shatter those around him and lord over the shards. Jason had stewed within his father's cesspool, coring in, ruthlessly hunting his own flaws, caulking the cracks in his armor. As Jason entered college, his father died of a stress-induced heart attack. Jason didn't cry at the funeral; he would not be betrayed by his emotions.

Instead, he channeled them into the sterile purity of mathematics and game theory. Even at Harvard, Jason's single-minded drive stood out. Markers tagged, Echelon came calling. Jason slotted into the clandestine world with faultless perfection. He was born to it.

Sachs pushed his musings away and prepped for the interrogation. In a projected image, he sped through Laing's life. Information was power. The coming hours would be too important to overlook some lever in Ryan's mind. A single misstep could scuttle an opportunity years in the making. He stared into the flow—inundated himself with Ryan Laing.

The man had risen to mythological status within Echelon. Born in Colorado, he lost his parents to the Fire. Nothing remained of his youth. Nothing in Colorado, probably nothing in the man himself.

Jason swam backward, delving into the causes of the inferno that had destroyed Laing's childhood. Years of improper land use had led to the catastrophe. As it became inconvenient for the occasional fire to clear out the habitat's detritus, the natural cycle of fire and regrowth was stifled. Lightning strikes were quenched with the latest in fire retardant, dropped from hovering helicopters nicknamed Hippos.

Able to carry half a lake in their massive gullets, they were designed in the early years of the twenty-first century after a particularly devastating fire season. Fires had whipped across the west, torching housing developments and polluting the pristine mountain air. The firefighting capabilities thrown at the inferno were insufficient. Smoke jumpers died in valleys when the fire turned on them. Fire lines were erected. The fire jumped them. Planes dropped payloads of fire retardant—to little effect. Only luck and a little rain quelled the beast.

Man had been to the Moon, plumbed the oceans' depths, created tech beyond the wildest dreams of those living even a decade before; it seemed ridiculous that human life should remain at the mercy of something as primordial as a forest fire. That summer fueled the expenditure of vast amounts to pacify the threat. And thus, the Hippo came into existence. Using the latest in aerodynamics, it was engineered to carry a payload many times its own size.

For years, engineers had studied the flight of the bumblebee. How it could rip its bloated body from gravity's grip had long been a puzzle. Unknowingly, it went about its life contradicting the most basic rules of flight. Breakthroughs had blown the bumblebee's secret wide open, and the H-107 was born.

The H-107 had little resemblance to the copters of its day. It was ugly, ungainly, utterly inelegant. And it could carry enough flame retardant to stop any and all forest fires. Years passed with Hippos patrolling the mountains, forcing human will on the cycles of nature. Nature didn't seem to mind.

Laing grew up in Silt, Colorado, a town whose heyday came and went—if it existed at all—long before he arrived. His parents, Jack and Bubbles, were a dying breed. Both had grown up in the valley. Save Jack's military service, neither had left. Jack's ranch stood line of sight from the small farmhouse where he was born. Bubbles—a name fitting only in its incongruity to the owner's demeanor—taught at the schoolhouse she herself had attended. They ran cattle, relishing a lifestyle on the brink of destruction. Each year, competing with the conglomerates' hydroponic meat plants became more onerous.

Laing grew up watching his parents cling to the past. He laid fence, ran cattle, worked the ranch, but only during his time in the flow did he feel rooted. Sachs skimmed Laing's history in the flow during that era. He saw it all, read everything.

For better or worse, the Fire ended the protracted tragedy of Jack and Bubbles Laing. It swept in, a tsunami of flame and heat, insatiable. Years later, after investigation and inquiry, it was discovered that the greatest natural disaster in American history had been triggered by human hands. An off-duty fireman hoping to make an extra buck started a small blaze in a box canyon. He got more than he bargained for. Dumb, blind circumstance turned that flame into an unrelenting firestorm. Within hours, the fire had rolled out and blanketed the whole county; it became the Fire. The Hippos did their best. They lost the battle. The west lit up.

Sachs paddled through currents of information collected during Laing's deep retrieve. Before entering the fold, Echelon agents were mapped. The process revealed any hidden neuroses that could gum up the works. Jason dove into Laing's recollection of the Fire.

Flames licked at the Laing Ranch. Jack and Bubbles thrust fifteen-year-old Ryan into a musty bomb shelter under the house. Built during the Cold War, it hadn't been used in years. Jack and Bubbles didn't follow. They scrambled to water down the barn, too little too late. A flash flame ran them down. Laing heard the fire's howl as it sucked oxygen from his shelter. That wail still haunted Ryan's dreams.

The wind shifted, and Laing emerged into a new world. Scorched earth, smoldering relics of a life that was vibrant only minutes before. The flames had struck with the chaotic force of a tornado—reducing the barn and house to carbonized skeletons.

Ryan stumbled to the barn. Cows twitched, neural pulses flickering through their mangled frames. Jason saw Ryan coming upon his parents, smelling them first, charred meat. Jason sampled the horror, the abject terror the boy had felt.

A shift in the wind and fire marched back toward the ranch—itching to complete the immolation. Laing got into the family's beaten-up F150 and drove into the eye of the storm. Aggressive suicide, Sachs mused. He drove into the flames, eyes closed, tears evaporating on his cheeks from the heat. Somehow, the gas tank didn't explode. Somehow, the firestorm parted, offered him a path through. Laing's truck crashed through the wall of flame and came out the other side, charred black. The Fire drove him, corralled the terrified animal he'd become. It dumped him at the gate to Cheyenne Mountain.

Deep in shock, Laing mingled with the crowd at the military installation's entrance. The flames encroached, picking off the outliers. Laing just watched, shock subsuming him. Then strong hands hefted the boy into a troop transport carrier. Massive blast doors opened for an instant, allowing the carrier inside before locking shut with a definitive thunk. Strong enough to weather an atomic blast and designed to accommodate a lucky few through nuclear winter, the installation easily accommodated the ragtag exiles that had survived the inferno. Outside, the Fire gorged itself.

Inside Cheyenne Mountain, the teenager met Christopher Turing, Godfather of Echelon—probably the most powerful man on earth. Once quartering NORAD, America's missile defense system, Cheyenne Mountain had lost much of its usefulness as the need to maintain a threat of mutually assured destruction wavered. With NORAD gone, the base was retasked for scientific research. Echelon, through a dummy front, used a portion of the base to pull data. Its low ambient radiation made the subterranean base a perfect listening post. During a routine visit to the facility, Turing was caught in the firestorm.

Despite Laing's shell shock, the young man impressed Turing. In mere hours, Ryan's world had become vacant space. Turing saw the boy's potential. He occupied the vacancy, opening Laing to a world his father had fought against.

Turing made Ryan a god in that new world. Jason mused that everyone who chose a life within Echelon must accept the deity's mantle. To not admit such power was to be undeserving of it. Turing brought Ryan into Echelon, into his family. Like any intelligence organization, it was a family formed of peacemaker thieves and visionary liars, all plying their trade for the greater good.

Jason smiled to himself. A rigid morality didn't apply to the scope of power Echelon wielded. Yes, Echelon stole humanity's choicest fruit to nourish its own agenda. Laing had done more than most to achieve Echelon's ends: the maintenance of peace and enduring stability.

Sachs relished having Laing before him, strapped to the sensor grid, helpless, his deepest thoughts betrayed by the impulses of his body and brain. Unlike Ryan, Sachs detested fieldwork. He was the chess master. You don't send the master to do the work of a pawn, or even a king. Just the same, he admired the older man. He was constantly amazed at the man's drive, his unwavering commitment to the job.

Ryan rose from unconsciousness. Reality eclipsed dream, snapping into place and holding fast. He'd been here before. Not all his missions ended in success. He'd fractured an occasional order in his career and paid for it with experiences such as this. Sachs looked on coolly. Young, gloriously handsome, his features looked too perfect, devoid of humanity. He could never be an agent, Ryan mused; he was unforgettable. The impression of Sachs' features lingered as he leaned back and closed his eyes, steeling himself for the ordeal to come. Ryan didn't hate Sachs for these little sessions. He understood their necessity. Despite the syrupy sweetness that Sachs oozed, Ryan saw grit in the man.

In a projection hovering before him, Sachs saw all these thoughts and more. The grid was far more powerful than anyone suspected.

"You know I hate this, sir," Jason said. He loved it.

"Just get on with it."

"You disobeyed direct orders. Why?"

"No choice. I wanted to get the job done."

"Turing canceled the mission personally. He monitored your transmission. You knew this."

At Turing's mention, Sachs' monitor lit up. For all his outward composure, Laing's emotions betrayed massive volatility. Fear drove Ryan Laing. A parasite deep in his gut that both impelled and preyed on him. The man bore it in silence, with shame. Fear made his appetite for the work insatiable. It was his greatest asset and his deepest weakness.

Though the grid picked up this emotion spike, Jason read it easily in the man's eyes.

"You saw something," Sachs said.

The monitors again went red.

"I did the job. The data haven is out of commission."

"Your job was to perform reconnaissance. Nothing more."

"That mission became untenable."

"So you destroyed it all."

"There was no other option."

Jason knew it was time. He had a fleeting urge to reveal the gambit he was about to initiate. He knew in his heart that Laing would approve. But it was not to be. A pawn couldn't know the chess master's strategy. Jason approached Ryan and began disengaging the grid. It took several minutes and he worked in silence. Finally, the two faced each other.

Ryan let Jason unhook him. He hated the tangle of wires that came with debriefing, hated knowing that Jason gleaned so much from them. He wasn't particularly self-conscious. Just the same, he didn't like anyone rummaging around in his head. But if it had to be done, Sachs was as good as anyone. Ryan saw something of himself in Jason. The fact made Laing want to avoid the young man, but unable to actively dislike him. Few others had a problem disliking Jason Sachs.

Inspector general of Echelon at the tender age of twenty-nine, Sachs excelled at rooting out dissension in the ranks. He worked with a barbed, cruel proficiency. Ryan didn't know Sachs' past, couldn't really believe he had one. Sachs was less man than mechanism. Ryan couldn't imagine Sachs beyond the confines of Echelon. The man had lost himself down Echelon's rabbit hole. He didn't go home to a wife and kids. Of that, Ryan was sure.

"Turing pulled you from active," Jason said.

"Link me to him."

"He's intractable. I already pushed the issue."

"There was no possible means of retreat."

"I was on your flow—I saw. You acted on the option with the highest possibility of survival—a fact I pointed out to Mr. Turing."

"Set a meeting. I need to get back out."

"I need your help," Jason said.

That took a second to sink in.

"You?"

"I'll get you back to active, but you'll be working for me."

"I—"

"If not, you'll have plenty of free time."

"I'm not Internal Affairs."

Jason changed tack. He needed to keep Laing on edge. Ryan was too dangerous when he had legs to stand on.

"How is it, dealing with the drones all the time? Does it get trying?" Jason asked.

"Sachs, is this part of my debriefing?"

"Sorry, no. I'm curious. I won't ask again."

"I respect you, and what you do. But I'm an operator."

"I'm aware of that," Jason responded.

"So what the hell do you want?"

Jason paused, took a deep breath and lowered his tone, "There is a conspiracy within Echelon."

Ryan's features masked out. He blinked repeatedly. He felt his adrenal gland release, infusing him with noradrenaline. The hormone made the drones twitch. Deep breaths calmed them.

"You can't be serious," Laing finally said.

"For several months I've been tracking a breach in Echelon's system core. A subtle shift in mission parameters."

"The fallout of such a—"

"Would be complete. I can't let such a disaster go down on my watch."

"Who else knows?"

"Just you," Sachs said.

"Your own department is unaware?"

"I don't have many allies, Laing. Those I manage find me especially repugnant. Goes with the job."

"So figure this out yourself. It is your job."

"If I start poking around, the culprits will smell a witch hunt. If you do it, they'll be none the wiser."

Ryan held. Jason prodded him. "The ramifications of a conspiracy within Echelon would be global. The stability we maintain would crumble in weeks. No one knows the cruelty of human nature better than you," Jason said.

Ryan stared through Sachs, the tremors within his mind occupying him. "I . . . Okay."

Jason smiled. "Good. Poke around. You know the drill."

"I know it. I . . ."

Images of his flight through the haven flashed into Ryan's mind. Images he wished he could forget. Maybe it wasn't a coincidence that Turing revoked the mission personally. It had seemed odd that the head of Echelon would patrol such an inconsequential op. And yet Ryan knew that Turing monitored all his missions. He felt Christopher's presence in the field. It encouraged him, comforted him, made him capable of extraordinary feats.

"What is it?" Jason asked.

Since that first day deep in Cheyenne Mountain, Ryan had never known real solitude. Turing had bored out a place in Ryan's world. He gave the boy an outlet for his pain. He nurtured that boy through the subsequent years.

"It's safe to talk in here. Is there something you want to say?"

"No. Give me a week."

Ryan hopped off the chair and made for the exit.

"Laing," Sachs said.

Sachs waited for Laing's eyes to find his own. "I'm serious about nabbing this fucker," Sachs said. "Wherever the investigation leads, you have my full support."

Laing held firm, only a quick blink revealing his anxiety. "Sachs, it never occurred to me that you were anything but serious."

Ryan exited.

"Good hunting," Jason whispered into empty space.

6

Ryan emerged into Los Angeles' muddled sunlight from a nook behind the Walt Disney Concert Hall. Designed by Frank Gehry, its strutting titanium plates and long, fluid arcs stood out as much today as when it had opened.

Ryan attended now and then. He liked losing himself in someone else's dream, shrugging off the itch, if only for an hour, and returning to life a little more settled. He preferred theater to digitainment. Theater was allowed to go its own course—mostly. He knew it was ridiculous that he should have an issue with manipulated entertainment, as he worked for the organization responsible for the manipulation, but he found it hard to let go if he'd seen the show's script on the morning's scan port.

Laing eased into the pedestrian crush, just another suit shuffling through his commute—a rat on the wheel. He let his face slacken to impassivity as his thoughts churned. Sachs had sparked a maelstrom. The mere possibility of an infiltration . . .

A fellow pedestrian jostled Ryan out of his reverie. He stumbled, careening off the woman. She didn't bother turning around, just hollered over her shoulder, "Watch it, asshole!"

"Uhh, sorry. I—"

"Fuck off."

Jammed together, there was little chance of that. Ryan contented himself with fading back into the scenery.

—*Making friends?*

Sarah's voice crashed through Ryan's mind, scaring the shit out of him. He jumped, again bumping into his walking companion. She glared at him, then whipped an electro-stick from her purse and gave him a solid jab. The shock made his teeth crack together. He didn't respond, just stood there looking like he'd stuck his finger in a light socket.

No one else in the packed walkway seemed to notice the assault. No one wanted to get involved. They all just wanted to get home and hunker down in front of the latest vid special.

—*Thanks, I needed that.*

—*What?*

—*Some broad just electro-sticked me.*

—*Well, stop groping her.*

—*Commuting's a contact sport out here.*

—*I'll bet. Wouldn't know personally, but I hear LA is jammed up solid.*

Ryan cut off the walkway, through the turnstile, and jammed himself into the people mover. Made to look like a train from the London Underground, it went so far as to issue a "Mind the gap" warning before shutting him in.

—*How'd it go in debrief?*

—*That what you're getting me zapped for?*

—*Hey, I was worried about you. I'm on my own time here.*

The doors sealed not half a centimeter from Ryan's face. Once locked in, the passengers collectively exhaled, their added girth pressing Ryan into the plexi. He had little choice but to watch downtown fade into haze. Only the Gehry building offered discontinuity. The other structures ascended from massive bases into ever-thinning spires—ethereal ziggurats rising into the stratosphere. Well, maybe not that far—but LA's haze gave the architecture an awe-inspiring solemnity. The sunsets weren't bad either. Ryan headed west on the people mover. He watched the ziggurats. He remembered Sarah.

—*Well, how was it?* she asked.

—*Went fine. A choke collar was just added to my short leash.*

—*You deserve it. I got reamed on my end.*

Ryan thought a grunt of exasperation her way.

—*I'm supposed to be your controller. That means I'm in control.*

—*I won't justify my actions twice. You don't like my tactics, bugger off. Get out of my head and heckle someone else.*

—*Charming to the last. I'm not buggering anywhere. I've got my orders same as you. I just choose to follow them.*

The mover pulled into Century City. Ryan fought to remain on board and not get swept up in the sea of passengers plunging into the sprawl's depths. There was a big Mormon settlement here. The tabernacle on the hill gleamed a pristine white. They must scrub that sucker daily, Ryan thought. Everyone needed to cling to something. If that something revolved around a guy who pulled off a miracle or two—

so be it. Laing didn't like it when they came to his door—which wasn't often—but he understood their motivation. Laing was an evangelist too. But instead of pulling in the odd housewife, he and Echelon forced the issue. Anything that wasn't Echelon-approved never made it to the door at all.

The gap was minded, the doors sealed and the electro mags engaged, rising up over the superconducting track. Laing shot west, toward the ocean.

—If you're so regimented, what are you doing in my head on your own time?

—I was worried! I mean . . . I was curious. Debrief can be grueling and you're—

—Not so stable?

He wondered if she could glean his inflection, or if his words just flickered across a monitor, sterilized.

—You're an exasperating man, Agent Laing.

—But you knew that going in.

—I did. Report to central on reaching your terminal. We will discuss your latest failure and work out something simpler for you to undertake next.

—Can I end this transmission?

—No, but you seem quite capable of ignoring me.

—True.

He let her diatribe fall into the background and concentrated on exiting the mover without getting electrocuted. The doors opened, and Ryan flowed with the sea rush. He emerged into the solitude of the Venice Beach night and ambled through the canals that had given the city its name.

A marketing ploy during Venice's heyday, the canals served no purpose other than offering a novel view from one's house. That had all gone to hell when the oceans rose. Now squatters, artists and misfits lived in the waterlogged husks of ancient mansions. Ryan's looked as dilapidated as the next.

Ryan had moved in immediately after his recuperation. It seemed more fitting than his old place in Sky City—which was firmly attached to the ground. In Venice, each occupant had devised some means of keeping the swelling sea at bay. The closer one got to the ocean, the more drastic these measures became and the wilder the inhabitants grew. Ryan's was right on the water. He had blown out the first of three floors, allowing the ocean to ebb and flow right through. Only the steel stanchions supporting the rest of the house remained.

Ambling through the salted wasteland, Ryan could feel a storm brewing. It would be an exciting night. He waded down the walkway, his biz suit looking more and more out of place in the environs.

—*With all of LA, how could you choose to live in Venice? Hear it's a total shit-hole.*

—*Sarah, I appreciate the personal treatment, but fuck off for a while, will ya?*

—*You're a piece of work, Laing. Remember who your fucking friends are. And that's strictly off the record.*

—*Nothing's off the record.*

—*End trans.*

Ryan sighed. Alone at last. Well, not quite. He sensed movement from one of the junks that plied the coast, hoarding and trading. After the rich had scattered, Venice became a trade zone for everything illicit. Of course, no one was free from Echelon's gaze, but this was purely small-time. Just the same, the brass were happy to have someone in the trenches. That Ryan chose to make the trenches his home was another matter.

A young man jumped from a junk and headed for Ryan. Tall and lean, he had the typical wharf-rat look: vaguely Asian, rope thin, steel hard, ready for a fight. A muffled splash behind Ryan alerted him that he'd been surrounded. A middle-aged man in a slick suit screamed easy mark. Ryan kept walking, the setting sun in his eyes.

One of the rats behind him lunged, bringing a pipe up in a wide arc and swinging it toward Ryan's concussion-addled brain. He caught the rod easily, twisting the arm attached to it and felling the attacker. Before the other assailant could register apprehension, Ryan's hand shot out and caught the man's Adam's apple. The man stopped short, unsure of what to do.

"Welcome home," the man approaching Ryan said.

"How's tricks, Tex?"

"Same as always, sir."

Ryan let Texas John approach. Heat seared between the two, then quickly dissipated into broad smiles. Ryan let his assailant go and warmly shook the man's hand.

"Apologies. Just biz. Didn't recognize you," Tex said.

"Wouldn't feel like home without a mugging at my doorstep."

Tex smiled. "Come. Invite me inside before we get pelted with waves. Then you'll give me a beer and I'll listen to all the bullshit you can ladle out."

"Sounds good to me."

Ryan led Tex into his home.

7

Sarah ripped off her flow goggles. The laser projectors firing info into her eyes shot a distorted image onto the ceiling before shutting down. Laing pushed her to the brink. She'd talk into his mind, worm deep into him, hunting for connection. He'd allow her in, only to rip her from their confederacy and remind her unceremoniously just how green she was. Asshole. She might be new, but she was still the Man. She ran him, not vice versa. She wished she had shocked him herself, and took a perverse satisfaction from having sparked the incident.

She was good in the flow, great even. Reality was another matter. In reality, purpose got clouded with desire, want and subterfuge. She liked the pure truth of numbers, stats, and decisions made on logic's bedrock. But her work with Ryan, their proximity via the drones, had entwined the smooth sterility of the flow with a mess of emotions. Jackass.

It was her own damn fault for getting attached. She was his controller, nothing more. And he was unstable, a loose cannon in her roster of armaments. Had Ryan not been Turing's pet, he'd be dead. Instead he'd been revived, pulled back from death's door and given another shot. He was a dinosaur. She was the new breed.

Sarah paced the room, her emotions fading to a dull gray. Despite her abilities, all the power and position she'd gobbled up, a pervasive depression had settled in. She could inhale only enough air to survive. In the flow, sifting through the crush of data, she forgot her asphyxiation.

On the grubby couch next to her, Elaine stirred. They occupied a spartan apartment in the city-scraper of Inverness, Scotland. It was a good deal all around. The university was on floors 658 through 660, and they had found this nook on the southeast corner of 657. That was the good news. Unfortunately, the rest of the floor was industrial. The unremitting cacophony took months to get used to. Now, Sarah barely noticed it.

It being early evening, Elaine was just getting up. They'd met in university, both thrilled to be accepted to the hallowed halls of New Rollins. That thrill had died quickly, and they bonded in dissatisfaction. Elaine expressed her rage by piercing every spare piece of flesh and becoming the lead singer of Agamemnon's Mitten, a screamo poetry band.

Sarah's abilities had led her to Echelon. She also played bass in Elaine's band. Since finding outlets for their angst, neither had much use for school. Strictly speaking they were still enrolled. Living off the university's tit, Elaine called it. In reality, they'd fallen into a limbo filled with masses of disgruntled youth looking to blow off steam, and get laid as often as possible. Elaine was tops on that score. Sarah was no slouch herself.

Fully awake, Elaine took a couple slugs off a half-empty bottle and offered it to Sarah. She declined.

"Kill the pacing. You're giving me a headache," Elaine said.

"Couldn't be the hangover?"

Elaine smiled, recalling slivers of last night's debauchery. "Well, you're not helping matters."

"You gonna be ready for tonight?"

"You gotta ask?" Elaine said.

"Good."

"Just need to put my face on."

Elaine ambled over to the WC. Putting her face on involved inserting the fifty odd earrings, nose rings, and so on that had to be removed before sleep at the risk of catching her face on the bedding, or on whoever might be sharing her bed.

Sarah was looking forward to the evening. She knew it was ridiculous, raging against a machine she secretly operated, but it was fun. She could be both Echelon analyst and rebel bassist.

She prepared herself. Unlike Elaine's megapunk style, Sarah rebelled through utter conformity. Onstage, she wore outfits of such sparing elegance that the audience, manic and throbbing with drugs and beat, saw her as an angel. She looked good playing her stand-up bass behind Elaine. No pussy electro shit for her.

Elaine emerged with a kilo of silver on her face. They trundled out of the apartment and into Clinton Hall. The industrial halls in Inverness were all named after American presidents, a subtle joke on the building planners' part that Sarah approved of. The Penthouse halls were named after Chilean dictators. Pinochet Place was particularly swanky, she heard.

Everywhere, machines churned. Their neighbor, a manufacturing company, made motorcycles at the rate of one per minute. Several days before, a cycle had been misplaced. The machinery couldn't account for it. Of course, Sarah could afford to buy one, but Elaine preferred nabbing it. She considered it payback for their sleepless nights.

It took half an hour to get out of the city building. Elevators, the lifeblood of the mile-high structure, ate up time. Fortunately, they had digitainment consoles so you could check out the latest show while commuting.

They emerged, hopped on the bike, and headed into the country. Negotiating the roads on the heavy bike took skill. Doing it with a bass strapped to the back like an engorged shark's fin was downright terrifying. Elaine liked to speed—just on principle. Sarah held on tight, let the adrenaline rip through her. She needed the amp.

In half an hour, they'd emerged from the building's footprint. It was a beauty. Had to admit it. So many millions doing their living and dying in the ether. The city-scraper allowed its residents all the benefits of a metropolis while preserving the Highlands for recreation. Over the years, though, people got used to living in the sky. It became the norm. Sky dwellers looked down on the earthbound. Why leave the culture, art and biz of Inverness for hills and dales? Besides, you could see most of Scotland from the higher floors. No need to get one's shoes dirty tramping through it.

The screamo poetry world embraced the lowlands, plodding gleefully through the mud. It felt like good, solid rebellion. And the venues were supercheap. Elaine and Sarah sped toward the village of Ross and Cromarty. Largely unchanged over the centuries, the little town's residents trundled along with no obvious means of support. Tonight they found themselves deluged in angry youth.

Outside the town, a grizzled husk of a castle loomed. Kinkell, once used as a fortified way station for sixteenth-century tax collectors, had fallen into disrepair. In the twentieth it had been revived by a pop artist. He had lived in the castle, slowly filling its grounds with his sculpture. Now, it had fallen back into the shambles of history. Sarah had studied Stonehenge—long gone now. In a few more millennia, Kinkell might be thought of in a similar light.

They pulled up just in time for sound check. The stage had been erected under one of the artist's monolithic sculptures. A massive bronze pyramid with a gentle vertical cut bored through the center, it made for a great venue. Didn't need anything other than that. Sarah didn't listen to Elaine psyching up the rest of the band—all equally pierced. There'd be some serious knife work in their future—just closing up all the holes. She wondered if they got waterlogged in the bathtub.

They headed into the remnants of the castle to party, waiting for the audience to get good and toasted before starting the show. Elaine then led them around the pyramid and onto the stage. A seething froth of groupies, moshers, and megapunks raged below them. Good to have a following. With a primal shriek, Elaine kicked them off, and Agamemnon's Mitten ripped into its first set. Elaine screeched out seared frustration. Norm, who went by Stump, banged his drums with tribal exaltation. Hell Cat, a smallish Nigerian, wailed on his axe—the kid was good. And behind it all, Sarah laid down the beat.

She wore a vintage, cream-colored pantsuit. She suspected that a blouse was supposed to be worn under the jacket but didn't bother. When not slamming into their neighbors, or being slammed by the sound waves, those in the front could catch a glimpse of her milk-fresh skin under the jacket. If they paused, they could see the briefest glimpse of her right nipple. The fierce energy of her figure, of that quick glimpse, added to the crowd's frenzy. She had her own set of groupies (male and female) who came for that alone.

The band played, and she kept the beat. About an hour in, they'd screamed, banged and picked themselves out. Sarah kept playing. She let her beat blossom. It expanded into a melody of its own. It rippled and curved. She fell into an ecstasy, slowly moving against the cool frame of the bass. The crowd moved with her.

She threw the strings out of tune, somehow managing melody in the resulting chaos. By the time Hell Cat joined back in, she had the bass back in perfect tune. Elaine launched another vocal assault, and Sarah faded into the background.

Shivering, the melody hung with Sarah, soft and malleable. She longed for time to revel in the feeling. Instead she played on, working back into the bone-jarring bite that was the Mitten's trademark.

The crowd surged with maximum energy, crested and crashed out in climax. Sarah wasn't a showman, but she faked it pretty well. She stepped back and spun the bass before her. The move saved her life.

The bass shredded mid-spin. Hot pain shot up her leg. Splinters ripped through her suit as bullets thumped up the instrument, marching for her chest. Adrenaline maxed panic. Pain scorched her side as she toppled into the crowd below her, desperate. Who the fuck was shooting at her?

Drowning in a mosh of feet and budding terror, Sarah caught Elaine's eye. Her vocals shifted to a panic-tipped scream on seeing Sarah drenched in blood. The fusillade of bullets continued—hunting Sarah. The crowd around her took body hits. With the blood and bullets came pandemonium.

A steel-tipped boot caught Sarah in the temple, driving her into the mud. She blacked out. In a mad impulse, Elaine plunged into the crowd and pulled Sarah from the dank turf. Bedlam rising, Elaine dragged Sarah behind a subwoofer. Crouched behind the massive speaker, Elaine smacked Sarah hard across the face. She came back reluctantly. Elaine pulled off her jean vest and draped it over Sarah's torso.

"Sarah, wake up! Someone's fucking shooting at us!"

"At me. They're shooting at me."

"But why?" Elaine asked, her voice quivering panic.

"Elaine, you need to get away from me—or you'll be a target."

"A target—what are you talking about? Who the hell are you?"

"I'm your friend," Sarah sputtered.

The shooter found them. Bullets ripped the woofer to shreds. Elaine slumped over, in shock. Sarah grabbed her hand and yanked them into the heart of the panicked throng. Safety there. She kicked and weaved, reaching what had once been a tranquil pond. It was now teeming with stampeding bodies. At the end of the pond an elegant, bronze Aphrodite rested on a marble pedestal. That would make good cover—at least until the shooter realigned. From the *thwak* of the bullets hitting the pond and the unlucky souls near them, Sarah knew the shooter was directly behind her. She dodged and wound through the throng, shoving Elaine behind the statue and landing heavily on top of her.

Sarah regained her footing and peeked around the side of the pedestal. In the millisecond before marble chips blasted her, she made out the assassin. The man approached steadily, gun held with a casual familiarity. Who was this guy? A crazed fan? Not likely. The killer was too methodical. Couldn't be her other job—because, well, that would mean someone knew about Echelon. And that was impossible. Then the gun came level and marble splintered. With the searing sting of shrapnel hitting her cheek, Sarah lunged back behind the pedestal.

Elaine hovered near shock. Fear-drenched jitters made her facial adornment jingle. Tears streamed down her cheeks, smearing her eyeliner. Her eyes held the crazed panic of a hunted animal. Trying to calm her, Sarah rested a hand on Elaine's back. The mere contact sparked Elaine's flight-or-fight response. There was no fight left in her. She had spent it all saving Sarah from the crowd. Elaine sprang to her feet and ran.

"No!" Sarah screamed, shocked at her friend's sudden bolt.

No time to spare, Sarah whirled, grabbed two rocks, and lobbed one at the assassin. It arced toward him, and despite his training, he looked up for the briefest second. Sarah used that second to fling the second rock at the assassin's head. The killer realized his mistake and dove, the second rock nicking his right eye. In spite of the pain, he rolled perfectly in the soft heather and came up in a firing stance. A silenced shot whizzed past Sarah. She felt more than heard the soft impact of bullet hitting flesh. Elaine fell. The assassin shifted his stance and trained his gun on Sarah. Her last memory would be of her best friend's death.

A single piercing shot echoed through the pandemonium. It took Sarah a beat to realize she wasn't dead. The assassin flew back, his head evaporating with the impact of a high-velocity hollow point.

From behind a tree another man emerged and loped easily toward the assassin. With little left in the way of rational thought, Sarah wheeled around and crouched over Elaine. For an instant, Elaine's fear-soaked eyes focused on Sarah.

"Elaine, I'm sorry," she sobbed.

But it was too late. Elaine's eyes clouded, and she shrank in Sarah's arms. Sarah felt the man approach and hunker down behind her. She didn't care. Let him kill her and be done with it. He crouched down and gazed at Elaine. Gently, he reached out and shut Elaine's unseeing eyes. Through her tears, Sarah looked into the man's face. In the moonlight, she could just make out his features. An old man's eyes stared back at her. It was a face she knew.

Christopher Turing had just saved her life.

8

Life wasn't fair. In fact, it was goddamned malicious. The thought hammered through Ryan's raw circuitry as he sought the courage to rise from his temperfoam cocoon. Sandblasted eyes and a syrupy mouth let Ryan know that his hangover hadn't yet matured to peak throb. It would crescendo in a couple more hours, leaving him groveling and sweat slick. So he had that to look forward to—which was nice.

He stared at the ceiling and tried to remember if he had done anything particularly stupid the night before. No, he'd stayed in the house, gotten thoroughly sauced with Tex. Beer after beer. Then something harder. Aged mezcal that Tex was hauling. Ryan doubted it got better with age. He wrested himself from the bed and stared into the mirror. Same could be said for yours truly, he thought, looking at the haggard shell before him.

It made no sense. Just plain cruelty—one more sick joke in the long series that had become his life. The drones made it very difficult for him to get drunk. Sensing a shift in brain chemistry, they fought hard to retrieve status quo. He bested them only through superior firepower. Bottle after bottle into the breach. And yet the drones helped not at all with his hangover. Nothing. They took a holiday and let him suffer. He supposed he could sample something harder, but it seemed like too much effort to find a new drug after so much experience with the bottle.

He doubted he'd been much company to Tex, but the kid didn't seem to mind. Lithe, jovial and always ready for the next con, Tex had come on the scene just as Ryan arrived in Venice. Ryan had immediately taken to him.

Ryan shuffled down to the main floor, a jumble of living room, dining room, and kitchen. Passed out on a couch, Tex snored deeply. From his pallor, Ryan gleaned that Tex's day would not be any cheerier than his own.

Ryan got himself to the kitchen before a wave of nausea flung him to the countertop. He hunkered down and suffered. It was worth it. In the haze of the previous evening, Ryan vaguely remembered a moment of peace.

He fumbled for the digipad that controlled the kitchen. Then he thought, Fuck it. Through his throbbing headache, he focused on feeling out the pad. The drones bristled. And there it was. It sounded like the soft chirping of a chick. It smelled like mezcal. Well, everything did at this point. He concentrated on the electronic controls and ordered breakfast: coffee, coffee, more coffee. The coffeemaker sputtered to life and Ryan smiled. Maybe there was some justice.

He stumbled off to the can as Tex awoke. The shower worked its magic. Ryan felt each heat-filled pellet thumping onto his battered body, a thousand fingers massaging him. He gingerly felt his broken rib. Nothing. And his fingers looked perfect—fixed and fully functional. The damn things were efficient. He probed the nature of his headache, realizing that it was purely alcohol induced. An aficionado of both booze and concussions, Ryan could tell the subtle difference.

The pellets pounded down, washing away his boozy funk. He chose lavender-scented cleanser. And then he splurged, rinsing with water. Honestly, he preferred the pellets. Drying off was a pain in the ass. He shaved and hunted down a clean shirt and a pair of jeans. He emerged to find Tex huddled over his coffee.

"Christ, Laing, I feel like hammered mule shit."

"Help yourself."

"I will, and I already have," Tex grunted.

Ryan poured himself a cup and moved over to the plexi windows that offered a view onto a very angry sea. Rollers hammered the stilts and gave the whole place a gentle sway.

"Storm's coming," Ryan said.

"Thank God. I thought it was the booze."

"You got work today?"

"A ship's worth of toy guns," Tex said.

Ryan gave him a squint.

"Hey, a man's gotta make a livin'."

Tex suspected that Ryan was an arms dealer. What other suit would live in Venice over Chatsworth Estates? Ryan did nothing to counter Tex's suspicions.

Suddenly, the whole house began to chirp. The downside of having everything connected was that an incoming summons lit the whole damn house up like a Christmas tree.

"Guess I better hit the clock myself," Ryan said.

"Don't worry about me. I'll let myself out."

Ryan liked Tex. Probably the closest friend he had. But there was no way he'd leave Tex unsupervised in the house for a second.

"Just the same, I'll see you out."

Tex smiled. He knew the score. Ryan saw regret in Tex's eyes; he'd wasted the night sleeping when he could have been snooping. At the door, Tex dropped into his dinghy.

"No words of wisdom to start my day?" Ryan asked. Tex was obsessed with America's Old West, hence the self-given nickname.

Tex gazed at the sea thoughtfully and retrieved one of his favorite cowboy sayings from the plethora he kept on call.

"Don't squat with your spurs on." With that, he shoved off.

"I'll keep that in mind," Ryan said with a laugh. He shut the door, replaced the sandbag, and ambled back upstairs.

The lights continued to flash. The appliances continued to chirp. He took another sip of coffee and stared into the churning ocean. He felt the anxiety rise. Never far off. Impending doom seemed to hover over him. Better get to work.

He climbed up to his loft, little more than a piece of floor cantilevered over the rest of the space. Gusts of wind buffeted the house, making it sway with the rising ocean swells. He sat on the temperfoam chair and picked up the only thing on his desk, a small visor. He put it on and clocked in.

For many, flow shift induced a moment of panic. The interstitial space between reality and the flow held demons. No rules, no boundaries, just endless space, an infinite blank. Ryan found it comforting. He opened himself to the black, letting it take him as reality fell away. Then the flow emerged from four cardinal points, sloshing over him and finally locking solid. An entire reality built block by block by the hands of man.

He sped through data streams, slowing only to check the front page of the "paper," an anachronism held over from the twentieth. Ryan hadn't seen real paper in years. All quiet. A small disturbance outside of Inverness, Scotland. Looked like a crazed fan had dispatched the megapunk band, Agamemnon's Mitten. Twelve spectators dead.

Ryan hadn't heard of the band. The buzzing in his head was music enough.

He continued on, pushing through the blocks and barriers, tunneling into the framework underlying the flow itself. At its center, he halted at an inconsequential entrance with a single moniker on it: IN GOD WE TRUST.

The door scanned him, matched his vitals to record, decided not to fry him, and opened up. Another plaque hovered in the half construct beyond: ALL OTHERS WE MONITOR.

Ryan pushed through the plaque and entered Echelon. He loved the place. No frills. No fancy rendering. Just a sea of cubicles surrounded by chrome walls. He shifted past other agents. Some stood brilliant—sporting the same tech-sensitive visor he wore. Others rezed scratchier—in low-rent, maybe even public 'ware. He nodded to a few, but that was the extent of his cordiality. Interoffice acquaintanceships weren't condoned.

He found his desk, a cubicle like any other. He settled in, checked his mail. Only six messages. Two notified him of his substandard performance on the last op. He'd been demoted, whatever that meant, and put on probation.

One was from Jason Sachs. It listed codes that Ryan couldn't believe the inspector general had access to. He committed them to memory and junked them in the shredder. Even such precautions were silly. Someone with Echelon access could easily put shredded data back together. But it took time. Besides, Jason had camouflaged his transmission.

The last message was the one that lit his house up. It was a summons from the man himself. Turing wanted to see him. Fuck.

Turing's office stood in contrast to the rest of the construct. Echelon was the core upon which the flow rested. It dealt in raw code. High-splash rendering was for civs. At Echelon, you never forgot where you were, awash in a sea of data.

Ryan walked through the cubicle maze, approaching one of the hundred or so doors along the hall. The brushed metal decor suddenly felt oppressive. Ryan almost ripped his goggles from his face, quelling a snap need to jump free, go back to bed, sleep the day away, anything. The door slid open, and Ryan entered another world.

Though he'd almost single-handedly constructed Echelon's current iteration, Christopher Turing hated the flow. He loved the elegance of pure math, but hated the cold sterility of data transfer. And so his office resembled that of a nineteenth-century professor. Oak bookshelves ringed the two-story space. A desk of rich Cuban mahogany dominated the room, the leather chair behind it cradling the man himself. Though little more than a dream made permanent, Turing luxuriated in his creation. This was his domain. The very shift of scenery made that clear. Echelon was Turing's realm. Turing didn't rise to shake hands. It wasn't done in the flow.

As Turing's view up-shifted, the papers on his desk went transparent, a security precaution. They would return to opaque when the visitor departed.

"Ryan," Turing said in a rich baritone. Warmth rolled through Turing's chocolate-brown eyes, the curve of a smile crinkling his aging skin. Then the emotion passed and Turing's tone settled into gray slate. "Sit," he said.

Ryan sank into a plush leather chair and looked up at his mentor. Turing made sure he was always the tallest man in the room. Ryan had a childish urge to grow his holo but decided against it. Turing dominated any room he entered. No one defied the height restriction; that would be tantamount to challenging Echelon's alpha male.

"I'm not sure you understand what a precious commodity you have become," Turing began.

"You mean after my years of training and service, or after getting mangled and put back together by your latest creation?"

No smile. No wrinkle over the left eye revealing amusement. Maybe he's turned his facial digitizer off, Ryan thought. Ryan wondered where Turing actually was. It had been nearly a decade since they'd seen each other in the flesh. Not that it mattered.

"That creation saved your life. And I'd appreciate it if you would call a spade a spade. Those drones swimming through you are not my creation. Like everything else in our roster, Echelon stole them."

"That's a bit harsh, isn't it?" Turing was a cynic, but rarely sarcastic.

"We stole them," Turing repeated. "We steal the best the world has to offer. Yes, we combine our loot in ways the original owners would never have imagined, but that's only because our cache is so great.

We gather the cream of human inspiration's crop and make it our own."

"You mean when we're not busy manipulating the data passing through our banks and shaping world affairs?" Ryan countered.

A hint of a smile from the old man. So his digitizer was still on. Interesting.

"Precisely," Turing said.

"I've already been through debrief."

Turing's eyes turned up and left. He scanned the report.

"I know. Says your disregard of a direct order was justified by circumstance. That you're to be returned to active duty. I don't agree."

"You don't?"

"Odd that the inspector general would think himself qualified to make decisions on your field capabilities."

"Have I fallen into a turf war?"

Turing paused. Far away, in flesh, Ryan's head throbbed. The coffee wasn't helping. He tried to push away the memory of Turing's data floating through the haven. He needed to keep straight.

"You were not authorized to raid that haven," Turing said.

"Authorized? To do my job? I find havens; I infiltrate; I drop the bug. Why would I need authorization to do my job?"

"Because you are different than you were. Because you're more valuable now. I can't afford to lose you over some second-rate storage facility."

"It was more than that," Ryan said. Might as well push a little. See where it leads.

"In spite of your lone-wolf mentality, you do not have access to the full picture. There are pieces missing."

"Fill me in, then."

"Sorry," Turing said.

"Keeping your cards pretty close."

"You ignored my direct order, Ryan. As such, you are not only barred from the field, you are to return to Op Tech for further testing."

"I'm no lab rat."

"Agent Laing, that's exactly what you are. You were an operative with access to Echelon's rips—to everything we pulled from the data stream and every manipulation we introduced. You were the best. You are now an experiment gone awry, a man who must be protected for his own good."

Turing emphasized this last sentence. Was there something missing here, or was Turing taking Ryan into custody?

"Listen, we need to discuss that data haven," Ryan stammered.

"Why would I bother with such trivial matters?"

"Because they concern you."

"Agent Laing, I operate a net that catches every single bit of data humanity creates. At some level, everything concerns me."

Ryan's blood boiled. He felt the cage bars rising around him. His chances of maintaining any semblance of sanity without being able to work were nil. Dave Madda would have a ringside seat to Ryan's plunge into the maelstrom.

"We both know—"

"You know nothing!" Turing shouted, rising from his chair. In his entire life, Ryan had never witnessed Turing raise his voice. The old man was unshakable, the mathematical genius who distilled everything into a chess match that he never, ever lost. Ryan's holo jumped in shock. A pang of fear goosed his adrenal medulla into action. Back in reality, Ryan swallowed hard, his throat scratchy.

Turing loomed over Ryan. "Between Madda's experiments, work up a report. If I have time, I'll read it."

Ryan waded through a quagmire of desperation, trying to maintain control. "Sir, I . . . You know I can't go back. I'm not Madda. Can't live in a cave forever."

"You have no choice. There's no other place for you."

"I won't—"

"Stop. It's already done."

Tingling through the backdrop of his consciousness, Ryan felt the flesh pull. Sound, light, movement. In his house. Pulsing hot fear, Ryan toggled a switch on his gear package. The image of Turing's office blurred, then sheared into a billion pixels. Laing's holo exploded into shards as he ripped free of the flow. His last image of Turing revealed a man noticeably older, a frown chiseled into his pallid visage.

"There's no other place for you, Ryan. I am sorry."

· · · · ·

It took time to reengage. Time Ryan didn't have. He heard the thump of a copter. Tremors ran through the house. Maybe it was just the storm. Then, through the raging tempest, Laing heard a second copter joining the ratcheting thump of the first. He had seconds to spare. Why was Turing doing this? Did he suspect that Ryan had seen his account in the haven? He must. And this was his response. Ryan had become a liability to be snuffed out. The betrayal stung. Rage surfaced. Laing wouldn't make it easy.

—*Go quietly.*

He'd expected the thundering baritone of an amplified soldier's voice. Instead, he got Sarah.

—*Et tu?*

—*It's not what you think,* she responded.

Suddenly, plexi shattered in every direction. Below him, seven soldiers crashed into the room, their umbilicals to the copters quickly detaching.

—*It's worse,* he thought.

Ryan knew his chances were minuscule. Taking down mercs was one thing. Seven Echelon agents was another.

"Fuck it," he said to himself, to Sarah, to Turing's invisible presence.

He vaulted over the rail of his second-floor perch. An agent broke the five-meter fall. Ryan crashed into him, rolled free from the tangle of arms and legs, and stood to face his end. Gel-composite armor flowed like greased silk over the agents' bodies, color shifting to match the environment.

They held back. One raised an odd-looking pistol. Ryan pivoted, closing the distance between them. He slipped around the agent, wrenching the man's arm as the gun discharged. An agent standing in the kitchen took the hit in the chest. Viscous liquid splattered over the man's suit and face. Couldn't be blood. He tried to rise, but stumbled and blacked out. They were firing tranq balls—enough to pacify a rhino.

Ryan continued his turn, twisting the man's arm back on itself. He felt a muffled pop as the shoulder came out of socket.

A second agent rushed him. Ryan pulled the man in his arms around, spinning him over his shoulder and slamming the bulk into his attacker. The two crumpled.

Ryan fired a back kick in time to thwart a third agent's attempt to lock onto his neck. Sooner or later, one of them would get tired of this and shoot him with real artillery. He wouldn't make it easy.

As the agents regrouped, Ryan made a break for it. He sprinted through the kitchen, an agent right on him. Laing snagged the refrigerator door as he passed. He whipped it open just as the agent fired. The tranq splashed on the door and all over the man.

—*Ryan. You can't escape.*

—*Then get it over with!*

—*They don't want to kill you.*

—*I know. I'm too valuable.*

—*Ryan . . .*

—*I'll give you a corpse, but that's all I'm offering.*

He continued his flight up the stairs and into the bedroom. A dyed-in-the-wool insomniac, Ryan's one indulgence had been the latest in bedding. The whole bedroom floor had been retrofitted. At the moment, it was in day mode, just a pillow and sheet puddled on a hard floor.

The men entered and surrounded him. As they moved in, he engaged his bad-ass bed. The floor under the agents buckled and went soft. The agents lost their balance, and he attacked. Unable to keep their feet, the agents could do little more than parry Laing's blows. They tried to lock on with their tranqs, but the shots went wild. I might just get out of this, Ryan thought. But his hubris was short-lived. The lead man, given an instant to recuperate, kicked off the floor and lunged to the nearest wall. His feet and one hand stuck to it like glue. That was new.

Entomologist Jeb Dorn had made the discovery mere days before at the University of California, Riverside. After years of fruitless exploration, he'd tripped the switch. The genetic coding of *Ornithonyssus sylviarum,* a blood-feeding mite, unspooled before him. He cracked through the coding of the ectoparasite's pulvilli, the sticky pads with which the mite clung to its host. Jeb made sheets of it. Echelon had it the next day.

The other agents took their leader's cue, lunging for the walls. Each drew his weapon and took a bead on Laing, now totally exposed in the middle of the room.

Shit. Ryan lurched left, then churned his feet. He hurled himself from the firing line and toward the bay windows. Tranqs whizzed past him, exploding off the furniture. He ran straight and hard. Behind Ryan, the leader steadied himself. He took careful aim, waiting for the optimal line of fire.

Ryan jumped, crashing through the window and into the raging seas below. Like a long jumper, his legs churned as he hit the apex of his arc. Then the tranq ball hit him. The back of his neck exploded in a rush of pain.

Ryan toppled over in the air, feeling the tranq's effect even before he hit the water. He crashed into the churning waves. He'd heard drowning was the best way to go—a smooth trip into the gray zone. As consciousness fled, he realized he'd soon find out.

—*Fucking stupid bastard*, Sarah said through the ether.

Ryan couldn't find the energy to respond as the ocean swallowed him. He was a sinker. Something about his body type.

As a kid, his parents had taken him to a reservoir named Ruedi, high in the Rocky Mountains. Splashing around the craft on which his parents lounged, he stopped moving and let himself sink. Cold water pressed in on him, shifting through blues and greens before settling into a tar black. He exhaled and sank deeper, into an intoxicating wash of relaxation. His tension dissipated into the murk. Then he broke the spell, kicking to the surface. His parents had dragged him into the craft, hugged him, scolded him and never returned to the reservoir.

Now, struggling through rough seas, that memory of peace lured him. He fought it. Must always fight. No choice in that. But the force of the waves and the effects of the tranq blast outgunned him. The surf pounded Ryan into deep water. He could sense the agents scanning. But even they were nothing compared to the force of the storm. He'd escaped their threat only to succumb to another. Cresting a wave, he took a huge gulp of seawater. It choked him. He thrashed. Then something hit him on the back of the head so damn hard he saw stars. He realized too late that he wasn't paddling.

9

"Goddamn it!" Sarah ripped off her flow gear and chucked it at the wall. Sweat glistened across her brow. She tried to smooth out the panic-racked hyperventilation she'd fallen into. As reality settled, she sucked in lungfuls of air and forced herself to calm down. She gazed at her surroundings, yearning for something to ground her. Nothing—a perfectly comfortable, utterly generic hotel room. She could be anywhere.

Mere days ago, she'd found Ryan's stubborn obstinacy mildly attractive. Tough, even cruel at times, he had that deep well of tortured baby-boy angst that she couldn't resist. Of course, Sarah never told him that. Now, his death infuriated her. Sarah's rage swelled, surged and finally washed out, receding into an abiding despair. She'd lost him. Another failure.

Sarah Peters' life had gone dark. She'd seen the potential for such on entering Echelon but never ran the numbers, never did the simulation to see just how fucked it could all get, and at such an alarming rate.

How does one say no to running on the inside track? How does one say no to engineering peace? To having an unknowing world owe you the greatest of debts? Sarah couldn't. Now, here she was, lost in a catastrophe that had shattered her life and threatened to spread like wildfire.

The nightmare at Kinkell felt distant, eons past. Her life before that night had evaporated. She could never return to her cramped hovel in Inverness. With Elaine gone, what was the point? Thinking of her brought fresh tears to Sarah's eyes.

On that night, huddled over her dead friend with Turing at her side, Sarah had tried to hold back. She wouldn't let herself cry in front of the stone-faced titan. But the pressure built, finally bursting free in great, hulking sobs. What the fuck, right? She wasn't a field agent. Turing wrapped an arm around her. The gesture was awkward, Turing uncomfortable with the contact. She pulled herself together.

And then Turing told her she had to die. She almost wished he'd meant it.

He collected her ID and retrieved the assassin's weapon. Sarah stumbled after him, lost in shock amid the roaring panic of the crowds. Turing found a corpse that vaguely resembled Sarah. Without pause he pumped five shots into the prone figure, blowing off her hands, feet and face. The raw gore curdled Sarah's gut. She retched uncontrollably. Turing slipped Sarah's ID into the corpse's moist pocket. It would take weeks for the cops to uncover the ruse. Until then, Sarah Peters was dead.

After that, a blurred revulsion settled in. Turing dragged her into the fields surrounding the castle. He gave her a new ID, told her to use it sparingly. Sarah asked him only one question: Why? Turing's response cut through her pain. It drew her into a conspiracy that threatened everything. Ryan Laing was the key.

Then, Turing disappeared into the night—off to the next battle. Sarah forced herself to act. She moved on autopilot. Somehow she cleaned herself up, got herself away from Kinkell and out of Scotland. Locked into her seat on the transport to Italy, she stared into flashing recollections of her shredded past and cried.

The Capri Hilton was well appointed. Every amenity supplied, every need anticipated. Sarah didn't wash up—afraid that a glance in the mirror would shatter her fragile stability. The dirt under her nails, the dust in her hair were all that remained of her life. Instead, she plunged into the flow. She shimmied through cracks in the flow, kept low—remaining dead allowed zero flow wake. Below the fields of information transfer ran undercurrents of slag, detritus floating toward destruction. She floated with it, inching toward her goal.

Nearing the connection point, she pulled from the deep-sea current and muscled into position. Madda had hidden the connection within an abandoned retail site. Amid crumbling code for refrigerators and athletic shoes, Sarah patched into the flow point hardwired to Ryan's drones. All that remained of her life in Echelon was her connection to Ryan Laing. The drones' recognition of Sarah's thought pattern could not be reprogrammed or deleted. It was a fail-safe Madda had demanded. Having the wrong person thrashing through Laing's mind would be catastrophic.

She arrived too late. Turing had already made his play. She tried to push Ryan toward the truth, but he was all fight. She'd been too little too late.

She supposed she could talk to Ryan as he died. Wish him well, all that. But he'd just spit some final vitriolic insult that would haunt her for the rest of her life. She couldn't bear it.

Sarah stretched back over her chair, her spine popping at each vertebra. She needed to get out—do something. She walked to the window and clicked the plexi off opaque.

Sarah looked down on a gentle ocean lapping at limestone cliffs. Her tears rolled. She wished Elaine could see the paradise before her. She wished Ryan wasn't drowning.

10

Ryan awoke. That alone confused him. Last he'd left off, things looked bleak. Survival hadn't occurred to him as an option. As consciousness returned, he went through the checklist. All his limbs seemed to be in place and willing to move on request. Headache. Yup, he was alive.

"Hell of a way to work off a hangover." Tex sat just off Ryan's bunk. The stink of waterlogged, fishy life infused the tight cabin.

"Now I know I'm in hell," Ryan scratched out.

"You're on my junk, partna. No hell here. We're strictly Buddhist."

"A Buddhist cowboy?"

"They broke the mold when they made me, old man."

"How did I—"

"Sorry about the head. Not easy ropin' a stray in those conditions."

Ryan gave Tex a quick glare, just enough to shove him out of the Wild West crap. If this samurai trade jockey had any idea how dumb he sounded to someone who actually . . . Ryan stopped himself.

"You banged into the side of the junk before we could grapple you," Tex continued.

Ryan became aware that his slice of reality was swaying dramatically.

"We're still in open water. Came out here to weather the storm."

"In open water?"

"Sure, nothing to hit out here. Well, nothing except some dumb-ass gringo trying to paddle to Catalina. By the way, you're a terrible swimmer."

"Evidently."

"Aren't you going to ask about that?" Tex asked.

Ryan looked down to see a large speargun dart protruding from his left shoulder. He was pretty sure he hadn't been born with it. The waves of nausea suddenly clicked.

"Fuck, that hurts!" Ryan gasped.

Tex shrugged, breaking into his customary half grin.

"A very good shot. I drew down, fired from the hip and got you before you slipped into the next trough."

"Thanks. I think."

"No other way, partna. Now, I want the dart back, unless you gonna buy it?"

Tex gripped the dart head and was about to pull through. Ryan grabbed his arm. Tex might buy that the current lack of blood was from the sea cauterizing the wound. But gray resin pouring from Ryan's re-opened lesion would be tougher to explain.

"Let me do it," Ryan said.

"Man, you crazy."

"Just fuck off for a bit. I'll do it."

"You like the pain, huh? Ripping that out will make you all hot. You some kinda kink freak."

"Tex, you know me too well."

"Let me—"

Tex made another grab for the dart. Ryan snagged him by the throat with his good hand.

"Now would be a very good time for you to leave."

"Okay, okay—just trying to help." Tex stumbled back and fell out the door. "There's Skin in the cabinet. If you live, I'm gonna kick some of your ass."

Tex closed the door, leaving Ryan alone to ponder his fate. Had he just been saved from his own agency by a quick-drawing, cowboy sea-farer who'd skewered him like a tuna? At least life wasn't boring.

Turing had betrayed him. The thought cracked through his giddy mirth. For his own good, Turing had said. For his own good he'd ordered Ryan's assassination? No, Turing had done it out of the single motivation that propelled all of humanity: the drive to save one's own ass. Power had finally toppled Christopher Turing. Corrupted absolutely.

Now or never, Ryan thought. He grabbed the dart's head in his right hand and yanked. Pain swelled through his shoulder and into every cell of his body. He pulled again and the dart came free, scraps of flesh clinging to its barbs.

Ryan lay back and let the pain take its course. He realized there was a mirror above him. Gotta be Tex's bunk, he thought. And Tex had called Ryan kinky. Laing watched blood spread over his chest and onto the white sheets. Maybe they died in the ocean, he thought.

Nope. Drones spilled out of him, a gray syrup, overtaking his lifeblood, dragging it back. He watched the jagged wound seal. Before the fall in Joshua Tree, Ryan had counted his miles by their mark on his skin. One scar from a rail gun hit off the coast of Goa. A slice on the thigh commemorating a particularly interesting year spent in South Africa. His flesh told the story of his life.

Now, Ryan watched the drones put him back together and realized that he'd never have another scar. In fact, his old scars had vanished. He'd lost his past and not even noticed. Flesh synched tight, and the drones retreated to wherever they went when he wasn't fucking himself up.

Ryan slathered Skin on his shoulder and back, but any close inspection would reveal flesh over flesh. The Skin spread on thick; he felt like he'd buttered himself. In seconds, it solidified. During the Fire, he'd seen corpses burned beyond recognition. Worse, he'd seen the survivors, their scorched features covered in leathery scar tissue. He tried to smooth the Skin out, make it a little more uniform. He might be a victim of betrayal, of attempted assassination, of conspiracy, but not of fire.

Deeming enough time had passed, Laing emerged from the cabin. Tex and his family hunkered over their meal. The wafting pungence of peanuts and shrimp made Ryan quiver with hunger. They all looked up at him. They hadn't expected their wayward passenger to be up so soon. An old lady, probably Tex's mother, silently rose and prepared a bowl of noodles. Peanut ambrosia. He slumped down to the low wooden table, and the others made room. Two younger brothers and a sister. None would make eye contact. Instead, they concentrated on their meals and pretended that the giant, recently mangled gringo wasn't taking up most of the galley. Or maybe they just didn't care.

"Excuse them. Not used to strangers," Tex said.

"Talk low, talk slow, and don't say too much." Ryan had a few cowboy witticisms of his own.

"Never miss a good chance to shut up," Tex countered.

Ryan nodded and fell into his meal. He ate until he noticed all eyes upon him. He'd probably just demolished the equivalent of their daily sustenance.

"I owe you. I owe you all for what you did," Ryan said.

"Yes," the wrinkled old woman croaked.

"I pay my debts."

Tex nodded imperceptibly to the woman, and she shuffled away, grumbling.

"Don't often find honest men swimming the channel in a storm," Tex said.

Ryan had already come up with an explanation—something believable and just embarrassing enough to ring true. "I, ugh, I thought it was you. Thought you'd forgotten something. It was a crew, sent to take me out. Trashed the place, kicked my ass up and down and pitched me through the plexi."

"You never struck me as a mark, Laing."

"I'm not. Not when I'm sober. And they were good."

Ryan paused. Shifted uncomfortably in his seat.

"They . . . I think they . . . had their way with me."

Tex's face registered surprise, then deep embarrassment. He went through six shades of crimson, tried to maintain his composure and came up with exactly nothing to say. When lying, make it embarrassing. People were less likely to push.

"I am sorry," Tex said.

"They'll be very sorry they didn't finish the job."

"You goin' feudin'?"

"Something like that."

"Ain't no money in revenge."

"There is for you, Tex. If you help me."

"What can a simple trader do for a man of your stature?"

"You already saved my life."

"And for that, plus room, board and medicals, I charge you ten thousand euros."

"Tell you what, help me and I'll triple that."

"A hundred thousand."

"Jesus . . ."

"You are in no position to bargain," Tex shot back.

"You have a point."

"You want guns? Armor?"

"I will. Right now, I want information. Are you in the flow?"

A kernel of cruelty twisted the young man's smile. Catching it, Ryan wondered if he'd underestimated Tex. Was he more than the congenial, if slightly odd kid who thought he was John Wayne reincarnated? Assuredly. How much more, Ryan couldn't tell. The glint faded to a jovial grin and happy nod.

Tex rose and led Ryan through the narrow gangway to a cabin in the junk's stern. The seas continued to rock the flat-bottomed ship. Ten-meter swells, Ryan guessed. A queasy need to blow his noodles all over the deck rose in his gut. Laing swallowed down his own bile.

Tex opened the door to reveal a tightly packed but well-appointed console. Ryan figured the pirate would have such a rig. Trading goods was just part of a pirate's life. There was also the hijacking of data, at which Tex was particularly adept. Ryan had watched several of Tex's raids through an Echelon feed. He liked Tex's style. The raids ran well below Echelon's official radar. Tex stole small pieces of code or swatches of science, which he sold on the open market. Nothing big enough to draw real attention. Ryan just liked to know who his drinking partners were.

Laing sat at the console and let Tex power it up. The low hum of recognition in his head told him this was a very fine machine indeed.

"Given my situation, I, ahh, I'd prefer not to let my continued presence be known."

"Wise," Tex said.

"I think it would be in our mutual interest for me to remain dead. My associates wouldn't take kindly to your involvement."

"Speak your mind, but ride a fast horse," Tex extemporized.

"Yeah, so, to keep my identity hidden, I'd like to, to use yours."

"In the flow?"

"Yes."

"That's big-deal trouble. For that, they lock you up and throw away the key."

"Maybe so, but my associates can inflict far worse."

"Two hundred thousand."

"You must be kidding! I could buy ten junks for that."

"Then do it and get the hell off mine."

Ryan sighed. It didn't really matter. He had plenty of money. Never really needed it for anything.

"Two hundred thousand."

Tex smiled. All his apprehension fell away and he pushed Ryan out of the way. He interfaced, screens and locales flying past. He landed, and an identity appeared before them.

"Meet Gwen." She was flow beautiful, hyperreal and bulging in all the right places. "My creation. I use her in just such circumstances."

In spite of himself Ryan ogled. He'd just escaped the salivating jaws of death, for God's sake. He had every right to enjoy any pleasure flitting by.

"You'll like being her. She's fully functional."

"Tex, how did you? Is she clean?"

"As a virgin schoolgirl, if there're any left. She's a Swiss citizen. No record. No tracers. Nothing. And best of all, she lives scattered through servers around the world. Even if someone caught on, realized she wasn't real, it would take hours to track her down, analyze her billions of parts and pull their operating source."

"Impressive."

Ryan knew about Gwen. He'd watched Tex run her. He just hoped Echelon hadn't bothered with her. She was purely small-time—like Tex. Nothing to worry about. Ryan had no choice anyway. He sat at the console, realized Tex was still in the room and gave him a look.

"Enjoy. I'll just leave you two alone," Tex said.

He bowed low and exited. Ryan locked the door behind him. He sat for a beat, then goggled in and dove. The world slipped out, and he rose up and into the flow.

Gwen stirred, rotated, and Ryan meshed with her. His senses shifted as he settled into the cyber being. He gazed at the flow through her eyes, tasted it on her lips, even felt data breeze over her skin, making her nipples stiffen. This was how you fooled the system. Masks within masks.

Ryan merged with the flow and began sifting, a difficult task when each hit made Gwen shiver in erotic spasms. Data itself kindled Gwen's pleasure sensors. Ryan wondered how Tex got any work done inside her. Had Laing been on his game, he might have felt a subtle shift in the data flow. His drones might have registered a filter. As it was, they were busy managing Ryan's hormone spikes.

Ryan lost himself, pursuing a million leads at once. He plunged through information, calling up bits helter-skelter. He pursued the splotches of data he recalled from his seconds in the haven. He pored over them, trying to find a link. Turing was guilty—the attempted assassination proved that. Before confrontation, Ryan needed to know why. What could make him turn after so long? Ryan bobbed, weaved and pieced together the true story of Turing's last months. No one was immune from inspection by someone like Ryan. Even Turing, with all Echelon's defenses, had made just enough mistakes to implicate himself.

But why? And then he found it. Bits of cached data, deleted but never erased. From twenty different servers he pieced together a money transfer. Then a hundred more, totaling billions. Despite a lifetime of working for the higher good, Turing had sold out. Could it be possible? Data doesn't lie. Turing had tried to kill him, after all—had tried to take out the one man who suspected. No matter that the man happened to be an adopted son. He'd been targeted nonetheless.

Ryan stared at the data. Despite its disconcerting nature, the current made Gwen tingle head to toe. The money transfers rising out of the filters Ryan had coded pushed her into a gushing tidal wave of sensation. Data peppered her from all sides, and each contact pushed her higher. Ryan had little choice but to tag along.

Trying to ignore the construct's sensory link, Ryan watched the final pieces of Turing's betrayal resolve. Gwen's eyes focused on the data, and Laing knew . . . knew beyond any shadow of a doubt.

❚❚

Christopher Turing watched his world crumble, helpless. How slow he'd been. How easily led. He'd seen each move, but failed to resolve the larger strategy. At least Sarah was safe. Sending agents to subdue Ryan had been a risk, but he'd had no alternative. It was late in the game, and Turing's moves were limited. He'd longed to tell Ryan everything, but couldn't risk revealing his discoveries in the flow—especially within Echelon's walls. For decades, Echelon stood unassailable. Turing had been lulled by Echelon's very power, and thus had sealed its fate. His error with Ryan marked the culmination of a botched career.

He would play the dupe no longer. Where he'd failed, others would succeed. It was time to turn the tables, to position his pieces for attack. Not head-on—he was far too weak for that. No, this would be a brazen gambit. Risky, but the alternative was unthinkable.

He unlocked the encryption package. A unique design, it had taken him years to engineer. Adapting it to his current needs hadn't been difficult. Turing engaged the package and linked it to the flow. It did its job, finding the data and binding to it, sealing it in chaos. His code weaved itself into the data, through it and around it until there was nothing but a black hole of 1's and 0's. Anyone who came close would be infected. The secret was safe, temporarily at least.

Move two. He linked out and made a call.

A voice, flinty with sustained panic, responded, "Yes?" Turing liked Sarah's voice. A shame he'd never hear it again.

"He's coming," Turing said, killing the connection.

Turing looked forward to seeing Ryan again, even if it would be under less-than-ideal circumstances.

No wonder he turned, Laing thought.

Ryan had never been much for the high life. For him, a perfect night entailed six cold beers and a bacon cheeseburger. Maybe two bacon cheeseburgers. But he knew class when he saw it. The Napa Valley in California's wine country oozed class from every vine. The grapes grown here remained genetically identical to those brought over from Europe centuries earlier. None of the bioengineered varietals held a candle to these ancient genomes. And after the crop infestations in South America, Napa became the pinnacle of wine growing. Like its grapes, the valley itself remained largely unchanged over the years, a theme park of gentility amid California's sprawl.

It hadn't been easy tracking down Turing's whereabouts. Even now, Ryan couldn't be sure he'd found the right man. Flesh contact between Echelon agents was discouraged, to say the least. Not much need for it when Echelon controlled the flow.

Ryan had a vague sense that Turing had been at the medical facility during his lengthy stay. The memory of Turing's baritone drawling out over hours, days and weeks of unconsciousness struck him now and then. In that drone-induced coma, Laing had been more than asleep, less than awake. The waters of his imagination had seeped up and inundated him with lurid fantasies, shattering terrors and wild speculations. And far in the distance, he'd seen the light of reality, inaccessible. In his battered mind, his death had replayed interminably. Unrelenting. Flashes of impact, and then a searing hot flood. Weeks had passed within that nightmare.

For a time, he'd thought he was dead—that this torture was his own slice of hell. But every now and then, searing physical pain had shot through his fantasies. Only life hurt that much. During these episodes, his recollections of Turing's calm voice ran strong. When Ryan emerged from the well, there'd been no sign of the man. Laing had learned of his new houseguests from Madda, but only Turing could have authorized the use of "Echelon's Great Experiment."

But why bother putting him back together and then attempt to kill him? Ryan could only assume Turing hadn't known the target of Ryan's data haven operation. Turing had found out too late and tried to pull Ryan out before he found anything incriminating. Disobeying the order to retreat had signed Ryan's death warrant.

Ryan understood disillusionment. He'd had little to cling to through the years. No family, no one he'd call close. He saw only the worst of humanity. He spent his time manipulating those who'd try to manipulate others, a puppet master, who himself danced on invisible strings. But he'd always thought his cause was just. He'd clung to that—it was all he had left, a simple goal of keeping humanity from destroying itself. Turing had killed even that.

Ryan had considered taking his findings to Sachs, letting the IG's office handle Turing. But Ryan had to know why. So he went hunting.

In the backrooms and shadows of the flow, he searched for data linking Turing to the flesh. The man wasn't interested in being found. When his identity finally came up, Ryan could hardly believe it. But then, Turing always said the best hiding place was right out in the open.

The man owned a winery. He was a mainstay of the Napa social scene and had been so for a decade. Ryan found him through a tenuous link between one of Turing's nefarious flow personas and a charity. Few criminals gave to the victims of pestilence in southern France. The charity happened to be run by Robert Auerbach, owner of the Auerbach Winery.

Auerbach was notoriously good at staying out of the gossip columns, but he'd overlooked the gallery of one of his high-society neighbors. In a shabby-chic locale in the flow, password protected and open only to blue-blooded users, Sandra Benjamin, art dealer extraordinaire, had a little showroom. Most of the gallery exhibited her clients' dreary art. In a side room, the select few could access stills from her most recent fete. In the corner of one still, masked by shadows, stood a man identified as Robert Auerbach, a man looking much like Christopher Turing.

Sarah tried to crack the ice locked around Ryan. She had to do something. Someone had wrapped Ryan's flow point in static, so many billions of bits that he became utterly inaccessible. No entrance, no escape. Even her link to his drones had been diverted. Turing had told her the attempt would be useless, that she would get caught up and drowned. She tried anyway; he wasn't her boss anymore. You can't boss a casualty.

She entered the flow and sailed over the abandoned retail site that hid her connection to Laing. No trace of it remained. Instead of shoe shops and software galleries, raw code seethed and ebbed, virus-tipped barbs bubbling through the site's detritus. Did Laing know how thoroughly he'd been iced? Probably not. He'd be staying far from his personal flow point, using other personas to hunt. If she could just get him a message.

She initiated her incursion software, and the scene shifted. Sarah dropped in just downstream from Ryan, relishing her interface. The flow transferred information, bits, data. How one chose to view and interface with that data was up to the user. For most interactions, environments were a mutually accepted constant. To enter public spaces in the flow, one had to submit to a common vision. You couldn't set up a dainty little shopping district and have users come in as Bigfoot and crush all your virtual flowerpots.

Dealing in base code, hackers had more leeway. Each hacker developed his own incursion environment. There was simply too much data for the mind to process the raw feed. For some, breaking through firewalls and encryption took the form of a battle in space, or an intricate first-person shooter. A hacker's interface said a lot about his character, and his prowess.

Sarah's interface veered from that of her brethren—possibly why it worked so well. Her software slotted her hacks into a white-water kayaking environment. Though she'd never actually run a river, she suspected that the commitment, risk and adrenaline of the sport mimicked that of her high-level incursions.

Applying her interface to the encryption that hemmed in Ryan's flow point, she cautiously paddled into the fray. Her proximity to the pulsing dam around Ryan Laing triggered a white rush of data. Sarah had to paddle hard to stay above water. The dam loomed over her, a speck within the flow stream. White froth tumbled down the onyx spire. The banks of Sarah's interface trailed into the abyss. She paddled up the spindle, awash in reverb, beyond which there was only the empty space. Her 'yak sliced effortlessly through most data streams, drawn of its own accord to the hard locks within the code wash that granted access.

She paddled hard, using the standing waves of code to surf her way upstream. The rapid grew stronger as she approached Ryan. Fuck, this guy was impenetrable. If only she could use Echelon—then she wouldn't have had to take this outrageous risk. Sarah let the thought go and focused.

She neared the dam base—even saw the hard point. And then all hell broke loose. A data stream erupted from the face of the dam. It loomed huge over Sarah, threatening to drown her mind in a tidal wave of bits. She'd seen hackers who'd succumbed to such a fate. Slobbering voids, unable to even speak through the inane backwash swirling through their heads. No extrication from that maelstrom. It was a one-way ticket down the rabbit hole.

Sarah's mind boiled, subsumed by the drive to react, to survive. She probably screamed, but the wave's roar drowned her out. Flight became the only option. She cartwheeled the 'yak, flipping it end over end to point downstream. And she drove hard, cutting through the churning data with her paddle. The wave gained. She looked over her shoulder and immediately wished she hadn't. "Fucking huge!" she repeated over and over. She abandoned any semblance of safety for speed. She flew off cliffs of impacted bytes, using the eddies beyond to catapult her forward. Another quick glance back, and she caught a crab, her paddle held under the torrent for the briefest instant. It was enough.

She lost control and shot out over a massive hard point, plunging into the seething froth below. She went deep; data ripped around her, churned through her. Bending forward and pulling her paddle to the hull, she arched back with all her might. Grudgingly, the 'yak yielded to her stroke and rolled through the white wash. Her head popped free and she paddled for her life. Nothing happened. The tail of her 'yak wouldn't come free—pinned in the churning hole. The front of the 'yak started to rise—her paddle not even touching the flow. And then she flipped. Consciousness ebbed after the third backflip. Data sloshed into her mouth, infecting her holo with a slow-burn virus. She felt the wave looming and did the unthinkable.

She pulled out, left the 'yak behind and let the flow take her unprotected. The force of the data shoved her down, scraped her against the hard point. The din enveloping her grew calm as her interface crumbled. She began to drown. But just as she'd given up, the hole released her, the force of the wave itself scraping her up from the deep and spitting her into the air. High over the flow, she felt the wave at her back, just meters away. And then she saw it: an exit point. Nothing to lose, she closed her form into a bullet shape and dove, the wave bearing down on her. If she missed, the wave crush would leave her vegetating in the backwash.

She didn't miss.

Sarah emerged in her hotel room, dripping with sweat, terrified and exuberant. She'd made it. She was alive. The very fact filled her with elation. But her failure quickly crested out the ecstasy of survival. She had failed to connect with Ryan. She hated that Turing was right, hated that she couldn't stop the inevitable. Sarah settled back into her chair, initiating clean directives to scrape the viruses off her holo and divert any trace protocols she'd activated. Sarah Peters had to remain dead. And Ryan Laing would have to do it the hard way.

12

Some maintained security as a pretense, just another means of displaying wealth and status. There were plenty such in Napa. A mecca for the rich and famous, the small valley was home to some of the wealthiest people on Earth. And so there were bodyguards aplenty, gates, fences: highly visible security devices, all of which could be thwarted. Auerbach's estate had none such. On cursory inspection Ryan saw little possibility of a successful incursion. Any intruder would be dealt with quietly and very thoroughly. He saw the traces of laser wire, optical scanners, biothermal imaging.

But there were other ways to skin a cat. If he couldn't beat them, Ryan figured he'd join them. He had all the cash he could need. And Tex was only too willing to turn that cash into a new identity.

Ryan checked into Meadowood as Norman Bass, one of the many heirs to the Bass fortune. The Meadowood resort defined old-world charm—a getaway for people who owned several getaways themselves. Posh, even compared to their myriad of estates, Meadowood nestled into the hills behind the small town of St. Helena. Ryan was shown to his room overlooking the croquet court.

Before dinner, Ryan wandered through the grounds, trying to get used to his new face and its accompanying demeanor. Gnarled oaks sprawled over the resort, lending it an enchanted elegance. White-clad gentlemen played croquet with the intensity of scientists striving to cure hepatitis G. They gazed up from their match and Ryan nodded, the gel over his neck undulating uncomfortably. He strolled into the dining room.

Operating with altered flesh made Laing chafe. Flash gel encased his face, slipped down his neck and generally made him feel like a hot dog trapped in an air lock. Echelon had more sophisticated means of altering appearance, but Laing steered clear of his employer. He wanted, needed, to confront Turing. Sachs would only get in the way. So, Ryan had turned to Tex.

A man of many resources, Tex had attained a vat of the gel on the black market. The gooey slop set Ryan back quite a bit. Worth it. Knife work, while reversible, was laborious and time intensive. Flash gel made life a lot easier. He'd fed Bass' image into the gel's interface package and, seconds later, pulled a molded impression from the slop. Placing the mold onto his own face, the gel linked and held to his skin, adjusting to his musculature. A pair of contacts rounded out the disguise. The mask wouldn't fool a thorough security check, but it would be enough to get him into Turing's den.

Sitting in the sumptuous dining room, Laing felt like he was playing dress up. He settled over his meal, falling into the part. Eating with gel-packed lips required concentration. Ryan's target sat across the restaurant.

Paul Leck was a fishing magnate and social friend of Norman Bass. Leck owned the salmon fishing off the Pacific Northwest—an empire scraped together by his father. The company operated thousands of fishing boats, each of which loaded its cargo onto a single massive factory ship that remained one of the largest seagoing vessels in existence. On Echelon missions, Ryan had used the ship several times. It had taken him months to get the smell of fish out of his body armor. He still couldn't eat salmon.

Ryan settled into his Norman Bass persona as Leck approached. Leck's smorgasbord of clashing plaids made Ryan's head spin, though his own outfit, a linen suit, was only slightly less ridiculous.

"Norm old boy, pleasure to see you."

"Paul, what a surprise," Ryan responded. The pitch and cadence weren't balls on, so Ryan covered his voice with a scratching rasp.

"But what are you doing up here? I thought you were sailing the seven seas," Paul rumbled on.

"Oh yes, well, going got tough, got sick as a dog. And you know what they say, when the going gets tough, the tough skedaddle." In fact, the real Norman Bass was now skirting the tip of Cape Horn in a catamaran. Not drowning would be occupying most of his time. Exactly why Ryan had picked him to impersonate.

"Here, here. Time for you to settle down anyway."

"You know me, Paul, always on the move."

"Well, I hope you're here for the weekend. I've set up a surprise party for Susan Bonnington. You must come. It's at Auerbach's estate. Everyone will be there."

Leck had been carrying on a not-so-torrid affair with Bonnington for about a decade. In this circle, sexual dalliances were mandatory, though neither Leck nor Bonnington put much energy into theirs. An affair of decorum.

"Oh Paul, I'd hate to impose."

"Nonsense, you're already invited. I saw you here and immediately had my secretary put you on the list. So, you see, you must come. You'll be Susan's surprise within her surprise."

"Does that entail hopping out of a cake?"

"Nothing so crass. But you know Susan's always had a thing for you. You mustn't disappoint her."

"Wouldn't dream of it. Glad to come."

"Wonderful. And now, I'll drag you over to my supremely dull table. You can tell me all about your adventures as I get thoroughly soused."

"Again, I'd hate to disappoint," Ryan said.

An amber sun tumbled down the valley's length. Hints of gold flecked off the oaks and vineyards. Not the wild Colorado mountains Ryan had grown up with, this was an ordered beauty, manageable, exacting, the product of humanity. Ryan felt in it an easy relaxation of the spirit. Even the buzzing in his head ebbed—slightly.

Laing's corporeal tenants plagued him. The drones worked constantly. They swirled, buzzed and bombarded him with unintelligible stimuli. The tumult gripped him, and he felt them manipulating his chemical makeup, amping the fight-or-flight response initiated by their very presence.

Ryan grabbed a glass of champagne from a passing waiter, downed it and grabbed another. The waiter gave him an odd look, and Ryan winked.

"Tough day at the office."

"Yes sir."

The waiter slid away, and Ryan continued sizing up his fellow guests. They grouped in tight cliques, chatting diligently. Every now and then, a courageous soul broke from his island, hovered over the seas of solitude and quickly found another atoll to glom on to. Ryan's guise as a slightly inebriated gentleman adventurer allowed him to meander through the camps. Norman Bass was a brave man.

The cocktail party spread over the veranda of one of Auerbach's buildings. Nestled on Napa's western slope, the terrace girdling the building offered magnificent views of the valley, a fact Norman mentioned several times in several conversations.

Passing thoughts voiced tonight held the livelihood of thousands in the balance. These were the movers and shakers. Laing recognized most of them, had in fact sifted through many of their most private secrets under Echelon's aegis. He had manipulated several, drawing them toward actions that enforced stability.

He noticed Jaqueline Burnham, owner of Cybex, whose discoveries formed the basis of the drones currently driving Ryan insane. Combining them with the guarded data of several other titans, Echelon had made a giant leap. If she only knew. She and the others here thought their cabal shaped events. Maybe they should be given the reins. Might do a better job.

Ryan's musings only aggravated his delicate psyche, and he'd need his wits to get through the night. Many of the guests knew Norman Bass, keeping Ryan on his toes as he hobnobbed. He'd dressed the part, again decked out by Tex. He wore a tight linen suit, off-white, with a maroon silk tie. Bass preferred clothing that hinted of his exotic exploits.

The guest of honor had been successfully surprised, though Ryan suspected she'd known something was in the works. Her birthday would never be forgotten, of that she could be sure. She basked in the spotlight, resplendent in enough diamonds to bore into the Earth's core.

Dinner was announced.

Ryan followed the guests around the building and into the dining room. A banquet table seating about seventy ran the length of the room. Ringing it, casks of aging wine stood sentry. The room smelled earthy and sweet. Candles glowed down the table, making the space shimmer. Ryan found his seat as the barn-style doors at the end of the hall split open, treating the guests to a tableau of the dying light silhouetting a gnarled oak, just off center. Ryan recognized Turing's touch—the whole building had been constructed around this view.

The guests sat. The hosts had placed Norman next to a woman of stark, unassailable beauty. She smiled politely. No doubt she would have been more than a match for the real Norman. Ryan basked in her beauty, enjoyed her scent and conversation, but other thoughts intruded. All work and no play, he thought.

At the center of the table, a frail man stood. Christopher Turing. He'd aged in a decade. When he spoke, all thoughts of fragility fled. He had the strong baritone of a self-possessed man who knew his way about this old world.

"Many thanks, friends, for coming tonight to celebrate our Susan's birthday. As to the exact number we're celebrating, I've been sworn to secrecy."

Laughter floated through the room, mingling with the flickering flames of a thousand candles. Turing continued on, the perfect host. Susan applauded his fine party, and Turing handed the mic off to a man who began a toast that quickly degenerated into a roast. The laughter grew raucous, and the roasts bawdier. The angel to Ryan's left threw him cautious smiles as if they shared a secret. Ryan let himself be drawn in by her. It was preferable to discussing the wiles of the gem trade with the man to his right.

Salad, duck, wine, dessert, coffee and toasts, so many that Ryan learned more about the guest of honor than he could ever possibly require. The party began to break up, and Ryan saw how the night needed to play out. He leaned close to the angel; her name had already floated from his mind. A subtle touch, his finger on hers. An offer of port on the terrace. They rose and moved away from the crowd.

Minutes later, Ryan and the angel had abandoned their drinks in lieu of more aggressive enjoyments. The woman pressed herself against him. Though the flash gel of his mask dulled sensation, Ryan found it hard to maintain focus with her lips brushing over his. How easy it would be to lose himself for a while. Ryan's rage wouldn't allow it.

Christopher Turing bid the last of his guests adieu and undid his tie. He enjoyed being Bob Auerbach. Napa suited him, as did the subtle art of winemaking. Manipulation and patience, the application of force over time. Napa's arid hills offered the perfect venue for growing grapes. Like many things in life, grapes needed a struggle to fulfill their potential. They required maturation under the harshest environment, just below their maximum tolerance. After years in the casks, all that pain and struggle blossomed into the most perfect aroma, the most wonderful taste.

Turing enjoyed the process. Though only a hobby, he found it vastly more rewarding than . . . other endeavors. As a vintner, he had an obvious goal. The wine emerged and was either good or bad. Each year was a project, a task that would be completed and, eventually, qualified. Echelon's goal, on the other hand, went on and on. The cultivation of humanity was a never-ending process. Threats were never fully suppressed; the human drive for self-destruction never fully crushed. How long could Echelon hold the lemmings from the cliff?

Turing nodded to his waitstaff and moved off to his private study. He swung the heavy doors open, still working on his tie. He had a long night before him. Hours to go before he slept. Beat beat drums, blow bugles blow, he thought. Time is short, and the call to arms is near.

Adrenaline flushed out his musings. A man sat at his desk. The man stirred, touched the light next to him.

"Hello, Ryan."

"Enjoy the party?" Turing asked lightly. Then he noticed a sleeping woman on his couch. "I see you did."

"She's fine. Your port has some kick to it. I suspect she'll recover in six to eight hours." Ryan paused, trying to keep his rage in check. "You won't be here to revive her."

"No, I suspect not," Turing responded.

"I needed to see you, to look you in the eye. You'd slip out of the IG's grasp."

"But not yours."

"No, not mine."

"Perhaps that's why you were induced to come. Ryan, you must know I never wanted to hurt you—"

Ryan cut him off. "Enough!"

Turing's face cracked, weight settling over his eyes. He blinked it away. No place for that now, he thought. I must play these moves precisely.

Ryan opened Turing's desk drawer and removed the antique, ivory-handled Colt .45 he had known would be there. Turing was obsessed with relics of the past, and this was his favorite. Ryan cocked the gun and aimed at Turing's head.

"You plan to kill me with Patton's gun?"

"Fitting, isn't it? Two commanders with delusions of grandeur. George Patton obsessed over power and conquest. What drove you to betray Echelon?"

"Nothing so grand, I assure you."

"What drove you to betray me?" Ryan asked, determined to keep his tone hard and steady. His face tingled from the latent flash gel, now slopped into the waste bin. He shook off the discomfort.

"You uncovered a secret that shifted everything. What you thought stood firm now sways in flux."

"Even your loyalty?" Ryan asked, struggling to maintain composure.

"Especially my loyalty. Such a tricky thing—loyalty to a cause," Turing said.

"Dammit, Turing, cut the shit. You pulled me into this, made me what I am, and then what? You turn into the very thing I've sacrificed everything to destroy."

"Ryan, I am the same man who found you in Colorado."

"Then why?"

"In the end, does it matter? Does it matter what one man does?"

"You promised me it did."

Turing smiled, remembering happier days. "That's right, I did. Maybe I have changed."

"We had a higher purpose, you said. Gave me a line about looking on suffering and doing nothing—"

Turing cut in. "We sit and look upon the sorrows of the world, out upon oppression and shame, the meanness and agony without end. All these we look upon, see, hear and are silent." Turing paused, savoring the words. "Not mine, I'm afraid, ripped them from Whitman. But he got it right."

"All bullshit."

"Games within games, Ryan. What the grape thinks is agony, the vintner sees as development."

Anger boiled over. "It's your turn for the press, Turing." Ryan cocked the hammer. "Now, I'll ask you again—why?"

"You know what they say about absolute power. We were given the means to play God. Maybe we weren't ready."

"But for money?" Ryan gestured to the opulent environs, "What could you be wanting?"

"We're all addicted to something. The sooner you find your own need, the easier it will be to accept."

"No justification for what you've done?"

"Reap your vengeance or vacate!" Turing shot back.

Ryan took a last look into his mentor's eyes, saw only the abyss, and aimed at the bald forehead before him. He would make it quick.

"No!" A scream burst through the tension.

At first Ryan thought it was the girl. Had he miscalculated the narc in her port? It was Jason Sachs. He spilled into the room, a flood of his soldiers following.

Jason stopped short, taking in the scene.

"Do not kill him, Mr. Laing."

"Finish it, Ryan," Turing countered.

"He's darkened key data. You kill him and it's gone forever."

"Ryan doesn't care about that. He's been betrayed. He wants vengeance."

Why was Turing so intent on dying? He was many things, none of which included suicidal. The inconsistancy stilled Laing's hand.

"Mr. Laing, he has encrypted the codes to your drones. Kill him and we'll never get them out of you," Jason said.

That brought everything to a thunderous halt.

"You mean, they can be removed?" The words caught in Ryan's throat.

"We think so, but not without the access codes."

Oh God, to have them gone. To have his mind to himself. The potential relief was enough to make him lower the gun.

Jason smiled. He glanced at Turing, eyes infused with victory. "Take the traitor away," Sachs said.

The soldiers cuffed Turing and led him out. As he exited, he wrenched around and took one last look at Ryan.

"I'm sorry I let you down."

In spite of his reeling fantasies of freedom, Ryan still found a slice of rage specifically cut for Turing. "You're dead to me," Ryan said.

"Bury me with your parents in the cemetery of your mind," Turing responded. With that, the guards dragged him away.

Ryan was left in the room with Jason. Stillness blanketed them. Laing let the gun clatter to the floor. Jason approached, put his foot on the gun and his hand on Ryan's shoulder. The physical contact felt forced and awkward.

"You did the right thing. You accomplished your mission, found the traitor," Jason said. "We'll get the encryption from Turing, and Echelon will once again be safe."

"Is Echelon in danger?"

"Turing's a crafty old bastard. I'll give him that. He darkened your drones, but worse, catastrophically worse, he encrypted the Key, Echelon's core software. Echelon is offline."

The implications sent a chill down Ryan's spine.

"Turing relinquished the future to the masses. But not to worry, I'll break him soon enough. We'll not let things get too far gone before we get back in the game."

"Jesus," Ryan managed.

"Tell me about it. We'll need you in the interim. Need your skills."

Jason gave Ryan's shoulder another squeeze and departed. Ryan stood in shock. The safeties had been removed, the gloves taken off. Humanity could never last. Why would Turing do it? Confusion swept over Ryan. With Turing locked up, Laing was out of danger. He could return to the life he knew. Somehow that wasn't reassuring. Ryan looked down at the sleeping angel. He longed for such peace.

Pictures of Susan Bonnington's fete found their way into the gossip mags. Many suspected she had seeded the mags herself—a notorious glutton for attention. At the end of the article outlining the latest in fashions, breakups, and hookups, a small bit was accorded to the host, Robert Auerbach. Despite the season, the article said he'd embarked on an African safari immediately after the festivities concluded. The mag bemoaned his absence; to have only one Auerbach party during the season was unthinkable. Nonetheless, the writer wished Auerbach well and bade him see many a beast on his extended journey.

After reading the article, Sarah packed quickly and exited the hotel without checking out. She hoped Ryan would find the clues, hoped that Turing had been able to drop them. If not, she was in for a long, cold winter.

13

Echelon worked Turing's encryption. From his sterile office in flow-space, Jason Sachs oversaw every aspect of the operation. Hackers hacked; engineers diverted torrents of data trying to unlock Turing's software. So far, they'd gotten nowhere.

With each passing day the world slipped, stability eroded. With no one to monitor information flow, violence emerged from the bedrock of human consciousness, found no impediment and blossomed. An as-yet-unidentified terrorist cell managed a spectacular suicide bombing in the heart of Paris. Jason watched news feed of the incident, mesmerized. Reporters stumbled over their words, caught up in the devastation, unable to decipher the language of violence. Even so, their ratings spiked.

The world's intelligence services stood equally flummoxed, having grown lax over decades of peace. They'd all been lulled into a false sense of security. False, at least, while Turing blocked Echelon from doing its job.

Damn him, Sachs thought. The old man had lost. Why couldn't he let the course of events play out? Jason acknowledged Turing's contributions, but it was time for new leadership, a new direction. Echelon had been in Turing's hands long enough. It was the dawn of a new era.

Proximity sensors blinked with Ryan Laing's approach. He entered and, together, they watched the Paris feed. The blast had occurred under the Eiffel Tower. Now, from the megalithic 'scrapers ringing the teetering structure, cameras caught the first exhibition of terror in a century. Blood, shock and horror filled the screen. It was hard to turn away.

Ground zero became a swirling fishbowl of dust and rubble. The feed panned up the 'scrapers' blast marks, out of the mayhem and to the civs, thousands of them, standing at their windows to view the destruction below. In the cloud-white 'scrapers they ogled, mesmerized. Sachs killed the feed.

"Turing has been remarkably effective against my interrogation tactics," Jason said.

"He won't break."

"I suspect he's conditioned himself to resist. Must have taken years."

"He saw this coming?"

"Possibly. I'd guess he was just being paranoid."

"Even paranoids have enemies," Laing responded.

Jason's lips cracked upward, as close to a smile as his stiff flow persona would allow. He analyzed Ryan with the biting accuracy of a surgeon. Laing seemed none the worse for wear. Stiff, formal bearing, lips curled thin, hands slung low at his sides, no flickering in his holo. And yet . . . Ryan's eyes swam. Jason, a master of the human condition, saw something looming behind those eyes. He should terminate Laing's tenure. Caging a tiger posed inherent risk. If that tiger had been wounded, the threat only grew. And this man was damaged goods. Yet Sachs couldn't relinquish a weapon of such potency, even if Turing had locked away his means of controlling it. He could keep Laing at bay until the old man broke.

"Is there something I can do for you, Mr. Laing?"

"I want to take some time off."

"I'm sorry, come again?"

"Time off. I need a break."

"Ryan, as far as I know, you've never asked for leave."

"True. But I . . . With Turing gone—I need to start over."

Jason stared at Ryan. Was that the source of his abyss? Was Ryan adrift without a father figure? Human weakness consistently surprised Jason. He'd respected this man, even thought of him as a mentor. And now, this display of vulnerability? Well, what could it hurt to let the wounded tiger hunt down his own pride?

"Colorado?"

"You know?" Ryan stammered.

"Ryan, of course I know."

"I, yes. I want to go home."

"Not much left."

"Just the same."

"We're slipping toward chaos here."

"If you need me, I'll come back. You know that."

Jason paused, pretending to deliberate. He'd already decided to let Ryan go. By the time he returned from this pitiful bout of introspection, Jason would have the drones' initiation codes, and he'd give Ryan a new set of priorities. Until then, best to keep him out of the way.

"Okay, go. Just see Madda first. Let him check your tech."

"Done. I'll report to LA ASAP."

"You're already in LA." Jason couldn't help himself. He savored the act of knowing. It made life worthwhile.

"How could you know that?"

"I'm not totally powerless without Echelon, Mr. Laing. Have a pleasant journey."

"A lie, to be effective, should be an admission of weakness. Bolsters believability." Turing had told him that years ago. Maybe a lifetime ago. Laing had seen the condescension in Jason's eyes and knew he'd be believed. And he'd escaped a debriefing. Echelon was simply too busy to deal with Laing. The loss of the Key was the most critical incident Echelon had encountered in its illustrious, if clandestine, history.

Ryan emerged from the public data port and reentered Santa Monica traffic. He'd stayed close to home, pretending to lick his wounds and sulk. To be honest it wasn't all that hard. His body felt racked. It had taken all his effort to remain calm in the flow. The drones amped him, growing more comfortable in their environment. They never shut down, swirling within him even as he slept. Ryan stopped eating dinner. He'd just throw it up. Moving was better. Constant movement. But he needed sleep. His body might not require it, but his mind longed to power down. It wouldn't be soon. Maybe Madda could help.

He merged into the pedestrian traffic along the Santa Monica Promenade. He liked people-watching here. An easy happiness pervaded. A young man, attractive if highly pierced, kissed his punk girl. An old woman emerged from Banana Republic weighed down with packages. Ryan watched, noticing a subtle shift that had evolved over the past weeks. An air of anxiety wafted over the ambient contentment. People were frightened for the first time in their lives. There was violence in the world. Confusion. Nothing catastrophic, but the novelty was disturbing. Men huddled over drinks in an airy bar that spilled into the mall, glued to breaking news reports. The netball game had been abandoned for a vid on the rising ethnic hostilities in the

Balkans. In lieu of splashy, colored amusement, scenes of rage and riot darkened the sunny establishment. The patrons watched wide-eyed, horror mingling with bloody fascination.

Ryan cut off the promenade, hopping a people mover east. It being off hours, he managed to find a seat, acceleration pressing him into the temper-resin. He'd deal with Madda immediately. Ryan longed to get under way, to scratch the itch that had been building since that night in Turing's winery.

Something had been off about that night. He watched the buildings of Century City slip by and reviewed the memory once again. Turing's death wish irked Ryan. Not at all like him. Christopher was rational through and through—even if he had become a crook and traitor. Not a rational move to further agitate an agitated man holding a Colt .45.

And then the numerous references to his parents. In their entire relationship, Turing had asked about Ryan's parents only once. In the shelter of Cheyenne Mountain, as the inferno raged overhead, Turing had simply asked their names. He sat over a dazed Ryan in a corridor turned makeshift bunkhouse. Misery filled the canned air, sobbing interspersed with anguished sighs. Ryan remained impassive.

"Jack and Bubbles."

The name drew a smile from Turing in spite of himself.

"I know," Ryan had continued. "Silly name. It . . . it didn't fit her."

Ryan remembered feeling the wellspring loosen. The names had released the bottled pain within him. Tears had poured down his face. Turing hadn't shrunk away. He'd reached out and taken a firm grip of Ryan's shoulder, the closest thing to a hug he could muster.

"I am sorry," Turing had said.

And that was it. Ryan and Turing had shared that single moment years ago. Neither discussed it again. They understood each other, and that was enough. But now, a lifetime later, Turing had dredged it up— in front of Jason and looking down the barrel of a gun. Why? To remind Ryan of his debt? To throw him off? Neither seemed likely.

Turing only spoke with purpose. There must be some reason the traitor had dredged up the past. Only one way to find out.

So he'd lied to Jason, making his return to Colorado into a quest to find his roots. Embarrassing for an Echelon agent to admit to such sentimentality—especially in a time of crisis. The perfect lie.

. . . . .

Ryan found Madda dueling in a cramped fencing hall shoved into a back room of his workspace. His opponent, a holoshield, wore the same getup he did. White fencing uniform, complete with mask and resin-injected lamé. Madda and the program flashed back and forth with blazing-fast strikes and parries. After a fusillade of thrusts, Madda landed a hit and the program crumpled, falling into an extended and morbidly amusing death fit.

"That's a little much, wouldn't you say?"

Madda spun, whipping off his mask. He beamed on seeing Ryan.

"Hey man! Didn't hear ya come in."

The program continued to twitch and moan, finally falling flat. The holoshield then disintegrated and re-formed in the corner of the room, waiting for the next bout.

"Sorry about Hal," Madda said, motioning toward the holo. I gave her a little more flair than your average opponent."

"Her?"

Madda smiled with mischievous glee and surreptitiously looked around as if others might be watching, which of course they were. He slinked up to the holoshield and removed the mask, which disintegrated in a sizzle of energy on being parted from the rest of the body. Madda revealed the delicate face of a Norwegian beauty.

"Before all this, I spent some time in Iceland. Big fencing tourney up there. Never forgot it. Never forgot her."

"I can see why," Ryan said.

"You know they wife swap up there? Genetic necessity."

"Lucky you."

"Hmmm. She's fully functional."

"I'd expect nothing less from a genius of your caliber . . . pervert."

Madda grinned. "You say that like it's a bad thing." Still holding his saber, his eyes lit up. "How about going a couple points?"

"Not really up on my fencing, Dave."

"A lost art, I know. But you should try it. Very good for the soul."

"I really need to get under way."

"Oh come on, the fate of the world can wait a couple points. Humor a man who hasn't seen the light of day in half a decade."

Ryan did like this kid. "Yeah, okay."

Laing grabbed a saber from the wall. "Where's my mask and suit?"

"Sorry, I only have one. You've got all those drones inside just itching for something to do. I'll see if I can't give them some puncture wounds to heal."

"You should work on your people skills. Getting a little rusty."

"Don't see them improving any time soon."

Madda stepped back into a fighting stance.

"En garde."

Ryan swished the saber through the air, trying to get a feel for it. He mimicked Madda's body position.

"Does that mean ready?"

Madda didn't bother replying. He shot forward. Even jacked on drones, Ryan had no chance. He managed a wild parry. Madda recovered immediately, and his second strike sunk deep into Ryan's left shoulder. Even as pain seared through him, Ryan felt the drones work the wound.

"Fuck, Madda! Do you have any idea how much that smarts? Lighten up on a beginner, okay?"

Madda just laughed.

"Been wondering how fast your enhancements made you. So far, I'm not impressed."

The little fucker's competitive, Ryan thought.

"Okay, you want a taste? Here it comes. On your guard and watch out."

With that, Ryan lashed out. Raw speed made up for a complete lack of technique. He took wild swipes at Madda, getting close on the second. But the force of his attack and Madda's flawless parries threw him off balance. As Ryan stumbled, Madda thrust. He let go of his saber and stepped back, admiring his handiwork. It had pierced Ryan's left ear and now dangled from it.

"It's a look. Should be huge next season," Madda said.

Ryan ripped the saber out. He tossed it back to Madda.

"This is gruesome."

"You really are terrible."

Instead of another wild attack, Ryan forced himself to concentrate. He centered his weight over the balls of his feet, mimicking Dave's body position. Ryan's world melted away. All that remained was his sword arm and the saber that extended from it. Madda would always beat him. Ryan's only attribute was his inexperience. He didn't know the rules, the techniques. That made him unpredictable.

Madda lashed out with a cross strike, which Ryan blocked, too easily. A setup. Madda threw another, again parried easily, but the move sent Ryan stumbling left. He thought he saw the hint of a smile through Madda's mask. The trap was ready. Ryan's flank stood wide open; Madda thrust. He found empty space. Ryan continued shifting his balance to his left. He threw out his left leg and pushed off a support girder, cartwheeling away from Madda's thrust and over the fencer's head. Ryan let his body move of its own accord. He landed, shifted right and then thrust upward, bending his saber into Madda's faceplate. Ryan rose, grinning like a madman.

"Mark one for the good guys!"

"Look down," Madda responded.

Sticking out from his shirt, Madda's saber had punctured Ryan's flesh.

"Shall we call it a draw?" Madda said, throwing off his mask.

"I can live with that," Ryan grunted out.

Madda retrieved his saber from Ryan's gut. The wound closed with a fleshy slurp that made Ryan cringe. Madda led Ryan to the examination room. For an instant Ryan felt clean. The fight had washed him out—stilled the drones' interminable static. Then they renewed their frenzy, and his mind locked down. The struggle to maintain his sanity forged on.

Madda lowered Ryan into a chair and began his examination. Everything looked fine. Everything except the eyes—eyes staring off into the maelstrom. This guy wouldn't need much of a push, Dave thought. Madda realized that his impromptu duel could have ended very badly. He made a mental note to never, ever push this dude again.

"You've looked better, buddy," Madda said.

"No thanks to you."

Madda stared into Ryan's eyes.

"I think I'm the least of your problems."

14

Sarah stared at what had been an expanse of scorched earth only decades ago. The Fire left devastation in its wake, the aspens and ever-greens all tinder to its insatiable flame. The land's history vanished; nothing of the time before the Fire remained. Nothing living, anyway.

Now the hills and mountains were cloaked in a blanket of new growth. People replanted, returned to the land and started afresh. There was an excitement to the land now, a feeling that the past had molted away, revealing something fresh and pristine. Golden waves of hay undulated with the gentle breeze. Columbine and Indian paint-brush dotted the mountains, rising from green underbrush in a rush of color: deep red, still blue and vibrant orange.

Sarah had arrived in Silt, Colorado, a day earlier, bunking down in a prefab hotel. The major cities had been rebuilt in that first flurry of ac-tivity after the Fire. Rural townships had taken longer. Thus, the build-ings in Silt were the latest in economical housing. Biocrete walls kept interiors at a constant temperature. Their slight undulation gave the town a ghostly quality. Silt shimmered, giving Sarah the sense that it hung poised on the edge of existence.

A phase shift from the cragged landscape of Scotland, Sarah found herself drawn to the topography—to its budding optimism. The peo-ple welcomed her. She ate dinner in the local watering hole. It oozed prefab modern and clearly hadn't been in the ground more than a few years. Just the same, the young woman behind the counter cooked up recipes her mother, and her mother's mother, had passed down. A group of locals dragged Sarah to their table. She gorged on their com-pany, gluttonous for connection. As she ate apple pie and listened to concerns about cattle and weather, she realized why this place at-tracted her so. She blurted it out before even thinking:

"This whole town is . . . is young! There's no one here over forty."

The comment ripped the joviality from the room. The gleaming faces around her paled. She wished she had a mint-flavored foot—yet again.

A man with burnt red skin took pity on her. "Most of us had family that died in the Fire. Some of us made it out. We returned after. We re-built."

"I'm sorry," Sarah said.

The owner of the diner put her hand over Sarah's and smiled. "We all have ghosts. Ours just hang closer than most."

"But after, not everyone came back—of the survivors I mean." Sarah hobbled over her words.

A tall, willowy rancher responded, "Some couldn't bear the memories. They never returned."

"We took their place," the waitress said with finality.

Sarah looked around and smiled. "Well, whatever happened before, you've made it right."

The patrons smiled. Slowly, talk returned to normal. Sarah excused herself before she could blurt out some other completely inappropriate comment.

She slept fitfully for the first time in days. Knowing she couldn't risk a trace, she hadn't hit the flow since arriving. She felt removed, almost unable to believe that catastrophe loomed over this new land.

She woke to a mountain-chilled morning and headed for Laing's ranch. She'd picked up the latest in transport—which made her quite a sensation in a town where many still kept horses. Echelon had used the tech for years, but now there was a commercial vehicle utilizing the device. She preferred it to Echelon's utilitarian design. This bad boy just looked tough.

She donned her jet-black leathers. A couple kids gazed at her from across the street, fascinated. She decided to give them a little show. Turing would have admonished her for making a spectacle, but any outsider stood out here. Might as well make her appearance memorable. Besides, she hadn't had her crowd fix in a while. The thought brought back images of Elaine. Tears welled, and she shoved them down. There would be time to grieve.

She threw a leg over the machine, and it conformed to her body line. From the saddlebag she pulled out a helmet, gave her hair a flick for the gaping boys' benefit, and locked it down. The machine itself had no instruments. Everything was monitored and controlled through the helmet.

She began the initiation sequence. Below her, the powerful electromagnet energized. The superconducting coil came online. The bike hummed, a massive electric charge building deep in its innards. Fully charged, the superconducting magnets engaged, generating massive flux density. The coil bike's field interacted with that of the Earth itself, creating a magnetic cushion. The bike rose, hovering over the pitted road.

She backed it into the street, clipped her feet in and eyed the throttle. After a tornado-ripping 360, she howled down the street. She thought she could hear the boys hollering over the field's static crackle. Looming cataclysm or not, it felt good to be admired.

Screaming into the countryside, she luxuriated in the coil bike's pure speed. The mountains blurred as she coaxed the howling machine to its max. No better way to fly.

She found the crossroad on her helmet's map and powered down. Sarah pulled the bike off the road, gazing into the hills where Ryan grew up. Unlike the land around it, Laing Ranch lay untended. Parking the bike, she found the burnt-out husk of a tempered steel plaque, fallen to the side of the road. Fire had scorched it, distorted the Laing name and brand. The wording below remained clear: NO TRESPASSING, SURVIVORS WILL BE PERSECUTED!

Sarah laughed. Maybe Ryan's caustic wit was genetic. She ambled up the gnarled road on foot. While vitality buzzed through the valley, the acres before her stood grave quiet. No one had been here in a long time.

She found the old farmhouse, or the chipped charcoal and skeletal girders that marked its passing. She felt like an intruder tramping through a sacred burial ground. Curiosity prevailed. She kicked through wreckage. Time had done its work. Little remained. She shuffled forward, working her way into what might have been the kitchen.

With a sickening crack the floor below her gave way and she plummeted into darkness. She fell hard, legs flailing. She landed on the needle point of a rusted rebar rod. The impact blew air from her lungs and arced her backward. She careened over and came to an abrupt halt.

Shock choked her. Finally, she willed her lungs to intake the fetid air. Sarah rose shakily, rubbing the points on her body where she had struck the rebar. Her temper-guard suit had saved her—just one more reason she was thrilled to have decided on the coil bike. She threw on her helmet, letting its light enhancers dredge the room from darkness.

The Fire had ripped through this room like all the others. But safe from the elements, it had remained in stasis for the past three decades. Everything was char black, coal dark. She let her eyes wander, roaming through Ryan's past. Her eyes fell on something in the corner. She hunkered over it, realizing that it was the remains of a small cattle dog. It lay in perfect repose, as if it had merely slept through the decades. She reached out to pet its fur and it crumbled in her fingers—a carbon shell. The head crumpled and disintegrated into powder. Sarah jumped away, bumping hard into something behind her—someone behind her.

She opened her mouth to scream. Before anything came out, Ryan Laing killed her. Sarah crashed backward into the remnants of the dog, which exploded into a plume of black.

Not a night went by that Ryan didn't ponder going home. The possibility would sneak up on him, touching the edge of his consciousness before he could drive it away. Its path would tingle through his mind. Then he'd grab the bottle and retreat into numbed oblivion.

The reality of his homecoming had none of the anticipated punch. He didn't feel anything. The town, the setting, all of it was different—totally new. It took him a couple passes to find his road. When he did, the presence of a coil bike made him sigh with relief. He wouldn't have to delve into anything deeper than aggression. His new life had infected even the remnants of his childhood. He would do his job. Sneak up on the intruder, subdue him and retrieve information.

He'd found the agent hunkered over Sunny, or what had been Sunny thirty years ago. Flash flame had carbonized the dog. When the agent crushed its head, Ryan lost it. He drew his shock cord and let the guy have it. The spark lanced out and hit its mark, blowing the intruder back. Ryan let it stick a second longer than necessary before recoiling the cord into the holster on his forearm.

He cracked a glow stick and gazed down at the agent. No chance he'd be getting up. Laing knelt and pulled off the helmet, allowing golden hair to cascade down from one of the most beautiful faces he had ever seen.

Sarah's body blasted into a convulsive lockdown. Then silence, deep stillness. She longed to sink into its embrace. But the shocks returned, harder and faster, lancing her. Finally, one ripped her from the abyss and she jolted back into consciousness, sucking air. Her eyes shot open and she skittered away from Ryan Laing. He knelt, small electrodes in his hands. She regained the smallest bit of composure.

Laing moved closer. He'd shocked her to death and then back to life. Fucker. She was no field agent. She didn't belong in a mucky basement with this killer.

"Welcome back. Who the fuck are you?" he asked.

She couldn't respond, not with his dam in place. Anything she said would get back to the eavesdropper. She couldn't risk her vocal signature being detected.

"I'll ask once more," Ryan said, his voice gravel.

He knelt over her, and Sarah did the first thing that came to mind. She lunged forward, lips slamming into Ryan's.

Ryan's shock gave way to arousal—a barely remembered need. He'd ripped away the top of her suit to attach the electrodes. Now, he could feel the press of her breasts against his jacket. His mind tried to analyze her as a threat; his body overruled the attempt. The intensity of his drone-augmented desire overwhelmed all other impulses. He could do little more than succumb. Sarah's desperation fueled him. The danger of the situation only titillated him further.

He let her rip off his jacket, his shirt. Within five seconds she'd thrown him on the ground, completely naked. But as quickly as she'd engaged him, she stepped back, standing up and over him, her breasts and stomach a milky white descending into black leather. Her eyes sparked. She put a hand to her lips.

Ryan tried to regain his composure. The reality of his location nailed him. He'd been driven to a sexual frenzy in the place his parents had died, by a woman covered in the ashes of his long-dead dog. Sick. He tried to grab his clothes, regain some dignity. But she got to them first and vaulted up the stairs. Her action surprised him, allowing her a precious second.

He pursued, emerging into the mountain air naked as a jaybird—just one more indignity to add to his list. The woman sprinted ahead of him, hurling every last stitch of clothing into the well. She turned and stared at him. He approached warily.

"Lady, you just signed your death warrant." Hard to sound menacing butt naked. He thought he did an admirable job.

She pulled something from her suit and he caught her hand in a vise grip. He stared down at her. But his anger dissipated with the look in her eyes. There was desperation. He also saw pity. She didn't squirm in his grip. He looked down at her hand. She held a flow visor.

"Do I know you?" he asked.

She continued to stare at him, and he knew that she wasn't a threat. He let her go. She put on the visor.

"Do I know you?" he repeated.

From within, he felt a stirring, then a voice he'd assumed long gone. A female voice touching his mind.

—*You should,* she thought to him.

He took a step back. The woman removed her visor and the link faded. He forgot about his nudity. What the hell was she doing here?

"I'm Sarah Peters," she said.

She retrieved some clothes from her bike. Sarah had planned on discarding whatever Laing was wearing. The tech that altered his clothes' characteristics to suit his environment had been coopted, made into a surveillance and jamming device.

Sarah tossed the new clothes to Ryan, then took his shock cord and sent a spark down the well, frying any remnants of the damming software. That done, she allowed herself to stretch out, her back against the well. She gazed out over the wrecked house and into the valley beyond. Ryan watched her, unsure of what to say.

"You were dammed in," she said. "Your clothes were encrusted. They precluded my getting to you on the flow. I tried."

"I gathered that." He settled down next to her. She gave him an awkward smile and shifted over slightly, adding distance between them.

"I'm sorry about before. About the basement," he said.

Ryan struggled to regain his composure. She too squirmed with embarrassment. That was some relief.

"My chest hurts like hell."

He had to restrain himself from glancing down at the swell of her breasts, now haltered in leather. The memory of her skin made him tingle. He'd spent hours with this woman in his head. But flesh face, he couldn't shake the schoolboy jitters.

"That was an—" He paused for a sharp intake of air. "—inventive means of getting me out of my clothes."

Sarah blushed crimson. She'd never done anything like that. It was desperation, pure and simple. Now the man stood before her and she couldn't do anything but stammer.

"Look, I'm sorry. I couldn't tell you. They would have picked me up."

"Who?" he asked.

Sarah breathed a sigh of relief. Biz. "Turing just said to meet you here—that you would supply all pertinent intel."

The name drew a renewed look of suspicion from Ryan.

"Turing was arrested—as a traitor."

"No!"

"I mined the data myself."

"Not possible. I was nearly killed in Scotland. Turing saved me."

"And I'm very curious as to why," Ryan said.

"If Turing's guilty, what are you doing here?"

"You tell me."

Fear coursed through Sarah's veins. Maybe she shouldn't be trusting this killer quite so much.

"Mopping up?" she asked, keeping her voice monotone.

He bored down on her, trying to find a chink in her armor. If she was a weapon Turing had planted, she'd been trained well. She betrayed nothing.

"No. I didn't know you'd be here," he said.

Thank God, she thought. "Well that's a relief. I try not to die more than once a day." The joke fell flat.

"So, what now?" Ryan asked.

"Not sure. Turing gave me this."

She rose and pulled a metal case from the bike. She opened it for him, revealing rudimentary controls, a slot feeder and a small screen.

"That's old school. I know Turing was into antiques, but that's beyond me."

"He wanted something inaccessible from the flow. A stand-alone. It's called DVD, or was back in the twentieth. I guess it was all the rage."

"And now all it takes is a little visor for you to crawl through my mind. We've come a long way, baby."

She looked away, silence blossoming into an awkward eternity. He looked down at the charred wreckage that used to be his home. Images from another lifetime filtered through. He saw his mother and father as they had been: happy, standing at the porch, waving to him as he rode up the valley. Pangs of regret tugged at him.

After the Fire, Ryan couldn't return. He chose instead to slip into a new life, the life Turing offered. A distant relative had sent him images of his parents' gravestones; he didn't go to the funeral.

Grief welled up from the dark place where he'd stored it so many years ago, and Ryan kicked himself into action. He'd see them now. He rose abruptly, startling Sarah, and marched up the hill behind his house and into the meadow beyond.

He used to play with Sunny here, mess with the cattle, screw around with his friends. Memories populated the meadow for an instant, then receded to reveal two simple gravestones. He approached. The stones held only the names. Too many gravestones to bother with epitaphs. He stood over them, longing for a release from the pressure. The pain simmered then waned, leaving him hollow once again.

He heard Sarah come up behind him. His eyes refocused and he noticed a small garland of withered flowers resting on his mother's headstone. Who else came here? He picked up the garland, the flowers disintegrating in his hands. Behind it lay a small package. Ryan picked it up. He peeled the plexi wrap to find a vintage computer disc and with it, a note written on thick fibered paper. It was in Turing's hand.

He read it aloud:

"I wish I had known her, Ryan. I wish I had known them both. Savor this time. Remember your parents. Heal. Then, when you're ready, you'll find the data to set things right. I'm sorry I can't offer a more elegant solution. Something that would keep you safe. But I had few choices and, I'm very proud to say, you are the best. Sincerely, Christopher Turing."

Little spits of anger coursed through Ryan. He was tempted to crumple the paper and burn it. Turing had betrayed him, then dragged his only pure memories through the filth. He hated the man for that. His knuckles whitened. He felt Sarah's small fingers over his.

"Loosen up there. You'll crush the disc," she said.

He probably should. But curiosity got the better of him. She took the disc from his hand, slotted it into the player and they watched.

In a halting staccato, Christopher Turing told them of a conspiracy far beyond anything they'd thought possible, a conspiracy so powerful and well organized that the master manipulator himself had been caught in its web.

Jason Sachs' image flashed across the screen.

15

Echelon's interrogation facility filled Laing with foreboding. Ryan had never been in this wing of Jason Sachs' domain. The subjects that wound up here came on a one-way ticket. The shadow-gray hallway sapped Laing's energy—a sharp contrast to Colorado's throbbing vibrancy. He forced himself to breathe. The pause allowed him enough perspective to see that the hallway itself was off-kilter. What should have been right angles skewed slightly obtuse, making him dizzy. Ryan saw Sachs' hand in the artifice—better to keep his subjects on edge.

Time had slowed for Ryan since viewing Turing's disc. After the startling revelations Turing had thrown at them, he and Sarah had been at a loss for words. They'd sat in the tall grass at the foot of his parents' graves, dumbstruck. Ryan's shock dulled even his drones' cacophony—if only for an instant.

Turing's disc pushed Laing back into the maze. With the information it forced on him, Laing would be on the run for the rest of what would now be a very short life. He had few expectations of fouling up a plan that had duped Turing. Ryan rarely bothered with the big picture. Echelon meant security for the human race. That was enough. It hadn't occurred to him that his superiors might be fallible—that they might in fact be part of the problem.

And then, under the headstones of parents he barely remembered, the old anger had returned. He hurled the antique DVD player at the nearest tree. It exploded into a shower of silicon and plastic. Sarah scampered away from him. The affront cut him. She had been in his mind, spent months slinking around in there. With the damming tech broken, she could link to him again. And yet, in the flesh, she was terrified of him. He had to admit, she too was unsettling. Her introduction via sexual explosion still haunted him. The memory made his drones—among other things—tingle.

Coming to the end of the hall, Ryan saw Jason emerge from one of his many offices. He kept them all exactly the same. One desk, one flow port, two chairs.

In that field in Colorado, Ryan had wanted to enter Echelon, guns blazing. An unexpected suicide attack might at least cripple the traitor. With the drones buzzing, Ryan had been only too ready to volunteer. Sarah convinced him that they had a chance to put things right. He didn't believe it, but he played along. She was the data rat.

"You look . . . better. How was Colorado?" Jason asked.

Ryan restrained himself from knocking Jason's teeth through the back of his throat. This little weasel, a traitor. But Jason didn't have the courage to mastermind such a coup. No, he was a lackey pure and simple. A very smart, very dangerous henchman. Jason had no will of his own.

"It was good to get home."

"Yes, I'm sure."

"I hear you are now acting director," Ryan said.

"I am director."

"Congratulations." Definitely a lackey.

"I didn't want to assume the mantle like this. We're shattered, Ryan. With the Key encrypted, Echelon is at a standstill. And without us, society is fraying at the seams."

"Maybe the world can live without us."

"We are a murderous species, Ryan. History makes that clear. Without Echelon to control our baser instincts, war will spread across the globe. Inevitable. That no one alive has actually seen a war is irrelevant. It's instinctual."

And all that blood will be on your hands, Ryan thought. Outwardly he remained impassive. The drones weren't sure what to do with themselves, so they jacked up his noradrenaline response. Ryan hoped Jason would mistake his flush for fear.

"And you can't break Turing?"

"He has proved resistant," Jason responded with a growl. He didn't like to admit defeat.

"You want me to speak to him."

"That's why you're here."

"Then I take it all other means have been attempted."

"Oh, Turing will break. We just don't want to risk destroying him to get a false response."

"I'm less than thrilled to chat with him."

"Nonetheless, you'll do it."

Ryan let some of his rage boil to the surface. Let Jason think that his anger was directed at Turing.

"Yes. I'll do it. But when it's over I want an assignment. I want active."

Jason grinned, nodding. "We need every field agent we can get."

Jason led Ryan through a nondescript door. They entered a room of such pervasive darkness that Ryan wondered if the drones had accidentally severed his optical nerve. Ryan felt the connection of an electrical circuit, and light poured forth. Emerging from a horizontal bank running the expanse of the room behind Ryan and Jason, each and every light was aimed directly into Christopher Turing's eyes.

The sight shocked Ryan. The man hung suspended in a viscous liquid, crucified. Jason and Ryan looked at him through a plexi plate. Turing had been outfitted in a black, temperfoam suit, his hands and feet covered in the same material. The suit ran up his neck and spread over his head. Only his face remained open to the fluid in which he floated.

"Sensory deprivation. Suspended in oxygenated fluid, the subject loses all sense of touch, smell, hearing and sight. First developed in the USSR during the Cold War, it remains one of the most effective interrogation devices in existence. Obviously, we've improved on the idea over the years." Jason could barely contain his pride.

Slowly, the fluid began to drain from the tank. Suspended upright, Turing's face emerged. He coughed viciously, expelling the liquid from his lungs. He kept his eyes clenched shut against the glare of the lights. The sight horrified Ryan.

"Oh, don't worry, telling the subject will not hinder its effect," Jason continued. "The technique works on our most primal instincts. That the higher mind understands what's happening means little. Tried it myself. Only lasted fifty-eight minutes."

"That's because you have nothing to occupy your thoughts." Turing's voice lurched from his waterlogged vocal cords. He opened his eyes and shot Jason a furious glare, his usually warm brown eyes now piercing. In spite of himself, Sachs jumped.

"How long has he been here?" Ryan asked.

"Twenty-one hours."

"A welcome respite from my normal duties," Turing quipped.

The fluid stopped draining as it reached Turing's shoulders. With another signal from Jason, it solidified over Turing's torso, locking him in place.

"As much as I'd like to give the order to crush your arms, the onset of pain actually hinders the process. Just the same, there's no reason to make you comfortable. Mr. Laing, the fluid has now solidified around the subject's body, constricting the diaphragm. As such, he'll have about ten minutes of consciousness, maybe less if he's feeling talkative, which he hasn't so far."

Ryan nodded. He was not used to interrogations of such precision. He'd dragged data from individuals while in the field, but that had always been under messier circumstances. This was an entire device built and honed to break a man. Ryan shuddered. Jason grinned, patting Ryan on the back.

"I'll leave you two alone."

He exited. The two were left in the glare of the light bank. Ryan extended his consciousness, let the drones find the circuitry for the lights and dimmed them.

"Not a good tactic giving the subject a concession without receiving something in return," Turing said.

"Sachs can play those games with you. He wanted us to talk, so we'll talk."

"Well then, I thank you."

Ryan was sure this conversation would be recorded in full three. He needed to be very careful. He glared at Turing, using his anger to cloud other emotions. He had plenty to spare.

"After all our years, this is how I'll remember you."

"Not too flattering," Turing coughed out.

"No."

To Sarah, Turing looked like ten pounds of potatoes in a five-pound sack. Goggled in, she hunkered over her portable computer and squinted into Ryan's view. After the last few days, she was glad to find herself in a place she knew—Ryan's head. It was a gamble, having her tag along, but with the Key encrypted, Echelon shouldn't be able to access their link.

In another life, high up in her Inverness apartment, Sarah had trained hard to operate and monitor Ryan. Blown into the drones'

hardware was a single outside link. Once it had been coded and initiated, no one else could link to the drones via the flow—a safety device
to prevent hacking an agent. She'd jumped at the opportunity.

They said a link was needed to give the drones a human face, to
allow the human subject to accept their presence. But only Ryan knew
if she helped. No one else had been given the injection, and there was
very little research as to how the mind would react to a binary onslaught.

Meeting Ryan convinced her that the setup was unstable. His lips
and the frantic grind of his hips haunted her. She had jammed her
head into the lion's mouth. This time, she'd lived to tell the tale. She
doubted that would translate to future security.

She just hoped she could keep him together until they figured out
what the hell was going on. That, or she'd go down by his side. Like it or
not, her future was irrevocably linked to a loose cannon. Just one of the
factors limiting her life span. She'd done some morbid calculations
based on current data. None of the projections had her surviving more
than seventy-two hours. In several of them, Ryan himself would kill
her. She'd keep her distance. She sat in a rear booth in the Colorado
diner and thought into Ryan's head.

—*Careful. Let Turing know you retrieved the package.*

—*And how should I do that, Puppet Master?*

—*Just stick to the plan.*

Well, at least his sarcasm remained intact. She concentrated on the
task ahead. Sarah could play Jason's game, maybe even Turing's. She
would do it through Ryan's mouth, but Turing would know the words
were hers. Hopefully, Jason would be none the wiser.

Ryan sat in the single chair facing the tank. The solidifying fluid
pressed in on the old man. His face blood-flushed. Arms outstretched
in a mock crucifixion, Turing had very little time.

"I'm suffocating," he said.

"I know the feeling. Terrible, isn't it?" Ryan responded.

Turing forced out a smile. Ryan tried to still himself, to force the
drones' buzz into the background. Sarah's renewed presence, now that
he knew her face, also set him on edge. He'd never considered her as

a person, more as an extension of the tech squirming through him. She and the drones had condensed into a single entity. Now he knew her, and the drones felt even more foreign.

Sarah counseled him. He didn't block her, but also wouldn't be led like a pig with a ring in its nose. She wants to play me, he thought. Well, fuck her. I'm no one's puppet.

"So the prodigal son returns," Turing said.

"I'm not your son."

"Ahh. Now that I'm a disappointment, you're falling back on your biologicals? Convenient."

"I went home. I saw them. Visited their graves."

Turing's eyes twinkled for the briefest second. He covered the slip with a burst of coughing.

"You've made me redundant so quickly? You always were resilient. Was it all you'd hoped for, this reunion?"

Ryan jumped to his feet, his right arm cocking for a punch without conscious thought. He reeled himself in at the plexi barrier. His anger would no longer have to be faked.

Turing laughed. "Like a child jerking his fingers back from a flame, your inclination is always toward violence. It's hardwired into your nervous system."

Just inches from Turing, Ryan bored into the old man's eyes. Games within games. Meanings within meanings.

"All this time. All these years, was I just your toy? One more tool fueling your megalomania?"

"I've abandoned you, is that it? So sorry."

"Listen," Ryan growled, "you are no longer the chess master, no longer the manipulator. Now you're just another criminal. Abandoned? You've done far more than that. You gave me a purpose. With you, I spent my life maintaining order, peace."

"But at what cost?"

"I never thought about it. Until now. I killed for you—" Ryan waved his arm at the door. "—for them. And now I see it's all bullshit. All your talk of order and stability, of giving—"

Turing cut him off. "Of giving humanity freedom from chaos, from war, from the depraved depths of its own capacity. Yes, yes, I know the speech, and if I may say, I do it much better myself. But, Ryan, now you see that's just the tip of the iceberg. Some lessons make you thrilled to be alive; some grind you into the dirt. It doesn't make them less true."

"Some lessons make me sick. You've taken it all. You risked everything Echelon has built. For what? What do you want?"

"Ahh, the billion-dollar question. Of course you know I'm innocent. That I was set up."

"Please. Don't patronize me. You saw all this coming. Why let it happen?"

"Choices were limited," Turing said.

"Well, you've had your day. Now give up the codes. Let us get back to the job."

"Ryan, did it ever occur to you that humanity might need chaos to evolve? We've had a century of peace. Where has it gotten us? More tech. More entertainment—so much in fact that we now refer to it in terms of oceans. And yet, no artists of note. No composers. No writers. Without plumbing the depths, we've been unable to achieve our heights." The words lurched out of Turing's constricted lungs.

"So it was all about altruism, your abandoning Echelon?" Ryan spat back.

"We were given the keys to regulating the human condition, allowed to play God. Maybe it's time to lock the door. Maybe the ultimate power is the Key itself." Turing's voice slipped, his mind scuttling along the edge of consciousness.

Ryan pounded on the plexi, shouted into it, trying to keep him awake. He needed all the data he could get. "You're losing color, old man! Soon you'll be back in the dark. Release the encryption and Sachs will let you die, keep you from losing what's left of your mind."

"Fuck you," Turing whispered. He never used vulgarity. So either Ryan had succeeded in pissing him off, or he was about to say something important.

"Fuck you, and fuck everyone listening. I'm a dead man. Have been for a while. Now, I've got nothing left but the fight. So let's do it. I'm not giving you the codes. Let's see how you all do without. No more control, no more manipulation, no more twisted cyborg freaks. That's right, Ryan, no more agents with drones flowing through their veins. You'll be alone. I've blocked our stock of drones from initiating within new hosts. They won't just go inert, they'll eat the host alive. And I've encrypted your own codes, Ryan. No deactivation. No relief!"

Fury streaking through his body, Ryan let his right hand fly. The impact with the plexi jarred him. Blood flowed from his knuckles. He punched again, knuckles crumbling under the impact. Blood smeared the plexi. Jason burst into the room with several guards, who pulled Laing away from Turing.

"Traitor," Ryan yelled. "Get them out of me!"

"Maybe I am a traitor," Turing gasped, consciousness slipping, "but there are those who'll gain from chaos. Those who want, who need, the Key."

Jason approached the plexi, making sure Ryan hadn't compromised its integrity. Satisfied, he motioned for the guards to remove Ryan. As they pulled him away, Ryan stole a last glance at Turing. This could well be their final moment. He'd done what was necessary, as had Turing. Ryan felt empty. Each step along this road had further opened the widening maw that would eventually swallow him.

Jason stood before Turing.

"You toyed with Laing and spit him out. He needed the cause. You took it from him. Now he's only good to us as a lab rat, and a bodyguard."

"Fuck him. Fuck you." That Turing could utter such profanity surprised Jason. He took it as a signal that the old man was breaking down.

"Unlike Ryan, I learned from you, surpassed you. We'll get what we want. From you, or from the source."

"Get on with it," Turing said with a groan.

"Gladly." Jason stepped back, initiating the sequence on his pad. He left Turing to the abyss.

Outside, a strong hand locked Sachs' shoulder in a vise grip. Two guards lay sprawled on the ground, rivulets of blood spreading onto the white flooring like veins in a leaf.

"Jesus, Laing! Did you kill them?"

"Of course not."

Jason turned to face the infuriated man—a loose cannon getting looser by the second. But he had skills and he had the drones. If Jason could just hack Turing, crack Ryan's drones open . . . With the drones under Jason's thumb, Ryan would be locked in an internal prison. An army of such men would be unstoppable.

But those were musings for the future. For now, Jason would continue to use Laing as a knight. Soon he'd be merely a rook, interchangeable and expendable. But now, he needed to be kept occupied. Occupied and off balance.

"Tell me, is it lonely without Agent Peters in your head?"

The fury left Ryan's eyes. For an instant Jason saw fear. Good.

"I haven't been on active."

"You're back on active. And she won't be joining you."

"Active?" Ryan responded, his voice rising with expectation.

Jason smiled. Like any addict, he was easily played.

"She's dead. Peters died in a tragic accident."

Laing's faced remained impassive. "What's my assignment?"

Jason stepped daintily over the concussed guards and led Ryan down the hall. He detected no reaction to Sarah's death from Laing. He only cares about the assignment, Jason thought. An addict through and through. Just the same, engineering Sarah Peters' death had been a good call. Sachs didn't need outside factors randomizing his scheme.

"With Echelon down, we've got our hands full. The world is disintegrating into a shit storm in rapid order," he said to Ryan.

"My assignment . . ."

"Your assignment is Michael Welton."

Ryan shot him a confused look. This was risky; Jason knew it. But there was no one more qualified. Despite all his bluster, Jason was confident Ryan could keep it together. Long enough to become obsolete, at least.

"Do you remember him?"

"Michael Welton, the exec at Calsoft?" Ryan asked.

Jason nodded.

"I remember his name. The information we captured from him led to my termination of Neil Buist."

"Among other things," Jason responded. "After Buist died, Welton engineered a hostile takeover of Calsoft."

"Unsanctioned?"

"Sanctioned. Echelon supported the raid. This is not a destruction order. I want Welton protected. Before Echelon crashed, we got SIGINT of a planned assassination."

"You want me to play bodyguard?" Ryan asked incredulously.

"I want you to keep one of the most powerful men in the world alive. Need I remind you that Calsoft controls most of the infrastructure that forms the flow? That and a good portion of America's western seaboard."

"You need not."

"Then go do your job. Keep him alive."

Ryan nodded. "What will happen to Turing?" he asked.

"We'll crack him. Do your job; I'll do mine. When you get back, we'll have the code to get your drones out. I promise."

Ryan nodded, turned and walked away from Jason. Inwardly, he breathed a sigh of relief. He had some time.

—*Get the hell out of there, Ryan. I've got something.*

Getting buried alive, the last ray of light was most terrible. Turing couldn't bear it and clenched his eyes shut. Darkness descended. All sensory input evaporated. He opened his eyes to the black. In spite of his training, a primordial terror overtook him. He strained to breathe, couldn't get enough air, and panic mounted.

As the tank refilled, the fluid around him lost viscosity. Turing managed a final gasp of air before sinking to the tank's floor. Then, the machines controlling his slice of hell calibrated buoyancy and he floated weightless. The oily liquid enveloped him. He drew it into his lungs, its weight alien. The act sent Turing into bucking convulsions. But, with each breath, his body grew more comfortable accepting the oxygenated liquid. In time, Turing's pain dissipated into the darkness. He floated—perfectly comfortable, and utterly alone.

To stem that first step into solitude, Turing ran through his conversation with Ryan. The boy had done so well! He'd found the disc; he was under way. Turing hoped Ryan and Sarah would decipher the clues he'd offered. If so, there was hope. Maybe, Ryan and Sarah could pull off the impossible and bring down the conspiracy. Maybe they'd even get him out. The possibility only amplified Turing's black isolation. He bit down on his lip, pain the only input left to him.

16

They waited for flesh contact before discussing the interview. Turing may have encrypted the Key, but Echelon had other means of eavesdropping. The risk was too great. Beyond that, Ryan felt uncomfortable letting Sarah into his mind now that he knew her.

It was one thing to have a stranger bopping around in there. Ryan often felt more comfortable in the company of strangers—no expectations. He'd enjoyed Sarah's banter, liked her company, maybe even dropped his guard to a point.

But now, with her scent still buzzing through his fantasies, he wanted Sarah out of his head. He told her as much on reaching their rendezvous. He couched it in security issues and hated that she saw through it. She didn't say anything, just nodded. Ryan was terrible at reading facial expressions. He kept his own blank.

Ryan's reluctance to respond to Sarah jarred her. She knew this man. She thought he knew her. Yet now that their lives teetered on a single tenuous thread, now that their reliance on each other was total, she realized she couldn't count on him for the human connection she craved. They'd missed some crucial step in their evolution toward intimacy. Ryan had pulled away.

Now he sat before her, his face locked. She could see his time with Turing had ground him down. He looked as though he was being slowly gutted. She longed to place her hand in his—to bridge the chasm between them.

Their meeting location further crossed her signals. Laing had chosen a lovers' retreat in California's Big Sur. Nestled on the coast south of San Francisco, Laing had used the retreat before. As it was on the way to Calsoft, it wouldn't attract Sachs' attention. Because it housed many an illicit affair, Sarah's quiet arrival lifted not a single eyebrow.

Clinging to lush cliffs overlooking the Pacific, the retreat's restaurant stood open to the fog-thick air. A gossamer-thin, transparent fabric sheltered the diners from the elements. Sarah gazed into the gray, its solitude overwhelming her. Around them, couples shared companionship. Sarah had little more than fear and sorrow to keep her company. She reached for Ryan's hand. Somehow, his expression grew colder—running sea gray. Sarah's hand fell short.

She thought of a song Agamemnon's Mitten had planned to debut the night Elaine died. "I Need Someone to Love Me—Just Not You." That about covered it. She envisioned dying next to Ryan—in a day, a week. Wouldn't be longer than that. She saw that she'd die alone.

Ryan watched Sarah's brow furrow. Had he done something wrong—upset her? The drones' onslaught distanced him, drew him inward. Maintaining any concentration required Herculean effort. He tried to let it go, gazing down to the rolling waves at the cliff's base. Ryan liked this place—its fuzzed monotone soothed him. Anger and confusion slid away for an instant. He savored it. Then, a flitting memory of Turing brought it all back.

"He looked horrible." Laing turned to Sarah's questioning eyes. "Turing."

"You think he'll hold out?" Sarah asked.

"Probably. Just to spite me."

"What?"

"I thought I was stuck with the drones—with this fuckin' barrage. Now, I find out they can be shut down and Turing's sitting on the kill switch. Puts me and Echelon in the same boat."

Sarah looked at him in shock. "Jesus, Ryan! Don't you see? He did it for you. He saved your life by locking the drones down."

"Saved my life? Please."

"With access to the drones' code, Jason would control you. He could reprogram your drones at will, force you to do whatever he wanted. Beyond that, he could inject the rest of the batch into other agents, creating an army of slaves. Turing saved you from that."

Ryan's stone face cracked. It sank in. He'd missed the obvious. There was no room for that kind of error.

"I'm . . . sorry. I'm not five by five, Sarah. They're eating me from the inside out. I can't concentrate on anything else."

"Ryan, I need you."

"I'll try. I'm not well."

"Join the club. We don't get the Key, we're all fucked."

Ryan looked on impassively. He tried to care, but the drones' dissonance sent him sprawling.

"The key to playing God. That's what Turing said," Ryan muttered.

Sarah nodded, her mind spinning. She needed to get Laing's attention, to drag him out of his inner turmoil. Maybe she should kiss him again. No, better to keep her distance. Guy's a fuckin' powder keg. Though a little rough sex might be okay. World's going to hell and all I can think of is getting laid, she thought. That made her smile. The smile confused the hell out of Ryan.

"What do you know of Echelon's history?" she asked.

Ryan felt foolish and unfocused. And now Sarah was babying him. "You looking to give me a history lesson?" Ryan's asked caustically.

Sarah remained quiet, waiting for him to focus. Laing took a deep breath and muttered through his recollection, "Initiated late in the twentieth century as a worldwide information net. Developed by the United States' National Security Agency in conjunction with England and Australia. It was designed to monitor the rising flood of communication surging across the planet. But it didn't work."

"Oh, it worked," Sarah countered. "Back then it was ECHELON, all caps—just a cog in America's intelligence-gathering machine. The ECHELON system trapped information flow very effectively. But its ability to pluck the needle of golden intel from a haystack of spam, blogs and bullshit was low."

"As I said, it didn't work," Ryan repeated.

"So what happened? How did ECHELON become Echelon? How did this slice of the American intelligence net become more powerful than the country that created it?"

"What the hell are you asking me?"

"The Key, Ryan."

"Listen, I'm not up for mind games. Just spit it out."

Once again Sarah surveyed her partner. He might not be up to the task ahead.

"The NSA was the darling of America's intelligence community," she continued. "Its crypto city outside Bethesda, Maryland, was the largest intelligence complex in the world. And ECHELON was its baby.

But even with the NSA's substantial computing power, ECHELON couldn't pull the clean retrieve we have now."

"We had, you mean," Laing corrected her.

"Right," Sarah said, annoyed with Ryan's intrusion. "Anyway, ECHE-LON sucked in terabits of raw signals intelligence—enough to fill America's Library of Congress on a daily basis. The NSA couldn't effectively mine the data load. As the information haystack grew, the needles of intelligence got lost in the mess. ECHELON sank in a quagmire of information."

"And then?" Ryan asked.

"No one's sure. A change, a phase shift. Suddenly, ECHELON's operators possessed the ability to access, mine and manipulate data on a massive scale."

Light dawned. "They had found the Key."

"ECHELON's operators plucked needles from the haystack with ease. Their dream of omniscience became a reality. Yet with total success, ECHELON's operators saw that America would use its control of information flow to dominate world affairs."

"As we've done for a century," Ryan said.

"Yes and no. The interests of a single country, or even three countries, were far too limited. The power to control information needed to be in the hands of an entity that had all of humanity at heart."

"So?"

"So, the operators of ECHELON did just that."

"They stole the code," Ryan said.

"About right. They engineered a system crash. On January twenty-fourth of the year 2000, the entire NSA system went dark."

"Heads rolled."

"You're damn right. Had a foreign power known how vulnerable the U.S. was, well, you get the picture. It was an enormous risk."

"Which, I take it, paid off."

"The plan worked. NSA systems rebooted—that's what they called it then—and no one suspected a thing."

"ECHELON became Echelon," Ryan said.

Sarah nodded. "The NSA came back online, information kept rolling in . . . except now NSA's ECHELON was itself being manipulated. The real Echelon, the one we know today, was born. It very slowly began to shift the flow of world events, sparking a brief flare of violence and chaos before life settled to smooth order."

"What happened to the engineers?"

"Who knows. Probably quit the NSA over time."

"So where does all this lead us?"

"The Key, Ryan. It leads to the Key."

Ryan lit up. "The code itself—that kicked it all off, that drew the needles from the haystack."

"Give the cyborg a prize."

"Cute. So where did it come from? Who developed it?" Ryan asked.

"No one knows. It just appeared. One day they were awash in data; the next they controlled it with an iron fist."

"They were given the power of God," Ryan mused.

"Those engineers became the architects of our modern society."

"So where are they?"

"Long dead."

"And where the hell did they get that Key?"

"That's what I want to know. I think the answer's in Echelon itself. I think the answer *is* Echelon."

Ryan shot her a confused, irritated look. Before he could voice his annoyance, she continued. "Listen, I've been lurking though Echelon's 'ware for a few years now. To us, Echelon's framework seems natural. Makes all the sense in the world."

"Your point?"

Sarah ignored the sarcasm. "I've been looking into the standards and practices of computing in the twentieth century."

"Let me guess, the Key was revolutionary."

"More than that, it was a complete fluke. The rest of the world still operates on concepts grounded in twentieth-century technology. Echelon uses an entirely different system."

"Hence our ability to manipulate the flow at will."

"What would seem impossible to a civ hacker, the Echelon agent does in her sleep."

"Not impossible, not magical—we just operate by different rules."

"Exactly. It's information necromancy. No magic involved— Echelon just operates under better rules."

"Rules that couldn't have emanated from concepts of the day?"

"It seems highly unlikely," Sarah said.

"So where did they come from?"

"Where does one find the Key to play God? I have a theory on that."

Ryan smirked. "I suspected as much."

Sarah beamed.

17

Calsoft's massive complex sprawled through suburban Seattle. The buildings had a ruddy modernism to them, avant-garde encrusted with a pocked ornamentation that spoke of stability and endurance. The lobby had an archaic, retro-chic aura. Approaching the receptionist, Ryan detected the intricate webbing of the tech at her disposal. She greeted him before he could say his name and told him to wait for Mr. Welton. Ryan sat on a curved bench that seemed wholly unsuited to its task. Oblong and slick, its back rose well above Ryan's head, slicing the lobby into compartments.

Laing fumed over his new role as gopher and decoy. While Sarah was off hunting the elusive Key, he'd be here, guarding Welton.

—*You're brooding,* her voice echoed through his head.

For their continued work, Sarah had jury-rigged a microscopic implant linking her to his jack point in the flow. Ryan had wanted to abandon the link entirely, to keep Sarah at a reasonable distance. Circumstance dictated otherwise. Laing accepted her return. In truth, he needed the company. Sarah cut the drones' static, which continued to sear through his head.

—*I don't like being the patsy. The situation requires it, but I don't like it.*

—*You just convince Echelon that you're in their hip pocket and let me handle the dirty work.*

—*You're not helping matters.*

—*I rarely do.*

He couldn't hear her laugh. Their link translated direct thought only, but he suspected a soft giggle. She laughed at her own jokes.

Ryan shifted on the bench. Furniture that sacrificed comfort for appearance annoyed him. And this was no beauty. The high back rose ominously over him, the bench slightly too short for his legs. Several of these curved monoliths linked into a blocky snake cutting up the lobby. He studied the massive thing, puzzling.

"A Cray 1-A Supercomputer." The voice pulled him around. Welton loomed over him. He looked different in person, whipcord strength exuding from his lean frame. Tall, sandy blond, forty-three, he possessed an unmistakable aura that Ryan hadn't picked up in the vids. Welton's luxurious suit couldn't contain the raw energy vibrating off him. Ryan understood why Welton's associates referred to him as "the King." His presence shifted reality, gravitation bending it to his will.

"Built in 1978 by the eccentric genius Seymour Cray, it was the most advanced computer in existence. Now, any wrist console has more operating power."

"Yesterday's cutting edge is your lobby decor," Ryan said, standing to shake the man's hand.

"An important lesson. One that should never be forgotten."

Welton gripped hard, locking Ryan's hand for an instant too long. Rams butted heads, lions bared fangs; men utilized subtler actions to assert their dominance. Welton was used to being top dog. During the brief pause in his levity, Welton's hard eyes bored into Ryan. Ryan didn't flinch. Then Welton's mask of congeniality returned, his eyes brightened, and he slapped Ryan on the back.

"That's the basis of my success, Mr. Laing. Be two steps ahead of the cutting edge. Ride that edge and it'll slice and dice ya. Now, what can I do for you and the Saudis?"

"I'm here to protect you, Mr. Welton. Nothing more."

"Really? Protect me, huh? I have the most advanced security system in the world and the Saudi Arabian government thinks I need protection?"

Ryan had decided to use his Saudi cover to access Welton. In recent years, the Saudis had been an ever-expanding player in world affairs. Their tech sector alone made them a force.

"We received credible intel that you're under direct threat. The Saudi royal family has deemed your value too precious to allow this threat to become a reality."

"And so they sent you? A single agent?" Welton led Ryan through the lobby and into Calsoft's inner sanctum.

"And so they sent me."

The doors closed behind Ryan with a satisfying *thunk*.

A sharp chill cut through layers of protective gear, wicking away Sarah's warmth, and much of her desire to save the world. Shivering uncontrollably, the whole thing seemed like a pain in the ass.

How had she gotten herself into this mess? Sarah longed for her life in Inverness, a life long gone and barely remembered. For better or worse, she was linked to a cyborg slowly losing his mind. But he was safe and sound at Calsoft, carrying out his orders, while she bounced through the freezing air. She mentioned this to Ryan when she could pull herself away from copiloting an antique airplane over a sea pock-marked with icebergs. That she had willingly retrofitted the tub into a giant gas can was icing on the cake. She'd burst into flames over the coldest place on earth. Great.

—*I thought we'd satellite recon this. I'm a flow girl. Get in, save the world and get out in time for a beer at the pub.*

Ryan had just described the cushy warmth of his office within Cal-soft's security complex.

—*They'd pick up a sat link. Who'd suspect a dead woman would fly into the Arctic in a Grumman Goose?*

The harebrained scheme had come to her a mere twenty-two hours ago. And now here she was. High over the Arctic Ocean.

—*Humanity isn't worth it.*

Sarah pulled off a glove to scratch her ear. The implant itched like crazy.

It was a long shot. Occam would rip her a new one. She'd expected Ryan to reject her plan out of hand. Now Sarah wondered if he'd taken it up just to piss her off.

"Echelon didn't create the Key," Sarah had said between bites of seared ahi. "Just as the flow rose into being, a code stream spread across the globe. It changed everything."

That conversation felt far away now. Sarah peered over the plane's nose. In the twentieth, a listening post had clung to one of the barren hunks of ice passing below her. The United States and the Soviet Union had both operated posts here. Signal-bounce off the ionosphere made the poles prime points to eavesdrop. Russians had listened to Ameri-cans. Americans had listened to Russians. And the listening posts had listened to each other. Sarah looked out and shivered. No wonder they called it the Cold War.

"This is hopeless," she muttered to herself.

"Well, I coulda told you that," Gilbert Ransom said, a broad grin plastered to his face. Stuffed into the pilot's seat like ten kilos of potatoes in a five-kilo sack, Ransom clearly loved the adventure, hopeless or not. "Finding a single iceberg? Hell, you got a better chance of winning the lottery." He looked out past Sarah. "Sure is beautiful, though."

Sarah grunted, shrinking down into her parka. She'd made her way up to Alaska, staying off-grid, pushing through the populated areas and into the hinterland. She knew getting out to her target zone would be an issue. She had few resources that wouldn't draw attention. The hunk of junk that she was now sitting in became her only option.

Sarah had found the Goose, and Gilbert, in a state of inebriated decay. The hangar was well ventilated—rusted pocks allowing ice-cold air to seep through. Once a military installation, Vigilance, Alaska, didn't get many guests. This fact became readily obvious on seeing the haggard state of the only airplane based there. Its owner didn't look much better.

—A Grumman Goose! Do you know how rare those are? It's perfect, Ryan had thought.

—I figured we'd need a plane. Didn't figure it would be older than my grandfather.

Sarah had stared at the ungainly plane, deeply dubious.

"I know what you're thinkin', but she flies like a dream." The plane's owner, Gilbert Ransom, had a face that could weather a thousand Alaskan winters—and probably had. He ran a hand down the Goose's flank.

Sarah clambered into the cabin and peered through murky light into the cockpit. "There's no digilink," she said.

Ransom's jowls flapped with his nod. "My Goose has no circuits, no silicon. She's all mechy."

"Then how the hell am I supposed to fly it?"

"You're not. I fly the plane. You want her—you get me in the bargain."

"What kind of range does it have?"

"What're you plannin'? Normally, I do the standard tourist loop. You'll get mountains, glaciers—the whole deal. And at a good price too."

"I've got something a little more . . . aggressive in mind."

The man's eyes lit up. "I'm all ears."

"I'm scouting a possible retrieval operation. Sat tracking leads me to think that a . . . rich target is locked into an iceberg northwest of us."

"Retrieval operation . . . ," Gilbert repeated in dull confusion. Then a grin formed, pushing his chins together into a collar of fat. "You're talking about treasure huntin'!"

Sarah stayed quiet.

"What're you lookin' for?"

"Can't say. Could be nothing." She let Gilbert's imagination plug the gaps in her story.

"So you need to find a single iceberg in a sea full of 'em fuckers?" Gilbert didn't let her respond. "That's got to be the craziest, most bull-headed crapshoot I ever come across. I love it." With that, he'd set about filling the Goose's hold with gas canisters.

Now, hours later, the plane bucked through pockets of turbulence, triggering waves of panic-tipped nausea in Sarah's stomach. Sarah sunk into the copilot's seat and snuck glances at Gilbert, grinning like a maniac, his hands playing over the plane's controls with a grace she hadn't expected in the big man. They kicked through another patch of turbulence.

"This thing flies like—"

"Like a fat old goose? Yup."

Built in 1945, the plane had languid, sloping curves, punctuated by two behemoth propellers mounted on the wings. Its flat belly and high wings allowed for water landings, making it ideal for Alaskan transportation.

"But it's a hardy bird. Won't let ya down in a pinch. I flown her for nearly two decades and not a scratch."

Sarah nodded, her stomach churning.

"Relax," Gilbert barked. "Stop fighting the motion."

Sarah took a deep breath and exhaled, letting the knot go. The Goose conveyed the feeling of flight more than any modern plane.

"Good. Now curl your fingers around the stick—feel her move with ya."

Sarah did so. In the rudder's vibration she felt the turbulence, the engines' whip and Gilbert's adjustments for both. Sarah fell into it, engrossed.

Ransom hummed happily. "She feels good, eh? The wheel's kick and the wind's song . . ." Gilbert trailed off. "All that romantic bullshit don't seem so hokey up here."

Sarah smiled.

Ransom tapped at the fuel gauge. "That said, this trick's comin' to an end. 'Less you want to spend some serious time on one of those bergs, we gotta get back."

"Just a little longer. We're close. I know it," Sarah said.

Gilbert shrugged. "What else have I got to do?"

Sarah stared down at her makeshift homing device—an off-the-shelf metal detector that she'd modified. North Pole 8 was out there—buried in ice, but there. The transmission had spread from that listening post.

Sarah's gizmo beeped, and she breathed a sigh of relief. Over the vast expanse of space between them she thought out to Ryan.

—*I found it.*

For a man on top of his game, Michael Welton had a shitload of enemies. In analyzing Welton's security reports, Ryan found six viable and immediate threats. Most traced back to a cadre of very disgruntled billionaires. Welton's takeover of Calsoft had been swift and bloody. Mere weeks after Ryan had watched Neil Buist die in South Beach's fetid waters, Welton had solidified his position as Calsoft's CEO. In a series of inspired moves, Welton had managed to pole-vault up the ranks. In the ensuing purge, egos had been crushed, lives destroyed, careers decimated. Those who'd once held the reins of power found themselves at Welton's mercy.

Their response arose from emotion, making it easy to track. They hired a solid merc. A man with plenty of experience in wet work.

—*I found it,* Sarah echoed through his thoughts.

—*Good hunting,* Ryan responded.

Gilbert circled the iceberg. Its sheer, white cliffs rose from the churning seas to a small, far too small, flat patch at the southwest corner of the expanse. Sarah's gizmo indicated metal just off the field; she saw only white. Lots of white.

Ransom initiated a low-level pass. "Lady, I'll give you a flyby—but that's as close as I get to that thing."

"Gil, I have to get onto that berg."

"No place to land on that ice cube and, with those swells, a water landing's out of the question. You get the flyby, honey."

Sarah glared at him. "Guess we go with plan b."

"You gotta be kidding. You're not actually gonna try that?"

Sarah pulled off her belt and headed aft. The plane kicked, sending Sarah sprawling.

"Gil, can't you fly this fucker?"

The rudder bucked in his hands. "I'm tryin', lady. Funky turbulence down here."

The Goose made a wide, high turn, then pulled out of the bank and leveled over the iceberg. Sarah hauled the hatch open—iced wind ripping her breath away. She ignored the cold shock, heaving her gear out of the hatch. It crashed into the hard ice, careened off its irregularities and finally came to rest. Pieced together as it was from Laing's gear stash, she hoped it would survive such abuse. She would soon bet her life on it.

Gil's yelling cut through the wind's howl. The hatch's added drag wrenched at the plane. Sarah was about to respond when she saw the cliff face approaching. "Too low" slammed through her mind— crescendoing into a tack-sharp vertigo. At this altitude, she could see the ground getting closer.

"Shit!" Ransom shouted as he wrenched on the rudder. "Help me!" Adrenaline ripped through Sarah. Two hundred meters, one hundred . . . Sarah dived forward, sprawling over Gilbert's bulky frame. She grabbed the stick and pulled with him.

"Down draft!" he yelled. "And it's dragging us down. Opening the fuckin' hatch didn't help!"

They pulled hard. The cliff loomed huge, filling Sarah's view. She felt the stick move, slightly. A half second later, the tail of the plane dropped and the nose kicked up.

"That's right, old girl," Ransom muttered through clenched teeth.

Sarah watched jagged shards of ice skim under the plane. Mesmerized, she failed to notice the thin spire off the port side until it collided with the Goose's wing. The plane bucked hard, teetering on the edge of a stall. Gilbert threw the throttle wide open, engine whining with the strain.

The plane soared off the far end of the berg and bit into the air, regaining some altitude. Sarah dragged herself into the copilot's seat. Gilbert, still heaving through asthmatic gulps of air, craned his neck to port.

"How we doing?" Sarah asked.

Anger flared through Gilbert's eyes. "Twenty years—not a goddamned scratch! You're bad luck, lady." Gilbert tried to calm down. "Good news is—the ice sheared clean. So we're still airborne. Bad news—port-side pontoon is fucked. And yes, that's a technical term. What the hell were you doing opening that hatch?"

"I need to get onto that berg." Fear forced Sarah into a stutter.

"Lady, you're too pretty to die out here."

"I'm going onto the berg—and you're going to help me."

"Now here's where I kick into a rant about how I ain't doing shit for your harebrained, stupid—"

Sarah cut him off. "That bag I threw out—it contained the balance of your payment, among other things."

Gilbert just stared at her. "Girl, you are beyond doubt the craziest fuckwit I ever seen."

"Take us back over. I only need a couple minutes on the ice—then we go home and you get your money."

"Goddammit!" Gil yelled. After a pause, he banked hard. "Whatever's on that berg—better be worth dyin' for."

Sarah stayed quiet.

The plane banked up into the wind. Sarah got into position and put on each and every piece of clothing she'd brought with her. Over that she lashed life jackets, three of them. It made no sense that the Goose carried jackets. Mere contact with the water would kill in seconds. She was glad to have them.

Finished, she trundled to the open cabin door. Wind lashed her. Her nose froze immediately and she reeled back, squatting down. She couldn't afford frostbite. And she wasn't too interested in sporting a gel nose for the rest of her life. Some things should not be removable.

She hauled her bulk to the hatch as the Goose swooped over the berg's face and skimmed the flat zone. Fuck the big picture, she thought, gutting up. Elaine's death wouldn't be in vain. If Sarah had to jump out of a plane to get the assholes who killed her, then so be it. At the very last moment, she relayed her plans to Ryan. He deserved to know.

Gilbert screamed to her. "Twenty minutes! Then I'm gone and fuck your money! I'll tip my wings on the last pass."

She nodded and jumped.

The wind smashed into her—a solid mass. Had she hit the cliff? No. The roar of the engines howled behind, then over, then past her. They gave her pain a soundtrack. They covered the terrified shriek exploding from her lungs.

Time slowed. She had a long moment to appreciate how painful impact would be. Then she hit ice. It felt soft compared to the wind. She skidded across the berg's flank, registering only gray speed. She jammed her feet into the ice, but that only served to flip her onto her face. Her right leg burned hot and wouldn't work. She didn't have time to ponder the disaster that a broken femur would be on an iceberg in the middle of the ocean.

The cliff neared. Sarah scraped at the slick ice. And she slowed, but not enough. A bump in the ice kicked her into the air. Her vision filled with gray water, churning hundreds of meters below. The ice disappeared and she fell like a stone. She flailed her arms trying to grab at the cliff behind her.

Then her world shifted hard, movement canceled. Her whirling, spinning view snapped to stasis. The general pain of friction yielded to a searing, white heat from her shoulder. She passed out for a second, maybe a minute, she couldn't tell. Couldn't have been long. The stink of burnt synthetics revived her. Her outer layers continued to smolder from the heat friction.

She hung in space, a gaping abyss below her. And above . . . above was worse. She had fallen about five meters down the face. Her right hand had jammed into a vertical ice fissure, arresting her fall and saving her life. Or at least extending it a bit. Shock slid over her like a warm blanket. She twitched, letting the pain of her dislocated shoulder jar her back to reality.

She found a small ledge, just enough for one foot. Gently, she stood up on it. The ice crackled under her weight, but it held. Waves of nausea floated though her gut as the pressure on her shoulder ebbed. System check. One knee throbbed, crunched a bit as she moved it. But it worked. Her hand was thoroughly jammed.

Reality stormed back in and with it, life. She was alive. A cocktail of chemicals flooded her. Her eyes opened to her surroundings, and she couldn't remember ever seeing anything more beautiful. The jagged ice cliff below formed an intricate latticework, contrasting with the sea's rolling gray. Sarah screamed into the perfection, and her echo drowned in the ocean. She didn't mind.

Sarah realized she had better get a grip, and quick. She bit down on her euphoria, twitched again, pain searing her. Pulling a small utility knife from her pocket, she cut off the remnants of the life jackets. Their singed husks fell down the cliff. She looked away before they hit the ocean.

Sarah turned her attention to her hand. She could wiggle some of the fingers in her glove. At least she thought she could. Her arm looked unnaturally long. Before she could do anything, she'd have to get it back into its socket. Not that she had any idea of what she'd do, but at least this gave her a goal. Relocate my shoulder and don't pass out. Simple.

She hopped around on her foot, turned away from the ocean, her breath freezing into the cliff face. She figured the shoulder would want to go back. She'd just have to give it some motivation. She went up on her toes and pulled. The pain increased. She became nothing more than hurt. She wiggled, squirmed. Her knee felt weak. Her view began to spiral inward. No, no, no, no! She gasped and pulled hard. *Pop!* The reverberation of her shoulder returning to its socket thumped through her body. More pain, waves of it. She threw up, chunks of breakfast spotting the perfect white cliff.

She let herself rest. She must have nodded off.

Ryan's thoughts drew her up out of unconsciousness.

—*You still out there?*

—*I am. You'd never believe the view from here.*

—*Where are you?*

She told him. She felt his silent panic. With it, hers returned. She could already feel the cold seeping in, finishing her off.

—Sarah! Get up, get up that damn cliff and get back here.

—I . . . I don't think—

—Don't think, just fucking do it.

She pulled her gaze up. Stood high on her foothold and tried to wriggle her hand free. It budged slightly, but she realized that if she got it out, she'd tumble backward. That didn't seem helpful.

—I'm stuck.

—You need to get above your hand. Get your feet up. Then jam your other hand into the rock.

—Rock? There's no rock within five hundred kilometers of here.

—Sorry, I meant ice. Move your feet up. Find a new ledge.

She looked around. Her teeth began to chatter. There was nothing, just slick ice. At least the view was good.

—What do you see?

She told him.

—And above you?

Sarah looked up. Above the fissure that had locked down her arm, maybe a meter above, a small ledge pocked out. Lot of good it did her. Her foothold began to crumble. She hated the idea of dangling to death.

—Are you flexible?

—Are you hitting on me?

He just waited for a response.

—Yes.

—Okay, Sarah. I'm going to tell you how to get out of this. But you owe me.

She smirked.

—I tell you what. You get me out of here and I'll be your love slave till the end of time.

She sensed his sudden discomfort.

—Sorry, I forgot you were so shy.

—Listen, do you want out or not? Just do as I say.

—All right, all right.

He then described a move so ridiculous that she laughed out loud. But what the hell else did she have to do? Her dance card wasn't exactly full.

—Okay, but if I die while kissing my own ass, all that karma's on you.

—Just do it before you freeze.

She hunkered down and focused. Might as well give it her all. Her right hand remained thoroughly jammed. Her right foot teetered on her little perch. This would hurt like hell. She grabbed her right wrist and used it as leverage. She hauled her left leg up the wall until it was bent into the rock by her chest. And that's when her right foot gave way. The flake broke off and she dangled.

She was too tired to go in for another adrenaline rush. She had seconds before she lost her will. Still grabbing her right wrist she shifted and squirmed, giving her left leg some room to move and, finally, to straighten out. She hadn't done the splits in years. Vertically, with her hand jammed into an ice fissure. She hadn't done that, ever.

—I'm splitting.

—Good. Do the rest. Quickly!

She took a fleeting breath and curled her left leg down and in, wrapping it over her right arm. The back of her left knee dropped in the crook of her right elbow. She felt like a very not-hot pretzel. The pressure of her body weight began to pull her arm free. Now or never.

A fleeting curiosity as to how Ryan knew such contortions flashed past. She flexed her left leg, using it to hoist her torso up and into the wall. Her right hand held. She continued to push, rising above it. Then her hand began to slip. As it released, she shot out her left hand and grabbed the ledge above her.

Her right hand popped from the fissure, her shoulder screaming hot pain. She barely felt it over Ryan cursing her to pull. So she pulled. Her legs scraped against slick ice. She got her right hand up to match her left. And she pulled. An eternity later she crested the ledge, wide enough to support her, and dropped into a heaving puddle of exhaustion. When the stars faded from her vision, she looked up. It was an easy climb from here. She stood and wriggled her way up onto flat ice. Sarah took a breath and looked into the gaping maw below.

—Okay, I owe you one. Were you a circus performer or something?

—Rock climber. She felt relief shuffling off Ryan in waves.

—Right. I forgot.

—Get back to work. Quit fucking around.

· · · · ·

You're all heart. Sarah's voice pounded through his still-pulsing head.

—A caring nurturer, through and through. Where would I be without you? Alone with my drone buddies.

—So it's all about you, huh? I'm back on the flat. Got about ten minutes to find . . . whatever it is.

—Well, get to it. I've got my own problems here.

—Do your job, soldier boy.

Her thoughts faded into a distant hum. She was less able to control her broadcast. When she had something to say, it came through loud and clear. Yet her silence was anything but. A spindling chaos of thoughts floated through her head. Ryan couldn't believe the sheer mass she dealt with. He almost asked her about it but decided not to, afraid of embarrassing her. He added her cacophony of broadcasted thoughts to his own, walled them off and let them have at it. He had work to do.

He settled over his console and reviewed Welton's security. It was good, impervious during his normal routines. Unfortunately, he rarely kept to such. As Calsoft's CEO, his presence was requested at all manner of engagements, of which he accepted an alarming number. The latest, and to Ryan's mind the most dangerous, lay in an offer to be the commencement speaker for Welton's alma mater. Welton would be leaving for Princeton, New Jersey, tomorrow night.

The air chilled Sarah's lungs. Ice-crisped clouds condensed on her face with each exhale. The sky pulsed a vibrant blue. Sarah slipped her way across the glare, her knee throbbing with each footfall, to North Pole 8. Amazing that such a rickety structure could weather the rigors of time and climate. She drew her laz gun and unfroze the most obvious aperture. Its ancient steel frame warped as the ice melted. Overhead, she heard the comforting throb of the Grumman's engines. It continued to circle, waiting for her signal. She had less than ten minutes.

Sarah dove into the aperture and peered around a room turned to glass. Under her glow light the interior flickered with an ephemeral delicacy. She walked through the crystal palace, everything perfectly intact, untouched, frozen in time. The Key had passed through this cramped shit-hole. Sarah hunted for its fingerprints.

She ripped through the mass of machinery and material strewn haphazardly across the room. The final unlucky residents of these premises had vacated in a hurry. Old code makers and breakers frozen into the walls. Devices to record signals bouncing off the ionosphere. She imagined the gruesome lives of the intelligence operatives who'd inhabited these confines. No wonder it had been abandoned. Had the Key been a flight of fancy? An inspiration of one of the people marooned here?

Minutes clicked away. She refused to leave without something, wouldn't admit that she had been wrong, that her calculation was off. But the more she searched, the less promising it all looked. Three minutes left.

She saw it. In a far corner stood an ancient console enshrined in ice. Made before goggles, it had a monitor sitting on top of the tower. She chipped away enough ice to get a view of the thing, then ripped the monitor away, revealing the tower. She thought of using the laz gun to dislodge it from the table. But that might fry its circuitry. Time ticking away, she cracked the shell, opening its guts to the frigid air. She took a wild guess, banking on her intuition. She worked the hard disk out, cracking it slightly in the process.

She pocketed it and bolted. The drum of the Grumman built steadily. She exploded into the fresh air. Running hard, she shoved the memory board deep into her pocket. Sarah reached the gear she'd chucked out of the plane. Her numbed fingers frantically disengaged the ropes binding it. The pain in her shoulder tore at her. She ignored it. If she missed her flight, she'd have plenty of time to obsess over her agony. She looked up to see the Goose tipping its wings. She'd get only one shot at this.

Grabbing the injection-molded backpack, she ran back into the open. The Grumman was about five hundred meters off to her left side. She struggled into the pack's harness, ignoring the leg loops. No time. She got her shoulders through, and clicked in the chest restraint with the Grumman less than fifty meters away.

She didn't have time to get scared. If she'd had all the time in the world, she probably would have psyched herself out of blowing the cord.

No such worry. She reached back and yanked on the yellow handle. Nothing happened. A wave of nausea rolled through her. A dud. Then her back exploded. The shock threw her forward, her hair singed by the quick flame. Above her, a tiny rocket shot into the sky. A slender line played out from her pack. As the rocket reached its apex, it expanded, floating. The gas in its ballast tank mixed and swelled, pushing at the soft rubber frame. What had been a rocket became a balloon. Sarah got to her feet, relief sweeping her. Optimal deployment. Gilbert banked slightly, locking on the target.

And then all hell broke loose. Emergency egress was not about comfort. The Grumman swooped over her. She could make out its ribbed hull against the blue sky. A small fork recently welded onto the plane's nose snagged the line between her and the balloon.

Sarah's sigh of relief vanished in an explosion of acceleration. The balloon caught on the fork and ripped Sarah off the ground. The straps dug into her chest and back. Her legs dragged for a beat and then she was flung into the air.

Below her boots, the ice pack vanished, replaced by ocean and a widening chunk of air. She tried to breathe, but her body had gone into shock; nothing worked. Blasts of wind ripped at her senses. Only the engines' roar broke through the howl.

The Grumman banked, turning toward dry land. Sarah swung out wide in a centrifugal arc, rising level with the plane. She caught Gilbert's hard eyes on her before plunging back in gut-wrenching free fall. She blacked out. Then something kicked over; some small piece of her cortex remembered that she was alive and desperately wanted to remain so. Warm adrenaline surged through her.

Her numb right hand lashed back and ripped at the pack. After several jarring attempts, she found it. She yanked, her hand whipping back into view clutching a red handle. The winch activated. It hauled her closer to safety. It also hauled her closer to the whirling props. Nothing came easy. The pull on her shoulders became unbearable. Turbulence pounded her as she neared the plane. Through her fog she tried to remember what she was supposed to do next, beyond staying well away from the prop blades.

The winch drew her closer. The gloves! Iron filings had been woven into their fabric. With a slap at her control harness, they magnetized. The wind bucked her. She flapped directly under the plane, continuing a shaky approach.

She counted on the turbulence to slam her into the hull and got her wish. But the impact was too hard. She couldn't get the gloves onto the hull before bone-crushing turbulance kicked her away. She hit again. This time she stuck. That she felt safer magnetized to the bottom of a plane in the middle of the Arctic illustrated just how long her day had been.

The open hatch gaped, agonizingly close. The winch pulled her as she crabbed over the plane's hull. One hand slipped into the cabin, then the other. She hauled herself inside. The winch stopped. The howl lessened. Safety.

Through a haze of exhaustion, Sarah groped at her harness. Numbed, she wrenched one shoulder free before the plane hit a pocket of low pressure and dropped. In the second before the Grumman's props regained thrust, the balloon popped free of the nose fork. It whipped back, the line trailing out behind the plane, still attached to Sarah's harness.

Drag ripped Sarah from the plane in a flash of speed and panic. She launched out a hand, snagging the hatch with magnetized fingers. Legs flapping, her body slammed into the plane's metal flank. Sarah squirmed against the balloon's pull. Her grip on the hatch faltered. She couldn't hold. Mind reeling in terror, Sarah arched back with everything she had left. Ripping her shoulder back out of its socket, the harness fell free. Dangling in space, she watched the balloon swirl in the plane's backwash.

Sarah tried to pull herself into the hatch, but had nothing left. She sank back, drag tugging at her. The ocean's gaping expanse filled her vision and she clenched her eyes shut. Her fingers lost purchase, ripping free of the hatch.

Sarah lurched back, then stopped short, Gilbert's meaty hand clutching her wrist. He dragged her along the hull, using his bulk to wrestle her into the cabin. Once inside, they sprawled backward in a tangle of limbs.

With a crackling wheeze, Gilbert got to his feet and forced the hatch shut. The howl ebbed. Sarah drew herself into a ball, shivering uncontrollably.

"I owe you one," she rasped through frozen vocal cords.

Gilbert stared down at her, panting. "Fuckin' A."

Sitting up, Sarah's shoulder popped into the socket in a white flash of pain. The sensation shattered her haze and she yanked the hard disk from her pocket. Outside the small crack, it remained intact. She hoped it was worth the effort.

Gilbert lifted her up and flopped her into the copilot's seat.

"Hope my money wasn't really in that backpack," he said as he crammed himself in behind the controls.

Sarah smirked. "It wasn't."

"Well, in that case, I won't drop ya in the ocean. But you're payin' for the damage, lady. And I'll tell ya now, the landing's going to be rough."

Sarah pushed back into her seat and closed her eyes. "Relax, Gil. The old girl'll do just fine."

Gilbert chuckled. "You got that right. Hell, I remember a flight over the Hubbard Glacier . . ."

Sarah was out before he could get to the good part.

18

The halls of Princeton University rested quiet. Ryan felt the potential energy of coeds running to and from class. But now, in the humid New Jersey dawn, the students were long gone, off to summers of sport and service or, if they happened to be seniors, sleeping off their final night of debauchery.

Ryan wandered the campus, relishing the solitude. He walked up grandiose slate stairs, through the Blair Arch and emerged on the commons. He looked back at the pointed arch. The evening before, Welton had gushed eloquent, or at least effusive, about his times in the rooms above.

"Four of us lived in that room over the arch. We had parties so massive you'd swear the building itself would crumble," he said.

Ryan merely nodded.

"And the kegs . . . We stored kegs of beer in the attic over the doorway. I wonder if they're still there," he mused.

"Mr. Welton, I think you should get back on the plane and cancel this engagement."

"But I have you to protect me."

"I can't protect you from your own stupidity."

For a moment Welton's eyes flashed a deep unsettling fury. They clouded back over with joviality before Ryan finished shivering.

"Einstein said that only two things were infinite: the universe and human stupidity. And he wasn't sure about the universe."

Ryan gave him the requisite chuckle.

"Besides, you've got me strapped into this girdle." Welton itched at the body-sock encasing his torso. Made of a carbon nanotube fiber, its tensile strength was one hundred times that of steel.

"It's not so breathable—I'll grant you that, but it's probably the strongest material made." Ryan found it easy to talk with Welton. He possessed an airy nonchalance that was intoxicating. Ryan tried not to get drawn in by his force of personality, but couldn't quite break away.

"Yes, I know," Welton responded. "Carbon locks into a stronger atomic mesh than any other element. Carbon tube fibers are functionally unbreakable."

Ryan nodded. "Same stuff chaining the Fenrir Space Station to the Earth. That's a lot of satellite, orbiting at forty thousand klicks, and that tubing is only millimeters thick."

"Well, I feel like I've been shrink-wrapped," Welton said.

"I think it's slimming." Ryan let a grin slip across his face.

"Everything will be fine," Welton had said, ending the conversation.

It all seemed fine. Sarah was making her way back. It took some work to get across the country as a dead woman, but she was managing. In the morning glow, even Ryan thought the whole mess could possibly work out. He sloughed off the thought. Optimism didn't suit him.

Laing continued his tour, meandering through the campus. He wondered what would have become of him without Turing's influence, had he come to a place like this instead. He couldn't see himself outside Echelon. And yet, that's exactly where he stood now.

He emerged onto the grounds set up for the graduation ceremony, an oak-pocked lawn hemmed in by Nassau Hall and a tall wrought-iron fence. He'd gone over the precautions to the point where local security thoroughly hated him. Take a number and get in line. He had little chance of protecting Welton in such an exposed position. Laing would have to spot the merc before he got a shot off.

"So, Bill Kneip's trying to do me in, is he?" Welton had not seemed too surprised when Ryan mentioned it on their rounds the evening before.

"He and several others in the previous administration have hired a merc to liquidate you."

"They lost in the boardroom. I wonder why they think they'd fare better in this arena."

"They may."

"Well, they won't be around to enjoy their handiwork. I run a tight ship."

"They already paid the merc."

"No matter."

Ryan learned later that Kneip died of a heart attack less than an hour after Welton learned of the merc. Wasn't Ryan's problem. He thought of Sarah and found it hard to concentrate on the task at hand.

He hoped her exploits would bear fruit. His ability to placate Echelon was not indefinite.

Several hours later, he'd made a couple more enemies. The chairs filled out with eager young men and women clad in their graduation gowns. Behind them, families looked on with pride. And yet, tension loomed over the proceedings. The world was encroaching on this little enclave.

The university's ownership of the land surrounding the campus kept Princeton's township mired in the past. Low-rise brick buildings dominated the quaint little town. Outside it though, Trenton rose up from the south and Newark descended from the north. Princeton felt like an aquarium, a capsule from another time fending off the two giants girdling it.

Now, as unrest spilled across the globe, Princeton became a flash point. That Welton was here only served to galvanize the frustrated masses into action. Picket lines and protestors flooded Nassau Street, the town's main drag, which backed up on the graduation grounds. Ryan had never taken notice of activists before. With Echelon in control, their impact was minimal. They were easily manipulated—information being their stock-in-trade.

Now, they seemed more ominous. Without Echelon, their information flow grew unfettered. The tree no longer fell silently, but crashed with the masses in attendance. The flow's smooth ripples of information had been easy for Echelon to manipulate. But now, without Echelon's governing hand, ripples gained force and became unpredictable. The protestors chanted slogans, ripping at every injustice under the sun, most of which they felt were related to Calsoft. They had a point. Ryan found Calsoft's aggressive opportunism hard to reconcile with a maintenance of order. Why Echelon had elevated the company confounded him.

Within the hallowed walls, commencement began. Outside, on the streets, protestors reigned. The shouts and chants made the families uneasy. Even for the parents, these past few days represented something new. An uncertainty had settled on the world, and they didn't like it.

Ryan sat in one of the bleachers, trying to blend with the crowd. The honorees had entered and taken their seats on an elevated podium.

Princeton's dean rose and flailed through a speech so boring that it put the entire graduating class to sleep, even seeming to calm the jittery families.

Ryan scanned. He knew the merc's face by heart. And to get through Welton's massive body armor, the killer would have to get close. There might just be a chance of stopping the guy.

Still, a visual ID would be a one-in-a-thousand chance. Picking out the energy signature of a device strong enough to bore through Welton's carbon body-sock was another matter. But to do that, Laing would need to open the floodgates. Ryan had never dared unfetter the drones in an arena so full of radiated data. Nearly everyone in the vicinity would have a device of some kind. The sheer mass of data waves made him shudder.

He breathed deeply and let his senses release. Stimuli rushed him. He heard the cacophony, smelled the smothering riptides of massed data. He tasted black. He was dimly aware that a new speaker had taken the stand. Was it Welton? Couldn't be. Language was wrong. It was a kid, speaking . . . was that Latin? He couldn't hold the thought as the drones probed further, flooding him with input—shock-waving through each and every sense.

An old lady took hold of his arm. "Are you all right?"

Sweat rolled down his brow, seeping into his collar. He pulled at it, desperate for air.

"Fine, ma'am. Just the sun," he heard himself say. He got up and made his way to the lawn. As he shuffled through linen pants and silk dresses, he felt it. The needle in the haystack pricked him so hard he almost yelped.

He hunted the source, and found it in one of the rows of students. Radiation emanated from a bulky man on the end of an aisle—good escape position. The man didn't know the students surrounding him. They rested on each other's shoulders, sleeping off their late-night excesses. But the man sat rigid. He glowed sharp orange. The orange began to pulse. His rail gun powered up.

An elegant gun, shooting a projectile at ungodly speed, it was the assassin's weapon of choice. The accelerator used a magnetic punch to propel a single metallic sliver at its target. No armor would be sufficient. Even the body-sock, if hit in a seam, would succumb to that kind of force. The rail gun's only downside lay in a single-shot capacity. Using such a weapon required commitment and skill.

Welton took the podium. The assassin fixated on him. Bad move. Ryan grabbed an extra gown from the table at the entrance and shrugged into it. He wandered down the aisle, drawing little attention, a graduate returning from the bathroom.

"We live in ominous times," Welton started out. The protestors' chanting bolstered his words. "You stand at the precipice of a new era. One that your parents do not understand. The status quo has grown so entrenched that few notice the subtle structures controlling our existence. We used to think that the explosion of information production, and easy access to it, would democratize humanity. Not so."

Ryan approached his target. The man shifted slightly.

"Instead, information has centralized, crystallizing around a single point of view."

A slight protrusion poked from the man's gown just as Ryan approached. He consciously stumbled and fell into the man.

"Sorry, pal," Ryan slurred, hoping the man would take him for an inebriated graduate. Though surprised by the intrusion, he responded quickly—like a professional.

"No problem," he said.

"Sam, that you? God, I'm still sloshed." Laing's voice rose, drawing attention. The man attempted to silence the disturbance.

"I'm not Sam. Fuck off."

"Fuck off, fuck you!" Ryan hauled back to whack the guy in the shoulder. Unconsciously, the man raised his weapon.

Ryan pushed with his right hand, while his left grabbed the rail gun and twisted viciously. The man let out a grunt of surprise, but it was too late. Laing found the trigger and fired. The silent shot hurtled from the chamber, through the merc's chest and out the top of his head with such speed that not a single drop of blood emerged. The projectile would continue well into the ozone. The assassin slumped into Ryan's waiting arms.

"He's under the weather," Ryan said to the kids around them. "Come on, Sam, it's back to bed for you!"

Ryan hefted the corpse and dragged him from the scene. Few took notice. The heat and excesses of the night before took their toll across the student body. Welton would be lucky to have any audience at all if he kept droning on. Ryan attempted to maintain his balance as he heaved the man through the crowd. They made it out of the central lawn before a security guard picked them up. He recognized Laing immediately.

"You playing doctor now?"

"Just making a drop-off."

"He got himself drunk, he can walk his ass home."

They moved into an alcove. No one would be able to see them. Ryan let the body fall hard.

"Hey! I don't like 'em any better than you do, but we're supposed to keep 'em alive. Till they graduate at least."

Ryan ripped open the man's gown, revealing body armor, the rail gun and a very clean hole in the chest.

"I don't think he'll make it. Pretty sure he isn't a student, though."

The guard's eyes widened. He took a step back, stumbled over his own feet and leaned into the cool slate wall. Ryan surmised that he had never done more than subdue coeds.

"Take him away. Call the police. Do whatever you're supposed to do."

The guard stammered, "Yes. Yes, sir."

Ryan left him gawking over the dead man. He walked back into the afternoon light and watched Welton pontificate. Grudgingly, Ryan admitted that he liked the guy, and was glad that things hadn't turned out differently.

"So this is the nature of a scale-free system. Our world is shaped by its internecine connections, not its parts. If a tree falls in the forest, its sound is shaped not by physics and gravity, but by how that sound is linked to the masses.

"In such an environment, success becomes elusive. Let me clarify your goal. Today, success can be defined as maximizing the information running through you. You must become a node—a hub through which the world's information flows. Those hubs that find an audience will, by their very nature, draw still more. Those that don't will fade into the flow's clutter and be lost.

"There are millions of news sites in the flow. Yet with such numbers, it is a very few organizations that shape the information you receive. Why, with all the offerings, are so few so immensely powerful? Because those sites, through advertising, content and lots of money, have built a larger web of links than the outliers. Once that web is formed, the site goes nodal and it's unstoppable. A critical velocity is attained, and these nodes begin shaping the information flowing through them.

"Without forging that tidal shove of connections, you will become that tree falling silently. No matter how you scream, you will not be heard. I wish you luck."

The audience broke from its torpor to give Welton a standing ovation. Ryan found himself clapping, caught in the man's aura. He held Welton's eye for a beat. Welton beamed. Ryan nodded. Welton descended through the throngs and into the secured area Ryan covered.

"Enjoy the speech?" Welton asked.

"Missed most of it."

"I saw. Remind me not to get on your bad side, Mr. Laing. That poor man never saw it coming."

"Like the man who hired him?"

Welton grinned. "Touché. We are both men of violence, then. We've survived the day's battle. Time to celebrate." Welton cuffed Ryan on the shoulder and ambled into the throng. Ryan followed behind.

Several minutes later, Welton was ensconced with his cronies in what he called an eating club. A row of mansions just off the university's grounds, Princeton's eating clubs stood as bastions of antique gentility and privilege. Welton belonged to the Cottage Club, a colonial-style mansion. On entering, Welton was saluted and shuffled from one sycophant to the next. Waiters passed appetizers. Well-dressed men and women joined the graduates in getting thoroughly drunk. That seemed to be part of the tradition.

Ryan tried to relax. His job complete, his cover with Echelon was safe. He could take some deep breaths and collect himself before Sarah arrived and the insanity kicked back into gear. And yet, something pricked at the edge of his consciousness. Beyond the ever-rising hysteria of the drones, a tingling uneasiness rose. He scanned the room. He'd learned over the years that instinct was rarely faulty. If honed, shaped by determination, it became a potent weapon.

Laing meandered, taking a beer from one of the waiters. He took a sip and nearly spat it out on the rich wood floor. Skunked. He tried another sip and it tasted better. It wasn't the beer that had fired his taste buds; it was the waiter himself. The waiter slipped down the hall and moved upstairs. The guy was carrying something that emitted all sorts of radiation. Reds and yellows swirled as the waiter ascended a large staircase.

Ryan followed. At the top of the stairs, a vaulted oak library filled with actual books opened to his right. He wondered why they bothered with such relics. Then again, the whole place felt like a relic— ornamental and fine but largely useless. The waiter skirted the library, moved past the snooker and pool tables. Ryan stopped to admire the sepia photographs along the walls, letting the man get out of sight before following.

Rounding the corner, Laing entered a shabby hallway with several doors leading off. The last one closed softly. Ryan loped down the hall and, in a single smooth movement, crashed through the flimsy door and into a small antechamber leading out onto a balustrade. The waiter had a small revolver aimed down into the crowd. He saw Ryan coming but stayed centered.

He nearly got the shot off. Jacked, Laing closed the two meters in a flash of speed. As he slammed his finger into the groove between the hammer and the firing pin, his other arm shot out, knocking the waiter to the floor. The man sprawled, but quickly shook off the strike and rolled into a crouch. Ryan had the gun. Too late, Ryan realized that it couldn't be the source of the man's aura.

"Ryan Laing," the man said with undimmed vitriol.

Great, one more fucker who knew more than he did. Ryan ran the face over in his mind.

"I know you?"

"Doubt it. We know you, though."

Ryan raised the gun, aiming for the leg. The man started to raise his arms in surrender. As they reached horizontal, a slim 'trode whipped from his cuff. It skittered toward Laing, glowing red, the source of the aura. He had no chance of evading it.

It latched onto his arm, blew something into him, then snaked back up the man's sleeve. Enraged, Ryan flung himself at the waiter, torquing his body and lashing out with a roundhouse kick designed to decapitate the fucker. It only concussed him. The man crumpled to his knees. Ryan loomed.

"Biokills won't work on me, guy. Just pisses me off."

When the man looked up, Ryan was shocked to see a bloody smile. "Just the same, you're starting to feel very off, isn't that right?"

"How the hell do you know my name?"

"We may choose isolation, but we've kept an eye on you."

"Huh?" Had he misheard, or was this guy just spouting bullshit? Something fuzzed Ryan out. The drones began to jitter.

"A virus, Laing. Not biological, digital."

Ryan stared at him in shock. This man knew about the drones. How else could he have engineered such a device? What the fuck was going on here?

"Particularly virulent from the looks of it."

Ryan crumpled as the man stood, trading positions. The man took the gun from Ryan's hand and sauntered back to the window.

"No . . ." Ryan slurred.

"Trust me, it's for the best. Welton's dreams must end."

A seething flame ignited in Ryan's core. The drones slithered through him, losing purpose. They triggered nervous reactions, sending him into convulsions.

The man looked down into the crowd. He raised his gun and took a bead on his target. Ryan saw it all from behind a film of slick fear, fried out. He lurched into a crouch and flung himself at the cause of his pain. Ryan slammed into the man's side, toppling him. The gun skittered across the floor. Ryan tried desperately to control his twitching body. The 'trodes holstered in the man's sleeves shot out, stinging Laing repeatedly. Ryan ignored the pain. Dying would be a relief. The man struggled mightily, thrashing.

"Die!" he screamed.

"I'm taking you with me," Laing grunted back.

"No! I must complete my assignment."

"Not on my watch, fucker."

Ryan beat away the man's flailing arms. He let the 'trodes sting him and clamped down on the man's throat. The man bucked hard. Ryan refused to be thrown. He gripped tighter, and the man's eyes glassed. A final kick. He stopped flailing. His face took on a glow of rapture, and he uttered a single word with his dying exhalation. Ryan barely heard it through his own pounding turmoil.

"*Elysium . . .*"

19

While being a ghost had its benefits, remaining ethereal posed a constant struggle. Getting from Alaska to New Jersey without triggering a trace would require some creativity. The Bullet wasn't an option; security scans would tag her. While Echelon may not be running five by five, Sarah couldn't risk generating any flow wake.

So she drove. She rented a car using Gwen, Tex's digital identity. While Sarah scoffed at the construct's erogenous link to the flow, she had to admire its engineering. The doll was a hell of a cover. Sarah assumed Tex had a thriving business creating such ether-dolls.

Waiting for the car to arrive at a haul stop outside Nome, Sarah fingered the hard disk she'd dug from the listening station. She looked around furtively, but no one seemed interested in her. She pried open its casing, losing herself in its mirror-smooth surface. Pulling code from the relic would be a bitch.

The car arrived, dropped in the lot off a hauler. Sarah paid for her stale coffee and headed outside. At the car, she punched in a pre-arranged code and the door popped open. It was no beauty. Dull green exterior with aged gray, faux-leather seats. She'd chosen a self-propelled model. Too many ID checks on the electrified superways.

Sarah got comfortable, keyed the ignition and hit the road, churning klicks. No one bothered to flow-link country roads. That meant she actually had to drive the car. While she readily admitted to a cycle fetish, cars bored her to death. She didn't like being boxed in. But after about a thousand klicks, and a liter of coffee, she sank into the relaxation of driving. Sarah fell into the easy rhythms of the countryside, the high plains of Dakota and enduring congruity of the Midwest. Her shoulder throbbed and her head hurt like hell. She hiked the climate control well above norm. If she never saw snow again it would be too soon.

Driving gave her time. Time forced recollection—something she wasn't quite ready for. She skimmed past fields of corn and wheat, skirting down and around the Great Lakes. She was born here, raised in Chicago. Topography settled, remembered and familiar. But the scenery pulled no emotional trigger. Childhood had been a void for Sarah.

Sarah's parents had loved her, satisfied all her material needs. They were both programmers for megacorps, code pullers. Her childhood had been fine, utterly average, grindingly dull. An eggshell happiness encrusted her memories, its brittle skin masking an emotional wasteland. Her earliest memories were discordant, filled with rebellion. Sarah didn't fit, couldn't embrace the cool economy of her parents' meager emotional output.

She had learned from them. They taught her the elegant purity of numbers and patterns drawn from chaos. Their knowledge shaped her prodigious abilities, honed them. She had her parents to thank for that. But her life was in the flow. There, she found friends, romance, connection. She'd left Chicago and never looked back. Every now and then, she'd link to her 'rents, check in. They didn't seem to care. The conversations gutted her.

Sarah stared into the blurred scenery, let the abyss take hold. The term Great Lakes was a misnomer, a moniker held over from another time. There was water in the lakes, somewhere deep in their center, engorged fissures that a changing climate hadn't quite sucked dry. The rest was a damp expanse descending in languid retreat from what had once been the shore. As a child, Sarah had explored the decomposed ships on those slanted plains—mostly because her parents had forbidden it.

She tried to shake off the memories, flick past them with the speed of her movement. She pulled an Agamemnon's Mitten tune from the flow. Mistake. Music blasted through the low-vibe angst her parents drew out. Replaced it with true pain, deep, swelling, threatening to engulf her. The song's rock sting seared through her; Elaine's anger and exuberance pulled a flood of tears.

Sarah stopped the car, spilled out and staggered to the road's edge, where pavement cracked into dirt. Silence, pervasive and total. No one used the back roads anymore—obsolescence hung heavy in the air. Through tear-filmed translucence, Sarah gazed into the distance. Sludge gray to the horizon. There, the expanse mingled with black nightfall, succumbing to it.

Ghosts populated the stifling silence. Elaine. Grief struck Sarah, hammered her down. She howled into the fading light. It didn't howl back. She screamed again—regurgitated anguish, loss, fear. Her cries percolated through thick air, their needle-sharp spark dulled. She stood defiant against the silence. But slowly, the absurdity of her act—standing on the side of the road yopping like a nutter—asserted itself. Her grief receded—retreating into her core. Tears stopped short, her throat felt chewed and raw. She slinked back to the car and drove on.

Moving again, she had a brief and potent desire to see Ryan. She almost linked to him, then decided against it. Whoever he was under all the drones—that being hung by a thread. She couldn't let emotions get the better of her analytical ability. Maybe she had more of her parents in her than she chose to accept.

Sarah ran some quick calculations and the weight of their conclusions crushed her into the car's seat. Their chance of surviving the next week ran only slightly above zero. Just as well, she thought. It's all going to hell anyway. Better to pave the way than eat dust. She kicked the music back on and drove. Slivers of reality flashed past. Her thoughts churned with the blurred topography, melding past, present and future.

Hours and a dull blur of kilometers later, Sarah approached the Princeton enclave. Trying to connect with Laing, she immediately sensed the virus. She didn't call it that, of course. She called it a blaze of high-pitched babble that ripped into her the instant she linked. Her headache was almost immediate.

—*Ryan, what the hell is going on?*

She got a response, but it wasn't human. If it was the drones, no wonder Laing was going nuts.

Uncertain of his location, Sarah sought Welton. She found him getting hustled from a colonial-style mansion. Before him, an EMT wheeled out a man in a body bag. Sarah's heart fractured. A snap knowledge of doom pervaded her. She sprinted up the cobblestones and ripped the bag off the corpse. Not Laing. Panic subsided, the scene around her filled in and she realized she'd become the center of attention. For a beat, even Welton's security sat stunned. Welton's own expression aroused new fears in Sarah. Surprise flickered across his face—then recognition.

Welton quickly recovered, his eyes fuzzing to static. He grabbed Sarah's arm and dragged her into his limo. She struggled for a moment but realized that would only draw more attention. When she saw Laing's crumpled form on the backseat, she allowed Welton to push her inside. The door closed and Welton settled in.

Sarah scrambled over to Laing.

"Ryan. Laing?!"

He didn't respond. His eyes didn't blink. Sarah turned to Welton.

"He saved my life. Twice," Welton said.

"What happened to him?"

"Injection of some kind. It's affecting his motor control."

"Where are you taking him?"

"I take care of my own." His eyes bored into her.

"Do you know me?" she asked.

Welton smiled. "Laing informed me that the Saudi Arabian security force might assign a second agent."

Sarah was fairly certain that Laing had done no such thing.

"Where are we going?" she repeated.

"I assume you'd prefer to keep out of the public spotlight?" Sarah did not respond, so Welton continued. "I own a building just up Washington Avenue. It has a full medical facility."

They sped along Lake Carnegie and out to an unobtrusive office building that had seen better days. Welton noticed Sarah's skeptical glance.

"It's more than it may appear. I picked it up years ago. Used to be an NSA lab."

The mention of Echelon's progenitor sent prickles up Sarah's spine.

"And now you own it?"

"I was hoping the walls could talk," Welton responded with a glint in his eye.

"Probably doing a lot more listening."

Welton laughed. "Maybe so. In any case, the building offers many advantages."

The car slid into an underground parking lot. A team helped Sarah haul Laing onto a gurney. They rushed him through the garage and into the bright fluorescence of the building's interior. There'd be little chance of escape. Welton would have augmented old systems with razor-edge tech. And it wouldn't take long for Welton's gurus to notice that Laing wasn't all human. Then Ryan would commence a new life as a lab rat. The gurney continued on its course, technicians swarming. Sarah had to fight to remain close to Laing.

They crashed through metal doors into a makeshift hospital room. A med plugged the gurney into the stat machines covering the wall behind it. Ryan's vitals blipped across the screens. None ran smooth. Each wave jolted through staccato punches. The med began setting up an IV. Sarah couldn't let that happen. As he picked up Laing's hand to insert the needle, Sarah elbowed herself to the forefront. She grabbed the med just as he punched the needle in, jerking his hand away and ripping the needle out in a single move. A trickle of gray blood slithered from Laing's wound. She slapped her hand over it, hoping no one had noticed.

The rest of the meds pulled back in surprise.

"Don't touch him! Any medical intrusion will trigger a self-destruct protocol."

"But he's dying," the med said, rubbing his hand.

"You'll have nothing to save if you proceed. Fail-safe installed on all SA operatives."

Welton stepped forward. "Saudi Arabia hardwires poison pills into its agents?"

"Of course. Everyone knows that SAs die before they can be broken. Makes them better bargaining chips than data sources. We don't lose many."

Welton bored into her. She held his gaze, hoping none of the techs had been in SA recently. Welton broke off and studied Laing's monitors.

"So we let him die?"

"I need to deactivate the pill. Let me have him for ten minutes, and then you can slice and dice all you want."

The med looked at Welton. "Sir, he doesn't have ten minutes."

"He'll make it if you let me do my work," Sarah said.

The beeps and buzzes of Laing's vitals pervaded the room. Finally, Welton nodded and the meds retreated. Welton lingered and Sarah remained still. He saw that she would do nothing in his presence, smirked and slipped out, shutting the door behind him. Sarah breathed a sigh of relief.

She stared down at Ryan. She slapped him across the cheek. Nothing. She tried their link and got slammed by his internal dissonance. Sarah heard every synapse in Ryan's head fire at once, and she fled. She needed help. Madda.

No way she could hack Echelon's defenses in ten minutes. She'd have to chance that he'd be in the flow. She made sure the door was locked, swung over to the terminal and goggled in. She filtered through Welton's security, circumnavigated the flow's matrix a couple of times to throw his dogs off the track and then found Tex's construct. Gwen was as radiant as ever. Perfect bait for a repressed supergenius. Sarah slipped into the construct, snuffing out the prickling desire it fostered on moving through the flow. She sifted through islands catering to fencing. There weren't many. Fortunately, Madda hadn't decided to play football.

She found him in a representation of nineteenth-century Portugal. Madda had a small studio that opened onto an ornate tiled patio with a fountain trickling in the center. Standing in the patio, she gazed in to see Madda jousting back and forth with an opponent. No time for subtlety, Sarah barged into the studio. The two men noticed her, but continued their duel.

"Looking for a teacher," she said.

"I'm busy," Madda replied. "Come back later."

"I need you now," she purred.

Her syrup-sweet voice made Madda stutter. His opponent pressed the advantage.

"Later," Madda gulped, recovering quickly.

Sarah had no time for this. She grabbed a saber from the wall, hefted it to get its weight and then let it fly. It rotated end over end across the room and buried in the opponent's back. The man arched in surprise, then buckled over, the protocols of the island informing him of his death and canceling his construct.

"Takes skill to throw a sword like that," Madda said, slightly stunned.

"Or very good programming."

"If it's that good, you'll be a hell of a student."

The opponent's saber rested at Madda's feet. He flicked it at her with a twist of his foot. She caught it in the air just in time to parry his thrust.

"Worthy indeed."

"Quit your bullshit, Madda. I need your help."

Madda's face paled. "How do you know my name?"

"We work in the same business."

Madda's shock turned cold. No Echelon agent would contact him outside the center. He charged her, his blade scorching the air between them. In the wake of this thrust, she tumbled to the floor, his saber's point at her neck.

"We have a mutual friend," she stammered. "He's in trouble. I can't go through channels—don't have time."

"I don't have friends." His voice chilled the air. He flicked her neck, drawing blood. Sarah's construct flickered.

"Not what Ryan said," she stammered.

The blade wavered.

"Who are you?"

"Doesn't matter. Here's what Ryan's got in his head. Tell me how to fix it."

She pushed the blade away and grabbed his hand, finding his link. She off-loaded a clip of Laing's chatter.

The shock blew Madda back. He reeled, slumping over, awash in static. Sarah jumped to him, slapped him hard.

"Madda! I need help now."

"Jesus, it is him."

"What's going on?"

Madda looked up, trying to decide if he could trust this nymph before him. The desperation in her voice convinced him.

"He must have picked up a virus. One that affects his . . . his friends."

Sarah realized immediately what he meant.

"Oh no."

"If their signals get corrupted, they could eat right through him."

"Can I uncorrupt the system?"

"Doubt it, not in time. You need to reboot."

"Reboot a person. How?"

"An electromagnetic pulse would work, but I'm guessing you don't have a nuclear warhead on hand. So, you need to shock him. And not a little. Restart will require a massive amount of energy. Enough to kill him a couple times over."

"Kill him? Can the drones pull him back?"

"I should know? But he'll be just as dead if you don't try."

Sarah wanted to grill him, find another solution, something more elegant. No time. She didn't bother with good-byes. Didn't even bother with a standard flow extraction. She just picked up the sword and rammed it into her own stomach. The last image Madda had was of blood pulsing from her perfect torso.

Ryan's thoughts ran tar thick. He clung to the last vestiges of his sanity in the black wash of data ripping him apart. No use. He tried to float, letting the black bits swirl through him. They pushed him under.

A white jolt shattered the darkness, and most of Ryan along with it. His psyche expanded like an object entering a black hole, stretching to infinite. Had he maintained a self, it would have been terrified. As it was, bits of him scattered through the emptiness, fading. Consciousness tore. He latched onto a single point of cohesion: speed. Wherever he was, whatever he'd become, all his bits were accelerating, moving in the same direction, faster and faster. He clutched the sensation with primordial ferocity.

A pinprick of light appeared in the winding sheet. He barreled toward it. He found a singularity in the black hole of brain death. The chaos of bits, memories and drone binary that formed Ryan Laing plunged down the rabbit hole. As he slid away from the nothing, Ryan began to recognize his own parameters. He remembered himself, dragged his thoughts, memories and flights of fancy back into form. Most of Ryan Laing emerged from the singularity. He had a moment of peace.

Then the drones reinitialized and their alien mist enshrouded him once again. He struggled through it. Finally, system rebooted, the drones settled into their arrhythmic background hum, and while that in itself felt like water torture, it was a torture Ryan could handle. He regained his ability to move, to live.

Laing awoke in the belly of the beast.

20

Sarah loomed over him, white-knuckling a set of crash paddles. She had ripped out the cord and spliced them directly into the room's central electrical outlet. Hit after hit, she had pulled death's shroud over Laing. With each shock, her mind reeled, bucking against premeditated murder. Hardwired ethics, short-circuited by an act of will. His vitals had gone flat on the fourth hit.

She girded up to jolt him again, eyes tearing from the pungent stink of burnt hair and ozone. Laing grabbed her hand before she could make contact. Sarah lit up. Relief washed over her face in a tidal flow.

Sarah's arm still locked in Ryan's grip, the door burst open and security stormed in. They grabbed Sarah, wrenching her back. Ryan lurched from the gurney, wobbled and lashed out at the closest guard. The man dropped heavily. Ryan swung as another man approached. He used the man's weight to flip him, in the process removing his gun from its holster. Laing bore down on Sarah's captor just as the man drew his own gun.

Welton burst in, breaking the standoff. "Calm down, Mr. Laing. These men are here for your protection. We thought you were being assassinated."

Shaky and out of synch, Ryan tried to find his bearings. He had little choice but to surrender. He dropped the gun and crumpled to the floor. Welton smiled and signaled for the guard to release Sarah. She ran to Laing and helped him back into the bed.

"With friends like her, who needs enemies?" Welton said.

She ignored Welton and the others, leaning close to Laing's ear. "It was the only way."

He pulled back, looked into her eyes and nodded understanding and debt.

Sarah wheeled on Welton. "The poison pill wouldn't disengage. This was the only option."

"Yes, yes, I'm sure you're right," Welton said.

The med studied Laing's vitals, still flitting across the screens. "Well, whatever you did, it shocked the man back on track. Must have been injected with a short-term neuro-destablizer. Odd that he's better so quickly. . . ." The med trailed off, lost in thought.

Welton paused for a beat himself, then turned to Sarah. "Come, we'll let the man rest. And you'll be my guest for dinner. I'm famished."

Welton motioned for Sarah to lead the way. Laing nodded, and she grudgingly departed, the retinue of guards trailing after her. Ryan and Welton looked at each other across the room. This was not a man used to gratitude; the very attempt contorted Welton's face.

"You're welcome," Ryan said weakly.

Welton's face smoothed out. He smiled. "Yes, well, this is just the beginning, Laing. We have many miles to go."

Ryan phased out, not bothering to respond. For the first time in months, sleep came easily.

They dined among relics. Tech from another era haunted the room.

"It's a crypt," Welton said, voicing Sarah's thoughts.

"What is all this?"

"Tools from another time."

"But why would a company like yours choose to own it?"

Welton smiled. "Try the corn. It's local."

Amid ancient computer terminals, a steel desk had been cleared and dinner placed upon it. The soft glow of the candles somehow emphasized the room's sterility. The Arctic listening station had more warmth. Sarah felt the case holding the hard disk cut into her side. How much would Welton pay for such a relic? Her life would be worth little on scale with such a piece.

"Thank you for . . . for helping Laing," she said.

"It was the least I could do. Very strange protocols you SA's have. You came very close to getting killed today."

"As did you, sir."

"And here we are, eating corn on the cob, surrounded by our grandparents' computers."

"Not too elegant," she said, looking at the blocky contraptions.

"True inside and out. Crude and ungainly. But at the time . . . the NSA was the very best."

Sarah's heart rate spiked. Surely Welton knew the rumors about Echelon, but he couldn't know that the organization existed, or that

Sarah was an agent. Though his game eluded her, Sarah knew gut-deep that he was trolling for something.

"Not too familiar with the NSA. I work ops, not signals intelligence," she said.

"Fascinating history. NSA's not much now—a backwater organization chained to an ineffective government. But it set the path. Now it picks through the scraps with all the other stragglers."

"While your Calsoft clan forges ahead?"

Welton chuckled. "No, Sarah. We're just cogs. Ants marching to orders we don't understand."

"Some ants understand more than others."

"True, but it makes little difference. One ant's comprehension means nothing to the whole—or to the fate of that ant, I might add."

"Such defeatist philosophy from the King himself?"

"I succeed because I understand the playing field. Few others see the patterns underlying our world."

Sarah gasped. She had little capacity to hide her feelings. They broadcasted across her face—as easy for a man like Welton to pick up as the latest soap episode.

She tried to play dumb. "Even as an intelligence officer, I see little in the way of pattern."

"That's because you view events from a limited perspective. Yes, we've had some dips and dives recently, but the pattern remains."

"Dips and dives? The world is crumbling. It doesn't take much perspective to see that. Humanity seems to have spontaneously combusted. If we're ants, the colony just got gassed."

"Maybe so." He eyed her. "Or maybe there's a duel between queens."

"There can only be one queen."

"Colonies can live for years with several. Of course, conflict is inevitable. And during that conflict, the colony suffers."

Thoughts rolled through Sarah's mind, confusion and fear hampering a distillation of cause and effect. This man was far more dangerous than anyone suspected. But, in lieu of terminating this threat, Echelon had fostered Welton, shielded him after Buist's destruction. It was Welton's slip that had drawn Sarah's attention to Buist in the first place. That single voice mail had catalyzed a chain reaction leading to Buist's death and Welton's meteoric rise. Had he dropped that voice mail on purpose? Impossible. But Jason Sachs had cut off her investigation after Ryan killed Buist. In the year following, Echelon propped Welton up, thrust him into power, protected him. Why? When he was so close to uncovering the truth . . .

"So if you're to be the new queen, who's your royal competitor?" Sarah fumbled through the conversation amid her swirling doubts.

"I've no delusions of grandeur, Sarah. I merely recognize the conflict and use it to my advantage."

Sarah fidgeted. She hated this.

—*Change the subject.* Ryan had rediscovered their link.

—*Gladly.*

"You've certainly done so. The wine is excellent. I don't get much chance to sample alcohol in Arabia." Saudi Arabia remained an oddly dissonant nation, mashing a fetishistic obsession with technology over the vestigial remnants of religious ferocity.

"Yes, I love it too. Found a wonderful winery up in Napa. Auerbach Estates. Have you been?"

—*Christ, this guy knows everything.*

—*He can't. He just can't,* Sarah responded.

"I haven't. I spend most of my time in Europe. Only get to America a couple times a year. I did some wine tasting in the French Riviera. Just beautiful there, don't you think?"

Welton's face relaxed imperceptibly, and his eyes glazed to a baby doll congeniality. She felt him slip away, only a bare minimum of attention remaining on her.

Sarah prattled on about her time in France, and he responded politely. Her fast-twitch tension had begun to fade when the music flipped into a remixed Agamemnon's Mitten tune. Sarah went white. Welton carried on, seemingly oblivious.

—*We need to get out of here, ASAP.*

—*This guy is colder than death. He's got something very nasty up his sleeve,* she responded.

—*He's easy to read. Wants money. Wants power.*

—*I hope you're right. And I am very ready to go.*

21

Welton forced them to stay through Laing's recovery. Under the circumstances, it seemed like a welcome respite. Ryan slept, ate and let the drones repair him. He was bruised and battered to the core. Each and every cell in his body needed work. The drones continued to broadcast at him, pounding unintelligible signals into his head, binary queries for which he had no response. He found himself lost in thought, literally. It took him long seconds to respond to Sarah, or to the world around him, so consumed was he by the slip within him.

Sarah sat at his bedside. They chatted a bit, about inconsequential matters, assuming surveillance. Sarah felt it in the physical presence. An orderly, guard, or med was always within earshot. Ryan knew it, the air around them singed red with activity.

So they chatted and, underneath, went over their next step. Sarah read him the news. Unrest spilled across the globe, pockets of discontent erupting into violence. Civil disobedience in Detroit. Riots through Mongolia. Religious attacks in Prague. Governments sat idle, unprepared for the force of humanity's fervor. Citizens cowered, fearing for their safety and unable to find an enemy upon which to focus their fears.

With each passing story, adrenaline-laced nausea flushed Ryan's gut. He forced restraint, squashed down shots of panic. Sarah stopped reading, laced her fingers through his with deliberate tenderness.

—*What is it?*

Years melted away; his iron-hard shell evanesced like that much smoke. Staring up at her, he was just a kid—back in Colorado—defenseless and out of control.

—*Everything burns. Echelon couldn't tame fate.*

What was there to say? She held his hand, let the moment pass.

—*We're not that far gone, Ryan.*

Sarah gripped down on his fingers, pulling Ryan from a backwash of flame-licked recall.

—*We need to decode that hard disk of yours.*

—*It's beyond me, Ryan. I'm no historian, and it's too dangerous to get help in the flow. We need an analyst.*

There's no expert in the world we can trust.

Probably not. We could give it to Welton. I imagine the technicians in this building could break the code out.

No.

Then I only see one option: Madda.

We can't reach him.

I already have, in the flow. And he saved your life. That honor goes to quite a few of us, by the way.

I'll try to stop being such a burden. How's the shoulder?

It ached constantly, augmented by tingling pangs of frostbite crackling over her body.

—*Stay on subject. We need Madda.*

—*Let's get out of here. Then we'll discuss which harebrained scheme to attempt next.*

—*Fair enough.*

As Ryan's strength returned, Welton gladly let them go, escorting them personally to the facility's exit.

"You're not out of danger, Mr. Welton," Laing said.

"None of us are, Mr. Laing. But you've done enough. Time for others to step in."

Welton gave Laing his hand, and kissed Sarah on the cheek. He promised to put in a good word for them with the Arabians. It felt too easy.

Welton disliked playing the idiot. Masks were his stock-in-trade, and he wore many. But wrestling his ego into this one required effort. The door closed on Laing and Peters, and Welton's easy gentility dropped away. Feet pounding across the concrete floor in staccato pops, his smile flaked away.

Welton retreated to his office and goggled into a private flow stream. He closed his eyes, reopening them to an infinite gray. Corners resolved, immensity relinquished. Two chairs materialized. A dark form appeared in the opposite corner. It condensed into a human silhouette. Neither man bothered with the chairs. They floated closer, constructed apparitions.

"They're coming your way," Welton said to the faceless form. "I attempted to read the hard disk but had no success. Seems easier to let them figure it out and lead us along."

The other man nodded. "Understood," he said.

With that, they both clicked off. The room was probably the most secure drop of flow in existence, forged from a forgotten piece of Echelon itself. Still, it didn't pay to tempt fate. Welton understood the price of hubris. It had become his primary tool in a plan so grandiose that even now, as it neared fruition, he could barely comprehend the power he would soon wield.

Welton threw his feet up on the table and took a long draft of the Auerbach merlot. It was exquisite. Rolling the wine over his tongue, he mused that Turing did indeed have the patience required to forge perfection. Welton understood the creation of perfection through pain. Now it was Turing's turn to suffer. Welton sipped again and closed his eyes, dreaming of army ants.

22

They stood on the prow of Tex's junk. Chop swells canted the deck, and Sarah brushed against Laing's shoulder. A shiver of excitement ran through him. It happened again and Sarah blushed.

Laing stepped away. The hormone shot spiked the pounding turmoil running through him. This was the last thing he needed. Sarah's blush ebbed. He watched her features shift from embarrassment, to acceptance, to determination.

Ryan returned his gaze to the Los Angeles sprawl. Riots started slowly here, feeding on the tonal undercurrent of uncertainty. Words like "melting pot" had long been used to define LA, the new colossus. Give us your tired, your poor, your huddled masses . . . And the world had done just that. Los Angeles became a city of exiles. But there was no golden door; Los Angeles fed on the world's carrion, masticating the undesirables, sapping them dry.

Echelon's vise lock on information flow had solidified the status quo. Under its thumb, the ebb and flow of human interaction nulled out. Inequity carpeted the forest floor of Echelon's world—even as trees of progress vaulted into the sky. Echelon squashed any controlled burn. Now, tinder dry, society stood poised to combust.

In Los Angeles, that tinder lay in the massive variance between the haves and have-nots. Los Angeles was no melting pot. It was a sifting pan. The middle and upper classes lived easy. They lived on the backs of a population with little ability to rise up the ranks. The poor, the uneducated, the immigrants—they were necessary, but they were given no quarter. Over the years, the striation solidified and resentment grew. Echelon made sure it didn't actualize.

But with Echelon out of the game, it had taken little time for a spark to ignite this latent rage. A private security captain beat a young Latina with carnal abandon. The event was recorded and hit the flow within hours. The reason for the scuffle was lost in the ensuing media storm.

When running five by five, an Echelon tracking program would have registered the incident and curbed its dissemination. Maintaining status quo was automatic. Echelon manipulated such incidents across the globe a thousand times a day. Agents got involved only in the more complicated operations.

But the unseen hand had vanished. Activists and demagogues alike latched onto the incident. "Kika," the young woman's name, became a rallying cry. Smoldering resentment and frustration ignited and bright hot violence raged.

Chaos blossomed with untamed ferocity. The city cannibalized itself. A demonstration turned ugly outside the offices for Population Transport. Trickling violence quickly became a flood, and the office burnt to the ground. In the ensuing turmoil, the people movers came to a halt, stranding millions of commuters in city center.

For some, the new environment was a homecoming. People like Tex, bursting at the seams all their lives, found themselves suddenly at home in a world they had never imagined. They reveled in it, realizing how controlled their lives had been just days before, trying to comprehend what had changed. Most of these people were criminals. They pillaged to their hearts' content. But there were others. Soapbox rallies popped up around the city, around the world. Some dredged the chaos for possibility. The disenfranchised found their voice. It was shaky from years of silence, but its resonance grew.

Ryan saw only destruction. He watched a silhouetted 'scraper go up in flames and couldn't restrain a shiver. Charred memories crowded him—damage he had worked so hard to paint over. Echelon was dead in the water, and the world crumbled around it.

The junk rocked again, and Sarah moved closer to Ryan, allowing her body to slide along his. Their hands touched briefly as the boat shifted. This time, he didn't back off. Sarah clasped and wouldn't let go. Ryan didn't squeeze back, but couldn't pull away.

"It's getting cold," he said.

—*I'm not a strong man,* he thought.

"I know, feels like Scotland," she said.

—*You're strong enough,* she thought.

Another burst of flames engulfed Santa Monica's promenade. Ryan shuddered and his hand twitched within Sarah's. She did not let go.

"We'll get Madda. We'll keep moving forward."

"Yes," she said.

"Madda will help us," he said.

—*We'll find a way to make it right,* he thought.

"Yes."

—*Yes . . . maybe,* he thought.

"The disk, the conspiracy, the traitor—we'll bring it all down." His voice wavered.

"We have to try."

—*Whatever happens, I'm glad to be near you,* she thought out. Her face stayed ice quiet. She felt like he was reading her journal as she wrote it.

"Yes."

The soft presence next to him seeped into Laing. She pervaded him, washing the fear away. He knew it would be fleeting, but the relief was palpable.

"I'm a husk, Sarah. I can't find much left anymore." The dry whisper hung in the air before him. His mouth felt sticky and fetid with rank panic.

Sarah put her head on his shoulder. "You're there. You're just scared."

"I hate that you see it."

She smiled into the burning night. "Ryan, we're all scared."

"You're not."

"We're all scared," she repeated. "You've just placed your fear at center stage. Most of us keep it in the background—laying down our bass beat. Your fear sings lead."

Torn between anger and acceptance, the walls Ryan had erected over a lifetime crumbled. This woman on his shoulder saw through them. Maybe the drones had rotted them out. Maybe life had. He squeezed her hand. He saw relief swim through her, tension dissipating. He felt worse, tighter.

"I need the fear," he whispered.

"You won't, not forever."

He turned and looked down at her. Fire raged behind him; electronic cacophony pulsed within. For an instant, it didn't matter. The face of the woman before him—the smooth, high cheekbones, the delicate nose, her sea-green eyes—they forced him into himself. She gazed at him, and he followed her stare. For an instant, he felt that place beyond fear. He recoiled.

—*The fear defines me,* he thought.

Her gaze fell. He watched hurt flit across her face and settle into resigned disappointment. She sees it now, he thought. She sees me and wants no part of it.

Then she shifted her eyes back to his, their luminescent intensity digging into him. Ryan looked away. Before he could break away completely, she cranked back and slapped him hard across the cheek.

"I won't watch you hate yourself to death," she said, rubbing her hand.

Before he could respond, she stretched up on her toes, her breasts touching his chest and igniting his skin. She crushed her body to him, but kissed him softly, just grazing his lips. The sting of his cheek mingled with the orchid delicacy of her lips. Her mouth slid over his, her tongue penetrating him. Everything in him responded—coming online after years of isolation.

Craving encased Ryan. He pressed into Sarah's small frame, crushing her to him. He lost himself in the newness of her lips, the familiarity of her scent. The drones in him pooled, yearning to flow into her. Laing tried to dam the flood—and knew he would fail.

The ship's intercom crackled to life, Tex's voice breaking through Ryan's need. "Madda's in the flow."

Ryan broke from Sarah, his desire receding to the dark place within.

"Saved by the bell. You're a lucky man, Laing." She patted him on the chest, gazing up at him with a smirk.

He forced a smile. A chameleon may change its color, but the disguise requires effort. Sarah saw that Laing's curtain had slammed back down. She showed him the courtesy of falling back into the task at hand.

Through trembling lips, singed from the kiss she had forced upon him, she said, "Okay, let's do this thing."

Sarah and Ryan spliced their feed into the flow, both sailing on Tex's construct, Gwen. Sarah had never done this before and found herself struggling with Laing to control the body. Laing let her take the lead.

They materialized in Madda's fencing studio. Empty. Sarah moved Gwen through the patio and out onto the street. Across the cobblestones, a sign hung over a pitted door. The Avalon. Sarah guided the construct across the street, wobbling on the uneven ground. She touched the door and it drew her through. The scene shift jarred her.

From the sandy gentility of nineteenth-century Portugal, the Avalon rezed out in full techno-hip. Sarah suspected Madda's handiwork in the 'ware itself. The rez topped the charts. Couches and tables more real than real scattered through the room. Wild swatches of color pulsed from the clientele's garments, supersaturated vitality streaming off them. Sarah moved through the bar. As with any meeting ground, pockets of energy rose and ebbed through the space. Sarah found Madda in the dreariest corner.

"Buy you a drink?" she asked.

Madda whirled, recognizing Gwen instantly. Fear flickered across his face. As she sat, the bartender materialized. No waiting in the flow.

Madda pulled his gaze away from the Gwen construct. He found the glass-blue eyes mesmerizing. "Absinthe," he stammered to the bartender.

The bartender pulled a small glass from behind the bar, along with a strainer. Then he gave Madda a sugar cube and a shot of the radiation-green liquid. Seeing that Gwen didn't want a drink, the bartender promptly vanished.

Madda didn't touch his glass.

"It's okay. Our friend survived," Sarah said.

Madda's tension flashed out. In reality, he took a long hard breath. His construct mimicked the action.

"But I need more help," Sarah continued.

Sarah then tried to sum up her experiences over the past days. As she spoke, Madda prepared his drink. With delicate fingers he placed the strainer over the glass and dropped the sugar cube on top. Then he languidly poured the absinthe over the sugar. On contact, the liquid transformed, shifting from green to milk-white. Sarah had seen vid on the Japanese tea ceremony. Madda worked the absinthe with the same ritualized fluidity. Sarah kept talking. Madda gripped his drink and listened.

Finished, she held silent, waiting for Madda's reaction. It was a lot to process. He gazed into swirling fluid, brought it to his lips and took the absinthe down in a single swallow. Of course there was no fluid to ingest. The action triggered a cascade of neural pathways, convincing his physical being that the illusion was real.

Madda could blow everything, turn them in. He stared at the construct before him, blank. Then, his digitized face creased, betraying an emotion Sarah didn't know Madda possessed: hope. On Madda it was eerily incongruous—a mole longing for the sun.

"I'd need to see the disk—need to see him," he said to her.

"You can't see him," Sarah said. "Not like he can just pop in for a visit."

Madda didn't respond. He slouched back, eyes clouding with the absinthe. "Look, it's just not possible to do this over the flow, and I assume you don't want to bring the piece to me. So, bring me to the piece."

Laing rose from passive and wrangled the construct's voice from Sarah.

"Impossible."

Madda looked up, staring into the beauty's eyes. He recognized a shift in the mask's ownership.

"Nothing's impossible. You have the means. I need out. Truthfully, I don't give a shit if Echelon is the good guy, the bad guy, or the fuckin' court jester. I'm trapped in a goddamned basement. Do it and we both get what we want."

"Or we die."

"I've got a whole life to look forward to, in a coffin. Death doesn't sound too bad." Madda glowered into his empty glass, lost in a feedback loop that had been spinning since he went under.

"Okay."

Madda looked up, hope again clouding his features. He swallowed hard. "I can do it, Ryan. I'll get that code for you."

The construct got up to leave, stumbling a little. Ryan's movement felt foreign, and Sarah tried to correct the balance, sending one of the construct's legs out too far. The doll rolled her heel and crumpled to the floor. Madda was there in an instant, helping her up.

—*Let me do it*, Ryan thought to Sarah.

He righted the doll.

"Not too smooth. Not smooth at all." Madda smirked.

"Just be ready," Ryan said.

The slice of fear Madda always felt in facing Laing filtered through the flow. He shivered spontaneously. "I'm ready," he said. He looked around the bar and noticed that most of the clientele followed their interaction. "Kiss me. We're attracting too much attention," Madda said.

Ryan had seen it as well.

—*You want this one?* Laing asked Sarah.

She was conspicuously absent, though he sensed a light chuckle running through his mind. Ryan manipulated the construct, lifted her arm and pulled a strand of hair from Madda's face. The rest of the bar took a communal inhale. She lightly planted her lips on Madda's. Madda lost himself in the kiss. The doll slid her silk skin along his cheek and nibbled his ear.

"Here I come," she whispered.

Madda's eyes shot open. He remembered who lay behind the mask. His fear returned, though now it twinkled with arousal and possibility. He nodded.

The construct stood, straightened herself and sauntered out of the bar, still tracked by the room.

—*Thanks for the help.*

—*Hey, it's about time you opened yourself to new experiences,* Sarah shot back.

Ryan forced out a mental grunt and kept moving. All the right bits jiggled; all the others stood at attention.

23

Suspended in the tank, Christopher Turing knew that body-temp liquid enveloped him. He couldn't stop shivering, cold seeping core deep. He knew darkness shrouded him. Light seared his eyes. He knew no sound could reach him. The pounding melody of Rachmaninoff's Second Piano Concerto pervaded his thoughts.

He had tried to keep his mind occupied, stemming madness with endless games of chess. When he could no longer hold the game in his head, he tried work, scheming plans within plans, predicting many futures and none. Gradually, logic faded into emotion. He resolved an existence around pangs of resentment, regret, hatred, even love. In time, those swings settled into a hardened solitude.

Then the memory came, a single repeating image cycling though his mind. Snow, ice, blood, murder. The image—a barely remembered past—occupied his eternity.

As a young operative, Turing had done his time in the field. His last assignment had taken him to Nepal, an oasis of peace wedged between warring giants. He was to aid a Chinese dissident crossing from Tibet, through Nepal, and into India. Turing remembered rising out of rhododendron-choked valleys and into the Himalayas. He forged rivers made furious by melting snows. White mountains loomed over him, materializing though cloud layers and vaulting into the sky.

At 4,800 meters, civilization petered out. Thriving villages faded into outposts for high-mountain herders. Turing brought no porters, no guides. His cover as a backpacker allowed no such. He blended with other trekkers, all questing for enlightenment among the peaks. But when they turned back, he continued climbing. He gulped air, unable to find satisfaction. Altitude-induced hypoxia melted his nights into wild flights of fantasy. His sleep grew erratic, the sound of his own hyperventilation rousing him.

At 5,500 meters, human cells can no longer divide. Turing crossed into that borderland, and slow death began. He worked through a moraine of frozen earth and ice-crusted rock, detritus regurgitated by the glacier before him.

Beyond the moraine, the glacier rose over a cliff in the valley's floor. The vertical shift generated mammoth ice blocks that Turing was forced to pick his way through. The ice quaked and shuddered in its slow tumble. He worked through the icefall, one painful step melting into the next. Exertion subsumed him.

A sharp crack ripped him from exhaustion. With a sickening groan, the ice under him gave way and he plunged into a crevasse. Acceleration screamed as the dark fissure sucked him down. Turing crashed against the crevasse's ice wall, ripping his shell. Then, before his scream crested, the slot cam exploded from his backpack, killed velocity and saved him from black oblivion. To balance a lack of experience, he'd been supplied with the very latest in mountain hardware. Sensing his fall, the spring-loaded camming device had discharged, studded tips burying into the crevasse's flanks. Now Turing hung like a shirt on a clothesline. He stared through his feet for what seemed like hours, gasping straight fear. Finally, he began the laborious process of extrication.

He reemerged into the maze of shifting ice blocks. For hours he had only the grating crack of the icefall for company. Finally, bruised and battered, he climbed onto the glacier proper. He trudged forward, crampons piercing the white. Rising over him, jagged peaks vaulted from the ice. He tramped over crusted snow, the only living thing among ice, rock and sky. A bronchial hack brought him to his knees. Pulmonary edema. If he stayed at this altitude much longer, his lungs would fill with fluid, drowning him.

He trudged on, finally catching the glint of a figure on the horizon. Turing quickened his pace, craving contact. Then the agency found Turing and altered his mission.

In the years since, Turing hadn't been able to bring himself to uncover the rationale behind the order he'd received. Maybe the man was a double agent, a plant, a traitor or a mole. It didn't matter.

When he approached, the first man Turing had seen in days, Turing pulled the small Beretta from his jacket and fired. The shot filled the universe, crashing through the dead zone, and dissipated completely. Turing was left standing over his victim, a gored cavity replacing one of the man's eyes. Blood staining the snow.

That moment, that murder, changed everything. An iced logic subsumed Turing's gut-rot. He returned to civilization to play the great game, cold and dispassionate. And now, years later, trapped in the tank, Turing's mind cycled over that image of death.

Extricating a man from Echelon was impossible. It had never been done. It had never been tried. Attempting the impossible had become standard practice for Ryan or Sarah.

"Each breath we take confounds the odds," Sarah said over a bowl of soba in Tex's galley.

"So let's go for broke," Laing replied. "Get Madda out and maybe Turing along with him."

"Why not? We've got nothing left. Besides, it's the last thing they'd expect."

Two hours later, Sarah was deep into regretting their decision. Slouched under rotted blankets in a downtown LA alley, she shifted on brittle pavement. She couldn't get Laing's operation of the Gwen Construct out of her head. He walked better in heels than she did. The thought cut through her discomfort, sparking a laugh that she amped up to a shrill cackle, marking herself as another broken mind wallowing in LA's refuse.

Black smoke slipped up the alley, the riot boiling through the streets. Holo shots and raging voices spread Kika's name and beaten form across the city. Ideology effervesced in the heat of violence. People rioted in lieu of acquiescence. Better to be the hunter than the prey. The confusion worked to Sarah and Ryan's advantage.

—*You take me to all the best places,* she thought.

—*Want to trade? You could go in and give Sachs the scare of his life.*

Only Sachs could grant admittance into Echelon's lair. To get Madda, they would have to dupe the inspector general himself.

—*Wouldn't mind seeing that. Though I doubt Sachs even has the capacity for fear,* Sarah thought.

—*Can't you just enjoy the view and leave me alone? Hard to concentrate with your psyche profiles filtering through my head.*

She shrank back in her blankets, her mung-crusted clothing eliciting a general itch. She hated fieldwork.

. . . . .

In the street, Laing moshed through the riot. Anxious, seething violence ran like syrup over the crowd. He flowed with the masses. As a child, he'd loathed fairs, amusement parks and the like. His parents had taken him to the Glenwood Hot Springs when he was seven. The hot springs maintained a megapool of bubbling sulfur stink. Bobbing in the pea-green water with so many others had driven Ryan to a near catatonic state of claustrophobia. The laughter of hundreds frolicking so easily became the roar of a mob intent on the kill. He'd known it as a kid. He felt it now.

Laing pushed and punched his way through the crowd, finally reaching the abandoned metro entrance on the corner of First and Olive. Normally, Echelon's security locks disengaged on an agent's appearance. Today the door remained locked. Ryan assumed the security 'ware couldn't lock on his ID amid the throng. He took a step back to shoulder the door, but as he shifted his force, a man fell between Laing's shoulder and the target. The door popped off its hinges and the two tumbled into darkness. They fell to a cement landing, blocked this time by a much more substantial gate. The man rose to his feet, wobbling slightly.

"What the fuck?" he sputtered, eyes doe-scared. He pulled a laz knife from his tattered suit, swishing it through the air with incompetent abandon. Ryan felt embarrassed for him.

"Scramble back up the rabbit hole, killer," Ryan said.

The man's lips pursed. He lunged at Ryan. Ryan dodged the strike and the man tumbled. But then he did the unpredictable. Instead of getting back on his feet, he rolled over and slashed out again. Ryan swiveled backward, but not far enough. The laz sliced through his thigh, and black blood poured forth. The man got to his knees, only to see the blood stop its flow and retreat back into the wound.

Dumb shock filtered through the man's rage. No doubt his life had crumbled in the past days. That physical constants broke down as well seemed no great surprise to him. He looked unblinking into Laing's glare. Ryan lashed out with his left foot and landed a solid kick to the man's head. He crumpled. Laing picked up the laz and retracted the blade. It folded in upon itself, the logo, Brookstone, embossed on the side. A yuppie toy. He slapped the man awake, picked him up and threw him back to the masses. The man stared down at him for an instant, amazed to still be alive. Then the sea of violence swept him away. Ryan closed the outer door and turned to the cage.

He placed his hand on a putty reader hidden among the refuse. It twitched. The putty melted around his hand, slithered up his arm and across his cheek. It moved over one eye and solidified for an instant, reading his identity through fingerprint, retinal scan and DNA. Still breathing hard, Ryan tried to get the man's face from his mind. Another week without Echelon and there would be little left to save.

Security check complete, the putty retreated. Laing barely made out the shimmer of a flexible tube shooting from the floor and encasing him. Then darkness and bone-crushing acceleration. He plunged through the floor, suction pulling him down and sideways, g-force crushing him into the tube's casing. Darkness and velocity canceled in a fraction of a second. The tube opened to a well-lit room, and he looked up to see Jason Sachs' smiling face.

"Mr. Laing, a pleasure as always. Though I'd prefer a little warning before you appear on my doorstep."

Ryan grunted as he got to his feet. His thigh stung and a large gash perforated his pant leg. Jason noticed it but said nothing.

"Don't trust the flow anymore. World's coming apart out there."

Jason considered it with dispassionate amusement, as if Ryan had just mentioned a football score. "Yes, well . . . we'll have that under control soon enough." Jason said nothing more, just looked quizzically at Laing.

"I want to see him," Ryan said.

"Impossible. No reason to let you near him."

"I need to see him."

"Turing's no longer the man he was. He's no longer much of anything—just a vault to be cracked."

Ryan's calm slipped. His eyes glassed; his cheeks tension-torqued, teeth grinding. "You couldn't get the key to a lunchbox from a preschooler," Laing growled.

Ryan shot for the door. Foolishly, Jason attempted to intercede. Ryan clamped down on his neck and raised him off the ground. The two guards in the room rushed Laing. Without releasing his grasp on

Sachs, Ryan dropped the man to his left with a side kick, then swiveled and threw an arcing heel kick that found the other guard's neck. He returned his attention to Sachs, letting his pent-up anger seethe, and noticing a speck of fear in Jason's cold eyes. Good.

"Ready now?" He let Jason down and relaxed his grip.

"Yes, okay," Sachs choked out.

With that, Laing unclamped Sachs' throat and wrenched his right arm up and behind his back, forcing the man forward. They entered the hall.

Turing remained trapped in his memory loop, his perception degrading with each iteration. The cycle began again—relentless. He approached his victim, drew the pistol, and fired—the man Turing was immediately lost to the gun, the bullet, and the moment after. Blood spatter. White ice, drenched in gore. The Beretta hung heavy in his hand.

Then the corpse vanished, leaving Turing alone. Only the blood remained, rotting down into the ice. Turing lived in that vision, trapped by it. A numbing cold seeped through him. He slipped into it, fading.

"Open the isolation chamber. Get that bastard out!" Ryan commanded as he hurled Sachs across the room. Laing turned to face the opaque tank that housed Turing. His grief boiled to hot rage.

Sachs scrambled to his feet, unwilling to back down. "I can't just turn on the lights, Laing. The shock would kill him."

"So it'll kill him. What do I care? Two minutes and I'll have the damn codes. I can't wait for you any longer."

"That's clear."

Ryan whirled on Jason, locking onto his throat again. Eyes bulging, Sachs sent a subtle hand signal to the guards that he was okay.

"Don't you get it?" Jason choked out. "There's nothing left of Turing. He's been inside too long. Isolation negated him. In a day or two, we'll retrieve his living corpse and troll his memories for the encryption coding."

"And how long will that take?"

"Could be hours, could be weeks. There's a lot of data in the old man."

"I want to see him," Laing growled, pulling Sachs close.

Sachs managed a slight head shake. "You'd just be looking into his coffin."

Laing flung the smaller man out into the hall and charged the tank. He reeled back and punched the plexi shell with drone-amped force. His hand broke on impact, flesh ripping off crushed bone. The plexi webbed out, then shattered, covering Laing in black, viscous fluid. Released from suspension, Turing crumpled to the floor, unmoving. Laing rushed to him, grasping Turing's head in his hands. He wiped away the oily fluid, and Turing emerged from the black—his skin a dull gray, eyes glassed and blank.

"*Turing?* Wake up, goddamn it!" Ryan bellowed.

Jason stood at the door, utterly shocked at Laing's aggression. "Jesus, Laing. What have you done?"

Ryan ignored Sachs as he pounded on Turing's chest, desperate to revive him. A frothy geyser escaped the old man's lips as he took in air. Drones oozed from Ryan's mangled hand, spreading through the tank's liquid and seeping into Turing himself.

Turing's glacier shook on its moorings, jarred out, then resettled. The shift drew Turing back from the abyss. He watched in astonishment as a single flower sprouted out of the puddle of blood at his feet. Turing centered on it. Its rich green stem surged up, growing in a passionate fit. He reached out, but immediately pulled back—terrified of destroying it. The flower ended his isolation.

It continued to grow, a delicate blue-on-white columbine unfolding into dead air. He knelt over it, reached out, and stroked its petals. On touching the flower, a voice filled Turing's mind. It sounded like Ryan Laing.

Sachs is right, Ryan thought as he knelt over Turing in a puddle of black fluid. The old man's a breathing corpse. Even as Laing raged for Sachs' benefit, despair gutted him. I will get you out, he promised. From far off, echoing through gibberish, a timid voice pierced Ryan's mind.

—*Don't.*

Ryan almost jumped out of his skin. Jason, still standing in the doorway, assumed psychosis. Ryan would have agreed.

The voice again. It wasn't Sarah's.

—*Let me go.*

Despite the distance and distortion, Ryan knew it. He just couldn't believe it. Turing had linked to him. The drones—diffused through the tank's black liquid—had generated a tenuous connection. Laing pushed through his shock and reached out to Turing.

—*Christopher, can you hear me?*

—*I'm cold.*

—*Listen to me. I can get you out. You need to wake up.*

—*No. They'll break me. They've broken me.*

—*I can't believe that.*

—*You . . . have . . . to.*

In reality, Laing sensed Sachs pulling guards into the room. One took aim and fired a tranq dart into his chest. Its force threw Ryan flat, black liquid splashing over him and Turing. The old man's voice wavered in his mind.

—*I failed you.*

—*No,* Ryan thought.

—*Make it right. Put an end to it—to me.*

—*I can't.*

—*No choice. I'm already gone.*

Ryan pulled his head around, lying face-to-face with Turing amid the swirling pool of black. The tranquilizer haze fuzzed the old man's features. Panic welled in Ryan. He couldn't do this thing. Turing stared through him with steel-dead eyes, his lips frothed and gray. Turing's thought filled Laing.

—*I will miss you.*

Laing couldn't respond, not if he was going to do what he knew he must. He bottled the pain, forcing it aside. The guards grabbed Ryan's feet and began pulling him from the room—away from Turing. Laing bucked—pretending to go into convulsions. Within his spasms, he pushed the drones to the surface. They spilled from his mouth, nose, ears, and eyes, infesting his flesh—and Turing's. The guards dropped him and backed off, horrified. In that instant, Laing unleashed the drones' power. Sparks flew.

Jason shielded his eyes. "Get him away from Turing!" he yelled to the guards. "He's overloading."

The guards tried to grab Laing but the drones blew white hot, singe-ing Ryan's face, arms, and legs. Energy built within him. Laing released it in an orgasmic pulse, lighting up the room. Electricity surged, arcing through Turing. For an instant, the old man's eyes cleared. Then his breathing sputtered out.

The guards regained their courage and plugged Laing with tranq shots. The drugs overwhelmed his drones.

Turing stood on the glacier, shouting into the flower and feeling utterly ridiculous. He would die yelling at a plant. His memory crumbled, the white beginning to give way.

Before him, the glacier morphed into rich darkness, sheltering and beckoning. Turing slumped forward, his knees scraping the ice. The agonizing cold ebbed, warmth surging through him. He basked in it. He forgot the glacier. He forgot Echelon. He forgot even the man he had murdered and whose blood still ran beneath him. His last thought was of the flower in his hand.

He watched it disintegrate, its blossom retreating, its thin leaves curling in upon themselves. This thing, this other, ate itself and grew again, transforming into its true nature: a minuscule machine, a single drone. Turing knew it for what it was—a piece of Ryan Laing—a piece of his son.

Love and loss swept over him. Then peace. Turing turned his gaze to the darkness. It unfolded around him. He embraced the abyss.

24

This habit of yours has to stop. How many times can you kill your-self?

Sarah ripped Laing from sleep. He awoke to nauseous rage. Thoughts churned through him. Turing is dead. I killed him. A welling vat of futility subsumed Laing's guilt. He couldn't bring himself to open his eyes.

—*He's dead,* Ryan thought.

—*You did the right thing. There was no coming back for him. Sachs would have retrieved the codes, and we'd be buggered.*

—*I'm pretty well buggered now.*

—*Make it through a single day without major trauma and we'll count it a victory.*

—*I doubt this will be the day.*

—*Dare to dream.*

Ryan opened his eyes. The clean sterility of Madda's lab felt vaguely comforting. Madda hunkered over a panel in the sleek room's far corner. Ryan let his pulse increase, and the monitors beeped. Madda dragged himself from his ruminations. He rose and approached the bed.

"Nice entrance," Madda said.

"What happened?"

"Full spasmodic convulsion."

"Huh?"

"You freaked out, big-time," Madda said. "Sachs is überpissed. I guess you fucked up some delicate shit in his little domain."

"I—"

"I don't want to know," Madda cut him off. "Whatever he's got going is none of my concern."

Madda probably had no idea that Turing had been labeled a traitor, let alone that he was now dead. Laing allowed himself a deep, indulgent sigh. The pressure eased.

Despite the gut-wrenching loss coursing through him, Ryan's planned had worked. He hoped Madda was worth it.

Madda hung over Ryan Laing, unsure of his next move.

"You going to let me up?" Laing asked.

Madda looked at him skeptically, unable to get past Ryan's grue-some appearance. "I think the drones broke through your blood/brain barrier," he said.

"Is that bad?"

"They're in your head."

"Tell me about it," Ryan responded, his levity contrasting the fear Madda saw in Laing's eyes.

Madda continued his cold analysis of the man before him. Laing of-fered a new life. Just the word "freedom" made Madda salivate. But the risk. Madda could do as ordered and keep Laing as a lab rat. No risk there. He iced the thought. In the end, life in a cellar wasn't going to cut it. Madda made his decision.

"If you feel light-headed or dizzy, it's back to bed."

Madda reached under the table and thumbed a control. The straps disengaged and slithered back into their holsters. Ryan sat up and rubbed his arms, then reached up to touch his face—which had to be itching like mad. Madda grabbed his hand.

"You have a ways to go there."

Madda motioned to a mirror along one wall, and Ryan swiveled to take in the slithering, metallic embossment his face had become. Drones engulfed him.

"They burned me," Laing said through his shock.

"The drones overloaded. Now they're correcting the error. It shouldn't happen again."

"Live and learn, huh?" Ryan attempted a smile.

The ghoulish mask made Madda cringe. "That's their nature. Con-stant adaptation. Instant evolution," Madda said.

Madda couldn't pull himself from Ryan's reflection. Ryan stared along with him—equally fascinated by the slick gray colonizing his face. Or was that revulsion running under Laing's metallic veneer?

In the street, an ancient hauler exploded and smoke filled the alley. It allowed Sarah an excuse to cry. The riot subsuming downtown crescendoed in a hysterical rage. Can fires billowed and cars burned. With Turing gone, what hope was there of setting it right? Another tear fell.

Sarah felt Ryan's loss on killing Turing. She would have done the same thing, or at least she hoped she would have. But the deed would hasten Laing's evolution. She didn't know where he would end up, what kind of balance he would find with the drones. Sarah suspected that he was moving away from humanity.

She craned her neck to see into the street beyond her alley. A middle-aged woman, frothing with terror and ferocity, shouted into the crowd. Her recently manicured nails dredged at an Asian girl's face. A Chinese man ripped the woman off. He beat the woman savagely and she crumpled. The man diffused back into the mob. The girl fled. The woman lay at the alley's entrance, her eyes fixed open, her outstretched hand twitching reflexively. Blood dripped from her ruby-red nails and gloved her hand. There was no sense to it. Why shouldn't Laing abandon his humanity? Look at them. At us.

Sarah shuddered, trying to shake off the horror. She was not religious, but she prayed that Ryan would emerge soon. She sucked at being alone.

Ryan tried to maintain his usual glib repartee with Madda. He felt the burn of Jason's eyes upon him and wanted to betray nothing. Waves of guilt cut through his tidal loss and submerged him. He didn't hide them. Jason would expect it.

If Echelon was Turing's bride, then Oedipus has got nothing on me, Ryan thought, stewing in cruel cynicism.

Ryan's face had healed; the new skin felt baby-soft and moist. He couldn't stop stroking it.

"You're freaking me out, there. Lay off the fondling," Madda said.

"Sorry, it's addictive. Want a hit?"

"That's as close to foreplay as I've been offered in a while."

"I thought you took a vow of chastity in exchange for all this." Ryan waved to the cramped, arcing confines.

Madda chuckled. "That's me, your friendly techno-monk."

They both laughed, then ran out of interactive energy. Ryan turned away. Madda went back to work. They had moved into the cylindrical lab space Madda called home. Originally a metro station, it had been transformed into Madda's personal playground. Scraps of next-gen tech lay around the room like building blocks.

"To you Echelon's one big toy store, isn't it?" Ryan asked.

Madda looked around almost wistfully.

"Yup. The products of the most advanced minds in the world come through here."

"And you tinker away."

"I transform them, combine them. I make miracles."

"Tall order."

"I made you."

"I'm no miracle, Dave. I'm just one more broken toy, ready to be decommissioned."

"I'll keep you on for a little longer. Who else can I practice my thrusts on?"

Madda had been working steadily, filling pockets and patches in an army jacket. He shrugged into it.

"Looking good there."

"I may be down, deep down, but I keep up with the fashions. This is the latest." Madda smirked.

Ryan approached and picked up a stylus and tablet. He began doodling. After a minute or so, he put down the tablet and wandered off. Madda glanced at the tablet and quickly erased it.

Jason leaned back in his chair, staring at his feed of Ryan and Madda. He hadn't expected Ryan to kill Turing. The events frustrated Jason; any glitch in predictability drove him to distraction.

Jason pulled a tablet from his desk and perched it on his lap. On it, Ryan's doodle appeared; Jason had pulled it from surveillance data. It was merely a set of numbers, a long flow. As Jason watched the two men, he went through the rote process of cracking the code. He worked it manually, hoping it would calm him. Rudimentary encryption, kid's stuff compared to the code Jason could pull. He jotted letters on the side, extracting order. He reassembled the letters and bothered to read them only when both men had gone into the train cabin that Madda used as his bunk.

He looked down at the glowing letters, and his eyes nearly popped out of his skull.

"Jesus Christ!"

He flung himself out of the chair and opened the comm system.

"Get to the lab. Now!" he screamed, then bolted from the room.

. . . . .

Madda liked computers, dabbled in flow structure, ate projectile weapons for breakfast, but his true love lay in propulsion. The psychs should have seen it coming. His breakthroughs shifted the size and power of such instruments on a fundamental level. In the cabin, cramped with years of crap, Madda and Ryan dropped their pretense just long enough to share a nod. No going back.

Their stare broke as Jason and a gaggle of guards burst into the lab. Sachs' eyes blazed.

"I knew that fucker was next door," Madda said to Ryan. "I felt his sleaze right through the walls."

Ryan gave Sachs a toothy smile and a salute, all the payback he could muster. Madda went for something with a little more flair. He bent over and gave the asshole a look in the mirror.

Ryan toggled a small switch and the train roared to life. It broke free of its moorings and rocketed up the track, Madda's propulsion generator tacked to its undercarriage.

"The train can't take much of this," Madda said through clenched teeth.

"It'll hold. We're not going far."

"They'll snag us at the next stop."

"Then enjoy freedom while it lasts," Laing grunted. Madda didn't react, and Ryan finally relented. "It's like Swiss cheese down here. Plenty of tunnels to get lost in." The train accelerated.

One-man coil bikes sped after them. As powerful as Madda's propulsion devices were, they had a century-old bucket of bolts to push. Laing stumbled about, pulling together pieces he'd snagged from Madda's lab. Fortunately, Madda hadn't gotten a housecleaning fetish since Ryan had last been a resident. He ripped out an armored body shell and snapped into it. He'd considered one for Madda, but rejected it. There was no time.

Their pursuers increased speed, homing in on the barreling compartment. Ryan allowed his drones to integrate with the suit. Then he jammed a hand into the door and pried it open. A torrent of ancient, skunked air belched into the cabin. Laing disregarded the death stink and continued to pull.

"What the hell are you doing?"

"We're making an unscheduled exit."

"What?! We'll be crushed."

Madda backed away from the door. Freedom suddenly became a nebulous concept over which to risk life and limb. Behind them, their pursuers fired magnetized grappling hooks that slammed into the compartment. Ryan toggled another switch and the car shot forward, teetering on its tracks. Laing saw Madda's apprehension. He pointed to the track ahead of them. A pile of rubbish filled the tunnel.

Time did not slow. Madda saw none of his life flash before his eyes. He noticed Laing's suit shimmering and found it oddly mesmerizing. He released indecision, refusing to die a coward. He shifted his weight, flinging himself at Ryan.

The timing had to be perfect. Laing's nerves jacked to fracture. He stepped back and enveloped Madda in a bear hug. Their combined momentum hurled them from the train. Ryan smelled the blast of air, saw the spattered cement of the station flashing beneath them. And then they hit. The force of impact blew Ryan's legs out from under him. He gripped Madda and rolled, letting his suit take the shock. Behind them, the compartment slammed into the dump, which effervesced into heat and shrapnel.

Ryan stretched into a long home-base slide, Madda resting on top of him. His suit grooved a furrow into the station's rotted cement. They missed the first column by centimeters, then crashed into the second. Ryan sucked the deceleration into his knees, which slammed into his chest. Without the armor, his knees would have pierced right through. As it was, Ryan struggled for breath. Madda's ability to scream seemed unaffected by the impact. Ryan released him from the bear hug, and Madda leaped away, furious at Ryan's recklessness—and thrilled to be alive.

Ryan stood, explosions ripping through the dank air. The coil bikes' twisted wreckage smoldered in the tracks. Their riders had vanished.

Ryan grabbed Madda, and the two sprinted for the staircase. They took the stairs two at a time, Madda huffing from the effort. No lights here, just stair after stair.

"I can't see shit," Madda said.

"Nothing to see. Keep climbing."

They began to hear sounds below them, then lights. Their pursuers had caught on. Ryan redoubled his speed. The guards gained. Ryan found the exit. He lowered his shoulder and rammed the door. It shattered, and darkness exploded into light.

Sarah, squatting a meter away, jumped to her feet and aimed the device. Nothing fancy, just a high-end Molotov cocktail. Sometimes the old tricks were the best. Ryan and Madda sprinted past her. The guards burst into the sunlight only to find themselves enveloped in flame. The heat wouldn't cut through their armor, but made it difficult for them to remain inconspicuous. She gloated for an instant, then turned tail and caught up with Madda and Ryan at the end of the alley. They sank into the riot and became anonymous faces in the frenzy.

In a gray room, the silhouetted men materialized.

"They're gone."

"Fine."

"It's a terrible risk we've taken. I didn't expect Turing's murder. Without his encryption code, we're lost."

"Turing wouldn't give it up. We'll regain the Key from source code. That's why we let Laing take Madda. It'll just take time."

"It's just, well, everything's collapsing."

"As it has in the past. Let the masses have their fun. It will all be over soon enough."

"I hope you're right."

But the other man was already gone, a digital ghost dissipating into gray. Jason shrugged and cut his feed.

25

Giddy, spasmodic flashes of euphoria bubbled through Madda. Freedom. He perched on the prow of Tex's junk, cantilevered over the cresting waves. He watched the ship cut a wedge into the ocean, gazed out on the vast expanse and let the breath of space fill him.

The burst of activity on escaping had stressed Madda to fracture. He'd grown accustomed to confinement—nesting deep into his life sentence. The frantic race through LA blew that silence apart. Winding through the maze of humanity, Madda overloaded. He clung to Ryan like a schoolboy, the colors, lights, sounds and mass crush of life blinking his system out. Laing said nothing, just supported him and kept moving.

After an hour or two in the cramped confines of his berth, Madda's panic subsided. Curiosity regained its familiar hold, and he emerged into the marina's thick air. He took up position on the prow and let the air beat at him. Massive cargo haulers dumped their contents onto the wharfs. Factory ships disgorged personnel and product. It stank. It was hideously ugly. Madda's heart leaped.

Sarah pulled him back to reality. "Duty calls, Madda."

He tore his eyes from the view, and she led him through the ship's labyrinthine corridors to a compact, well-appointed console.

"All right," he said. "Let's see this antique you're so nuts about."

Sarah removed the cracked hard disk from its protective shell and placed it before Madda. He looked at it for a long time. The craftsmanship, while primitive, had an intrinsic elegance to it. This is what archaeologists must have felt uncovering a new set of hieroglyphics, he thought. The virus that shifted the course of history had slipped into the world by means of this fragile wafer.

He sat down and worked. His world spiraled into the ten centimeters before him. He ran the disk, hunting down each lead, seeing the piece not as it was, but in flow-space, as the sum of its uses. Setting the interface was like trying to converse with an amoeba—an attempt to meld wildly variant spheres of complexity. With the graphic user interface online, Madda started his hack.

The encryption was laughable. He threw raw computation power at it. It soon buckled and gave way. Then the fun began. Within the flow structure he had programmed, he saw the disk's data raining down upon him. He had coded a saber, capable of cutting not flesh and bone, but information. With it, he dodged and shifted, slicing through the random streams of code. He let the data flash past him. Now and then, he'd skewer a piece of code that looked interesting, only to slough it off on further analysis. It was like hunting a leaf in a hurricane. After five hours, Ryan pulled him out.

"I can get it. Just can't say when," Madda said.

"Keep at it," Ryan said.

The disappointment in Ryan's voice grated Madda. "Got the code and tech broken down. Now I just need that bit of luck—literally." Madda laughed to himself. Laing remained stock-still. "I'll keep up the fight, but this Virgil's a hard nut to crack."

Ryan grunted and made for the door. Sarah caught his arm.

"What did you say, Madda?"

"Virgil. It's the programmer's ID—hooked his tag into the code. Hackers still do it today. Kinda like signing a painting."

Sarah gripped harder on Ryan's arm. She looked at him with a burning intensity. "The assassin who infected you—what did he say before he died?"

Ryan shrugged her off. She didn't seem to notice.

"He said something about Elysium. Where are you going with this?"

Sarah popped on her flow visor and allowed Madda and Ryan to piggyback. She melted into the library complex of her old university. Unintelligible words skirted their vision. In the shabby data nook of a library stack, she pulled a book and showed it to them.

"Virgil was an ancient Roman poet. He outlined the underworld, life after death. One of the places he journeyed was Elysium, a place where the virtuous went after they died."

"You think they're connected?" Ryan asked.

"Probably just coincidence," Madda said.

Sarah didn't register. She chucked them from her flow stream and dug. Madda went back to work. Laing, suddenly useless, retreated to his cabin.

When Sarah emerged hours later, she found Ryan lying on his bunk, staring at the ceiling's wood grain. She shook him from his reverie.

"We need to buy this boat," she said.

"What? This piece of shit? Why?"

Tex magically appeared behind them. "This is no piece of shit. May look like a nag, but she's pure thoroughbred."

Sarah nodded. She already knew. "Laing wants it—and your services. He'll pay top dollar."

Sarah and Tex commenced haggling. It cost Ryan almost everything in his copious account and further indebted him to Tex—a man he couldn't trust. Well, that wasn't quite correct. Ryan trusted Tex implicitly—to do exactly what was in his best interest. If your interest merged with his, Tex was an amenable guy, and a great drinking partner.

Only when the exorbitant price tag had been finalized did Ryan find his bearings enough to ask Sarah why they needed the junk.

Sarah ignored him.

"Do we have a deal?" she asked Tex.

He took his time, mulling over the small fortune he stood to make. He raised his hand. Sarah nodded to Ryan, her eyes betraying only intensity and assurance. He hated lagging behind, but Sarah hadn't been wrong yet. Laing extended his own hand and shook Tex's. The deal done, Sarah relaxed.

"Good." She turned to Laing. "We're going to Thailand." The word dropped heavy, filling the cabin.

"What?!" Tex shouted.

Sarah didn't pull her eyes from Laing's. "Elysium is in Thailand. It was connected to the Key's creation. And it's still around—your assassin proved that. Whatever Elysium is, whoever inhabits it, we need to know what they know."

"Thailand is dead," Tex sputtered.

"He's right," Laing said. "There's nothing in that region. There won't be for centuries."

"You're wrong, Ryan." Her eyes pleaded. "Thailand holds the answer."

"What's the question?" Laing shot back.

"Ryan, we don't know who created the Key. It's no small feat, hacking out a virus that shifts the course of human history. So why create it just to hand it over to Echelon on a silver platter? We know the rules of the game, but what's the larger goal? Elysium could hold the answer."

She held his gaze.

Ryan nodded, then turned to Tex. "We sail tonight."

And that ended the discussion. Tex sulked off, mumbling to him-self. He busied himself with offloading his family and readying the junk for a stealth run. Sarah smiled and returned to her console.

As promised, the ship held far more power than its ungainly appear-ance let on. A true smuggler's rig, it offered blinding speed in a cruddy package. After trundling into open ocean, the junk rose out of the water, hydroplaning on a single wing that extended lengthwise from a squat keel. With so little drag, the rocket propulsion system sliced ocean.

Madda continued to fence with the code, and continued to lose. He came to the junk's prow to recalibrate. The vibrant sea air refreshed him. He inched out onto the bowsprit, gripping the tension cable that held the forwardmost lugsail in place. It vibrated a speed-induced hum. Madda leaned over, his senses inundated by the frothing energy below.

A school of porpoise, perhaps caught in the same maelstrom, rose from the depths and surfed the wave preceding the junk. Their sleek bodies melded with their environment. In teams of two or three they surfed down the face of the wave, then disappeared into the froth. The junk quickly outpaced the porpoise, but their vitality suffused Madda. That they would soon enter a death zone seemed unfathomable.

26

Inactivity did not suit Ryan. He bucked against it. For many, angst bred an inability to make split decisions. Ryan drowned his angst in action, a phoenix addicted to the raw pain of ashing out. It was the lag between conflagrations that tortured him. In that downtime, his mind stumbled over blocks that would not budge.

He retreated to the darkness of his cabin, unable to look his cohorts in the eye. Familiar anxieties flashed past. He wanted to wring chaos' slippery neck, to assert control. But that thirst could no longer be quenched. Echelon had fallen into the quagmire it had spared the world for so long. Now, it was merely part of the struggle.

The drones' dissonance pounded through him. Laing had grown used to the vibration within, though it grew louder by the day. Turing's death had ended any chance of pulling the drones. Turing's death . . . The words fell lead-heavy through his thoughts, dragging him down.

Pure, searing loss froze his heart. In the cabin's wood-scented darkness, his world emptied. The loss sucked essence from the ether, made life less. His soul shriveled. He reached out to touch his memories of Turing, grasping at impressions. They eluded him. Grief rolled in his mouth like a marble. He felt its weight but could only taste its glass surface. It expanded, choking him. He swallowed it down, and there it sat, still and foreboding. He shut out the pain, curled around his pillow and allowed sleep to empty him.

Sarah didn't want to go. She bucked against submitting to her desire. She occupied her mind with work, pushed herself and Madda, helping him work the chaos of ones and zeros. She hated that anything could worm so deeply into her. Her self-image crumbled in the face of this new reality. She was not indomitable.

Sarah had always been comfortable with life's betrayal. Nothing touched her core. She floated along life's surface, acknowledged entanglements along the way, but never dropped anchor. Now, longing weighed her down. She churned, refusing to let it take her.

She sat with Tex for long hours. In the galley, they played poker, betting outrageous sums. Her mind, honed in Echelon's service, could process thousands of facts at any one time, hunting linkage. She wove interlocking webs, manipulating the facts she controlled to trap those she didn't. Putting such a mind to the mathematics of poker was like regulating a ditch with the Three Gorges Dam.

Now, she watched Tex handle a grubby deck. Beaten and nicked by thousands of hands, the cards seemed to play the players. Calculations flowed through her head, but she couldn't hold the numbers. She lost—hand after hand. Finally, Tex threw in his cards.

"Quitting while you're ahead?" Sarah jibed him.

"Play—or pack it in. You're elsewhere, and it's cheapening my win."

Sarah hardly noticed Tex's departure. Hunting for distraction, she shuffled and reshuffled the cards. Their ticking flap soothed her, but she knew it wouldn't last.

She slapped down the deck and headed aft. Passing Laing's door, she stopped, unable to move farther. Her fingers hovered over the knob's tarnished metal, gripping it one finger at a time, hesitant. She ran her other hand over the door's grooved wood, each sensation drawing her closer to submission.

Sarah opened the door, bolting into Laing's cabin before she could change her mind. She kept her face to the door, quietly shutting it behind her. Over the junk's ambient wash, she could make out Laing's short breaths.

She moved to the bunk and sat next to him. He did not look angelic in sleep, but twisted and racked. Growing accustomed to the light, she saw Laing's eyes clenched tight, shutting out, pushing away. His chopping breaths crescendoed in a long sigh, an admission of weakness Ryan would never have allowed himself while conscious. Sarah's hand extended of its own accord, her fingers lightly touching his eyelid. For an instant, his face relaxed. His eyes unclenched, and a single tear rolled down the profile of his face.

The tear shimmered gray, fought the tug of gravity and drew back toward his eye. Sarah gulped down surprise. She stopped the tear's retreat with a finger. The droplet, infused with drones, swirled over her fingertip, lost.

Ripped into consciousness, Ryan grabbed Sarah's wrist. In the soft light he saw his tear on her fingertip. A base revulsion swept across his features. She felt him retreat, even as his fingers tightened around her wrist. She bent slowly, her thick hair sliding off one shoulder and down over her face. She held his gaze, his proximity intoxicating. Her lips' soft upward curve twitched. She took the tear into her mouth.

He pulled a sharp intake of air. His fingers relaxed. His eyes lost tension. He released her wrist and tried to turn away.

"Sarah, I . . ." His voice sawed through the dying light. She halted him before he could continue, grabbing his wrist in turn and forcing it over his head. She descended on him, her hair enveloping his face in a soft tickle. Her lips found his.

Her desire rolled through him. His mouth opened to hers. His rapture mirrored her own. He fell into her, swept away by her mouth, her tongue, her scent of fresh sea and lavender—the press of her breasts on his chest.

In their kiss, drones flooded her, swirling through her mouth. Like another tongue, they slipped over her, drawing her closer. They swarmed and flowed, and then she felt them linking to her, tunneling into her mind. Ryan opened the gates, and every drop of him assailed her. She wanted to cry out. She pressed harder into him. His desire became the froth on the wave of her own. His longing melded with hers until she could no longer differentiate her motivation from his. In his kiss and his eyes, she knew love. Warmth filled her, and she no longer cared that he had invaded her. She was he.

She released his hand, broke their kiss and stepped back. The drones stilled, their connection severed as she pulled her lips from his. The flood of emotion pouring from him slipped away. Without Ryan's flesh link, the drones went inert. The pang of that loss nearly crushed her. Then it ebbed into a longing soon to be fulfilled. She slipped out of her white blouse, fingering each button.

Ryan watched the shirt fall. It floated through the auric light, settling in a pool at Sarah's feet. She reached behind her back, unclasping her bra, and letting it slip off her shoulders with exquisite languor. The soft glow of her torso contrasted with her black, coarse jeans—the fly a slender vertical drawstring of leather. She fingered it, releasing the knot with smooth deliberation. With a sway of the hips, her jeans fell to the floor. She stepped free. In only a G-string, she grew shy, uncomfortable with her display. She shed her panties in a quick shrug. Naked, she regained her poise. The cramped cabin hugged her form, framing her.

—Now you. Even her thought rasped with desire, her need irresistible.

He held bone still, savoring her, holding her in his mind. Sunlight leaked into the cabin from a porthole over her shoulder, highlighting her profile—a delicate collarbone descending to a slender arm whose hair glowed like cilia, the soft curve of her breast, her tight stomach arcing out to smooth hips and flowing down along a single, perfect leg. Ryan's drive to act, to touch this half being dragged him from reverie.

He ripped his covers away, revealing his own nude torso. The light hit him dead-on, and Sarah gasped. The coarseness and barbs of his character didn't match his body, which glowed soft white, his muscles flowing under baby-perfect skin. He reminded her of Adam's languid form on the ceiling of the Sistine Chapel. A man's form, but fresh, newborn, unblemished. She shrank from it.

He exploded out of the bunk and enveloped her, hesitation abandoned to desire. They regained connection, their mouths locking. He needed to feel every part of her. He buried his face in her hair, kissed her neck, nibbled her ear. Her desire soaked him through. His mouth descended to her breast, tongue circling her nipple, coaxing it to erection. Her small hips ground into his. He sank lower, kneeling before her, kissing her flat stomach, ripples of muscle clenching involuntarily at his touch.

She shook, her fingers burying in his thick hair. His tongue touched the folds of her skin. She raised a leg over his shoulder and arched back, pulling him closer. He tasted her. He gazed up at her, taking in the geography of her body. She dragged him up to her and sank her tongue into his mouth, tasting herself inside him even as his drones swirled.

She climbed him, throwing her arms over his shoulders and pulling herself up his body. He shifted with the extra weight. Wrapping her legs around his torso, she opened to him, and he sank deep. She enveloped him. Movement, pure and strong, growing frantic. They approached the edge, both longing for release, neither wanting it to end. Ryan let out a low howl and Sarah dug her nails into his back. They locked into each other, exploded, died and returned.

He gently lowered her to the ground and guided her to his bunk. She lay down with her back to the room, sinking into the foam. Ryan matched his body to her curving profile. He slipped back into her, slowly fucking her.

She pressed against him, sighing as he wrapped his arms around her. A slow serenity engulfed her, but couldn't extinguish her desire for him—all of him.

"Ryan, what did you see? When you died?"

Ryan buried his face in the warmth of her neck and let his body melt to hers.

"I fell," he said.

"After—"

"I only remember the fall."

Unable to stop the memory flow, he relived pieces of the fall. Impressions swarmed. Something stuck. Searing heat as the rock broke away.

Ryan's eyes shot open. She sighed and shifted closer. Her breathing lengthened.

He said nothing.

Skimming over the South China Sea, their ship seemed a single point of peace in a disintegrating world. When not wrapped in Ryan's arms, Sarah floated through the flow. Laing was reluctant to follow. He found the change too gruesome. He'd made a life of slipping that last block into its proper position. Now, the blocks had scattered, and none fit true. With each passing day Ryan lost touch with the nature of the world. He rejected it, banking on their efforts to bring Echelon back online.

Sarah plunged in, renewed by her connection to Ryan. With him grounding her, she could face anything. Even as fear pulsed from him in waves, their link made her stronger, more secure. She spent her time journeying through the newness of his body, and that of the world around them.

At first, she couldn't escape the pervasive destruction. The riots in LA dissipated, but Seattle went up in flames. Shock coursed through the world community as Israeli militants struck military installations in Palestinian Jerusalem. Waves of violence washed over the Middle East. Ancient rivalries erupted without Echelon's vigilance. In Europe, environmentalists crippled a nuclear reactor, wreaking havoc on the continent's power grid. In Asia, Sino-Korean relations slipped toward war even as Chinese leaders contemplated expansion. The great powers began to flex, asserting their dominance. And the less powerful countries found their populations hating these renewed giants.

Sarah floated through a flow swirling with paranoia and fear. She tumbled in and out of bars, classes, meeting rooms. Empty sections of the flow suddenly filled with revivalists. Words like "apocalypse" and "Armageddon" cropped up in bare warehouse spaces, quickly programmed to accommodate growing numbers of zealots.

In classrooms across the flow, students and professors alike tried to comprehend the shift that had occurred so quickly. Here too, fear reigned. But, lurking invisible in the wings of book-lined constructs, she felt tingles of new understanding.

In the boardrooms, the shifting landscape led to radical action. Large corporations, entrenched for decades in bureaucratic slumber, burst onto the new world scene, led by innovators. Some succeeded wildly; others failed and crumbled. What was a plodding stability now ebbed and surged in fits and starts, the world bucking toward a natural equilibrium.

Periodically, Sarah checked on Madda, who remained lost in his universe of numbers. Every few hours, she slid into Madda's fighter bar, the Avalon. Even here, she noticed a shift in atmosphere. The swordsmen seemed less interested in flash and dazzle. In corners, they read through old works on Bushido and chivalry, hunting for something to ground them.

Sarah slipped past the patrons and into the bar's framework. The farther she went, the less realized the construct. Finally, she approached a door, floating in blank flow-space. As she reached to open it, she picked up peripheral movement. She whirled around, but found nothing. Triggering her history-tracking program, she stuck her hands into the gray flow-space. She found trace scans and attempted to follow their footprints. But without Echelon, her tracking skills didn't have much bite. She quickly lost the scent. Sarah pulled her hands from the liquefied space and returned to the door, unsettled.

The door read her signature and drew her in. Code assailed her. She remembered going to a planetarium as a child, sitting back in the recliners and listening to narration shift through the wash of stars. Looking up into the massive dome Madda had programmed, she felt a similar sense of vertigo. Ringing the dome, billions of distinct calculations attempted to crack through the chaos in the hard disk Sarah had found. The products of these calculations then floated up the walls into the dome's center, allowing Madda to analyze them, combine the solutions, edit and adjust. He lay on the floor of the room, sunk into the material so that only part of his head remained above the surface. His eyes buzzed the dome.

It took him a while to realize that Sarah stood over him. He blinked several times, more a series of facial twitches, and grudgingly refocused on Sarah.

"I could get a lot more done if you'd stop bugging me," he said.

"It's been six hours. Just making sure you hadn't turned to putty." She motioned to his current condition. His sharp features protruding from the matte-black floor set Sarah on edge. "I feel like Dante walking through the frozen sea," she said.

"Who?"

"Need to brush up on your classics, Madda. Dante—you know—the poet who journeyed through hell and heaven."

Madda's face remained blank. "Long trip?"

"He thought so. In hell, he found a sea of ice, within which sinners froze for eternity."

With the perfect fluidity of honed flow-sense, Madda rose out of the floor in a single smooth arc.

"Well, this has only felt like an eternity, but I think—"

Sarah cut him off. "It's quite a world out there. Hell in a handbasket, you might say. Everything's shifting so quickly people are grasping at threads."

"Well, I think I found—"

Again, Sarah stopped him short. "New world. New rules. Everyone's gotta look out for their own, you know. Never know who's after you."

Madda shot her a quizzical glance. "And you thought I'd gone crazy?"

She just stared at him, forcing Madda fully into the present. He found the meaning under her words. "If you're concerned about the security in this room, rest easy. Even if Echelon were active, it would take them days to get in here."

Sarah sighed. "Good. I found traces of a hacker outside."

"Impossible," he said.

Sarah didn't bother arguing. Madda reminded himself that he was no longer secure in Echelon's crypt. "Probably just a lurker, randomly accessing flow-space."

"Maybe."

"No one knows I'm here."

Sarah shrugged it off. "What have you found?" she asked.

Madda lit up. "I think I found the string, the path back to the initial virus, before it mutated."

He gazed up into the numerical heavens, and the code began to gel into a single progression. Sarah tried to follow the logic but found jumps she couldn't fathom and theory she'd never seen.

"This is . . . this is new. How did you come up with this?"

"I needed a vise to crack open the chaos, a starting point to begin reverse engineering. Nothing in modern number theory worked. So I went beyond it."

"So now you're a visionary?" she asked, poking fun at him.

Madda went serious. "Inspiration." He paused, staring up into the numbers with something approaching rapture. "All that time in Echelon's labyrinth and I could only riff on others' achievements. But now, scared shitless and slamming across the ocean in a smuggler's rig, I snag a whisper of inspiration."

Sarah put her hand on his shoulder, and they both stared into the dome. She didn't possess such lofty goals. She analyzed. Ryan acted. Madda created.

"Put you, me and Laing together, and we just might become a full person," she said.

He continued to stare into his creation as a smile spread across his face.

"Tell me about the original program. Describe the Key."

Madda retuned to her. "It's not completely clear yet. Still need some more time for regression. Basically, I found clues in the hard disk."

"Clues?"

"Most of it was too damaged to read. The clues hinted at a fundamental shift in the nature of information flow. So, I sampled pieces of modern flow-space and regressed them back over the centuries."

"And?"

"And the data this disk captured initiated a planetary virus. Nasty bugger too, spreading across every mainframe, computer and node."

"But there's no history of a planetary crash."

"Oh, it didn't crash anything. It organized information, subtly shifted the flow's nature."

"You mean Echelon rose from that single transmission?"

"Looks like it." Madda nodded. "The hacker at the virus' incursion point, ground zero, was given the keys to the castle."

"The listening post, Virgil."

Madda nodded again. "The virus begat the Key," he said.

"Who programmed the virus? Who sent it?"

"That's the billion-dollar question. And I don't have a clue. This was way beyond its time. Beyond our time."

"Can you spark the virus into a second run and retrieve the Key?"

"You mean make our own Echelon?" Madda was suddenly on guard.

Sarah's own hackles went up. Would Madda take the Key for himself? The urge to play God was difficult to resist.

"I, I don't know, Dave. I just want to understand the extent of our options. If you get the Key, you'll become the most important piece in the puzzle."

Now it was Dave's turn to gulp. "I don't have it yet."

Sarah nodded.

"As I said, further regression is necessary," he said.

They stood, two figures awash in code.

"Do me a favor, Dave. When you crack this thing, don't say anything to anyone. Just let me know you've done it."

Dave's suspicion blossomed again. "You want me to keep it from Ryan?"

"No . . . Yes. I mean, I think we have a hitchhiker. Someone's on our tail. They know enough to track you here and attempt entry."

"You think it's Laing?"

"Of course not," Sarah lied. Not a lie, really. Her heart ripped jagged at the thought of Ryan becoming a conduit for Echelon. But despite her emotional backlash, she knew it was possible. "Laing's got a lot going on that he's not necessarily aware of. If Sachs broke Turing's encryption, Echelon may control Laing's gadgetry."

"Doubtful."

"It'll happen. If they haven't broken it already, they will soon enough. Ryan's on borrowed time."

"We all are."

"True enough." She paused and reached for his hand. Even in flow, the connection reassured him, a slice of humanity in an ocean of code. "Will you do it?"

Madda looked around him and shuddered. He nodded.

Isolation desiccated Ryan. Standing at the cabin's doorway, he watched Sarah and Dave lost in flow. Chaos closed in. The drones grew fiercer. Even intimacy couldn't stop his disintegration. He wanted to be whole with Sarah, but felt his sanity slip. The fingernails of his rational mind were ragged. He couldn't hold on much longer.

Looking at Sarah and Madda, he felt inconsequential. They had jobs, something to do. He was yesterday's news. Old hardware—software on the verge of overload. The two were locked in, attached to the world. He was lost.

Tex clapped a hand on his shoulder, and Ryan jumped. That anyone could sneak up on him showed just how far he had fallen.

"Land in sight," Tex said.

27

Thailand . . . The dead zone.

Known for centuries as Siam, Thailand had a long and illustrious history. Coalescing in the fourteenth century, Siam settled into a country long before its neighbors. Siam managed to fend off the European imperialism of the eighteenth and nineteenth centuries. Instead of being colonized, it gelled into a society rooted in the ancient but thrusting toward hypermod. Thailand became a hotbed of technology, both legal and black bag. The rich and famous flocked to its skin shops for resets, literally wrenching the years away. Thailand's Buddhism bent with the times, not buckling under the pressure of innovation as Western religions had. It became a promised land. In the twenty-first, immigration skyrocketed. Prosperity reigned alongside a beloved king.

Now, entering the restricted country posed no problem; leaving would be an issue. The junk sailed past the Star Wars system's event horizon without a scratch. Developed for missile defense, the particle-beam curtain now hung over Thailand. But instead of keeping missiles out, it kept everything in. Nothing emerged from the event horizon.

Tex maneuvered the junk into Chao Phraya River, which spilled into the Gulf of Thailand after journeying down the length of the country. They passed the port town of Samut Sakhon, then entered Bangkok. The rattle of the junk cracked the still life that Bangkok had become.

Sarah joined Ryan on deck, compulsively checking and rechecking her mask. On Ryan's look, she dropped her hands and gazed out. The silence was crushing. She tightened the seals of her mask one more notch. A once-prosperous nation had become the dominion of ghosts.

Sarah sidled up alongside Ryan, leaning into his shoulder. His stare remained fixed, but he leaned back, the contact warming in this expanse of death.

—*I've seen battlefields, massacres. This is more horrible,* he thought to her.

He couldn't bear to crack the silence with his voice. Plus, the masks made speaking uncomfortable.

—*Do you remember the clips they showed in school?*

Ryan shook his head. He'd avoided class on days when Thailand was discussed.

—*They were cleaned up, for educational purposes, but still . . . devastating.*

Though the air in her suit hovered just below body temp, she couldn't stop shivering.

—*At least it was quick,* he thought.

—*It was. One day, all fine, life as normal. The next, everything's dead. They say the virus spread through the country in hours, burned through the jungles like a fuse. Millions tried to flee. But Thailand's neighbors rushed its troops to the Gulf, shot down planes attempting escape, forced ships back to harbor.*

—*I think they bombed the harbor, actually.*

—*Right. An entire nation under quarantine. So every Thai festered and died. Bangkok went dark. Then the firebombing began. A perimeter went up around the country. One hundred klicks in every direction, the ground and seas scorched clean. Not a single organism survived. To this day, it was the most intensive air campaign ever waged.*

—*Against a mere virus.*

—*Against weaponized HIV—a killer totally devoid of sympathy.*

—*It was one of Echelon's early failures. That it let the virus be created.*

—*But it was a successful mop-up. A unilateral, coordinated effort to extinguish an entire nation and wipe out the worst threat humanity had ever encountered. Couldn't have been accomplished without Echelon greasing the wheels.*

The junk slunk on, boring into the dead zone. Once past the harbor, even the devastation vanished. Those buildings infused with scrubbing microbes remained pristine. Older skyscrapers sprouted layers of vegetation. Bangkok felt like a country house shut in for winter. It stood empty and still, ready to accept life, waiting for someone to pull the sheets off the furniture. White powder cut a great swath along the banks of the river. Against the shiny black of the newer buildings and the mossy green enveloping the older ones, it contrasted out bright and clear.

"Beautiful," she said. Her muffled voice percolated up through the still air, imbuing the tableau with life for an instant.

"They're bones. Millions died on the river. Their bones turned to sand."

Sarah looked upriver. Streaks of white rode the banks as far as she could see.

Tex maneuvered the junk into a slip far too small for the ship, but it was the only one left standing. Automatic grapplers extended from the hull, securing the ship. Tex approached Sarah and Ryan, who leaned out over the side watching the action.

"Impressive," Ryan said.

Tex's grin couldn't be tamed by the requisite mask. It filled the clear faceplate, pushing his other features into the background.

"Cost me many shipments."

"But effective when loading ship to ship on the high seas," Ryan said.

Tex's grin broadened. "Some shipments best to change hands beyond the stares of stevedores."

Sarah cut in. "We don't need to know about your smuggling."

"Miss Sarah, my other interests have served you well."

"Maybe so, and we've paid you better."

"Nothing is free in this world."

"Nothing is free in *your* world," she responded, her smile never wavering.

Tex's grin hardened for an instant, then settled back into a mask of levity. Ryan stepped between them.

"Let's get the wheels onto solid ground."

Tex clapped Ryan on the shoulder and sauntered off. "You da boss."

Once he was out of earshot, Ryan turned on Sarah. "What was that?"

"He's dirty."

"He showers as much as the next man."

Sarah rolled her eyes. "You have a miserable sense of humor," she paused. "In fact, you have a corny sense of humor. Wouldn't have pegged you as corny."

—*Sarah, why push Tex? We need him.*

—*And he knows it. The guy's dirty. My gut says to get as far from him as possible. For our continued survival, the action of highest probability would be to destroy him.* She let the statement hang.

—*Now who's the cold one? I won't kill him, and I won't let you hurt him. I know he's got a certain moral flexibility. But he's okay.*

Sarah just shrugged. "Your call."

Ryan tried to glower at her, but Sarah had turned her attention to the unloading, forcing Ryan to glower out into space. He relished frontal assault. But arguing with Sarah turned into a web that invariably encased him. He'd won this argument, and yet . . .

—*I'll have Madda keep an eye on him while we're in country.*

—*That'll help. Madda will be surfing the entire time, and even if he wasn't, Madda's a geek.*

—*He can take care of himself.*

—*I'm sure.*

At this Ryan threw up his hands and retreated to his cabin. From the bridge, Tex watched their interaction, stone-faced. Laing would have been surprised at the frost in those eyes.

Ryan took a last check on his gear. His black bio-suit felt bulky and claustrophobic. The thought of living within it for the foreseeable future did nothing to lighten his mood. Designed for long-term space exposure, it was definitely overkill.

As space-based industrialization expanded, the Moon's stock of minerals became a sought-after prize. The ensuing mining rush forced extraterrestrial innovation into high gear. It also set off a complex and potentially threatening struggle between corporations, countries and miners, all trying to claim ownership of what had been a useless hunk of rock. Echelon had manipulated the parties into a negotiated accord. Now, minerals flowed from the Moon.

Strong and light, the suits allowed miners to spend entire days beyond airlock. They had internal oxygen sources fitted with rebreathers that recycled exhaled O_2. They also had intakes for water and food. On the reverse end, they collected waste and recycled the water while ejecting the refuse. Miners always walked side by side.

Ryan watched Sarah squirm in her suit. At least he had a partner in

misery. He waddled to his wheel, threw a leg over the saddle and settled in, letting it assimilate his balance points. Sarah did the same, her
eyes gleaming with the speed rush this vehicle promised.

Ryan looked over his shoulder at Tex and gave him the thumbs-up.
Immediately, the grappling hooks released the pier and the junk
slipped into the bay. Tex would take the ship back into the Gulf, well inside the event horizon, and wait.

Through a porthole, Sarah caught Madda's face. He looked like a
bird who'd bolt the second its cage door opened. It had taken all her
rhetoric to convince him to stay behind. On land, he'd only hold them
back. And his work needed completion. Without the Key, exiting Thailand would pose serious problems.

Sarah nodded to Madda. His expression did not change. He placed
his hand on the porthole's plexi. Sarah turned away, clicking her legs
into the wheel's locks and leaning forward. The wheel moved with her
weight shift. Ryan came alongside her as they crunched over the
chalky powder and out onto the road, still littered with vehicles.

"Ever ridden a wheel before?" he asked.

"Nope."

"Well, you're doing great. It will shift and move with your body
weight. Lean forward, you speed up. Back, you slow down. Right and
left like this." He leaned to his right, and the vehicle arced under him.

The wheel possessed a single chubby tire over which a sleek en-
casement covered its motor and gyroscopics.

"I had a unicycle as a kid. My parents never let me take the training
wheels off," Sarah joked. She jerked and swerved, getting a feel for the
machine.

"That's good. You're doing fine. Just keep it slow and you'll get the
hang of it."

Sarah gave Laing a devilish sneer. "No training wheels now."

"Sarah, no!" he shouted.

Too late. She thrust her weight forward, and the wheel shot ahead.
In seconds she was weaving between dead cars, buses and tuk-tuks.
Over his link, Ryan heard a gleeful yelp and reluctantly cracked into a
smile. He leaned forward and tried to follow the black-and-white
streak fading into the distance.

. . . . .

For millennia Bangkok had been a hive of activity. A crossroads for travelers, traders, merchants and money, it had bustled with energy. The outbreak stilled its exuberant heart. Pollution had blanketed Bangkok in its prime, the three-wheeled taxis, called tuk-tuks, eating low-grade gasoline and belching exhaust. Now, the air was wiped clean.

From maps set to memory on the junk, Laing knew his way around. They entered the legendary travelers' ghetto surrounding Ko Sahn Road. What was a street bursting with peddlers and bars selling everything from cheap suits to trips into the Golden Triangle had become a museum. Ryan gave up pursuing Sarah. She could find him when she finished hotdogging. Her actions infuriated the field agent in him, but he also felt a gentle tug in his heart, and lower, for a woman with so little fear.

Ryan dismounted his wheel, which bobbed back and forth like an inflatable punching bag. He ambled through an outdoor café. Plates remained on the tables; remnants of clothing littered the floor. At the bar, old bottles of Singha, Thai beer, gathered dust. He sat down on a wicker stool that disintegrated under his weight. Wiping himself off and making sure Sarah hadn't seen him fall on his ass, he shuffled over to a table, drawn by a book lying open. Laing turned the page, mesmerized by the visitor's guide. The waxed paper crumbled in his gloved hand.

—*It breaks my heart,* Sarah thought to him.

Sure enough, she'd doubled back on realizing that her pursuer had given up. No fun without a little competition. Ryan pulled his gaze from the tableau of backpacker life.

—*It's peaceful,* he thought.

—*Peaceful? This is what you consider peaceful?*

—*All the pull and tug is gone here. The air smells calm.*

—*That's canned air you're smelling.*

—*All the better.*

"I won't let you do it, Ryan." Her voice cracked the scene. "I will not let you find solace in this coffin."

—*You think that's what I want?*

She knew it was. "Struggle has merit."

Ryan shrugged off her look and stepped into the street. Stillness suffused the ghost city.

"I'm tired," he said.

"Which also has merit."

"I could stay here."

"I know." Sarah looked out on the desolation and shuddered.

The city had a necromancy to it, the promise of accepted degradation. Entropy proceeded here without opposition. Every spring within Sarah loaded against its call to let go, to give up. She stared down the street with Ryan, slowly reached for his hand and gripped it through the layers of protective gear.

"You'd stay here over my dead body," she said.

Ryan didn't move for a long time. He felt the lure of this place, the potential release of pressure. Sarah squeezed harder.

"I see devastation. You look around and see a nice place to summer," she said, breaking the mood.

Ryan couldn't help but chuckle. "Peace, quiet, what else could a guy want?"

"We could reach the address I dredged from the flow, find Elysium, and get the fuck outa here."

He squeezed her hand back and remounted his wheel. The machine settled with his weight. He twirled to face Sarah. "You'd beat me to the target over *my* dead body."

With that he leaned far back, flinging the wheel into reverse and hurtling ass first down the street. Sarah grinned devil wide, clicked in and shot after him. Ryan twisted back around and accelerated down the road. He zagged off the main drag, clogged with abandoned vehicles, and onto the sidewalk. Sarah stayed right on his tail. At the last possible instant, he careened to his right, driving his tire into the pitted cement and veering down a tight alley.

She canted hard over, but the building's wall filled her view. Sarah wouldn't make the turn. Instead of pulling back, she pressed into the cement, then lifted out of the saddle with all her force. She torqued sideways and her spinning tire went horizontal, gripping the wall and slingshotting her forward. With gravity's tug, she wrenched the wheel back under her just as she touched down. The move pulled her even with Ryan.

They raced through the alleys, weaving and kicking over the detritus of a city long forgotten. Sarah veered into an old warehouse, snaked through its crusted crates and burst back into the street, sailing off the concrete loading dock. Impacting the pocked roadway jack-knifed Sarah's body, slamming her weight forward. The wheel shot out from under her, its action off the shock sending the machine up and over her head.

Ryan turned the corner to witness Sarah doing a full backflip, still attached to the wheel. Only at the end of the arc did her feet break loose from the clips. She tumbled over the rutted pavement, the wheel slamming dangerously close to her head. She spread-eagled into the flaking wall of an old house, which buckled slightly before stopping her sprawl. The wheel went into a long slide, throwing up a shower of sparks.

Ryan's grin melted. He stared at Sarah's still form, the dark place in him cradling the idea of losing her in this husk of a city. With such a calamity, he could break down—let it all go. Then panic shoved his black thoughts aside. He was not religious. Man made God. Man imbued the deity with power. Ryan had spent a lifetime reclaiming that power. Yet now he found himself slumped over Sarah, praying for her survival.

He turned her over, wiping the grit from her faceplate. She looked like a cloaked angel. Then her eyes shot open and she burst into laughter. She hugged him hard and pulled herself up. The suit, made to withstand the hazards of mining, had taken the fall in stride. She vigorously brushed herself off, not noticing Ryan's gaze, his silent thanks.

"Holy shit! That was a hell of a spill. Never done anything like that—even back in my biker-bitch days." Adrenaline jacked her, made everything brighter.

"Sarah, you could have killed yourself," was all he could say without betraying himself.

She looked at him, finally recognizing his anxiety. Sarah flashed him her best smile, large and genuine, just hinting at a smirk. It made him want to laugh, even while feeling that the joke was on him.

"I'm fine, Ryan. Just got carried away. And I win, by the way."

She pointed to a blocky apartment building across the street. Its shattered windows and chipping concrete sprouted a lush blanket of rhododendron. A multileveled street blocked their full view. The traffic here had been the stuff of legend. With no space to move outward, the engineers went up. Highway stacking had turned the city into a labyrinth.

Sarah righted her wheel, trying to hide the pain in her left shin. Even with the adrenaline spike, she felt the jittery relief of having dodged a bullet. She quietly checked her suit for punctures. All systems operational. She walked through her pain, annoyed that she'd put the mission in jeopardy. She also promised herself a wheel of her very own, if they made it through the week. Always need something to look forward to.

"We traveled across an ocean and into the dead zone for this?" Ryan asked as they made their way toward the dilapidated building.

"This is the only connection to Elysium I could dig up."

"Looks promising."

Even as he spoke, Ryan sensed radiation floating from the building. His drones had been unusually quiet in their race through the city. There'd been nothing to report. Now, the tingle returned. Someone was in there.

"Quit bitching and help me find the door," Sarah said.

It took longer than expected. The vines formed an impenetrable wall around the building. Finally, Ryan reached out with his other senses. He felt an electrical impulse emanating from a dense patch of foliage. It smelled like oatmeal. He reached into the thicket and flipped a switch, making a note that oatmeal equaled secret door. A crack appeared in the foliage. Sarah and Ryan crouched down, peering into the dank, shadowed interior.

"After you," Ryan said with exaggerated gallantry.

"What a gentleman."

"Chivalry is not dead."

"You will be if something bites me in there."

Ryan chuckled. They entered the decrepit building and allowed their eyes to adjust. The door rammed shut behind them. A staircase rose from the darkness. They approached it and gazed up the spiraling steps into the gloom.

Ryan bent over the stairs. "There's been traffic here. Recently." He pointed out a mess of footprints.

They began the long climb. Ten floors in, their suits' went slick wet with their perspiration. Ryan felt the catch pockets sucking it in, processing it and filling his canteen with warm, sterile water.

"This is about as far from Elysium as I could imagine."

—I don't think it's here, she thought.

Ryan stopped, picking up on her choice to go subvocal.

—If it's not here, what the hell are we doing?

—I picked up traces of Elysium all over the flow. Hints and allusions in the übertech zones. They led me to a hacker named Minos. The dude hid his tracks pretty well, but I cracked him. Minos' signal originates here—somewhere in this building.

—Minos? Who comes up with these names?

—Minos was a king of Crete in Greek mythology. When he died, he became a judge in the afterlife, deciding who should be sent where.

—According to whom?

—Virgil, she thought.

—So Minos is the gatekeeper to Elysium.

—That's my guess.

—Okay, so we find this Minos, who judges us worthy and we're off to Elysium.

Sarah recommenced their upward plod.

—Maybe.

—Maybe?

—It's just that anyone who would choose Minos as a tag is probably an asshole.

—You said he was a judge, Ryan returned.

—In the afterlife. In life he was cruel and self-centered. The gods punished him by making his kid into the Minotaur.

—Okay. So he's a prick judge.

—I'd say so.

—Hopefully, he's a prick judge that doesn't live in the penthouse.

After another half hour of slogging, Ryan gave up on that wish. Looking up, he caught radiation blooms from the top floor. Heavy tech up there. About a flight below the penthouse, Ryan and Sarah heard clomping feet. The sound of another's presence spooked them both. They'd grown used to isolation. The footsteps grew closer. With nowhere to hide, Ryan pulled Sarah behind him.

The clomping materialized into an obese figure who filled the stairway. No getting around this guy. The man stopped, wobbling slightly and taking in the black-clad figures below him. The man's girth made an impression, but his outfit was mesmerizing. Unlike Sarah and Ryan's slick bio-suits, his was a patchwork of bits and pieces. He looked like a massive quilt project, his gut challenging the material's tensile strength.

The man swayed, drunk. His sweaty features bore down on Sarah and Ryan. Then he stumbled to arm's length and threw his arms up. Ryan jumped back, ready for an attack, but the man was saluting them.

"Newcomers! Welcome to Tortilla Flats!" The man spoke in a lazy drawl.

Shock flashed between Sarah and Ryan.

"This is the Flats?!" Sarah exclaimed in surprise.

—*Can't be,* Ryan thought.

Everyone knew Tortilla Flats. A meeting place for the worst of the worst, its location was one of the few mysteries that eluded Echelon. Finding the locale had been low priority, but had developed into an obsession for several analysts. No one thought to look in the dead zone.

"Welcome to the Flats," the large man repeated, his words slurred and muffled through a rotted mask and several liters of liquor.

"Why do you think we're new?" Sarah challenged.

The fat man laughed, his quilted bulk jiggling merrily. He pointed to their suits. "You got virgin skins, and you're uncomfortable in 'em."

"You're used to yours?" Ryan asked.

"Course. It's life. Get used to it, or it'll drive ya nuts. I seen newcomers tear their suits right off. Don't bother me none. I can always use the extra material."

"True enough," Sarah shot back.

The man's expression turned dark. Ryan gauged just how much

force would be required to hurl this man over the banister. But the man burst into another geyser of frothy laughter. He shifted his bulk past Ryan and clapped his arm on Sarah's shoulder.

"You'll fit in just fine up there, ma'am. You sure will."

"You spent much time here?" Ryan asked.

The man grudgingly pulled his eyes off the bulge of Sarah's breasts. "That's the kinda question'll get you killed."

Tension sparked, which Sarah jumped in to dissipate. "The Flats is pretty tough?" she asked.

Delighted to return his attention to Sarah, the man broke into a toothy smile. "Tough? The Flats is so tough, they frisk you when you come in . . ." At that, the man pulled a relic of a handgun from a fold somewhere around his belly. Ryan tensed.

"And if you don't have a gun," the man continued, "they give you one!" Before Ryan could hurl the man over the edge, he flipped the gun around, handing it to Sarah butt first.

"My compliments, miss. Consider it a sample. Known around these parts as a man who can get what you need."

Sarah smiled and took the gun. She tucked it away and inched by the man. "Thanks. I'll remember that."

The man pretended to doff his cap, taking another long gander at Sarah's physique before turning back to the stairs and plowing his way down amid sloppy laughter.

"Yes ma'am, you remember that. I'm sure I'll be seeing you both soon."

Ryan and Sarah shared a look and continued more cautiously up the stairs. Sarah handed the gun to Ryan. He checked it. The gun's barrel housed enough crud to ensure a misfire, or worse. He threw it down the stairs, its clattering descent accenting the muffled laughter.

They reached the top of the stairs and entered a long hallway. Noise emanated from the room at the end. They approached a standard apartment door, the number reading 107. No sign, nothing indicating that this was the entrance of the most notorious bar in the world. Ryan put his hand on the knob and turned. The door opened to a scene that would linger in their memories for a long time to come.

· · · · ·

"You bring me to the nicest places," Ryan said.

Sarah couldn't help smiling. She felt like a gunfighter entering a saloon in America's Old West. Before them, Tortilla Flats teemed with transients. Sarah supposed it made sense. With the event horizon locked down, Thailand became the ultimate haven. For those on the run, Thailand was the perfect asylum. It was also the end of the line. Once inside, there was no chance of escape.

The bar spilled out onto the tented roof. Antiques dripped from the walls; no space remained bare. Telescopes and neon signs, sports paraphernalia, and one of the most impressive exhibitions of taxidermy Sarah had ever seen plastered the entire place. Patrons lounged in old barber's chairs, hunkered over drinks that they distilled and disinfected in numerous, bizarre manners. Not a single piece of flesh lay exposed. Each and every person was encased in hazmat paraphernalia. Their clothing ranged from old to ancient. Mr. Stairwell seemed chic in comparison to the great unwashed before them.

Sarah half expected the music to stop and everyone to give them their best cold stares. More disconcerting, however, was the patrons' complete disregard for their presence.

Ryan knew that each and every person had clocked them on entering, and would be only too happy to help them part with their suits, their riches and their lives. He took Sarah's arm and walked into the bar. Ambling through, the Flats seemed less like a bar and more like a domicile whose owner threw a constant party to which all were welcome.

A group of locals had taken over the far corner. Ryan saw the delicate features of the indigenous population through their masks. This crew had the oldest suits, patched together over the years as their wearers grew. The Thais lounged, utterly comfortable.

An itching unease pervaded the rest of the bar, the patrons shifting constantly, less accustomed to their outfits. Ryan saw a corner table and steered toward it. It had a full view of the room. They were about to sit when a gloved hand grabbed Ryan's arm. He whirled to find a small Thai man with a particularly ratty suit and beautiful face looking up at him.

He nodded toward the kitchen. "Get a drink."

"I'm not thirsty."

"Not thirsty? Bar's wrong place for you. Get a drink or fuck off."

Sarah maneuvered Ryan away from the Thai and into a seat.

"I'll get it," she said.

She ambled over to the kitchen, opening an antique refrigerator to find bottles of Sang Tip and Singha beer. She selected the whiskey, figuring it would be harder for anything malicious to grow in it. Strolling back, Sarah payed particular attention to the Thai man and his entourage. The slope of his arm over a chair, the droop of his eyes when the conversation wasn't of interest and twenty other impressions led Sarah to the conclusion that this man called Tortilla Flats home.

She sat down with Ryan.

—*I think that's Minos.*

—*He's got the asshole part down.*

—*We need to get him alone. For that, we need to become good customers. And for that . . .*

—*Yes, I know. I may have done this once or twice.*

—*I just hope the whiskey doesn't kill us.*

—*I've had Sang Tip before. It just might.*

Ryan opened the bottle and removed a valve-and-tube system from his suit. Sarah did the same. They plugged their valves into the bottle and sucked on the tubes in their helmets. The whiskey drew out of the bottle and was processed by the suits' filtration system before rising up into the mouthpieces. Ryan took a hard swallow, the liquor scalding his throat. Sarah did the same, but her stomach rejected the poison outright. She coughed hard, and it splattered all over the inside of her mask. The action elicited quiet laughter from the men around their table, who had been pretending not to look. The liquid slid off her faceplate, finding its way to her boots before the suit absorbed it.

"That's a hell of a cure for athlete's foot," Ryan said, adding to Sarah's humiliation.

She glared at him, taking another long draft, which she forced down without choking.

"That's better darlin'. Looks like you got the hang of it." A leather-faced giant loomed over them.

Here it comes, Ryan thought. The man took a good look at the couple and tried to pull a chair out to sit down on. Ryan locked it with his ankle, forcing the man to put all his weight into the tug. He did so, sitting down triumphantly.

"Don't mind if I do. Name's Shrek."

"What?" Ryan asked.

"Old vid character my mom liked. Said I look like him."

"How proud she must be," Laing said.

"You got quite a lip on ya, boy. Get ya in trouble round here."

"That so."

"Better have a drink to cool the nerves."

Shrek pulled two shot glasses from his patchwork and smacked them down on the bar. He waited patiently until Ryan poured the drinks.

"What do we drink to?" Laing asked.

"At the Flats we don't drink to nothing. Ain't no future worth the booze. The question is, What do we drink for?"

"For?"

"How 'bout that pretty little thing there. I don't like seeing a lady spit, but she looks cute enough."

"But . . . you're stuffed in a suit. What would you do with her?"

Shrek rolled his eyes. "Fuckin' newbie. Got the capsule over there. Hop in, get irradiated back and forth, up and down, in and out, then get to the good stuff. Shit, that's all we got left. Drink, fuck, scheme a way out, then get your shit zapped off tryin'." He stared at Ryan, then broke into laughter. "Ha! You think you're a short-timer. See it in yer eyes. Well, newbie, there ain't no such thing. No escape from the beam, man. You're stuck here. And here, life is cheap. Very fuckin' cheap."

"Ryan . . . ," Sarah said, getting nervous.

"Shut up, woman," Ryan snapped back. He turned to Shrek. "What's in it for me?"

"I'll let you live through the night."

Ryan let fear glisten in his eyes. "Yeah, okay," he said haltingly.

Shrek smiled viciously and raised his glass. "Then this here's for the girl." He slammed his suction valve over the shot glass and sucked it down. Ryan did the same.

The night wore on. Ryan drank, slowly ingratiating himself with the exiles who called this wasteland home. Being the prize and not much else, Sarah had time to study the people gathered around this table. She marveled that anyone could inhabit such an environment. Already, her body twitched with an itching need to break out of her suit. She understood a goldfish's plight.

Most of the patrons were scum, the dregs society couldn't stomach. Shrek certainly fell into that cadre. They had fled from the law, or worse. Thailand was their final option. Now, they lingered, scheming escape from the moment they arrived. Getting past the particle beam was possible—but not for this crew. If they'd had the tech and brains to crack the beam, they wouldn't have needed asylum in the first place. No, they'd die here, a way station on their path to hell.

Others seemed content with their locale. They didn't fidget or look longingly at the capsule, hoping to find enough cash to get in there, with or without a partner. Instead, they chatted and laughed. They oozed freedom.

She was pulled from her musings by the drinking bout's ignominious finale. Ryan had taken another pull, and Shrek, on the brink of delirium, exploded with fury. Hauling himself up, Shrek ripped the table out from between them and stormed Ryan. "You cheating!" he screamed. "No one outdrinks me!"

Laing leaned back and kicked his right leg straight out, his boot slamming into Shrek's gut. Shrek's breath left him in a long whoosh.

"Maybe you need stiffer competition," Ryan responded, doing his best to slur.

Shrek's eyes glazed with dull rage. He grabbed Ryan's boot from his belly and wrenched it. Ryan lashed out with his other foot, connecting with Shrek's chin. The blow stunned the giant but didn't fell him. Shrek continued to haul on Ryan's boot, threatening to rip it off. So Ryan gave Shrek the boot—let him lift it up and went with it, twisting at the last second and scissoring Shrek's neck between his thighs. They crashed to the ground, splintering the table.

Shrek sank his weight into Ryan and pulled out a laz knife. Ryan caught it centimeters from his chest and, more important, millimeters from his suit. A single twist and Laing relieved Shrek of the knife, which he kept hovering between Shrek's legs. The two rose slowly. Shrek had little choice in the matter. Shrek's buddies made a move to join in. Ryan twitched, sending the man onto his tiptoes.

"*Wow!* Whoa, there, boys. Back off now. We's just had a misunderstandin'. Nothing to get steamed over."

The boys backed down reluctantly. Ryan inched the knife away from Shrek's pride and joy. Shrek exhaled in relief, then passed out cold. The crowd broke into laughter, and Shrek's buddies set to work hauling him away. Ryan retracted the knife and pocketed it. He gave a nod to Sarah, and they resituated themselves on two barbershop chairs.

The owner watched the goings-on with vague interest. Now that the activity was over, he unfolded himself and stood, arms flopping down to his sides. His face blank, he walked over to Sarah and Ryan and leaned back on the counter, taking in their full measure. Thirty seconds passed in this way.

28

Unlike most of his brethren, Minos had traveled. Thailand was supposed to be vacant, a barren zone left to the Weapon. The virus had made end times a reality. The karmic cycle had been uprooted. Now, and for decades to come, life was day-to-day, each moment a gift. His brethren knew it. With survival being so tenuous, few found it necessary to court further risk by traveling.

Years ago, Minos had felt isolated from such peaceful acceptance. His suit chafed. Through childhood, he played the explorer. His longing to see, to touch, shaped him. As childhood matured into adolescence, he grew distant, unable to share in the peaceful joy of existence that came so easily to others.

So he moved from zone to zone. Most offered only the charred husk of life immolated. He moved north, up past the skeletal cities of Chiang Mai and Chiang Rai, into the Golden Triangle. Occasionally, he met other survivors. They augmented his endurance, either by offering their knowledge or testing his will to survive. Always, the drive to move seeped through his suit and forced action. He longed for vision without the haze of a faceplate, for touch unhindered by his glove.

He continued north, determined to crack the beam, pass through the event horizon and leave his mask behind. He got close enough to see the moonscape that surrounded his country. He threw rocks into the kill zone and watched the beam fry them. Crackling heat shot down from the heavens; the rocks vaporized before hitting earth. For him, there was no escape. He turned his back on the event horizon, afraid that he'd make a break for it if he lingered. A suicide run. He resorted to life in the jungles, letting the effort of existence subsume him.

Then he met Rachael. She was like nothing he had ever seen, or even imagined. She was older than he, probably midthirties, with dark curly hair and milk-white skin. Her green eyes dazzled him. She hunted the Weapon. She needed a guide.

He led her through the jungle, feeding her, sheltering her. Gradually his curiosity returned. Questions rolled off his tongue. She answered every one. She was looking for the village of an extinct hill tribe, the remainder of an ousted Chinese legion driven from their country by Mao Tse-tung in the twentieth. For decades the tribe had survived as opium traders. But, as high tech exploded through the region, they had found a new commodity: bioware. At the time, HIV plagued Thailand. This tribe weaponized the virus for sale to the highest bidder. Their work was inspired. Their security protocols were not. That village became ground zero for the plague. The Weapon spread, mutating flash-fast. By the time it reached areas with population density, it was indomitable.

Rachael now hunted for the original strain. He had little interest in such things, but found the adventure to his liking. He helped Rachael get to the village, where she found what she needed. He accompanied her south, way south, to Elysium.

Elysium had changed everything. From that day on, he craved the place like an addict. It fueled him, gave sensation to his life. But he couldn't stay. He'd grown used to suffering and couldn't live without it. He abandoned his own name and took another: Minos. He returned to the wastelands and opened Tortilla Flats. There he stayed, the ache to return to Elysium spicing his days. He obtained whatever Elysium needed from the outside world. His slice of the death zone became the last stop for the world's refuse.

Now, Minos studied the two before him in silence, letting tension fill the space. Neither seemed particularly bothered by the act. The woman had passion, some driving need that scorched her features. The man, aside from faking inebriation, swirled. Everything in him spun. Proximity to such a man held little future. Minos wondered if the woman saw it.

"This your place?" Ryan slurred.

Minos held silent for another beat. "Drop the act. You're not drunk."

"After that many shots—"

"I'm an expert on drunk, and you aren't there. Probably have a siphoning pouch somewhere in that fancy suit."

"And why would I do that?"

"Obviously you suspected just such a reception. And you'd never give up the woman."

"Pretty perceptive for a bartender," Sarah said.

"I tend nothing. People get what they want and I watch."

"Must be fascinating," Sarah said.

"It has its moments. Today, I'm fascinated by you."

The remainder of the clientele shuffled out. Minos gave a slight nod to his entourage, and they too ducked into the stairway.

Minos studied the two. "Where did you come from?"

"Suffice it to say that we passed through death to get here and there's no going back," Sarah said.

To Minos' eye, the two seemed to be communicating, sharing a conversation that welled under verbal.

"I'm Laing; this is Sarah."

"I'm Kukrit."

"You go by another name," Laing said, taking up Sarah's gambit.

With that Minos whirled, smoothly drawing a handmade gun from the folds of his suit.

"If you know that, then you must realize the peril you're in."

The two didn't look at each other, but Minos knew they had agreed on action. He was up against a beast with two heads. Minos took a step back, ready to fire.

"We have passed through death, paid Charon and crossed the Styx," Sarah said. The words came off with an awkward cadence. The code sounded silly. Minos didn't seem to agree.

"You may not like my judgment," Minos responded.

"We have no choice," said Sarah.

"Some places are reserved for ancient heroes."

"Yet must be renewed by new blood," Sarah said.

"I'm not just, or lenient."

"Nor was your namesake," Sarah continued.

Minos laughed, and some of the tension sheared away.

"We need access to Elysium," Ryan cut in.

"Of course."

"They hold the Key."

"Some locks are better left unopened."

"The world is crashing down on them," Sarah said.

Minos smirked and waved his hand around their surroundings. "What could that do to us?"

"That could destroy the peace of the dead," Sarah said.

Minos stared at the woman. She saw so clearly, yet could not know.

The two had the fortitude and intelligence to get here. But could they keep the secret? How strong were they?

Minos chose a middle path. He would take the woman. The man, the whirlwind, would not see the dawn. Minos raised the gun and pulled the trigger. Or he thought he did. Glancing back several seconds later, he felt sure of it. But his memories might have been clouded by the pain racking him.

Ryan unsheathed the laz knife, slicing the gun in half, leaving the grip and trigger in Minos' hand. Before the barrel hit the floor, Ryan buried his foot into Minos' groin. The small man buckled. Ryan shot forward and grabbed him by the front of his suit, holding him at eye level. Ryan watched Minos' pain settle, saw the waves of nausea even as his face remained impassive. Minos gazed increduously at the severed weapon in his hand. He reeled from Laing's strike. Such speed was . . . inhuman.

Ryan pulled Minos close, shield on shield. Then, with deliberate poise, he shifted the knife and forced it into Minos' hand. He guided the shimmering blade to his own heart and let go, giving Minos control of the weapon.

"We came here for a favor. If the price is my death, do it. Then take the woman to Elysium."

"You would die for her?"

"I would, but this is not for her."

Sarah got close enough to feel the knife's heat through her suit. "The world has crumbled around you. You can't see it, because this place is already dead. Elysium may be able to help."

Minos stared at the two, felt the heft of the blade in his hand, pondered sinking it into the man's chest.

"Two hundred fifty baht," he said.

"What?" Ryan and Sarah said in unison.

"Two hundred fifty baht: what you owe me for a night's worth of whiskey. That you're still sober is no fault of mine."

Ryan relaxed his grip on Minos' suit, and Minos lowered the knife a fraction.

"You take credit?" Ryan said.

The knife came back up, but Ryan saw the hint of a smile chiseling through Minos' stone face.

29

They moved through the city, tracked by the rising sun. Ryan carried Minos on his wheel. He'd assumed the gatekeeper would have his own transportation. Minos had merely shrugged and settled himself onto the small bulge protruding from the front of the vehicle. It took some work for the machine to find balance. It also required that its operators move in unison. After several crashes, drawing fits of hysterical laughter from Sarah, Ryan let Minos take control. He wrapped his arms around the little man and let him guide.

Now they plunged into the thickening jungle that encroached on the city. Sarah wobbled beside them, muted laughter erupting from her periodically. Minos looked like a tie-dyed hood ornament. The twin glares from Minos and Ryan only added to her mirth.

—*I think everyone will want a Minos next season. It really fills out your look.*

—*Anything to amuse, Sarah.*

—*Oh, lighten up. You're here in a beautiful jungle, friends around you, hugging a Thai man for dear life . . .*

—*I know—these are the best of times.*

Sarah grinned and did a few pirouettes around them before shooting ahead. They left the city and fell off the map. They followed cracked highways for a time, swooping between petrified vehicles. After half a day, the highways gave way to jungle. They slipped into rutted cart tracks, then what looked like animal trails. Finally, they had to abandon the wheels and go on foot. Minos didn't seem to notice the crushing foliage impeding them. He slipped through without effort. Ryan and Sarah struggled behind, tripping and tugging themselves through the jungle's vise. Eventually, Ryan strapped the laz-knife to a stick and slashed a path from the green.

At night, Minos foraged. He diverted streams to harvest freshwater shrimp. He even managed to catch jungle squirrels every now and then, which he seasoned with wasp larvae. After his foraging, he cut down one of the towering bamboo stalks surrounding them and built a fire. He used sections of the tree as pots, expertly fashioning chopsticks and bowls as well. The meals ran just short of inedible. Neither

Sarah nor Ryan cared much. They plugged bites into the pockets of their suits and ate the irradiated sustenance.

Lying under the jungle canopy, Ryan finished his meal and lay back. Sarah followed, her helmet clicking against his. Minos slipped away. He had grown used to their silent conversations.

Sarah made out a few points of light breaking through the blanket of palm fronds.

—*You can almost see stars,* she thought.

—*I only take you to the finest places.*

Sarah sighed. "This is a fine place. I always wanted to travel."

Ryan rolled on his side, wanting to look at Sarah as she looked into the sky. He forgot the sweat-cramped claustrophobia that gouged deeper each day he wore the suit.

"You've traveled all over the world."

"No. Not like this," she said.

"You mean in the lap of luxury? I admit the larvae brought out the jungle squirrel's nutty undertones."

Sarah laughed, free and easy. "No. That part I could do without. But this. This is all I want."

She gazed up into the foliage, her eyes flecked with excitement. He let her take up the thread of conversation in her own time.

"I've moved from one place to another," she continued. "But this . . . This is traveling, exploring. Feels like no one's been here before. We're off the map."

"I could download exact coordinates."

"Don't. I know it's an illusion. People lived here, cut into the wild and made it theirs. But for whatever reason, they relinquished it. Now it's ours to discover again."

"This makes you happy?"

Sarah turned to Ryan. The fluttering firelight and their masks' glare gave his face a blurred elegance, only his essential features slipping through.

"The map's gone dark here. We've gridded ourselves to death. No place left to explore, nowhere to expand. We've illuminated every nook and cranny and succeeded in electrocuting ourselves. This may be an illusion—a theme park—but it's all we've got. A hint of what life used to be."

"But you live in that electricity. At least, you used to."

"A substitute. The only thing left that's wild and new is the environment we've fashioned in the flow. So I explored there. But it never sated me."

"Is that why you played in the band?" Ryan asked.

The jolting memory of Elaine, and gut-shot pain of her absence, crumpled Sarah.

"How did you . . . ?"

"Had plenty of time to myself on the junk—so I caught your show on feed."

"Did you like it?"

"I . . . No, I didn't."

Sarah's lips set. She swallowed hard, shaking off the slight, needing him to understand. "Maybe that's why I played. For that primal, unpolished energy. I spent the day ordering the universe and at night ripped it apart."

Ryan scoffed, cutting Sarah further. "Sorry," he added, flat blank.

"What scares you so deeply?" Sarah asked, her voice spined with frustration.

Ryan looked away, anger rising.

—This—Echelon—isn't a game, Sarah. Not something you can turn on and off. It's serious. It's everything.

Sarah grabbed Laing's helmet, forcing him to look at her. "Speak to me," she said.

Ryan hadn't realized he'd been using the drones. He hated that she saw him so clearly—and made him so vulnerable. Better to lock the pain down, to remain untouchable. But now, looking into Sarah's eyes, he couldn't hold. The dam within him cracked.

"What scares me? Life scares me, Sarah. I'm petrified of this chaotic fucking maelstrom we're all caught up in. Life has no rules, no assurance. It's not fair. It's not just. It's all pain and fire."

"Your parents," Sarah said, trailing off.

Ryan couldn't bring himself to say yes. He sat up, words gushing. "Turing offered a way out. Become the controller, the manipulator. Grasp life with both fists and wring order from it. And I did. With everything in me and every drop of energy. I tamed the chaos."

"But where's the release in that life?"

"Release?"

"The freedom," she said.

"Freedom is for the bold."

Sarah sat up and forced him to look into her smile, even as tears formed at the corners of her eyes.

"I don't work for Echelon," he continued. "I am Echelon. It defines me. Its cause is mine."

"Echelon is gone, Ryan."

Ryan blinked hard, tension crushing his features.

"How can you say that?" he said. "Don't you see what that means? Without Echelon, entropy wins."

"Maybe. I don't know anymore. Echelon hooked me too. I saved lives every day I worked there. Every single day. And every night, I played in that stupid band. Sure, it was meaningless rebellion, just kids slamming. But it fueled me."

"You want anarchy?"

Sarah laughed. "Of course not. I'm just thinking that the help we offered, the peace Echelon gave to the world, became a crutch, and then maybe the disease itself. I don't want anarchy. But there's something to that edge beyond order."

"Don't you know what's on the other side? Meaningless pain, death. Cacophony."

"I never thought of you as eloquent."

"Sarah . . ."

"Sorry, I shouldn't have said that. I know what Echelon did. How much it helped. But I wonder if there's more. I lie here in reclaimed wilderness, looking at you, and I feel empowered. I wish I could smell this place."

"You look at me, but you don't see. I'm nothing. I'm the war. I'm cored out—a wind tunnel."

She held his gaze. Gray tears welled and fell down his face, only to stop mid-descent and scuttle back into his eyes. He looked down in shame, and her heart broke.

"I love you," she said.

Ryan could only shake his head.

"I know what you are and I love you." She gripped his shoulder, trying to infuse affection across the barrier separating them. She felt him recede. Sarah removed her hand and stood. She looked down on him.

"I see it, Ryan. You're bubbling with repressed energy and can't control the drones coursing through you. You're a mess. Statistically, you're a far bigger threat to my survival than the conspiracy we're after. Any Vegas bookie would bet on a full Ryan Laing breakdown. Beyond that, you haven't realized quite how powerful you've become. You don't see the scope of your abilities. You could well be the most dangerous man alive."

Ryan sank into himself. "Maybe I need to die."

"If Echelon existed, if I were sitting at my console in Inverness, that would be my analysis. I'd have compiled the facts, worked the stats and determined that you're far too great a risk. I would have imagined the ramifications of the report I'd just submitted. I'd see you in this place, running scared. I'd feel the beat of copters, imagine the marksman's finger caress the trigger, watch the bullet pound through the bamboo and into your brain. And then I would walk to the bathroom and throw up. I'd find Elaine in there, doing the same thing, hung over. In another hour, we'd be in front of a thousand kids, and I'd forget you. I'd add you to all the other great things I'd destroyed. I'd be just a little less than when I'd started the day."

Ryan said nothing.

Sarah's voice softened. "But Echelon does not exist. I'm not an analyst anymore. You've changed that. You've changed everything. Now I get to lie here with you. Now, I get to feel your body against mine. I get to stand beside you."

"What an honor," Ryan croaked.

"I see what you are beneath the pain, the loss, the drones, everything. I see it, Ryan, and I love it. I'd risk anything, even my own life, to be near it."

The words beat into Ryan. Something in him clicked over. He found the will to look up at her and then out into the canopy beyond.

"Thank you, Sarah."

Sarah nodded. Ryan rose, drawing close to her. She did not back away. He unclasped his suit's rigging, he groped for the lever at the back of his helmet, found it and pulled hard. The airlock released, and he removed the helmet. He pulled down the suit's top and stepped from its leggings. His naked body glimmered with perspiration. Ryan opened his arms to the night and took a massive gulp of air. He felt the drones stir, felt their call to arms and their battle with the Weapon. He let the war wage within him; he allowed his center to move beyond it. He heard the teeming life in the jungle. The staccato input thrilled him. He looked at Sarah. Her eyes never left his. For an instant Ryan saw himself through her eyes. It was enough. He inhaled.

"It smells peaty and thick. Something sweet, a flower maybe. It reeks of life. It's overload." He paused. "I like it."

Sarah's tears flowed. She leaned forward, resting her helmet on his forehead. Then she pulled him down and let him curl into the crook of her shoulder as she lay on her back.

Ryan drew in the smells of the jungle, describing them in an unending stream. His description grew rhythmic, part of the landscape itself. She fell asleep, drenched in the fragrance of his words.

30

Minos was not surprised by Ryan's new outfit, or lack thereof. Laing had chucked his helmet and wore only the pants, tying the upper half of the suit around his waist. Few had the fortitude to accept the suit as second skin. Minos had seen it so many times that Laing's oncoming death barely raised an eyebrow. The Weapon had him. In an hour or two, he would wither. Sarah wouldn't be able to pull away. Minos saw the promise of her own suicide in her glances at Ryan. If they had only waited. If Elysium chose them . . .

But it was too late for that. He led the dead to their graves. He made the pretense of starting the day as usual. He broke camp. There was little to take with them. The jungle offered all one's imagination and skill could harvest. Minos walked into it with nothing, brushing past Ryan and Sarah, who talked without words. There was necromancy in these two.

"We go as long as we can," he said over his shoulder. He looked at Ryan. "We'll stop when you tire."

Ryan nodded gravely. At least he understood what he had done. And yet, hours passed, morning turned to steam-slick afternoon, and Ryan showed no signs. Every now and then a pustule would pock his face and Minos would breathe easier. He did not wish for the man to die, but if he lived, it would spell the end of Minos' world. Settlers would pour into Thailand, and its flanks would glow electric. But the man did not falter, and when Minos looked minutes later, the abscess had vanished. Maybe it had been wishful thinking.

They stopped for lunch. Minos hunted. Sarah sat heavily, cooling in the shade of a banana palm. Ryan offered to help Minos, who blushed and looked away. Laing's exposure distracted him. Minos squelched a carnal longing to touch Ryan. Flesh contact was not shunned here; it was simply impossible. The mere sight of flesh pushed at Minos to abandon his own suit—an itch that hadn't gripped him in years.

Awash in ones and zeros, Madda hunted. He slid into the task, let it consume him. Symmetry tugged at him, then faded before his eyes. He hit the island of data with torrents of processing power, boring in, ripping it apart, coring down and finding nothing. He fell asleep in the flow and dreamed electric.

Back home, when he'd been just another hacker jockeying for notoriety, he'd dabbled with full-shift operation—all the kids had. In their little cubicles, nestled into San Francisco's Tenderloin, they slipped reality and lived in the flow. They grew well versed in the intricacies of IV tubes and catheters.

Madda couldn't last more than a couple days. His need for physical action pushed him out. That need embarrassed him, made him weak. But his innate ability to slip dams kept him in the club. Soon, he got spotted, picked off the rookie rosters and stuffed into a corporate coding gig. He lost track of his slum buddies; none made it. It took Madda another year to see that the corporations that hired him were being driven by a single force. At that exact point of realization, Echelon contacted him. He abandoned everything to live out his life on the cutting edge. But the longing never vanished. He couldn't live in the flow, and couldn't be contained in Echelon's lab.

Only now, utterly awash in his task, did he experience complete flow shift. The flow became his reality. He lost himself within it. Madda cut extraneous audio and visual interfaces away, seeing only code. It rippled and transformed with his commands, and Madda began to see shape to the chaos.

Like an ancient stereopticon image, the code shifted dimension, extending in space. But try as he might, he couldn't resolve the image. He welled out code for the mother of all waves and hurled it into the fray. But his assault was cut short. Tex's hardware simply couldn't handle the size of the operation. As it crashed around him, Madda made out a glimmer. He felt a watcher.

Before Echelon, Madda understood that his every move could be observed. Concepts like personal privacy went out with the twentieth. The only protection lay in being a tiny piece of flotsam on a great big sea. The vastness of the data the world generated was a hacker's best defense.

Once inside Echelon, Madda knew that his every move was watched. He'd become adept at sensing the briefest flickers in flowspace that signified surveillance. Inside Echelon, his only defense had been a retreat into his own mind, wherein he lived a different life. Outside, he knew that each and every action was scrutinized. The pressure of such attention drove him to flee.

And now, as he cursed the frailties of the machine crashing down around him, he saw that flicker, sensed the watcher. Instead of saving the system, he let it go. As it spat him out and rebooted, he placed a very subtle tracer behind him. On initializing, it pinged red. He turned in flow-space to see Ryan's ethereal frame floating off his left shoulder.

"Jesus Christ," Madda spat, "you scared the shit out of me."

"Sorry to interrupt," Ryan responded.

"I won't be tracked. You want something from me, ask."

"Haven't been tracking you. Just stopped in to check on your progress."

Madda's anger melted into anxiety. Ryan saw it. "Someone else is onto you?" Ryan asked.

"Must be."

"Can you cut them out?"

"I can stall them."

"Are you close?"

"Well, I've cracked pieces of the virus, but the Key's hard to pin down. Basically hitting it with a binary holocaust, but nothing seems to be—"

Ryan cut him off, "Are you close?"

"No."

"Well, keep pushing."

Madda nodded. "How's jungle life?"

"I'll keep you posted."

"Be careful."

"You too."

Ryan faded. Madda compulsively swiped at the space the ghost had occupied. Nothing remained, not even residue. Madda shuddered; Ryan was accessing the flow directly. He wondered if Ryan would flow shift when this ended. No human could be more suited to the environment. Madda turned back to his target code.

From the cabin's door, Tex watched. As did two shadows in a small gray room.

· · · · ·

Ryan left Madda and surfed the flow. He allowed the drones to lead him. The slow steady beat of progress had disintegrated. Instead, bursts and fits of energy sparked and receded. Radical advances in mechanics, lofty speculations on philosophy, rich debate on the future. And with each came the inevitable tumble. War sprouted up. Fear regained its footing, and anger followed. Even as achievement shot sparkling light into the gray, so explosions dragged it into black. Ryan watched, felt the drones trying to make sense of the shifting data set but even their near-infinite capacities overloaded.

He tried to quell the tyranny, to get out of the flow and shut down the drones, or at least quiet them. Their power grew. He forced his eyes open, and the jungle's night sounds suffused the chatter within, confounding both.

He sensed movement near him, but couldn't resolve specifics. Overload. He waved a hand before his face and saw not only the movement of his fingertips, but the gentle flux of air currents around him, and the fluttering of the fronds over his head made by that flux. The drones processed the shift in the nature of existence precipitated by his tiny movement. The ballooning ramifications of his action drove Laing to stillness. He began to hyperventilate, unable to lock out the expanded consciousness the drones forced upon him. Their access to information and computing power dwarfed him. He drowned.

Sharp beats of pain drew him up and out. He locked into the sensation. He did not wake up; if anything, parts of him fell asleep and he was able to find his own small slice of reality. Currently, that reality consisted of Sarah, hunkered over him and slapping him in the face. The filters snapped back into place. Each ripple melded into the approximation of reality that Ryan recognized as his own.

"Okay, I'm up!" he said. The tingle in his cheeks was scintillating.

"Where the hell were you?" she asked. "You scared the crap out of me."

"I—it's hard to explain."

The fear locking Sarah's jaw into a grimace relaxed slightly. She massaged the palm of her gloved hand.

"He's gone, Ryan."

"Minos? It's a little early to start out. Not even light yet."

"No, he left." She pointed to the smoldering pit of their fire. Next to it was enough food for several days. "I think he's gone for good."

Ryan looked around the campsite. Minos' meager belongings had vanished. Even in the morning twilight, the dense jungle hid everything.

"After all this, he left us? He led us on a wild-goose chase," Sarah said.

—*Maybe,* he responded.

—*Maybe? Definitely. That little shit dragged us out here to die. Elysium's probably in the opposite direction.*

Ryan let himself venture out, keeping a tight hold on his senses. The jungle lit up.

—*No, Sarah. He did it.*

—*Did what? Stranded us? And why are you in my head?* "Talk to me, damn it!"

—*We're here, Sarah. We're in Elys—.*

Ryan's signal cut short as a searing light blew through his left temple. His body convulsed. His eyes bled. He threw up. Sarah's silhouette loomed over him and then everything faded to black.

From a palm several meters away, Minos watched Ryan fall. He held his breath as the jungle disgorged a small band of people, their skin shimmering with sweat. He felt the greasy confinement of his suit. Minos watched them close in, saw the wavy brown hair of the woman who had filled his thoughts since that first meeting in Chiang Rai all those years ago. She felt his gaze and stared into the trees. Through the glint of his mask she seemed an apparition: more real than real. She nodded to him, beckoned. His head sank. He descended and turned his back on the woman.

Minos longed to go with them, to be free of his suit and even the task that defined him. But he could not. He needed a center, a core. He needed to worship them. It was all he had. He broke into a fast trot, heading back to the city and to his world. He imagined Rachael looking after him as he faded into the jungle. The thought made him light. He ran fast.

Ryan twitched at Sarah's feet. The speed of his fall stunned her. She'd grown used to his invulnerability. She felt her surroundings shift, sensed numerous enemies closing in. She grabbed the laz knife and made her stand—knowing the act would be futile. If her attackers had the power to turn Ryan into a fizzled husk, they would dispatch her with little difficulty. She'd go down fighting. She cursed Minos and struggled against a flood of despair.

The jungle belched out a dozen men and women. Sarah whirled, trying to keep them all in her sight line. It took her a second to realize that none of them had suits. In fact, they didn't have much clothing at all. Several held guns of a make she didn't recognize.

A woman with rippling brown hair stepped forward. She was obviously the leader, and Sarah lost no time. She charged the woman, unsheathing her laz blade. The man next to the leader raised his weapon, but Sarah closed too quickly, getting the blade on his barrel an instant before he pulled the trigger. With nothing to guide the projectile, it exploded in his hand. Gore covered Sarah's faceplate, slipping off in meaty globs. She turned on the leader, lunging wildly. Fire raged in the woman's eyes. She dodged Sarah's attempt to grapple her, spinning with slippery fluidity. Sarah whirled around in time to see the woman leap into the air and send out a side kick. The woman's heel smashed through Sarah's faceplate, and Sarah tumbled backward.

Sarah sucked in lungfuls of air. Her face burned. She tried to get to her feet, but a man grabbed her shoulders and held her down. The leader loomed over her. She looked at her injured man. Another had scurried in and wrapped a tourniquet around the man's spurting stump.

"If he dies . . ." The woman's voice rang ice cold.

"What?" Sarah shot back. "I'm already dead."

A cruel smile spread across the leader's face. "That's true. As are we all."

With that, the woman unsheathed a dagger from her belt. She raised it high over her head. Sarah watched her death coming with removed fascination. The woman glowed above her, naked flesh shimmering in the morning light. Sarah saw that the blade was in fact a large needle. A droplet of liquid gathered at its tip and fell onto Sarah's chest. The woman's arm wound like a coiled spring, then released, driving the needle down. Sarah felt more than heard the sickening crack of the needle piercing her sternum. Light and dark warred in her vision. She fought and relented.

The woman jammed the needle deeper into Sarah's chest, and Sarah arched into it convulsively. The woman depressed the plunger. It flooded her, froze her. Consciousness slipped in a flood of darkness and pain.

"Welcome to Elysium," the woman said.

31

Sarah awoke to the rich funk of moist grass and dirt. The smell intoxicated her, offering a moment of contentment before memory kicked in. She opened her eyes, finding herself in a small thatched hut, sprawled over a straw mattress. She jerked upright and bolted for the door. The sharp yank of a cord attached to her wrist told her all she needed to know. She was a prisoner.

She settled back and took stock. Her clothing had been removed. In one corner she saw a pair of gossamer white pants. She struggled to jam her cramped legs into them. No shirt. As decent as she could muster, she scanned her body for the telltale pustules that signaled the Weapon's first bite. One such nodule had formed on her arm, but it seemed to have healed. Impossible. She scanned the rest of her body and found nothing. Her chest ached. Radiating veins of blue and black spindled out from a puncture wound over her heart. She touched it, cringing.

"The bruising will recede."

Sarah hadn't noticed the woman standing in the doorway. Her voice resonated through the small room, too large for the enclosed space. She was dressed in an outfit similar to Sarah's: thin cotton pants, hers augmented with a sash of luminous green. Her chest hung full and voluptuous. Her tanned skin and dark hair offered a stark contrast to Sarah's pallor. The woman coursed with barely contained energy.

"Who are you? Where's Ry— Where's my friend?" Sarah demanded, arching up and attempting to regain some sense of control. The effort felt ridiculous.

The woman smiled, deep grooves forming at the edge of her mouth. "I'm Rachael. You're not dead because I administered the vaccine—something I don't usually do."

"You've let others die?"

"Many others." Rachael's dark eyes offered only reflection. Sarah found herself unconsciously cowering before the woman.

"Well then, I guess I should thank you."

"Not necessary. Had you not come with . . . your friend, you'd be dead too."

"You knew we were coming?"

"I know a great deal."

Rachael dropped to eye level with Sarah. Reflexively, Sarah shrank back. Rachael caught her arm and pulled her close. Sarah locked into those eyes, caught by the animal force before her.

"You are not welcome." Rachael's lips nearly touched Sarah's. The faint scent of mango weighted her breath. "But we knew you would come. You and Ryan."

Rachael stepped back, and Sarah realized that she had removed the wrist restraint. Sarah got to her feet, rising a full head taller than Rachael. The height difference did nothing to diminish Rachael's dominance.

"How do you know his name? Is he okay?"

"He'll live, Sarah. I'll take you to him."

With that, Rachael turned on her heels and exited the hut. Sarah emerged into hot, moisture-thick air. She took in her surroundings, trying to keep up with Rachael. In spite of herself, she couldn't help watching the bounce of Rachael's breasts as she marched. Around her, others moved by, filling out village life. All wore the same outfit.

"We call it Elysium, named by our great-grandparents," Rachael said.

"You've been here that long?"

"Since the Weapon."

"And you had the antidote all along?"

"My parents lived under the mask."

"But why not offer it to the world?"

"For what possible reason?"

Sarah looked astonished. "Civilization could return."

Rachael said nothing. Sarah had just answered her own question. She let her gaze wander. Elysium was situated on a narrow peninsula jutting into the sea. At the far end of the peninsula, the ground rose to a knobby spire of limestone. Below the looming formation, the village of Elysium hummed with activity. Moving toward the mainland, the spit again rose into mountains. Above the lush peaks, the air warped and glimmered. Rachael noticed Sarah's gaze.

"A barrier field covers our peninsula. If someone came looking, which they never have, this area would appear deserted to even the most sensitive of instruments."

"Impossible."

"As an Echelon analyst, you know it isn't. Echelon has been working on the same tech. We just figured it out first."

Sarah's jaw dropped. Rachael smiled. "As I said, we know many things."

As they approached the cliffs, Sarah saw that climbers peppered them, lithe forms snaking up the rock. She and Rachael came to a large thatched hut and entered. Immediately, the temperature dropped. Sarah felt like she'd discarded the blanket of moisture she'd lived under for the past weeks. She shivered. The air had lost its vitality.

"This is our sterile room," Rachael said.

In the corner, Ryan lay on a pallet, dead pale. Then his chest heaved and Sarah allowed herself a sigh. She approached and slipped her hand in his.

—*Ryan?* She attempted to contact him but felt nothing.

"The room also dampens all radiation. Your connection will not work. His drones have settled into hibernation."

Sarah whirled and stared down Rachael, who didn't bother to return the gaze. "How do you know?"

"You must suspect. If you didn't, you wouldn't be here."

Sarah had a thousand questions, all shoved aside as Ryan ascended to consciousness. His eyes flickered open. On his chest, a bruise similar to Sarah's spread. Sarah stroked his hair, letting him come back slowly.

She watched the past hours flood Ryan's mind as he attempted to connect. She watched him feel the stillness within as he struggled to rise. He breathed heavy, inundated by relief. A single gray tear fell from his eye and dropped onto the hard pallet. He fell back onto the pillow.

Ryan lay still. The terrors racking him slackened. He felt drugged by the lack of input, the drones' silence intoxicating. He slept for hours, lolling in lazy stupor, unable to care about anything beyond his release. Sarah grew impatient.

"Go, check out the village. I'll watch Ryan," Rachael said. The way she said his name drew pangs of jealousy from Sarah. She shook the feeling off, stood and left the room, never looking at Ryan. For hours after that, Rachael merely sat with him. He longed to hold the moment, to stay in this bubble of peace forever. Rachael seemed willing to let him do so.

Finally, he spoke. "Why aren't I dead?"

"You interest us. And as long as you're here, you pose no threat."

"Your henchman seemed willing enough to kill me in Princeton."

Rachael looked up, as if trying to remember some inconsequential bit of data. "You should have let Robert finish the job."

"He almost did." Ryan massaged his head.

"We weren't after you, Mr. Laing. We wanted Welton." The way her mouth lipped the consonants of his name made Ryan tingle.

"Welton? But why?"

"Some of us felt it was time to reenter the world, to help. I was against it."

"And now?"

"Now, I've prevailed. We will remain separate."

Ryan stood and walked the perimeter of the room. He approached the open door, felt the sizzle of electronic interference as he neared it. He looked out at the small village spilling onto a white sand beach and perfect blue bay. Mushrooms of limestone rose from the water. He saw the climbers. He began to walk out onto the veranda, but halfway through the door, the surge of data hit him. He reeled back, unprepared for the drones' bite.

Safely within the room, their blitzkrieg abated. Silence regained. Laing reached his hand beyond the door, felt the drones' surge in his fingertips. He held it there, testing his will, seeing just how much he could take. Rachael silently moved in behind him, her breast brushing his back. She did not shy away from the contact. She pulled his hand back into the room. Soft inebriation returned. Ryan sighed.

"They cannot be removed," Rachael said. "But here, in this room, you'll find some peace."

"What is this place?"

Laing let Rachael's words flow over him, their low harmony heating his skin. "This is a refuge, Mr. Laing. From the glare of the world. A retreat to simpler times. A place where emotions come clean—not bottle-fed in supersaturated, scripted, and easily ingested formula.

"How do you know what society has become?"

"We watch, Mr. Laing—those of us who continue to care."

"But not you," Ryan said.

"My father's father rejected that world. I do the same. I know the truth and choose this place."

"What truth?" Ryan turned to Rachael, felt her proximity, her vitality sparking through him.

"This is the only place left that's free."

"From Echelon."

Rachael laughed. "Echelon. The puppet master, controller of society, arbiter of progress," she said with mock awe. "Yes, this is the only place beyond Echelon's control—until recently."

"You know about Echelon," Ryan said, trying to maintain his calm.

"Of course we know. We created it."

Ryan's mouth dropped open. A flood of questions began to spill forth. She quelled them, putting her finger to his lips.

"In time, Mr. Laing. You have all the time in the world." She let her finger slide down his lips. Heat swelled between them. Ryan stepped backward, but Rachael followed. She leaned into him, and her lips found his.

Through the luxurious embrace, a small part of Ryan stood apart. He heard a creak in the floorboards and looked up to see Sarah staring at him from the doorway. Shock spread across her face, quickly replaced by anger. He saw the anger directed at him; then her rage turned within. She turned on her heels and stalked into the village. Ryan broke from Rachael and chased after Sarah. But the cacophony at the doorway stopped him. As potent as an electric shock, he didn't have the strength to pursue.

Days passed. Ryan watched from his prison. Rachael visited often. She didn't mind the silence. Ryan would stand at the door and track life in Elysium. At first, Rachael's kiss had infuriated him. But in watching their society, he saw that there was little stigma against sexual expression. Men and women casually exchanged embraces as they would handshakes in Los Angeles. Sex was just part of daily life, a pleasurable respite between chores.

Sarah stayed away. He caught glimpses of her as she moved through the community. He saw Sarah's lithe frame shift up a limestone cliff, roped to a well-muscled woman.

"Climbing is part of life here. The rock surrounds us. We'd be fools not to use it," Rachael said, answering his unasked question.

"I climb."

"Then you know."

She left it there; she left most things hanging or unfinished. Time melted into moments. The pressures of the world beyond Elysium grew ephemeral. Ryan settled. He watched Sarah do the same. Elysium's tech occupied her. It possessed a slippery, wild quality that frightened Ryan. This little band had broken off from society a century ago. Their tech had thus become a language wholly its own. It was like visiting an alien planet.

One night, the moon rose full and the village turned out for a party on the beach. Ryan watched from his doorway. As darkness settled, the villagers sat in a circle, laughing and talking. They drank mushroom tea. A glass was brought to Ryan. He sipped the tangy beverage, realizing immediately that it was poison. His stomach curled around itself. Rachael approached and raised her own glass.

"What is this?" he asked.

"A mild psychedelic."

"I tried 'shrooms once. It felt like a cheap parlor trick. I was watching an old vid and for the rest of the night, everything pixilated. I couldn't wait to go to bed."

"Well, this should be different. Are you sure you won't join?"

Ryan longed to; he inched to the door. He looked out into the circle and saw Sarah watching him. At the door he recoiled. Sarah looked away, embarrassed to have witnessed his retreat. Rachael returned to the circle.

No one ate. The mushrooms prevented it. Some of the villagers picked up oddly shaped musical instruments and began playing. Like everything else, the harmonies of this place rose stark and contrasted, left to grow on their own. The music possessed a spectral resonance. Sarah found something resembling a bass and joined in. Soon, she lost the old rhythms and adopted the Elysians'. Her beat evolved, became something all her own. The other musicians drank in her novelty. It inspired their own. People swayed to the beat, the music and drug forcing movement.

Two men stood. Each held chains, at the end of which fire danced. They began to swing these flaming orbs around their bodies. The flames melted into circles of light that twisted and writhed. Their chests gleamed with perspiration. They synched with Sarah's beat, augmenting it with flame slashing through damp air.

To this beat, to the circling dance of the fire, people stood and spoke. Ryan was no poet. He found little place for such things. Now he listened. The words hit him and hurt him, then soothed the ache and offered insight. Later he couldn't recall what had been said. He remembered only one thing—inspiration. Unfettered, these poets, musicians and dancers ascended. Ryan watched in awe. It never occurred to him to join.

A woman rose. Slight—with taut, bunched muscles that exploded into pulsed action—she spoke. Ryan watched Sarah's face fall. Longing replaced rapture. Even from a distance, Ryan recognized loss in her eyes, in the furrow of her brow. She stared at the woman, locked into the staccato thrust of her words. Each one hit Sarah. She took the pain, accepted it, coveted it.

When the woman finished, Sarah dropped her bass and kneeled before her. The woman looked neither surprised nor offended. Tears rolled down Sarah's face. The woman's hand shot out and caught a tear falling from her chin. It splashed on her open palm. She closed her palms over the tear as she knelt. Sarah slowly clasped her hands over the woman's.

They rose onto their knees, their lips meeting over clasped fingers. Beyond the music and the whirling flame, augmented by the nether-reality of the drug, the kiss drew the crowd's attention. A purity existed in that act that dwarfed the others. People around them drew their neighbors into similar embraces, inspired. Ryan held.

Sarah wrapped her arms around the woman's neck, her frame shuddering in great sobs. The woman held Sarah. Sarah closed her eyes and buried her face in the woman's chopped hair.

Ryan inched to the door, his breath skipping. He stepped onto the veranda. Input flooded him. He let it fall away. He looked only at Sarah.

—*I miss her,* Sarah thought.

He felt her thought, her longing for what could never be reclaimed.

—*I know.*

Sarah did not open her eyes. She hugged the woman harder, melting into her.

—*I miss you.*

Ryan took another step. Data stifled him. He began to hyperventilate. He wanted to take that next step, to go to Sarah. But the onslaught was too much. He retreated, cut off the flood, regained control.

Her link with Ryan snapped shut, flooding Sarah with loss. The psychedelics both clouded and clarified, drawing her desires to the surface. She danced across them like a water strider.

The woman in her arms drew closer. Even her smell reminded Sarah of Elaine. Staring at the woman in the moonlight, her face shifted with the lapping waves into that of another.

"What is your name?" Sarah asked.

"Does it matter?" she said.

She was not Elaine, but she was comfort. Their lips reconnected. Sarah softened to the woman's urgency, and the knotted grief eased.

The woman lay Sarah back, kissing her chest and breasts in sharp onslaughts. Sarah inhaled the sea air in long currents. She gave in, let pain and pleasure flow through her. The woman took one of Sarah's nipples in her mouth, and Sarah rose to meet her. With perfect timing, the woman pulled Sarah's pants over her hips. She broke away, knelt back and pulled the pants free. People surrounded them. Sarah didn't care. She savored the moonlight on her skin.

The woman spread Sarah's legs. No foreplay, she dove into Sarah's core. Sarah arched back. Grief rolled off her, beating at the waves and dissipating into the water. Sarah felt Laing's eyes on her. The swirling newness of the environment and the freedom of the drug dissipated her inhibitions. She wanted him to see her, wanted the comfort of his eyes if that was all he could give.

The woman drove deeper, and Sarah shrieked, tears streaming down her face. Her body arched in ecstatic tension, then exploded into a million shards. The dancers' swirling flames filled her, scoured her, wiped her clean. Her cries diminished to hulking sobs and finally into deep gentle breathing. She rolled onto her side, and the woman curled around her. Sarah looked through the fire to the doorway. Ryan was gone.

A simple hammock hung in the corner of the room, positioned under a window. Ryan slumped into it. Sarah's face, her grief and joy, pervaded him. He stared into the night sky, the moon's brilliance overpowering all but the most powerful stars. He relaxed, let his need go. The stars began to dance—psychedelics taking hold. They shifted and swayed to his internal rhythm. He tried to control them—to force them into stasis. But the stars refused, jittering like fireflies trapped in a jar.

He sank into their dance. Slowly the stars blurred, recombining into a latticework of entwined light. Each point connected to the next, pulsing in smooth rhythm. He watched mesmerized by the creation of his mind. Its perfection startled him. He closed his eyes and the images continued. Their spindling web stretched before him—his alone. He fell into the infinite capacity of his own thought.

32

Dave Madda hadn't had this much fun in years. He relished the impossible problem—the only challenge worth accepting. And now, after days in the flow, his efforts had started to pay off. Little by little chaos yielded to order. It seeped in from the edges, like the frame of a jigsaw puzzle. Madda probed the data, massaging it into position. He routed over dead ends, only to get stymied by a massive chasm. He backtracked and began again.

But he'd tipped the scales. He couldn't stop the cascade if he tried. Even as he watched it coming together, the elegance of the virus shocked him. Its absolute perfection reflected pure balance. He touched the software, dipped his fingers into the flow stream and tried to grasp the majesty of this string of ones and zeros. It had required the computing power of most of the western United States to crack. Madda wondered smugly what panic he had created by sucking so many computers offline.

As he watched the code unravel and re-form into the basis of Echelon, his mind stumbled over an inherent impossibility. It had taken everything at his disposal to crack the code, and even then he admitted that a great deal of luck was involved. The task would have been impenetrable using the feeble tech of the late twentieth century. So how the hell did Echelon's progenitors get the Key? He watched the final pieces of code materialize, packing it into the hilt of his saber.

Seconds later, after a blurred rush of data, Madda sat over a drink at the Avalon. He deserved it. While watching the antics around him, he tried to contact Sarah, but she didn't respond. Madda tried a link with Laing. He'd agreed to let Sarah know first, but had little choice. He didn't want to hold the Key for too long. The temptation to slot it already tugged him. What he could do with such control . . .

To forget the itch, and as a celebratory treat, Madda decided to hit the mat. He pulled up the board of patrons and scrolled past the regulars. Madda wanted something new. He found a name he didn't recognize and booked a room. Newcomers usually meant easy marks—though this one claimed to be a kendo master. Madda's saber against a katana's curved blade would be a challenge. Anyway new was new, and Madda craved the interaction.

He faded from the Avalon and rezed into a standard fencing suite. Oak walls lined the room. A thin swath of red carpet marked the fencing strip. Madda smiled. This was home. He unsheathed his blade and began warming up. No need to loosen the muscles here. This was about loosening the mind. It had taken Madda a while to accept the rules of the flow. Slightly skewed from reality, they had thrown off his timing. No longer. He felt his mind relax, lost himself in technique.

A man appeared in the far end of the room. Clad in black, he'd shadowed his face. Madda shook his head. Rookie. Novices used the strategy to shield any giveaways their eyes might offer. Madda thought it bordered on cheating.

Dave gave his saber another flick and stepped to the center of the room. The man joined him. Many liked to chat before commencing. Madda preferred to speak after, once the battle was over. The man seemed of the same persuasion. He pulled a soft leather gauntlet from his hand. Madda grinned with schoolboy glee. Maybe his opponent did hold a surprise or two. The man threw the gauntlet at Madda's feet.

Madda picked it up with his left hand. "I like your style—" His words cut short. The glove dissolved, slipped into Madda's own code, locking onto the representation of his hand and jacking his system. Before Dave could adjust to the incursion, the man whipped his sword high and attacked in a series of clean swipes that took all Madda's resolve to deflect. Dave parried and dove, but the man's katana broke through his defense, gouging Madda's back. A burning jolt shot through his nervous system. He stumbled to his feet, only then realizing that their environment had shifted.

The room went gray. A single desk with two chairs shoved in a corner. The man in black circled, hands gripping his weapon, poised to attack. Madda's mind stung.

"What the fuck's going on?" Madda coughed out.

"We're dueling for the prize."

"You hacked me. Who the hell do you think you are?"

The man paused for an instant, letting his shadow drop.

"You?!" Madda said, stunned.

"I want it," Tex responded.

"What?"

"You have the Key."

Madda probed the gauntlet digesting his hand. Perfect coding. Indestructible and untraceable. Like any art form, raw code betrayed the idiosyncrasies of its maker. The gauntlet had Echelon written all over it.

"You've been with them all along?"

"Of course."

"But you protected Ryan," Madda sputtered, desperately trying to understand the depth of Tex's betrayal.

Tex chuckled. "He wasn't the target. He was the weapon. Now, I suspect he's outlived his usefulness."

Tex grinned and shot forward, breaching Madda's defenses with a clean strike. A black gash sliced down Madda's left shoulder, and pain scorched his mind. The room hadn't been coded for blood. Madda rolled away and shot out with an unexpected attack, catching Tex in the hip. He flinched. At least they could both be hurt.

"What is this place?"

"Our arena. No entrance, no exit. No controls. Every hit jolts your brain. Die here, Madda, and you'll be just another vegetable I throw overboard."

"Where are you?"

"Sitting right next to you. We're shoulder to shoulder."

Sure enough, Madda could sense the subtle pressure on his arm, just enough to let him know that something touched him back in the real.

"I won't give it up."

Tex smiled again. "You will. I'll beat you, and then the real pain will begin."

"I could just use it—slot the Key myself."

"Go ahead."

Madda guessed the room was rigged to record. Tex grinned maniacally and attacked. Madda let him approach, stumbled even. He needed to draw this fight out. Beating Tex wouldn't grant him escape. There'd be other blocks. This gray would become another cell, a personal hell around which everything he'd worked for would crumble. Madda's past days in the flow, his bone-deep exhaustion, all faded.

He initiated a double game. In the room, he attacked and parried, marking Tex's weaknesses, of which there were frustratingly few. In his mind, he accessed the room's code and started a run. He set the run as another duel, better to maintain consistency. In the duel with the code he only attacked. Its defenses were prickly and barbed. Each thrust seemed only to grind the gauntlet's virus deeper into his system.

Tex saw his attention diverted, kicked off a wall and flew straight at Madda. Madda bent backward, letting Tex tumble over him, the katana's point gouging a nick down Madda's forehead. Tex crumpled against the far wall, and Madda attacked. Yet another ruse; Tex rolled out and threaded the katana past Madda's defenses and into his soft abdomen. Pain ripped through Madda. He lost his balance and fell into a chair, his saber clattering onto the floor.

Gasping, Madda felt death looming. Death here meant sub-servience. He'd be defenseless, unable to fight. Tex would heap pain on him, carve up his inert body, glazing him with agony. No passing out in the flow. Torture here offered no respite. It would last until Tex got the Key. Not a pleasant way to lose your mind.

Subsumed by twin battles, Madda struggled to banish his dread. Pain caked him, encrusted him in confusion and terror. He tried to shove it aside, couldn't. Then a flash of inspiration. He could use it! The pain itself offered escape. If he could hack the code, he could bounce back to reality along the thread that was now racking him. He slumped, appearing beaten.

"It's over for you."

"I don't have it," Madda said.

"I know. You stashed it. As I would have. Well, serve it up."

Tex approached cautiously and raised his sword to Madda's neck. Madda slumped farther, leaning into the sword, letting it cut him. Pain bit, and he traveled the course of its signal. It forged a path—not quite wide enough to get him back. Another failure. He had seconds. Madda dropped to the floor and rolled to his saber, a thick gash across his neck. Tex jumped high and swung his katana down for the final blow. Madda reached his own sword with his left hand and managed to parry the blow. The room swelled then settled. Tex stopped his attack, looking at Madda's hand. Slender nerves extended from the gauntlet and latched onto the saber.

"So that's where you hid it," Tex said. "I should have guessed."

Madda felt the gauntlet sapping the Key. He tried to rip the saber from his tainted hand, screaming in fury. The sound erupted as a gurgling cough. Tex spun and arced his sword into Madda. Madda dropped, raising his left hand. The amputation was clean agony. Madda bellowed into it.

Madda yanked his sword from the severed, virus-laced hand. Pain blossomed around him, and this time, the link held.

Tex grinned, raising his sword for a killing blow. He brought it down hard and fast. He swiped at nothing.

Tex ripped out of the flow—too late. Madda leaned against him in the cramped cabin, his left hand hanging useless. It was the other hand wrapped around his neck that worried Tex. Tex tried to squirm free, to no avail. He felt Madda's determination. A thousand images burned through asphyxia. All his work wasted. So much effort to betray Laing, and for nothing. He'd had no choice, he reasoned fleetingly. Just a cog to be twisted and flexed at the machinist's whim. Of course the promise of wealth had greased his motivation. But now, his greed and pride fell away. His thoughts centered on the faces of his children, the face of his mother. They dimmed, fell into silhouette and, finally, blinked out.

Madda gripped Tex's throat until he ran out of strength. He let go and slumped down, fading into a cool river of unconsciousness. When he awoke, Dave found himself much worse for wear. The interface had caused permanent damage to his left hand. His mind had seen its amputation and could not relinquish the illusion. Madda fashioned a sling and stuffed his arm into it. He had no time. Echelon had sapped at least part of the code from his saber. It wouldn't take them long to initialize it and get down to business. He estimated his chances of survival if Echelon regained the Key. Not too good. The decision wasn't difficult.

He accessed Laing's location log, which had ceased working several days earlier. He stumbled onto the deck and pulled a grimy canopy from the capsule. Basically a cannonball with wings, Tex used the capsule as a delivery device for illicit goods. It wasn't designed for human transport. Madda plugged in the coordinates and crammed himself into the cylindrical container.

The roar of ignition blew out his hearing; the massive thrust slingshot him into the wild blue. G-force and turbulence rattled him. Teeth chipped. No windows. Didn't matter. He couldn't see through the pressure. The container arced high, hung weightless for an instant, then plunged. Acceleration built, the anticipation of impact interminable.

Tugging jolts as the ball crashed into the jungle, its foam-dampening system deploying in time to save the capsule from decimation. A lurching cancellation of velocity.

The ringing in his ears told him the ride was over. He opened the hatch and spilled into the moist earth. He saw signs of a fight around him, noticed remnants of Sarah's helmet. He stumbled forward.

By the time he reached Elysium, blisters pocked his face, skin flaking off in bloody sheets. His world went fractal, a series of flickering illusions. He felt himself hauled downhill, saw the thatched ceiling of a hut. Ryan loomed over him.

"They got it, Ryan. I'm sorry. It . . . It was Tex." Then he felt nothing beyond a searing heat shooting into his heart.

In a gray room, two men hunkered over the gauntlet, still encasing a severed hand.

"Will it be enough? We only pulled partial code. Madda got the rest out with him."

"It will be enough," the other man responded.

33

Laing paced the hut, flashes of undirected fury forcing activity. His mind scattered. He found himself unable to maintain a train of thought. Fear and fury meshed. He approached the door, hovered near it, but couldn't bring himself to exit. The respite had sapped his will. He couldn't bear to reengage the dissonance.

"We have no choice, Ryan," Sarah said. When Madda had arrived, she'd realized how dire their circumstances were. Even if the conspirators had regained incomplete code, they would be able to reconstruct the virus and the Key. When they did, there'd be nowhere to run. Even Elysium's carefully forged cloak wouldn't hold. Not with Sachs hunting them.

Still, Ryan stood trapped, unable to relinquish his peace. "I know, Sarah. I know." It was all he could say. Fury lanced him. His terror made him weak; his anger made him dangerous. Laing's ability to impose discipline, to restrain desire from expression, grew tenuous. The rift between thought and action shrank. His hands clenched and un-clenched, longing for violence. He turned from Sarah, afraid that a single tendril of cause would cascade into a reaction for which he could never forgive himself.

"Coward," she spat.

Laing did not watch her exit.

Swaddled in blankets of rage and impotence, Ryan held. Twilight faded into night; then the moon rose and the bay slithered with lustrous vitality. Ryan's heart was beat out, slung gut low, while his lungs felt high and flighty. Time passed him up. He felt it, the slippage. For so long he'd struggled to hold it, to exact penance from time by bloating his life with action. Now he slipped into torpor, unable to pull himself from cycling bouts of self-hatred.

"You need a kick start." The voice ripped Laing from the whirlwind. Rachael stood in the doorway, backlit by the moon. Ryan hated that she saw him like this, as a victim. She entered the room and knelt. The smell of her, sweet and peaty, washed over him.

"Kick start?" he said.

"Old term. On motorcycles, there was a pedal that you had to kick in order to spark the engine to life."

"How do you know that?"

"I like old vehicles."

"But you never go anywhere," he said.

Rachael looked down. Ryan pressed. "You've made a nook for yourselves here, safe and isolated, and you've lost the will to engage, the will even to help those around you."

Rachael drew up and laughed. Even as Ryan's fury rose, her smile drew him in. She didn't need to say it; Ryan had just described himself. The rage blossomed, grew ripe and wilted. Ryan laughed with her.

Rachael leaned closer, her breasts tingling against Ryan's skin. He felt the inevitable rise. "Walk with me," she said. She uncurled and held out her hand. Ryan took it. He stepped out of the room and into the moonlight.

He was meters away, lost in Rachael's aura, before he felt them. They slammed down, flooding him. He struggled to maintain. His breathing sharpened into staccato shots.

"Don't fight it. Let it come."

"You . . . don't know," Ryan said through gritted teeth.

"Let it wash over you."

"I'd drown."

"No."

Ryan couldn't do it. He felt the old barriers slam up, lost pieces of himself in the struggle to keep the drones from his mind. Rachael led him as he stumbled. He found himself at the base of the limestone cliff, stretching up into the night. He uncurled his hand from Rachael's and gripped the rock. Cool and sharp, it calmed him, pulled him to other times, to a forgotten self.

—Belay on?

The voice in his mind shocked him. He whirled to see Sarah step from the darkness. Clad in a black, skintight body-sock, a simple harness hung over her hips.

A smile crossed Ryan's face, its reflection broke on Sarah's. She tossed him a pair of shoes. He bobbled them for a second, finally managing to scoop them out of the air. Climbing slippers. He sat in the sand, pulled them on.

—*I climb alone.*

The smile fell from Sarah's face. The resigned inevitability returned. Waves lapped onto the shore, beating rhythm from the silence.

"Sarah wants to climb with you, to share a rope. You're refusing?" Rachael asked.

Both Ryan and Sarah whirled on Rachael, her intrusion unwelcome. Ryan looked back at Sarah. He tugged at the slippers and stood. Again, he put his hand to the rock, gripping it. His feet longed to rise, the desire for movement welling in him. He turned, grasping the harness that Sarah held limply in her hand. In a rush, he stepped into it, buckled it down and knotted the rope linking him to Sarah.

—*On belay.*

Her eyes brightened.

—*Climb away,* she responded.

He nodded, a simple movement that he hoped conveyed apology. He turned back to the cliff. A stalactite drooped fanglike from the overhanging rock. He grasped the slender tendril and pulled himself off the ground. His left heel found purchase just under his hands. Using both arms and his leg, he lunged, flinging himself upward. With all his experience, the move should have been flawless. Now, he flailed in the air, the tips of his right hand just barely finding the hold. The force of his momentum slammed Laing into the rock, its nobbed grit gashing his side. He held, fingers trembling. Then, his left hand found purchase and he managed to pull his feet under him.

The moment crystallized. He lost everything, felt only the slice of rock surrounding him. He lived in it, exalted and flung himself into the night. Move after move, forcing him to the very limit of his ability. Finally, Laing reached the belay point. He clipped into the anchor and called for Sarah. He put her on belay and pulled the rope taut between them. His hands moved of their own accord, drawing rope as she rose. He gazed onto the moonlit bay, sucking it all in, letting his world refill to the rhythmic tug of Sarah's ascent.

The drones' cacophony echoed through his mind. Instead of looking away, blocking them out, he faced them head-on. A roar of data rushed him, ripped through him. His hands wavered. Data flooded him. He refused to turn away.

Finally, lost in the maelstrom, he found something to cling to. Laing grasped it and held, finding a single point of connection between his mind and the drones. The drones registered the connection, their shriek spontaneously reconstructing to a sweet, perfect tone. Understanding gelled between man and machine. Laing basked in its resonance.

Something pulled him from first contact. A sound in the back of his mind, and a friction on his hands, a word wafting up the cliff: "Falling!" Rope whistled through his fingers.

Sarah tumbled back and over—the overhang too much for her. She'd known she couldn't make it. But more than success, she needed to believe in Ryan's ability to hold her fall. Through the flash of speed and adrenaline, she caught snap images of the beach rising to meet her and clenched down, anticipating impact.

A tug at her harness, at first tenuous, then firm and steady. Her plummet ripped short. The force pulled her arms and legs down and away, arching her to the moon. She savored the elasticity of the rope, the thrill of betting right. Only then did she sense the pull on her hair and realize that it was wet from the waves lapping onto the beach. She hung suspended, centimeters off the ground. Above her the stalactite loomed, and beyond it, she could make out Ryan's silhouette protruding from the cliff, personifying it.

"Are you okay?!"

She held silent for a beat, then righted herself and yelled back to him, "Climbing!"

She grasped the stalactite. The rope drew taut. Its movement tracked hers, and comfort flooded her. She climbed with newfound confidence. After a gritted eternity, she muscled through the bulged crux. Sweating and triumphant, she pulled into the indentation where Laing sat. She hunkered down beside him and clipped into the anchor.

"Off belay."

"Belay off," he responded.

She sat next to him, faced out and breathed sea air. While laced with pathogens, it smelled clean to her. She pressed into Ryan, savoring his warmth.

"I got through," he said.

Sarah pulled herself from the view and looked at him quizzically.

"The drones," he continued. "The noise, the static, it's gone. I understand them, and they . . ."

Sarah saw the tension fading from Laing's features. She'd never seen him without it. She smiled, wrapped an arm around him and drew close.

"I think they've become part of me. I feel different. I feel ready."

Ryan and Sarah stared out over the bay, savoring their peace, knowing that it would not last.

34

"You knew all along and just sat on the sidelines?" Madda asked as he devoured a sandwich, tearing pieces away in ravenous chomps.

"Yes," Rachael replied.

Madda's eyes bulged. To have a power and not use it was inconceivable to him.

"You seem to have recovered," Sarah said from the doorway. She and Ryan filled the entrance to the sterile room, which Madda had taken over. Madda jumped up and bear-hugged the both of them.

"Goddamn, I'm glad to be back. Thought it was all over."

"Good to see you too," Ryan said.

The mere resonance of Laing's voice cut into Madda, reminding him of his failure. He stepped back, regained composure. "We have no time. They'll have the Key in a matter of hours, if not already."

Madda looked down. All heads turned to Rachael. Sarah stood ready to confront her. Laing took Sarah's arm, holding her back. He then slumped into a wicker chair next to Rachael's. She stared out at Elysium with unblinking determination.

"Thank you," he said.

"I didn't do a thing." Sour regret cut her words.

Ryan put a hand to her arm, gently pulling Rachael from her thoughts.

"You did for me. You forced me to help myself."

A soft glow washed over her, drenching her words in warm satisfaction. "The drones . . . You've expelled them."

Laing shook his head. "I've accepted them, and they, me."

Rachael's flush blanched out, his words—his presence—suddenly tarnishing her.

"And who's in control, Ryan?"

"I am. For the first time."

Rachael responded with a dry sardonic laugh.

"They're part of me. Rachael . . ."

She cut him off. "Will you stay? Will you all stay?"

Madda and Sarah remained silent.

"No," Ryan said.

"How can you go after seeing this?" She waved her hand, encompassing the whole village in a single gesture.

"We built a world out there, Rachael, or at least propagated it."

"You've built nothing!" She wheeled on them, jumping from her chair. "You sapped the world. You sucked humanity from it!"

Sarah stepped forward, facing Rachael down. "Who are you to condemn us?"

"We're the people Echelon forgot. We made it so, and we'll keep it so."

"Echelon forgets nothing," Madda said.

"Echelon forgot its progenitors."

Silence settled through the room, clogging out the light.

Rachael shook her head and continued. "We stand outside. We saw the alternative and chose this." She paused. "You found the virus in the listening station?"

"You know about—"

Rachael cut Madda off. "My great-grandfather sat at that station. Called himself Virgil. He was NSA. The Key came through him."

"And then he abandoned his creation?"

"His creation," Rachael scoffed. "Virgil knew what he had found—the promise it held, and the danger. He wanted the cadre of engineers and hackers in his circle to forget what they had seen—to let it go. They had other ideas. To them, everything was a calculation—everything controllable. They could stem the chaos, play God. So they stole the code—crashed the NSA and sank into the arteries of data feeding our world. Everyone involved left the NSA. Not everyone returned to Echelon."

"Virgil walked away?" Madda asked, incredulous.

"He saw the future and wanted no part in it."

"That Echelon would crumble," Laing said.

"That Echelon would succeed. That it would harness humanity."

"But the lives Echelon saved," Sarah said.

"Yes. Lives controlled, shaped and limited."

"But we were imploding," Sarah responded, "killing ourselves. Just look at the time before Echelon began its work. War, famine, terrorism—we stood on the brink. And now it's started again—we're headed right back into the fire."

Rachael laughed. "Maybe we need that fire. Maybe from it, we're reborn."

"Oh, come on," Ryan said. "That's just philosophy. We're talking about carnage, genocide—real death."

"Stasis begets stasis," Rachael spat back. "Echelon ground our progress to a halt. Yes, that progress was painful. Yes, it was destructive. But that's how greatness comes. And that's what we've lost. We've given it up for stable mediocrity. I mean, don't you find it odd that the great thinkers of our time died more than a century ago?"

Rachael stormed out, bursting into the open air. Sarah, Madda and Ryan followed. Ryan caught up to her and grabbed her arm. She wrenched it free, steaming hot.

"You're right, Rachael."

Her fury wavered. "You're something new, Ryan. Echelon didn't realize what they were creating. They didn't see the ramifications of—"

Ryan broke in. "Of infesting me with drones?"

"Yesterday you were infested. You and the drones occupied the same body but operated on the lowest operational mandate—stay alive. Higher symbiosis was blocked in their babble and your resistance. No longer. Today, you're a cyborg. The first true cyborg. You and the drones have meshed. You're no longer human."

Her words cut Ryan. He recognized their truth. A wave of loss crested within him. He found himself mourning Ryan Laing even as he let that old self dissolve into the sand. Already, his thinking had shifted.

Ryan shook free, pulled himself back to the present. "Help us, Rachael."

Rachael shook her head. "We interfered before—trying to kill Welton. It didn't work. We'll not try again." She stood firm.

"So you'll let humanity slide back into subservience? More manipulation, more control—and further stagnation. When will it end?"

"It has ended, for us."

"And you call me inhuman?"

Rachael refused to respond. She turned from him and stared into the bay.

"I can stop it," Ryan said softly.

Rachael wheeled around. "You won't. I see it in your eyes. You'll just be another overseer battling for control. The web will grow and humanity will suffocate in silk."

Dave and Sarah approached. He gave her a quick glance, looking for approval. Sarah nodded. Madda turned to Rachel. "I have the Key," he said. "Help us use it."

"No! Hold it. Bury it!" Rachael blurted.

Ryan laughed derisively as he stopped to pick up a handful of sand. He let the sand slip through his fingers, staring at the tumbling grains as he spoke. "Maybe you're right, Rachael—about Echelon—about me. Maybe I'm not human. But I won't let humanity sink under a new wave of domination."

Laing opened his hand, sand falling away to reveal a serrated piece of seashell. He gripped it, staring at Rachael with cold anger. "I won't sit here and watch. I will fight."

Rachael's eyes widened as she stumbled backward. Ryan grinned cold. But, instead of pursuing her, he whirled on Madda, grasping Dave's hand in his own. The shell, sandwiched between their palms, drew blood from both men. Dave yelped, trying to pull away even as their blood mingled and Laing gripped tighter.

Their link went active.

"Take me to it," Laing said. "Give me the Key."

Laing tumbled into flow-space, dragging Madda along for the ride.

Madda fell to the sand, lost in the phase shift between reality and flow-space. Drones invaded him, stripped away his sensory input, deadening him to the world. Dave gulped straight shock. He sensed Laing's hovering presence as the flow's familiar environment settled around them.

"You . . . How did you do that?" Madda sputtered. His voice welled up from far away—his physcial being far off—removed. "No console, no goggles, just zap, boom, and here we are?"

"Take me to it," Ryan repeated, hanging off Madda's shoulder.

"Jesus, Ryan," Madda said. "Yeah, okay."

Madda shook out, oriented himself and pushed forward, folding space to reach his fencing hall. Madda's sword hung on the wall, the fencing software resetting after his battle with Tex. Madda pushed in, lifted the sword, hefting it.

"Are you sure you want this?"

"No," Ryan wavered. Then, "Yes."

Madda whirled on Ryan, driving the saber into Ryan's chest, inject-ing the code. Laing sank to his knees. His torso glowed hot. Ryan erupted. The shock force blinded Madda, blew out the fencing hall and sent Dave sprawling into empty flow-space. The connection between Madda and Laing's immolated form shattered.

When Madda's senses returned, he found himself curled fetal, screaming into wet sand.

Ryan collapsed next to Madda, Sarah hovering over them both. Rachael stood behind them, horrified. Madda's screams faded, misting into the vegetation. Ryan remained still, arms spread, legs curled under him. His face bore pain, then peace, then nothing. Sarah slumped over him.

"What did you do?" she hollered at Madda. He shook his head.

Rachael answered, "It's in him now. The Key. Hopefully, it'll kill him."

Sarah vaulted over Ryan's prone figure and slammed Rachael, driv-ing her into the dirt. "Fix him!"

"I can't. Won't," Rachael shot back.

Sarah rained blows down on Rachael. Rachael bore them.

"Stop," Ryan's voice cracked.

Sarah turned. She disengaged from Rachael, scrambling to Laing's side, desperation shifting to relief. She took his head in her hands and slowly brought her lips to his.

"Does it hurt?" Sarah asked.

"Yes. But I can handle it."

Sarah drew Ryan to her, holding him tight.

"You may even think you control it," Rachael said, recovering from Sarah's attack. "But with it running through your system, who controls you?"

Ryan got to his knees and crawled to Rachael. He looked on her without pity.

"Where did it come from?"

"We don't know," Rachael said.

"You suspect. It's why your progenitors left Echelon."

Rachael remained silent, staring deep into the being before her. "Who offers the means to play God? Only God himself."

"You believe that?"

"I believe that we were given a power we are incapable of wielding. I believe that it has decimated humanity's will. Now it wreaks havoc as we fight over it."

"You see a pattern," Madda said.

"I see an end. Subjugation. But not through force. Willing, gladly granted and complete. Then, they will come."

"You think this is an invasion—a first strike by remote?" Sarah said incredulously.

"Can you think of a better way to dominate?" Rachael retorted.

Sarah croaked a laugh. "But aliens? Really . . ."

Madda didn't seem so surprised. "It explains a lot. The virus' radical perfection. No human could have conceived it—way too advanced."

Ryan nodded. "Doesn't matter who coded it. It was deliberate. It was an attack. And it worked."

"You're part of it now," Rachael said. "You ingested the Key. Before, you were just a cog. Now you're the factory itself." Ryan tried to stand, but Rachael pulled him back.

She kissed him hard, drones flooding her mouth, sifting through her, linking her to Ryan. Ryan tried to pull away. Rachael refused, clawing to stay connected. She used the drones' link—extending toward Laing's mind.

—*Or, you could be the sabot,* Rachael whispered into his thoughts.

She structured a thought in her mind, a memorized line. Rachael pulled Ryan closer, his emotions swirling through her. She responded, implanting her thought into the drones' coding.

The transmission arced out over Laing, twining into his mind. Laing reeled back, stung. Their bodies parted, and the drones in Rachael went dead, losing connection with their host. Rachael shivered, the connection severed.

Ryan stumbled away, stumbled into the next fight, his final fight, a piece of code echoing in his head. Rachael had shouted it into him.

35

Jason Sachs found himself reluctant to exit the gray room. He'd spent more and more time there as the days passed. Addiction gripped him. He liked the view from the ziggurat's pinnacle. A true throne room. From here, the virus would seep through the flow—pervading it. And then it would all be his.

Jason had spent the last three days working out the imperfect code retrieved from Madda. He rebuilt the virus slowly, poring over each line. Tedious work, but necessary. He felt like a restoration expert examining the soot-stained ceiling of the Sistine Chapel. He scrubbed, filtered and fiddled, finally revealing a perfect beauty, long forgotten.

Finally, the Key blossomed before his eyes. Sachs reached out, touched the code, let it inundate him. As he did, the virus initiated its run, spreading over the room and out. Its viscous dissemination left no trace. The virus poured over Echelon, then down into the flow.

Jason looked down from the throne, saw Turing's encryption shatter and Echelon come back online. Systems rebooted, controls reengaged. He sensed the sigh of relief spreading through the world. All would return to normal.

The coup he had orchestrated would never be known. The manipulation would be subtle, undetectable. Echelon would become one more piece of a larger puzzle, just as the NSA's original had. Even now, Jason initiated protocols blocking and shifting Echelon's data retrieve. Echelon would know what he wanted it to know.

He knew Turing would appreciate Jason's silent coup. The manipulation of society had become easy, pat. There was no secret in how to smudge humanity into a single mass. The real game, the interesting game, was who would wield that thumb. It had been Echelon. Now it was Sachs and Welton.

Yet at the moment of their success, Welton stood noticeably absent. Jason didn't mind. Though he responded to Welton's will and ability, Sachs didn't like the man. Jason refused to fall for Welton's force of personality. Always harder to kill those you admire. Jason had learned his lesson with Turing.

From on high, Jason watched the virus seep into the flow and out into the world. His fingers tingled. He felt the game of his life moving closer to checkmate. Just a few moves left. Plans within plans. Deceit within deceit. His mind flew. He disengaged grudgingly, pulling out of flow-space.

Back in the dank control office of his Echelon fiefdom, Sachs pulled the 'trodes from his eyes and readjusted to the dead light. He realized that he hated this place. He'd never thought about it before. Now he couldn't wait to be gone. He stepped into the hall and crossed into the tech center, once Madda's. The firefight had decimated the room, but its rudiments were back in place. A technician approached.

"Fantastic to be up and running, sir. Echelon is back in action."

"Yes, Mr. Johnson, I know."

The technician opened his mouth to say more, then thought better of it and scurried away. Jason smirked and entered the vault's pass control.

He stepped to the scanner. It sifted through his vitals, the locations of his organs, the specific nature of his brain waves identifying him as Jason Sachs. Moments ago, Turing's encryption would have blocked access. Now, Sachs was free to do as he pleased. The bolts released, and the vault's door slid open with pneumatic languor.

Jason stepped into the room, the door hissing shut behind him. It held a single canister. Jason approached it and looked down through the clear lid. Oil-slick gray slithered over itself. Jason lifted the lid, watched the drones adjust to the atmospheric shift.

Sachs took a deep breath and reached into the swirling mass. He cringed at their cool torrent, then plunged in deeper. The drones snaked up his fingers. The mass slithered over him, pervaded and permeated him. He drew cupped hands to his lips and drank.

He gorged on them, and they on him—Turing having laced their initiation protocols with his virus. Gut wrenching pain racked Jason as the drones ate through him. He fell to the hard metal floor, thrashing.

Then he injected the Key into his thoughts. He saw the Key, spoke it. Suddenly, the drones revived, recoding to suit Sachs' will. The drones recognized the pieces that made the man and were subsumed.

Ryan Laing had been injected slowly, over a period of days. Sachs hadn't time for that. The drones flowed into him, seeped through his internal barriers, permeating his system. His flesh gave in grudgingly, the machines invading him cell by cell, linking to DNA, becoming part of the fabric making up the man. Jason lost himself in the maelstrom. It didn't worry him greatly. He relished only his need, which remained strong.

The drones sifted through his mind. He felt their chill. He blew past it. The drones meshed with his thoughts, his drive. They tapped the data he'd gleaned over the past days. They ate the virus, found the Key and regurgitated power. They fed on it and he on them, parasites masticating each other.

He rose and sank a hand into the canister. Drones slithered between him and their tidal pool. He blew in new programming, irreversible. Each and every drone from this batch became his to control. Now, as other agents took the injection, Sachs would have a back door into their minds.

He had plans for the drones—mass implantation. Everyone would spit gray. Sickness would be a thing of the past, surgery and even death forgotten vestiges of a barbaric past. People would clamor for the elixir—the fountain of youth gladly given. Then, Jason Sachs would regulate information on a cellular level. Sensory-input control. People would see, hear, smell and taste what he wanted. Sachs would control humanity from within. Perfect order.

Drones slithered off Jason's body. His outer shell regained normality. He straightened his tie and exited. Sachs stumbled through the tech room and back into his office. He slumped into his chair and closed his eyes for a moment, feeling new power surge through him. He focused, using the Key to program a final piece of coding into his drones. Their operating system fought against it. He felt their resistance, but his hack would hold.

Sachs heard footsteps. He took a final look around the room. Already, he saw himself from on high. He pictured his image from that gray room that was his true home.

The comm at Jason's door crackled with his technician's nervous voice: "Mr. Sachs. I have specs on the retrofit for your approval."

"Come in, Johnson."

He felt the man pause. "Yes, sir."

The locks disengaged, and the man entered, head down. It took him a moment to see that Sachs held an old gun in his left hand. At that moment, Johnson knew his life was over. He backed away, stumbling over a chair and crashing to the floor.

Sachs rose and came around the desk.

"Please. I'm innocent. Whatever it is," Johnson cried.

"Innocent?" Sachs replied, his voice cold steel. "We're all innocent. We're all guilty as hell."

Sachs brought the gun to Johnson's head. The man squealed and pulled back, cowering. When nothing happened, he raised his eyes to Sachs. Sachs brought the gun around and, looking right into Johnson's eyes, shot a hole into his own chest. The force of the explosion ripped the gun from Jason's hand and blew him into the pea-green wall. Sachs slid down it, blood slick. Great torrents spilled out of him, pooling. In his décor, Sachs had never used primary colors. They offered too pure a vision. Now, red spread across the floor.

Johnson scrambled to his feet and fled, urine drenching the leg of his pants. He didn't care. Johnson bolted through the intertwining corridors to an emergency station and tripped the alarm.

In a gray room, Michael Welton tracked signal intercepts of Sachs' demise.

36

The plane skimmed ocean, Ryan flexing the flow's ether to cover their tracks. Laing floated over the action, lost in dual worlds and removed from both. Sarah stared out the cockpit's plexi, lulled by the waves below.

Before she and Ryan departed Elysium, Madda had pulled her aside. "He's way gone, man," Madda had said. "The Key gives him total access. Nothing's beyond his reach. No one can handle that kind of data yield. Think how much processing power Echelon required. That same amount of information is going through him. He'll be a vegetable in hours."

Sarah had looked across the room at Ryan. Gone was the anxious pain, the desperation. He sat in a corner, staring out into the bay and beyond to a world at his command. She tried to link with him but reeled back, struck by the torrents of data surging through him. He didn't hold any of it, just let it wash over him like a stone smoothed by the ocean.

"He'll be all right," Sarah responded.

"You know he won't."

"What can we do? We need him to end this."

"And if he wins, what then?" Madda asked.

"You think we created a monster."

"I think a good man can become one. I think it doesn't take much."

Sarah shook her head. She didn't take to faith easily, but right now she had little choice. Just the same, she contemplated having to kill Ryan Laing, or whatever was left of him. The thought made her sick.

"There's a saying about absolute power, Sarah," Madda continued.

"I know it."

"Let me come with you."

"He'll be okay, Dave. I can handle it. Besides, you're needed here."

"I can hack anywhere."

"True, but protecting a location you happen to be in will give you added motivation."

"You're one cruel bitch, Sarah Peters."

Sarah smiled, throwing an arm around Madda. "Oh, come on,

Dave. Could you dream up a better place to hang for a couple days? The sky is blue, the ocean warm, and the women . . . willing."

"You think?"

"Trust me, you'll be very popular."

Madda looked out across the bay, then locked on a passing woman, her tanned breasts bobbing with her gait. "Well, the scenery is pretty good." He turned back to Sarah, trying like hell not to look down and get caught ogling. "Doesn't matter, though. I'll be locked down until you guys get this done."

"How long can you hold out?"

"They cracked the Key, and unlike Echelon, they're actively searching for Elysium."

"But there's no data on Elysium for them to find."

"Exactly. There's a hole in the flow—a place with zero input. Everything's linked, Sarah, even in this wasteland. But this spot was cut free. The lack of input will paint a target on our chests."

"Is that what you've been looking for, the target?" Sarah smiled while Madda blushed crimson. She kicked back to shop talk before he stopped breathing all together. "Can you block them?"

"Yes, for a while. I'll fill the hole, open others. But they're already sniffing. In two days this place will be toast. Cracking the event horizon for you and Laing will only draw them faster."

"Then I guess we better get on it," Sarah had said.

That was six hours ago. The parting had been awkward. Rachael seemed reluctant to let them go. After that whole kiss thing, it was all Sarah could do to keep from knocking her block off.

They snagged Elysium's only transportation—a five-person airplane of a design Sarah had never seen before. The plane's hangar had been hollowed out of an indentation in the limestone mushroom. The cave extended about thirty meters back into dank humidity. Sarah and Ryan stumbled their way inside, knocking into the craft before someone deigned to turn on the lights.

They found a bulbous pod, suspended above a set of superconducting tracks. The wings seemed woefully inadequate to keep the capsule aloft.

"You've got to be kidding me," Sarah said.

"It will be fine," Ryan said.

"And how would you know that?"

"I've accessed the operating protocols."

"Well thanks then, Mr. Roboto. I feel much better."

Ryan ignored her, lost in his preflight checklist.

She shook her head and crammed herself into the capsule. Ryan ripped the rear seats from the plane, lightening the load. He settled in and interfaced directly with the machine. Sarah watched him, accessing his mind briefly, then shuddering back out. She couldn't seem to find him in there. They strapped in, and the plane's magnetic propulsion engaged. The pod rose, floating over the track.

"Get ready. The acceleration will be extreme."

Sarah had time to suck in a single breath. Then her world blurred in a snap rush of speed. The craft shot forward. Sarah's vision tunneled down. She felt her blood and body pressed back, knew unconsciousness was seconds away. From the corner of her eye, she saw Ryan, staring straight ahead, drones hazing the whites of his eyes.

Black blasted into pure white and then, finally, a blue sky. The craft shot into the atmosphere. It arced up, slowing, finally stalling. Sarah's heart floated in her chest for a gut-wrenching instant. Then gravity hunted them down and they pushed over into a negative-g dive. The sky fell away, replaced by a much harsher, rougher blue.

Sarah shrieked as they plummeted toward the ocean. Terror gripped her. The capsule began to rumble. Sarah closed her eyes, gritting for the final shock, rage coursing though her. Madda was right; Ryan had lost it. Now she would get a front-row seat to his suicide.

—*Fuck you, Ryan.*

Deceleration hit her. She crumpled into her seat. And . . . nothing. No crash. No death. She opened her eyes to see waves just meters below them. She found it hard to accept her continued survival. She looked out of the capsule. Extending in either direction, graceful wings cupped the moist air. Impossibly long and arced downward, their tips hovered over the water. Whirling in her seat, she saw a giant propeller humming behind her, extending from what had once been a smooth exterior. She looked at Ryan in shock. He pulled from his haze, remembering that she sat next to him.

"Wing-in-ground effect," Ryan explained coldly. "It's what keeps pelicans from crashing into the ocean. This plane uses it to fly long distances."

Sarah allowed herself to breathe. She gazed out beyond the clear capsule, watching the ocean roll by. Her body finally caught up with her mind's mad rush. She reached forward, snagging a barf bag—and filled it. Then she unbuckled her restraints and shifted in her seat to face Ryan. His gaze roved over her, analyzing her with cold sterility.

"Feel better?" he asked.

She reared back and hit him with everything she had. The impact ripped a gash at the corner of Ryan's eye. He stared at her in bewilderment. The wound had vanished by the time Sarah lowered her hand. She rose from her seat and struggled into the cabin's rear.

She hauled open the only door in the pod to reveal a toilet optimally designed for a three-year-old. She tried to slam the door behind her, but it thwacked against her thigh and offered only a dull thump.

Inside, Sarah chucked her barf bag and crouched over the toilet, letting the tears come. The weight of her solitude threatened to crush her. It had flickered out over the past weeks. Now it returned lead heavy. She found the sink and splashed water over her face, rinsing the disgust and terror from her mouth. Could Ryan last the fight as an automaton? She felt an overwhelming urge to let him go, accept his loss and finish the assignment. She fought it.

37

Laing tingled with anticipation, his drive for conflict overwhelming. The conspiracy would end now. Or it would end him. The flow sloshed around him, through and over him. He felt the pull of his own gravity, sucking data to him, sifting it, manipulating it. He became the nexus. A vague unease rose from the far end of the flow—another weight building. Sachs.

Sarah's soft breath warmed Ryan's ear. "Does this roller coaster have an autopilot?" she whispered.

"Yes."

"Then get back here."

"What?"

"Get back here," she repeated.

"One sec. We're coming up on the zone."

Ryan extended deep, held the satellite beams at bay as they passed through the sterile zone. They cracked the event horizon and flew into open ocean. After sewing up the hole, Ryan pulled himself from the whirlwind and engaged the autopilot.

To stay cloaked in the flow, he needed to maintain constant vigilance. The low-grade battle hung in the back of his mind. He unlatched his restraints and slid out of the cockpit. Sarah knelt in the cabin's center.

"What is this?" Ryan asked. He dropped down to his knees in front of her. The cloud hazed over him, his mind pulled in all directions.

"Your last chance," Sarah responded. "I know you're itching for a suicide run." She looked into his eyes, almost faltered, then drove on. "If that's all you have left, I'll help you succeed."

Ryan blinked, an ice shot of loss tearing through his fog. "You care so little?" he asked.

Sarah's rigid posture softened infinitesimally. "I care, Ryan." She couldn't say the rest.

—*I love you. But what's left to love?*

Her thought beat into him. It crashed through the sea flood, tunneled deep and found the drowning man. He leaned forward, hovering just over her.

"I'm here, Sarah." Ryan's voice regained emotion. "I'm still here. It's just—a little busy in here."

Relief flooded her. She touched his forehead with hers, her stifled chuckle becoming a sob. He lifted her head up and kissed her.

They hovered over the ocean, wrapped in each other. Sarah undressed him deliberately. Then she pressed into him, allowing her body to melt to his. Warmth flooded him, recognition flowed back, and he regained something lost. She knelt over him, letting him fill her. There was no need to move; the blanket of air buffeted them.

She opened herself, his thoughts colliding with her own. She swirled with him in the data rush. She watched him rematerialize. He arrested his spread over the flow, retracted perception. She saw what he could have become and didn't. It both thrilled and saddened her. Such awesome power, renounced for one mind, one body. Then she forgot about the struggles, the deaths, the future. She relished that single moment. When they finished, he curled around her and fell asleep in her arms.

Ryan wasn't a homebody. Home meant little to him after the Fire. He preferred to think of himself as an insulated unit, capable of living in any environment. Los Angeles was merely a place to hang his hat, if he'd owned one.

"Good to be back," he said to Sarah, surprised that he meant it.

They skimmed the water, competing for airspace with actual pelicans reluctant to give up their habitat. They reached Santa Rosa, a channel island off the coast of Santa Barbara. Ryan pulled the plane up and over the gnarled spit of rock, diving back down and banking into the channel itself. They hugged the coast. Sarah pointed down. A pod of dolphins frolicked in the waves below them.

"We'll be detected, Ryan."

"I've bubbled us out. We won't show on any system."

Sarah pointed to stunned gawkers on the beach, so close that Sarah could have thrown confetti at them. "There are limits to your power, Superman."

Ryan chuckled. "I'm not worried about them. They'll have no place to tell their story."

"So if an enormous winged pod flies down the coast and no one's able to lock it into the flow, it doesn't exist?" she asked.

"Thousands can see it. If they can't tell millions, it doesn't exist."

"Truth tempered by dissemination."

He nodded.

They cruised on, passing the hills of Malibu and entering Los Angeles proper. The channel filled with commercial and private ships.

"True or not, you're going to decapitate one of those thousands."

Ryan leaned in. The stick felt good in his hands, firm and reactive. "I'm taking us down."

"Tell me there are water skis on this thing."

"There are water skis on this thing."

Sarah harrumphed and tightened down her straps. Ryan initiated a series of S turns, spilling altitude until they flew just centimeters off the water. Before them, a monster tanker loomed, filling their horizon. Sarah squirmed.

Ryan said, "Trust me."

Sarah managed to uncurl her fingers from their death grip on her harness. "I do."

The tanker grew, its mass looming over them. Sarah could just make out sailors on the bow, waving frantically. With meters to spare, Ryan touched a button. The wings shimmered, then shrank. The metal buckled, folding in on itself and retreating. The throb of the giant propeller ceased. The knobby hull chugged toward them, meters to impact.

They dropped—a full eight centimeters. The capsule smacked into the ocean, skipping once. The nose rose up, and Sarah was sure they'd nail the tanker. Ryan threw the stick forward, sending the nose into the breaker pushed up by the tanker's mass. The capsule burrowed into the water. The tanker's hull became their sky, their horizon. It neared with sickening speed, even as they dived. Barnacles scraped along the canopy, grinding out a screeched wail. The capsule wavered for a beat, then dug into the water and continued its dive. Ryan pulled up and hovered. They watched the behemoth move over them.

"That dent's coming out of your salary, mister," she said.

"Normal wear and tear," he countered.

"You never were much on returning your gear in operating order."

"Bill me."

"Can I take it out in trade?" She grinned at him in the swamp light, her hand rising from his shoulder and playing gently with his ear. He shook it off.

"You're insatiable," he said in mock exasperation.

"And that's a bad thing?"

"I could learn to live with it."

"That's exactly what you'll do; live with it."

Ryan's grin faded. He nodded, wishing he could guarantee that, wishing he could foresee a long life with the woman next to him. He saw only the next hours, and a fight that would be his last.

They rose between the pylons of Ryan's Venice Beach abode. Ryan unsealed the hatch and stepped onto the moist dock, offering a hand to Sarah. He sent a signal to the capsule, and it sank into the surf.

"You'll be able to call it up in the flow," he said.

"Me?"

Ryan shrugged it off. "Come on. We've got work."

Ryan led Sarah into his house. The mercs' incursion had aerated the structure. Looters had taken care of the amenities. Sarah sifted through the remnants of his former life, reminiscing for him. He went upstairs and keyed in the codes, luxuriating in physical contact with his past. A door slid open, revealing his flow console and beyond that, his armory. Sarah followed him inside.

"Wow. You're ready for World War Three."

"Lot of good it did me."

The console drew Sarah, as Ryan had known it would. He shook off his worn clothing and found a clean T-shirt. He added a pair of black pants and his old leather jacket, which he filled with implements of destruction.

"Nice rig," she said, ogling the console.

"Best in the biz." He was ready. No use stalling the inevitable.

He reached for Sarah, pulled her close.

"I love you," he said. She looked at him with a mixture of affection and doubt. "You don't believe me?"

"Prove it to me over the next decade," she said.

He smiled; she stood stone-faced. She knows this is the end, he thought, careful to block her out. He sent her only warmth, which made her more nervous.

"We can do this, Ryan. We can do this and live."

"I know," he said.

He pulled her tighter. Her arms wrapped around his back, fingers curling through his hair, her touch deliberate, a declaration. He savored it, even as his heart solidified. He bent down, his lips grazing hers. A tingling joy radiated through him. She pushed into him. Their mouths melded. For an instant he forgot himself. Then, a twitch in the back of his mind and he iced out.

Ryan kissed her deeper, opening his drones to her—exploring her body, her mind.

—*Ryan—What are you—*

—*I'm sorry.*

He blew data into her. The onslaught nailed her and she writhed in frantic desperation. He held her tight, maintaining the connection. It ripped through her, brilliant intensity. Her eyes went shock-wide, then hazed. He pulled away and the link severed; the drones in her went dead.

Sarah came to in the chair facing the flow console. Ryan was gone. She felt dizzy, as if she'd eaten a whole turkey dinner by herself. Data gorged.

—*Get it out of you. Quickly.*

His voice slipped from the ether. She tried to respond, but the drive to expel the data engulfed her. She snagged the interface and tunneled into the flow, regurgitating great chunks of code into Ryan's dock. It streamed from her mind, clearing her. She breathed into it, a euphoric adrenaline rush building with her purge. Sarah's head spun making it hard to focus. She read the code Ryan had implanted.

—*Ryan, this is crazy!*

—*It's a poison pill. A hunter-killer. Rachael's design—why she kissed me.*

—*I know what it is. Rachael is using you like all the others. You're not her weapon. I won't let you do it!*

—*You're right. You have to do it. They'll hack me, Sarah. I might not be able to initiate the run.*

—No! No, this is a full burn. It will shock you out.

Nothing from Ryan. Quiet acceptance. She ripped off the interface. She could hear him just outside the door, head resting on its tempered steel. She lunged for the door, smacked the button. Nothing.

—It's locked. Initiating the run will disengage the door.

—Ryan?!

—There's no other way.

Tears welled, falling down the steel. She put her hand on the door.

—Don't do this. Please.

He was already gone. She felt him slip through his decimated past and out into the ocean air. She felt him pause, turn. He looked up at the place where she'd be. She reached out to him. He turned and walked into the floating city.

38

No one cried over Jason Sachs' demise. He had no friends, no relatives. He'd made no permanent connections, no lasting bonds. Sachs had lived on cold honed need and raw intelligence. Social interaction, family, love—all weaknesses to be exploited. Sachs remained pristine, untouched. He craved nothing beyond the game. Echelon drove him. A shut-in with delusions of grandeur. Well, maybe not so delusional.

Ryan watched attendants lower Sachs' coffin into the ground. It was a nice spot, on the crest of a sloping hill. He'd look down on a sea of graves. Several Echelon operatives stood by, pretending to grieve and scanning the area for suspicious activity. Standard protocol. It was a cushy assignment that they longed to finish quickly.

Sure enough, the moment Sachs was in the ground, they split. Ryan slipped back into the mausoleum he had selected as a hideout. The waiting began.

He longed to link to Sarah, felt her blinking in and out. But what more could be said? If she hesitated, even for an instant, the game would be lost. Better for her to hate him. Easier that way to see the big picture, and do what she had to do.

At half past twelve, Jason's heart started beating. For the past fifteen hours, drones had undertaken the job of shuttling oxygen and nutrients to his vital organs. Now, he hung in darkness and let his body heal. He had not factored in the embalming fluid. The drones worked overtime to eject the toxins. He coughed out formaldehyde in torrents.

As Sachs' body healed, he let his mind explore, opening to the flow. Data poured into him. He felt the comings and goings of each and every person, zeroed in on random actions, spun out to societal trends. He watched Echelon recapture humanity, tame it, bring it back under control. Wars that only hours ago seemed imminent, evaporated through expeditious diplomacy. Conflicts subsided. He felt a communal sigh of relief.

Above that, he saw the shift. Welton had been hard at work. Echelon's data was not quite accurate. It had been filtered. Jason delved into raw code, found Welton's prints all over it. Unsubtle. He would do bet-

ter. He fixed the inherent contradictions Welton had accidentally initiated. Sachs' lust grew. He let his desire guide him, his drive for power
nearing repletion. In a coffin, buried two meters into the earth, he
shifted the future's course to suit his ambition. His experiment would
be perfect. Not a stopgap measure like Turing's. Nor a blind grab like
Welton's. Sachs was beyond that. He thought bigger.

First things first. Decimate the opposition. Sachs zeroed in on his
enemies: Elysium the first and most obvious. The zealots were far too
dangerous to continue living. Code buzzed through Sachs; terabits of
information snapped by.

As he chewed into the code stream, he realized someone was blocking his hunt, encasing Elysium in mounds of dissonance. Couldn't be
Laing—too sophisticated. Madda. His stamp was all over this citadel of
babel. Sachs left part of his mind to the task. The tower would crumble
with his onslaught. Sachs had more immediate necessities.

His body recovered sufficiently to perform. He kicked his knee into
the faux-silk lining of his coffin. The cheap bastards hadn't deemed
him important enough for the real thing. His knee cracked the coffin.
Soft dirt spilled into the casket. He bucked, kicked and punched, soft
flesh made firm by the drones. In minutes, he broke free of the casket
and began the terrible scrape to the surface. Dirt filled his mouth and
lungs. He sucked it in and kept digging. His mind cycled through
waves of claustrophobia, then opened into the vastness of his new dominion. Character dissolved with the flash shifts. There was only desire.

His hand broke the surface. He ripped himself from the grave,
hacked dirt from his lungs and rose reborn. Free. He brushed himself
off, a futile gesture, then turned and refilled the hole. Once finished, he
sauntered through the cemetery.

Sachs opened his senses, not just to the graveyard's sights and
sounds, but to the data emissions around him. Nothing out of the or-
dinary. Slight blips here and there. A blank zone every now and then.
He shrugged it off and concentrated on his next task—destroy Michael
Welton. Sachs hadn't risen from the dead to rule by committee.

Ryan tracked Sachs through the cemetery. He hid himself in code jumble, knowing Sachs didn't have the field craft to physically spot him.

Just the same, Jason's prowess in the flow grew exponentially. Ryan's edge slipped by the second. Soon, Sachs would sniff him out. It didn't matter. Jason would welcome the fight.

Ryan let instinct guide him. His mind tunneled out, hitting the flow and surveying Elysium's dam. Sachs hammered at it, cracking order from Madda's barrier. Leaks sprouted. Porosity multiplied, integrity faltering. With every shift Madda pulled, Sachs countered. Elysium's isolation neared its end.

—*Three hours, tops,* Sarah echoed into him.

—*Good to have you back.*

—*Repeat, two hours, maybe three until Sachs cracks Madda's dam. That's best guess. When he does, Nepalese missiles could take the place out in minutes.*

—*It won't get to that.*

Silence from Sarah. Ryan continued his pursuit.

Madda ripped off his interface, terror mounting. He heaved out of the chair, muscles seizing after ten hours of sitting, and exploded from his hut to find . . . nothing. Daily life went on in Elysium. Children scampered about. Men and women chatted on the veranda. Teenagers splashed in the ocean.

"We need to evacuate," he said to the people mingling on the porch.

They gazed at him as they would an exotic animal in a zoo.

"Leave here?" a tall man said, incredulous.

"I can't hold the dam."

Everyone looked to Rachael. "We won't leave," she said.

"What?! If Sachs finds us, we're all dead."

Another man took up Rachael's mantra. "We've staked our claim. This is ours."

"He doesn't see it that way," Madda responded.

Rachael smiled. "Then we have just time enough to prepare a glorious lunch."

Madda's shock shifted into a stunned fury. "You're choosing suicide?"

"You're welcome to leave, David," Rachael said.

Madda considered it. He could bolt, flee Thailand, and run a gauntlet through the world and across the flow. He'd lose that marathon.

"There's nowhere to run," he said.

Rachael nodded. "Do what you need to find peace. Lunch will be waiting when you're ready."

"Fuck lunch. I may see the writing on the wall, but I'll spend every last breath erasing it."

He whirled and slammed back in. He'd lose, but with teeth bared and claws gnashing. He found his battleground. Sachs had him surrounded and was slowly tightening the net. Madda fought back, code flying, move to countermove. He shifted strategy. Unable to hide any longer, he attacked. Sachs would overpower him. But with luck, Madda could draw out the execution long enough for Ryan to do his job. Either way, it would take Sachs' mind off a more immediate threat.

39

Sachs caught a maglev west. Ryan followed. California faded into Nevada. Rail stretched to the horizon. Population density grudgingly gave way to the mandates of the desert. Where there was no water, there was no life. Despite all humanity's advancements, the simple truth remained.

Ryan slipped into the flow and watched Sachs. The man spilled out, suffusing. There wasn't much left of him, just a gaping maw, swallowing bytes, panning the flow stream. While Laing had meshed with the tech inside him, Jason had been subsumed. All that remained of Sachs was a single need, an insatiable hunger that drove and focused the drones within him. Ryan pondered following Sachs down that path. He could surrender his mind to the drones, spread into the flow and envelop Sachs. The mere thought bucked Laing out. Something within him refused such submission.

—*Don't*, Sarah thought.

—*I know. I'd lose.*

—*You'll lose anyway.*

Her thoughts chilled him. Laing hoped he'd fare better in the physical realm, but Sarah was probably right. Laing had harnessed the drones' capabilities. Sachs gave them free rein. Statistically unbeatable. Sarah knew it. Laing was too stubborn to concede.

He let his expectations fade into the blurred scenery. The maglev slowed, and Ryan sensed Jason's movement. He no longer needed to keep a visual lock on Sachs. The node growing around him continued to expand. Ryan could track the energy signature kilometers away.

Sachs rented a car, luxury model, and sped west. Ryan followed on a motorcycle, at Sarah's insistence. Electrified highway slipped into two-lane roads and finally into a single dirt track.

Laing sped past a desiccated sign reading BRYCE CANYON NATIONAL PARK. The NATIONAL PARK had been crossed out. Under it read PRIVATE PROPERTY. Ryan accessed their whereabouts. The park had been purchased by a revivalist Mormon faction decades ago. They'd abandoned technology and lived blind.

Ahead, Sachs' car pulled to a stop. He emerged and stood at the edge of a gaping cliff that spilled into an amphitheater of jagged sand-stone. With no place to hide and no reason to draw this out further, Laing went for a dramatic entrance. Ryan opened the throttle, barrel-ing toward Jason. At the last possible instant, he slammed down on the brake pedal and skidded to a halt, sending up a plume of dust that en-veloped Jason.

Ryan lunged from the bike, grabbed Jason's collar and smashed him into the car door. Jason sputtered but didn't resist. Ryan jacked his arm into Jason's neck. Sachs' eyes bulged. He grabbed Ryan's arm and began to push. His force halted Ryan's attack.

"Crude, Laing. Always the showman."

"You picked a beautiful place to die."

Ryan redoubled the pressure, but Jason easily held him at bay.

"I've been dead once, Laing. It wasn't so bad."

With that, Jason shifted his grip and torqued Ryan's arm. Ryan kicked off the car and did a backflip around his wrenched arm, manag-ing to roll away with it intact.

Jason grinned wildly. "My death was very instructive, Mr. Laing. I picked up a few things in that hole. Thrilled to try them on you."

Jason leaped into the air, twisted and whipped his foot around, bringing it down on Ryan's shoulder with hammering force. Ryan reeled back, the blow clean snapping his collarbone. Jason lunged again. This time Ryan dove sideways and Jason landed only a glancing blow to Ryan's leg. Pain shot through Ryan; the force of Jason's attack stunned him. He scrambled back, trying not to let fear slow him. He got to his feet only to find himself in a whirlwind of Jason's blows. He blocked into blinding speed. A single left hook slipped through.

Coming to his senses, Laing found himself suspended over the gap-ing maw of Bryce Canyon. The cliff stretched in a half-moon around him, descending into a coral reef of sandstone. Jason held him by the neck with one arm. Statistically unbeatable.

"You've possessed this power for so long, and have so little capacity to use it. Frankly, Mr. Laing, my admiration of you slips with each pass-ing moment."

"There's nothing left of you, Sachs—organic slop ruled by a digital master."

A twitch at the corner of Jason's eye, some recognition of truth. Subsumed. The stare went cold. "Your obsession with control is your un-doing," Jason said, gripping down on Laing's neck.

Ryan's world tunneled down. "No," he sputtered.

"Didn't quite hear you, Laing." Jason pulled him closer.

Darkness encroached. Ryan sensed Jason's balance shift and com-mitted everything. He wrapped his legs around Jason's torso and arched back. Jason's eyes went wide. He lost his balance, toppling for-ward, tumbling over the cliff with Ryan wrapped around him. In his mind, Ryan heard Sarah's screams. He felt nothing. He and Jason tum-bled down sand-red scree. Impact was sudden and devastating. Legs snapped; organs bled. For Ryan, a sense of déjà vu slopped out over the pain.

The two lay crushed into the earth, head-to-head, dying. Neither breathed, spinal cords severed. Drones swarmed out of them, covering the area in slick gray.

Jason jettisoned his broken carcass and plunged into the flow. Laing followed. Images jittered and twitched; Ryan felt the devastation of his body, doubted anything could fix such calamity. But the drones granted him time.

Jason ascended into a space Ryan had never noticed: a point above the flow, linked to it by streaming tendrils of data and looming over Echelon itself. Flashing up to it, Ryan felt its nodal draw. Jason plunged inside. Ryan hacked his way through.

Walls closed in on him. Gray matter bolted him down. A room rezed in from the cardinal points. Gray on gray. A single table and two chairs. Jason stood in the center. Someone else hung in the shadows.

Jason pulsed with fury. "You can't kill me! That husk lying beside you is nothing. I'm here now, all of me."

Ryan's image wavered. The drones' dual work of keeping his body alive and interfacing with the flow taxed them to their break point.

Jason continued. "Not you, though. You can't give it up. You'll stay locked in that flesh box. You'll rot in it."

Laing watched Sachs shift. Jason's simulacrum melted. In its place a new being emerged. The image of a man, but skewed. Jason became a processing point, the processing point, a cavernous mouth, a tunnel into chaos. Ryan reeled from the creature. It reached out, touched him.

In that touch Laing tasted bedlam. He screamed. It bellowed canned laughter.

—*Do it!* Ryan pleaded.

Silence.

—*Please, Sarah.*

—*I can't, Ryan. Fight it! You have the strength. I know you do!*

—*No. I don't.*

Fear and rage surged through Ryan as the creature became a vortex of blazing chaos. It sucked Laing closer, its pull inexorable. Ryan locked into the room's gray code, fighting against the anarchic power Jason Sachs had become. Swatches of Laing's flesh ripped away, opening his raw code to the torrent. The force tore through him. Eyes clenched, Ryan held. Jason's laughter rippled through Ryan's pain. Strength ebbed. Desire snuffed.

Ryan's memory crashed. He lost his past, knew only a tack-sharp present. It bored into him. A whole life defined by one single action. One choice. Ryan let go. He dove into the maelstrom.

Churning chaos racked him. Plunging into the whirlpool, Ryan opened his eyes and stared into the blinding embodiment of his terror. It ate through him, insatiable. To rein it in would be to wrangle the sun. Instead, Laing released his fear and embraced the chaos.

He rode the wave, operating beyond his limitations, free of the barriers that had defined him. Laing drove into the whirlpool's heart. There, in the storm's eye, Sachs blazed. Torrents of code pulsed from him, powering the maelstrom. Beyond fear, beyond rage, Laing found the single line into the beast's heart. He broached Sachs' barrage, broke through the onslaught.

Eye to eye, Laing latched onto Sachs' neck. Jason's eyes went wide in shock. He struggled. Ryan gripped tighter. Laing became the destroyer, tearing through Sachs. The maelstrom blew apart, subsumed by Laing's will. Jason's laughter faded to a bellowing howl, then a final silence.

Ryan fell into that silence, exhausted.

Far away, in the Utah desert, the drones that comprised Jason Sachs stuttered and went inert, core lost.

. . . . .

Black became gray, consciousness returning. Ryan found himself sitting in a chair, his head supported by the matte-dull table before him. At his feet lay the mangled corpse of Jason Sachs—simulacrum regained.

Slow, deliberate clapping. Hands emerged from shadow. A face followed. Michael Welton. His perfect blue suit drew out from the gray.

"Well done, Laing."

"Welton."

"Thank you for solving yet another problem."

"You wanted Sachs dead?" Ryan asked.

Michael smiled. "Jason was a loose cannon. Necessary, but expendable."

"And now you reign."

"The world is mine to control."

"I suppose you want me to join you."

Welton laughed. "Why on Earth would I want that?"

"I can do to you what I did to Jason."

Welton's face grew dark. "I'm no chess master, Laing. I'm the guy who'll blow your head off with a sawed-off shotgun hidden under the table."

As Ryan started to laugh, Welton whipped across the table, snaking his hand around Ryan's, transferring data. Ryan saw missiles locked on target: Elysium.

"Call them off," Ryan said.

—*Sarah, it's time.*

"No, I don't think so. Choose to die. End it in front of me, and they'll die easy."

—*I can't,* she responded.

"Or, I'll drop gas on them, let them writhe—as you did on that rock in Joshua Tree. As you're doing now in Bryce Canyon. You have a penchant for suffering, Laing."

Exhaustion didn't weaken Ryan's realization. "You cracked that rock in Joshua Tree. It was you behind the laz gun."

Welton smiled. "It was my man, yes."

"But why?"

"I knew what Turing would do to save you. What you would become. I used it to achieve my own ends. Your death was the butterfly wing that produced a cyclone. And now the storm has passed and we've come to an end—your end. Time to renounce Turing's gift."

—*It's done, Sarah. There's no other way.*

"You win," Ryan said, lead-heavy.

Welton beamed. He twisted his grip into a handshake. "Well, then. Good-bye, Laing. I fear you're the last man who'll know what I've done."

—*I love you, Ryan.*

—*Good-bye, Sarah.*

Sarah triggered Rachael's program. The hunter-killer belched into the flow. Its effects rippled out, rose and bucked at the corners of the gray room. The zenith quaked, its resolution fading.

Ryan looked up into Welton's eyes. "You're right; no one will know."

Welton jerked upright through the fault slip. Terror boiled up, shocking his eyes wide. "No! You can't! You'd sacrifice the world because you can't have it?"

The zenith swayed, losing integrity.

"The world isn't ours. I have no right to control it. Neither do you."

"Everything will crumble!"

"Then we'll go down fighting."

"Chaos."

"Chaos or submission. There's nothing else."

The gray walls blew out, leaving them suspended over the flow. Welton shrieked. Ryan gazed down, marveling at the beauty of Rachael's creation. The hunter-killer flashed through the flow, freezing every stream instantaneously. In that moment, its target, the Echelon virus, sizzled. It rose from frozen bits and effervesced into static. In every corner of the flow, the virus that founded Echelon, that held the world for so long, dissipated into the ether. Echelon crashed. And above that, the gray room tumbled.

Ryan spiraled out, unable to right himself. The drones within him writhed from core loss, Rachael's hunter-killer wiping their code as it had Echelon's. Anything related to the virus ripped away, leaving Ryan's drones without an operating system. Their babble suffused Ryan. He lost himself within it.

. . . . .

On a beach in Thailand, David Madda watched, stunned silent. With a single worldwide system stutter, Rachael's hunter-killer wiped the virus from the flow. Echelon was gone. The conspiracy to steal Echelon's power, gone. Even the drones within Laing himself—wiped. Nothing remained of the virus caught long ago by an Arctic listening post. The flow came back online, re-formed on a newly leveled playing field. Information flowed free.

Madda removed his interface and left the cabin. He emerged into the blinding sunlight in time to see a missile pod coming fast, then banking into the ocean just as quickly. Rachael stood behind him.

"We're safe," he said.

She reached her arms around him, pressing into his back. He gripped her hands, and she softly kissed his neck.

"Lunch is ready."

40

Ryan awoke on the canyon floor. Breath shuddered through him in quaking rasps. His body longed to die. His dogged obstinacy refused to give up the ghost. With their system wipe, the drones lost purpose, cutting off their triage within him. Crushed ribs and internal bleeding bloated his abdomen. Gritting through the pain, Ryan heaved himself onto his arms and looked into the distance. Tucked into the valley, surrounded by sandstone turrets, stood a small house. Welton would be there. Had to be. Just time enough.

Ryan abandoned the flow, forgot Echelon, forgot even the drones. He inched toward his mark, unwilling to let Welton escape. He crawled, then dragged his feet under him and stumbled. Reality throbbed. He couldn't maintain balance. He made it to the ranch house. Bones crackled within his shattered body.

Laing slammed through the door's desiccated frame, toppling a tall man bolting for the exit. The man righted himself and jabbed viciously, pinning Ryan to the floor.

"You just refuse to die, Mr. Laing," Michael Welton said.

Ryan tried to fight Welton, but his body betrayed him. Welton rose to his feet, drawing a small pistol from his pristine blue suit.

"The virus is out there, sailing through the galaxy," Welton said. "It will return. You only delay the inevitable. There will be another Echelon—another Turing. And another me."

"You are nothing like Turing," Ryan croaked.

"Men like Turing beget men like me."

"And after? When we're subsumed, helpless?"

"Then, they will come." Welton raised the pistol. "Inevitable."

He cocked. Ryan gazed into the gun's barrel, ready. An explosion rocked the house. Ryan's pain did not fade. Instead, Welton blew forward, crushing Ryan. Laing used the last of his strength to push the man away. Sarah stood in the door, a double-barreled shotgun smoking in her hand.

"You?"

"You're not the only obstinate fucker in this relationship."

"But how . . . ?" Laing trailed off, too weak to continue.

"I hired a copter," Sarah said. "Landed on the ridge and followed you here. Pretty good timing." She looked down on him and smiled. "By the way, your encryption sucks. Cracked that lock on your door without breaking a sweat."

Blood-filled lungs shifted Ryan's laugh into a spasmodic coughing fit. Sarah bent over him.

"Dying," he muttered.

"That's not true. Use the drones."

"They're lost."

"They need an operating code. Give them yours. Make them part of you."

He shook his head. She leaned over and kissed his frothed lips.

"Please," she said quietly.

Through exhaustion and his body's ruin, Ryan struggled to see her. She hung over him, beautiful, slipping into darkness. He held her as long as he could. Then vision faded into the void. He felt the sea pull and relinquished the fight. The ebb and flow lessened. He stopped thrashing and became the moon. Fear yielded, gave him up. He felt Sarah's warmth, the pressure of her need.

A single tear welled. It gained mass, filled with gray and slipped into the dry desert air. The droplet fell down his cheek, then stopped, hovered and snaked back into his mouth. He cried the same tear over and over. He abandoned release. There would be no absolution. He allowed them in, and they made him whole. He closed his eyes, knowing Sarah would be there when he awoke.

ACKNOWLEDGMENTS

My loving thanks to Barbara. You make it all so much fun. To my agents, Sarah Self and Matt Williams, thank you for letting me make up stories and call it work. To my editor, Betsy Mitchell, thank you for helping me hone that work into something worth reading. I'm indebted to Jud Grubbs for his creativity and advice throughout the process. I must also thank my think tank: Martine, Mom, Steve, Erik, Jeb, and Amanda. Dave, our travels made this book possible. Paul, thank you for your friendship and advice. As the first "industry people" to read the book, my gratitude to Mary Alice Kier and Anna Cottle for their assistance and encouragement. And my thanks to Jerry Katcher for his unwavering support over the years.

Born in 1974, JOSH CONVISER grew up in
Aspen, Colorado, graduated from Princeton
University with honors in anthropology, and
has lived in Europe and the Far East. An
experienced mountaineer, he climbed in
ranges across the world, including the
Himalayas, before giving up the mountains
for the jungles of Hollywood to pursue a
career in screenwriting. He is the executive
consultant on HBO's series *Rome* and has
several films in development. *Echelon* is his
first novel. A second, also featuring Ryan
Laing and Sarah Peters, will follow.

ABOUT THE TYPE

This book is set in Utopia, a typeface designed by Robert Slimbach in 1989. It combines the vertical stress and pronounced stroke contrast of eighteenth-century Transitional types like Baskerville and Walbaum with contemporary innovations in character shapes and stroke details.